SABRINA JEFFRIES
KAREN HAWKINS
CANDACE CAMP
MEREDITH DURAN

What Happens Under the Mistletoe

POCKET BOOKS

New York   London   Toronto   Sydney   New Delhi

Pocket Books
An Imprint of Simon & Schuster, Inc.
1230 Avenue of the Americas
New York, NY 10020

This book is a work of fiction. Any references to historical events, real people, or real places are used fictitiously. Other names, characters, places, and events are products of the authors' imagination, and any resemblance to actual events or places or persons, living or dead, is entirely coincidental.

The Heiress and the Hothead copyright © 2015 by Sabrina Jeffries LLC
Twelve Kisses to Midnight copyright © 2015 by Karen Hawkins
By Any Other Name copyright © 2015 by Candace Camp
Sweetest Regret copyright © 2015 by Meredith Duran

First Pocket Books paperback edition November 2015

POCKET and colophon are registered trademarks of Simon & Schuster, Inc.

For information about special discounts for bulk purchases, please contact Simon & Schuster Special Sales at 1-866-506-1949 or business@simonandschuster.com.

The Simon & Schuster Speakers Bureau can bring authors to your live event. For more information or to book an event, contact the Simon & Schuster Speakers Bureau at 1-866-248-3049 or visit our website at www.simonspeakers.com.

Interior design by Leydiana Rodríguez

Manufactured in the United States of America

10 9 8 7 6 5 4 3 2 1

ISBN 978-1-4767-8608-7
ISBN 978-1-4767-8612-4 (ebook)

Contents

THE HEIRESS AND
THE HOTHEAD

Sabrina Jeffries

Sweet emblem of returning peace,
The heart's full gush, and love's release;
Spirits in human fondness flow
And greet the pearly *Mistletoe*.

—Anonymous, from *The Mistletoe*

Chapter One

Lord Stephen Corry, youngest brother of a marquess, might be considered too radical for polite company, but clearly he still had some credit in society. Otherwise he wouldn't now be a guest at the manor house of American artist Jeremy Keane and the man's new wife—Stephen's old friend—Lady Yvette.

He entered the drawing room to find Yvette directing footmen who were hanging a large painting on one wall.

"Ah, there you are," she said. "And just in time for the unveiling of my new portrait. Jeremy hasn't seen it framed yet, so I'm surprising him by showing it off to our guests. The gentlemen are changing clothes after a day of shooting, the ladies will arrive any moment from shopping in town, and this must be hung before I can summon Jeremy from his studio."

"He didn't go shooting with the men?"

She laughed. "Jeremy is *not* the shooting sort."

Stephen well understood that. "I fear I'm intruding on your house party."

"Nonsense. Clarissa was absolutely right. It's absurd of you to spend the night at the village inn when we have so much room here."

What would Yvette think if she knew that her best friend—his cousin—had her own reasons for wishing him here? It had been a stroke of luck when he'd run into Clarissa earlier in the day.

I'll convince Yvette to invite you if you'll kiss me under the mistletoe in front of Edwin, Clarissa had said.

Why on earth would I wish to attend some society house party? he'd asked.

You told me once that you wanted to meet the owner of Montague Mills. Well, she'll be at this party. I'll introduce you.

Though Stephen hadn't been sure what Clarissa was about with Edwin Barlow, the Earl of Blakeborough, he'd found the promise regarding Miss Amanda Keane, Yvette's sister-in-law, impossible to resist. He had an article to write, after all, and he'd have no chance of meeting the American mill owner otherwise.

By all accounts, she was a colorless spinster with a hard-nosed view of life, who ventured into society as little as possible. He'd heard she'd be leaving England in a couple of weeks, so this would be his only chance to interview her.

"Well, I promise not to cause too much trouble," he joked.

"Somehow I doubt that. Between our tendency to provoke people and the way women react to you, I imagine there will be trouble aplenty." She grinned. "Fortunately, I enjoy a lively party. As does Jeremy."

"Wait—how *do* women react to me?" he asked, genuinely curious.

Yvette eyed him askance. "You know perfectly well that every lady you meet wants to fall into your lap. The older you get, the more unobtainable they find you, and now that you're nearly thirty, they're practically salivating to catch the elusive Lord Stephen."

"I'm only twenty-eight," he said sourly.

"Close enough. Especially when you stalk about with that air of dismissive impatience that perversely attracts them all."

"Have you been reading gothic novels again?"

"No, as a matter of fact," she said lightly. "I've merely spent years watching you trail women behind you as though you were a prodigal son pied piper."

The prodigal son part certainly fit. And it wasn't *his* fault that his pursuits left him no time for the fairer sex. Or that his lack of interest only seemed to attract them more.

Sounds of horse hooves crunching on the snowy drive outside wafted to them. "We can continue this discussion later," Yvette said. "That's the carriages bringing the ladies from town, and I'm sure the gentlemen will be down soon, too. Go corral everyone and move them into the drawing room quietly, so as not to spoil the surprise, will you?"

Before heading off, Stephen asked, "Does my brother know I'm here?"

"How could he? When I arrived earlier, he was still out shooting with the others. But I'm sure he'll be happy to see you."

"I doubt that." Ever since Stephen had begun writing for *The London Monitor*, he and Warren had been at odds. "He thinks me a dangerous radical determined to foment revolution and destroy England."

"He does not. He merely worries you'll do something rash and get yourself killed."

Stephen snorted. Granted, some of his speeches had been known to rouse tempers, and his series of articles regarding the poor treatment of workers in mills hadn't been well received by his peers, who cursed him for his lack of loyalty to other Englishmen of his class. But no one would murder him for them.

And once he interviewed Miss Keane and demonstrated that American owners were no better than English ones, people would see he wasn't just throwing stones at his countrymen. That the situation in English mills mirrored an equally bad situation in America. Perhaps *then* they would finally regard working conditions in the cotton industry as a problem that spanned continents.

Perhaps then they would finally *do* something about it.

He entered the foyer to find chattering women everywhere, stamping the snow off their boots as footmen hurried to take their bonnets, cloaks, and capes. Some gentlemen had already come down, including Blakeborough.

Overhead hung a kissing bough, a ball of evergreens with a bunch of mistletoe dangling from it. Here was Stephen's chance to discharge his obligation to Clarissa. Now, where was she?

Ah—there she was, with her back to him; he recognized her forest-green cloak and deep-brimmed bonnet. She was near the earl, so she must be setting up the scene she wanted him to play for Blakeborough's benefit.

Making sure that the earl was looking on, Stephen strode up to his cousin and spun her around. "I've been looking for you everywhere, you little minx!"

But as he bent to angle his head under the bonnet's brim, he caught sight of a freckled nose that was decidedly *not* Clarissa's.

That arrested him—especially when the woman gave him a startled look from eyes the color of a sparkling brook. With her sweet-featured face turned up to his, he could now clearly see the curls beneath her bonnet.

A low simmer began in his blood. Her hair was vibrantly, gloriously red. His favorite. Besides, they *were* under the mistletoe, and he couldn't balk at kissing her now or it would look as if he'd found her lacking.

Everyone had fallen silent to watch what he would do. So he pressed his lips to hers. For *her* sake, of course.

He enjoyed it, too, despite the tittering and whispering around them. Her mouth was soft, supple. She smelled of apples and tasted of cinnamon. And when she raised up slightly to meet his kiss, it made him want to stand there forever with his lips sealed to hers . . .

God, what was wrong with him? He had no time for this.

Pulling back, he reached up to pluck the requisite berry from the kissing bough, then forced a smile for his blushing mistletoe miss. Or perhaps *not* a miss. Damn it, what if he'd kissed someone's wife?

Seeking to recoup, he handed her the berry. "Thank you for that, madam."

She took it with a look of confusion. "Pardon me, sir," she said in an accent he couldn't quite place. "Is this some quaint English custom for greeting guests?"

English custom? Wasn't she English? "Actually, kissing under the mistletoe is a quaint *Christmas* custom. I take it you were unaware of it, Miss . . ."

"Keane. Miss Amanda Keane."

That froze the simmer in his blood. "Miss Keane," he said disbelievingly. She certainly didn't *look* like a colorless spinster. "Owner of Montague Mills."

That seemed to amuse her. "As a matter of fact, yes. And sister to the man of the house." Removing her bonnet, she handed it to a nearby footman. "Though I don't believe we've ever met."

"No." This was bad. She would think him a complete idiot to be kissing a stranger, and then he would never get his interview.

She was even more fetching without the bonnet, her hair a flaming beacon in the foyer. She had the sort of freckle-faced country girl appearance that fired his blood and made him want to tumble her in a haystack.

God save him. He hadn't reacted this fiercely to a woman in a very long time. Why did it have to be with *her*, of all people?

Then Blakeborough stepped up to cast Stephen a chastening glance. "Miss Keane, this is Lord Stephen Corry. Knightford's brother. I'm sure you've heard of him."

Her smile faltered. "*You're* Lord Stephen? Who writes the articles in *The London Monitor*?"

"You've read my articles?" This got worse by the moment. How had a woman with her family connections encountered a radical newspaper? That would make it damned hard to get her to answer his questions truthfully.

"Yes, I have." Her pretty eyes hardened. "Every ill-considered, blustering word."

His temper flared. "If that's how you feel about bettering conditions for workers," he said coldly, "then I suppose I know where you stand on the matter of reform."

"That's how I feel about your depiction of *mill owners*, sir." She was a tiny thing, but somehow her voice expanded to fill the room. "You write only about the worst ones, then tar the rest of us with the same brush. I've toured several English mills and have seen none of the things you describe."

He laughed harshly. "And who arranged these tours? The owners? Because they aren't about to show an esteemed foreign visitor how matters really are."

"Yet they're willing to show it to a lord whose idea of hard work is writing an article?"

As he bristled, Yvette hurried up to take Miss Keane's arm. "Come, Amanda, your mother has been asking for you in the drawing room."

Sparing a disgusted look for Stephen, Miss Keane let herself be led away.

She'd so roused his temper that he'd already started after her when someone grabbed *his* arm. "Leave her be," Clarissa muttered.

He halted, though his eyes followed Miss Keane as she marched purposefully into the drawing room. Like a man. Or a woman with a very firm will. Oddly, that attracted him even more.

No, he was *not* attracted to the termagant. How could he be? She was an *owner*, for God's sake.

"What were you thinking, to kiss Miss Keane so blatantly?" Clarissa went on. "I realize you were under the bough, but still—"

"I was thinking to do *you* a service." He dragged his gaze from the doorway through which his mistletoe miss had disappeared. "It wasn't *my* fault I mistook her for you."

"How could you? We look nothing alike."

"She was wearing your cloak and bonnet."

"Not mine. Her own." She scowled at him. "Yvette bought matching sets for the three of us. She thought it might be fun to have them for Christmastide."

"How was I to know that? I saw Miss Keane from behind."

Clarissa rolled her eyes. "You could have actually paused to speak to her before you put your mouth on her."

"In hindsight," he snapped, "that does seem the more sensible choice. But you weren't in the room, so I assumed she was you, setting the scene for Blakeborough."

"I forgot my reticule in the carriage and had to go back for it," she said defensively.

His eyes narrowed. "How fortuitous. Did you plan this?"

"Oh, for pity's sake." She huffed out a breath. "Yes, I planned for you to sneak up on the poor woman and kiss her senseless without stopping to think."

When she put it that way . . . "I wouldn't exactly describe her as a 'poor woman,'" he grumbled.

"No," Clarissa said with a faint smile. "Unlike most of the ladies who set their caps for you, she actually has a mind of her own."

"I noticed. And it's dead set against me. I'll never get my interview now."

"Well, I've lost my chance, too. Edwin is going to be highly skeptical about your interest in me if you're kissing every other woman in the house."

"Wait, is that what this is about? You're trying to make Blakeborough jealous?"

She blinked. "Don't be ridiculous. This is about . . . something else."

"If you say so." He headed for the drawing room door. "Whatever it is, it looks like we're both on our own from now on. And I, for one, mean to try again with Miss Keane."

There was more than one way to go about this. Her reaction to his kiss before she'd learned who he was had been decidedly enthusiastic. Perhaps he could use that. Flirt with her. Tease her. Gain her trust so he could find out what he needed to know.

That's right—this is all for my cause. It's not because of any attraction to her. No, indeed.

She was a means to an end, no more. And he would do whatever he must to achieve that end.

With that resolved, he entered the drawing room. Unfortunately, he was immediately confronted by the one person sure to ruin his plans: the Marquess of Knightford.

Who was also his eldest brother, Warren Corry.

Chapter Two

Amanda Keane stood in the drawing room, pretending to study the portrait her brother had done of Yvette, while she strained to hear the low-voiced argument taking place between Lord Knightford and Lord Stephen.

Oh, what she wouldn't have given to know what Lord Knightford was saying to his arrogant, self-satisfied younger brother. She hoped he was flaying the ass alive.

Not for his flirtations, no. At twenty-six, she'd had enough experience with the male sex to appreciate a fellow who was good at kissing, especially when he managed to do fluttery things to her insides. But once she'd found out who he was . . .

Leave it to a man to ruin a perfectly good kiss by being an awful person.

With a scowl, she opened her hand to stare at the white mistletoe berry Lord Stephen had handed her. Why she was holding on to it was a mystery. Honestly, she should have tossed it back in his face.

Hopefully his brother would toss *him* out. Or coax her

own brother into tossing him out. Wasn't that what their new St. George's Club was for—getting rid of unacceptable suitors to their sisters and wards? Though Lord Stephen wasn't her suitor, he'd made it look as if he was. And *unacceptable* certainly fit him.

She sneaked another peek. What a pity the man was so infernally attractive, with his firm jaw and sensual mouth and wavy brown hair. Not to mention his smoldering green eyes.

How appropriate for a firebrand. He made a profession of speaking out on matters he knew nothing about. She hated men like that. Especially when they condescended to her, like her late father.

Thrusting that lowering thought from her mind, she slipped out the nearest door into the hall. She must avoid Lord Stephen at all costs. Otherwise, she was liable to brain him with the nearest poker the next time he opened his mouth.

Or tried to press it to hers.

No, she mustn't think of that. It wouldn't happen again, if she had anything to say about it.

Fortunately, avoiding him proved remarkably easy. At dinner she was seated between her brother and Mama, nowhere near the argumentative Lord Stephen. And once the ladies retired to the drawing room, she was able to slip away, pleading a headache.

But it was early still, and she was too agitated to sleep. So she went to what had already become her favorite place in Jeremy's new manor house: the conservatory. She entered and went to peer out the window, glad that the moon was bright enough for her to view the lawn outside.

How lovely it looked at night. Snow frosted the cedars and holly hedges, and icicles sparkled along oak branches, reminding her of the Christmas trees people decorated in her native Pennsylvania.

Her stomach clenched. She missed Montague, even in winter. She missed the firs and the iced-over lakes, the log cabins and the elk. She didn't belong here in elegant England, with these elegant people and their elegant ways.

Unfortunately, of the two aims she'd had in coming to England, only one had been reached—getting her brother to agree to come home long enough to help her settle Papa's affairs.

But her other aim—getting information about how English mills achieved their success so she could make improvements in her own operation—had eluded her. The English were wary of having their advancements stolen by Americans—there was even a law against exporting English designs.

As much as she hated to admit it, Lord Stephen had been right about one thing: what she'd been allowed to see on her mill tours had been carefully orchestrated.

"It's beautiful, isn't it?"

She whirled with a little squeak to find the man himself leaning against the wall next to the lone candle lighting the room. "Are you mad, sneaking up on me like that? You nearly gave me heart failure!"

"Sorry," Lord Stephen said, but the golden light spilling over his face caught the unrepentant twinkle in his eyes. His lovely, intriguing eyes.

Curse him for those. "How did you find me?"

Pushing away from the wall, he strolled toward her. "I asked Yvette where you might go, and she told me this was your favorite room."

"That traitor," she grumbled.

"Hardly. She merely realized that we should talk."

"Why, so you could insult me again?"

His face was in shadow now that he'd moved in front of the candle. "Are you referring to when I kissed you?"

"Not that." She could barely see him, but still she caught his sudden smile and realized her mistake. "I mean—"

"Too late to take it back." He stepped closer. "So, you didn't mind the kiss."

"It doesn't matter if I did or not." Deliberately, she turned her back on him to gaze out the window. "You didn't mean it. You were just adhering to some silly English custom."

"There was more to it than that, and you know it." His richly accented voice spilled over her like fine wine. "I enjoyed it. As, I believe, did you."

She swallowed. So he'd noticed, had he? "Why wouldn't I? You kiss well enough . . . for an Englishman."

If she'd thought to prick his pride, she'd sorely miscalculated. He laughed. "So Americans kiss better than the English, do they? And how exactly do you know that?"

"I've been kissed often enough to make comparisons." She couldn't prevent the bitterness that crept into her voice. "As the only heiress for thirty miles around my home, I've had more than my share of flirtations."

With men who wanted Montague and all it stood for. Having seen what Mama had been forced to put up with after marrying Papa and handing him her family's mills, Amanda wasn't about to follow in her footsteps.

"That's not why I kissed you," Lord Stephen said irritably. "I did it because you were under the mistletoe."

"And because you thought I was someone else."

That brought him up short. "What makes you say that?"

"Your familiar manner of speaking to me when you turned me around. And your surprise when you saw my face."

A long silence passed, as if he were deciding whether to admit the truth. Then he sighed. "It wasn't an unpleasant surprise, I assure you." The low thrum in his voice sent a delicious shiver through her.

"Until you found out who I actually was."

"True," he said frankly. "Though I believe you were equally annoyed."

She faced him. "I still am, as a matter of fact. Now, if you'll excuse me—"

As she started past him, he caught her arm. "I came in here to apologize. And I haven't yet had the chance."

Pulling her arm free, she stared expectantly at him. Goodness, why did he have to be so attractive? Why must his coat fall crookedly and his cravat be slightly askew, as if someone had mussed him up on purpose to make him more appealing to her?

And why must he thread his fingers through his wavy ash-brown hair until it stuck out, making her want to step forward to smooth it down?

"Well?" she asked, annoyed by her reaction.

He stiffened. "Forgive me for implying that you are as unfeeling as the rest of the mill owners."

"Apology accepted," she said curtly, though it wasn't much of one. "I'll see you at breakfast."

"I'm not finished." His jaw tightened. "I admit I made assumptions about you . . . but only because I don't know you well enough. I should like to remedy that, so I can form a proper opinion of you and your mills."

She cocked her head. "You mean, so you can write about them—and me—as harshly as you've done all the others."

He looked startled.

"I'm no fool, Lord Stephen. Since all anyone wants to discuss these days are the difficulties of the textile trade, sometimes the press actually deigns to interview a female like me. I presume you wish to do the same."

He crossed a pair of rather impressive arms over what looked to be an equally impressive chest. "And if I do?"

"I shall regretfully have to decline. I have no desire to see you portray my mills as scenes of unspeakable horror because it suits your purpose."

A smug expression crossed his face. "So you're afraid of what I might learn by talking to you."

"Certainly not!"

"Then why not let me do it?"

Did he think her a complete fool? "Because you'll twist my words into an indictment of a business you know nothing of."

He recoiled as if she'd slapped him. "I may not run a mill but I know plenty about them. That's why I came here in the first place. To see if what I've been hearing about Hanson Cotton Works is true."

"And what is that, pray tell?"

"Why should I tell *you*? You don't want to tell me a thing about *your* precious mills." Triumph glinted in his eyes. "Besides, you can always go on one of your special tours, can't you? The ones where they show you everything."

Arrogant rascal. "I suppose Yvette already told you that Mr. Hanson refused to give me a tour at all."

"Did he, indeed?" His eyes narrowed. "It doesn't surprise me. If what I've heard of him is true, he wouldn't want anyone, even a fellow owner, witnessing his methods."

Drat it all. Lord Stephen couldn't have garnered her interest more effectively if he'd offered her actual designs of English machines. She wished she could dismiss his sly hints, but she knew full well that he discovered things no one else did. *Someone* on the inside was always willing to talk to him. It was how he exposed cases where laws were ignored, how he brought great injustices into the public eye.

"If he's so secretive," she said, "how have *you* happened to hear of it?"

One corner of his mouth kicked up provocatively. "Wouldn't you like to know?"

Ooh, he was infuriating. But maybe she was going about this all wrong. As Mama was so fond of telling her, one could catch more flies with honey. Maybe she could make use of him, and in the process teach him a thing or two about responsible mill owners.

"I *would* like to know, actually. So much so that I might even be willing to agree to your interview."

That certainly made him take notice. "Really?"

"But only if you introduce me to your sources of information and let me ask them as many questions as I please."

His face closed up. "I can't guarantee they'll answer you."

"They're more likely to if I'm with you, aren't they?"

"Perhaps." He tilted his head, still wary. "And I suppose you expect to be given some measure of control over what I write about you and Montague Mills."

"Is that a possibility?"

"No," he said tersely.

"What a relief. For a moment, you had me thinking that members of the English press can be bought. In America, we believe that they shouldn't be stifled." He was still blinking at that remark when she added archly, "Although obviously someone should have considered stifling *you* long before now."

He burst into laughter. "You do speak your mind."

"As often as I can." And he was the first man to say so without its sounding like a criticism. To her annoyance, that softened her toward him. Somewhat. "So? Do we have a bargain?"

"Not yet. There are some things to work out first. For one, you and I cannot wander the town alone together speaking with my sources."

She shrugged. "My mother can chaperone."

"For another, I heard that you're leaving England soon. So when exactly do you mean to do this?"

"I'd like to begin tomorrow, if you can."

"In the middle of the house party?"

"Certainly. I'm not exactly the kind of woman who enjoys sitting around making silhouettes or embroidering gloves. And I doubt you're the kind of man to enjoy shooting or fishing or whatever else gentlemen do during a house party."

"On the contrary, I enjoy such activities upon occasion." A slow smile curved up his lips. "But I confess I'd much prefer squiring you about town."

The rough timbre of his voice affected her most tellingly. "Well, then," she said as she strove to ignore that. "Are we agreed?"

"I believe we are." He marched forward, forcing her to back up or be run down. When he halted, his gaze drifted unexpectedly to her lips. "All that's left is to seal our bargain with a kiss."

That fluttering in her belly began once more. "Why would we do that?"

With a broadening smile, he pointed overhead. "Because we're under the mistletoe again."

She looked up, dismayed to see there was indeed another kissing bough hanging from the ceiling. Goodness, how many of them were there?

Then it dawned on her. *That* was why he'd maneuvered her in this direction, the arrogant devil.

And just his mention of a kiss had her heart pounding again, even harder than before. She couldn't gather enough air to breathe, and what air there was seemed rich and thick, heavily perfumed by the Persian irises and Christmas roses of the conservatory.

Or maybe it was just the heat simmering between them that made it seem so. Good heavens, she didn't want to feel this for *him*, of all people.

"Oh, very well, get it over with," she said, trying for a dismissive tone.

As if he saw right through her, he smiled. Eyes gleaming in the dim light, he tipped up her chin with one hand. "Rules are rules."

Then he took her mouth with his.

And oh, what a kiss. His lips were harder this time, commanding rather than entreating. So when he ran his tongue along the seam of her lips, it seemed perfectly natural to open her mouth and let him in.

Everything got more interesting then. His tongue sank inside to play with hers in slow, silky caresses that warmed her blood and banished any lingering reluctance. He slipped his arms about her waist to anchor her against him; she looped hers about his neck to bring him even closer.

It was *amazing*, like no kiss she'd ever known. His mouth consumed hers with long, hot strokes that made something heady and wanton curl up from below to entwine her like steam.

This must be what desire felt like. Oh, help.

"Lord Stephen, we shouldn't," she whispered against his lips.

"Stephen," he corrected her, brushing kisses along the curve of her cheek. "And why shouldn't we . . . Amanda?"

If her brain had been working properly, she could have summoned up any number of reasons. But it wasn't and she couldn't, and now he was kissing her again. That alone kept her from answering.

And when Lord Stephen . . . *Stephen* was plundering her mouth, he turned into something other than an insufferable English radical. He became a man, who tasted of brandy and smelled of wood smoke and wool, who knew how to kiss very, *very* well.

Who made her blood run hot and her knees wobble.

A noise in the hall arrested her. She pushed away from him. "Stop that," she hissed. "Someone's coming."

"I hope not." With a grin, he reached up and plucked a white berry, then pressed it into her hand. "I'd say there's at least . . . oh, ten more of these. We might be here all night."

That sent her pulse into a shameless scamper. She'd never expected Lord Stephen of *The London Monitor* to be such a flirt, though she was beginning to understand that *Stephen* was an outrageous one.

She closed her fingers about the berry. "What have the berries got to do with anything?"

"For every kiss, a berry must be plucked," he said huskily, "and once they're gone, there can be no more kissing."

That was the silliest thing she'd ever heard. "What's to stop a woman from plucking all the berries from the mistletoe while no one's watching?"

He chuckled. "For one thing, that would be cheating. For another, the women like the game, too."

No point in denying that; he'd know she was lying. Because she was rather enjoying having a man tease her. The men she'd known in America were far more interested in telling her what a woman ought to do, and how she ought to do it.

Yet this English lord was definitely *flirting* with her. Maybe it was time for her to try flirting back. It certainly seemed more enjoyable than fighting.

With what she hoped was a coy smile, she held out her hand. "Well, then, if there's to be no cheating, you must play fair. By my count, you gave me *two* kisses. You owe me another berry."

His amused gaze darkened into something more provocative. Keeping his gaze locked with hers, he reached up and plucked a second, then a third.

When she regarded him quizzically, he took her hand and put one berry into it. "This is for the kiss we just had." He lowered his voice to a seductive murmur as he placed the other berry in her palm and closed her fingers over it. "And *this* is for the one we're about to have."

Oh goodness. If he kissed her any more, she would end up doing something she was sure to regret. Best to retreat while she still could.

"Thank you for the warning." Slipping her hand free, she ducked around him and headed for the door.

"Hey, that's not fair!" he cried from behind her.

She paused in the doorway to blow him a kiss. "There you go."

"That doesn't count," he growled and started toward her.

"It's not my fault you plucked the berry prematurely." She waggled her fingers at him, delighting in his scowl. "See you in the morning for our trip to town."

Stifling a laugh, she flew down the hall and up the stairs. She heard him grumbling behind her, but she knew he didn't dare pursue her. There were too many people about.

Remembering the look on his face, she entered her room and collapsed into laughter. That had been fun. She'd never had fun with a man before. Maybe it was time she did more of that, too. Flirting and fun might be a nice change.

She threw herself down on her bed with a grin. And if in the process she also got to torment Lord Stephen Corry for his rigid opinions, so much the better.

Chapter Three

Alone in the breakfast room the next morning, Stephen swallowed some regrets along with his eggs and toast. He shouldn't have kissed Amanda in the conservatory. He shouldn't have kissed her more than once. And he definitely shouldn't have had erotic dreams about her that would rival the activities in a whorehouse.

Bloody hell. While his mind feared that Miss Keane was as ruthless as any other mill owner, his damned body didn't want to believe that *Amanda* was anything but the sweet, artless woman whose mouth he'd ravaged beneath the mistletoe. That same mouth had featured so luridly in his fantasies that just remembering them made him hard as a—

"Good morning," a familiar female voice chirped. "I'm glad to see you didn't forget about me and Mama going into town with you today."

Oh, God, could this get any worse?

"I didn't expect you to rise so early, though," Amanda added.

Rise? Could she actually *see* his arousal?

He groaned. Of course not. But she *would* see it when he stood, which he must— Oh God, and now her mother was entering the room, too.

"Good morning, ladies." He rose and bowed in one smooth motion, hoping that it was enough to shield him, then waited until they'd swept past him to the buffet before straightening. By the time they took their seats, he was safely ensconced in his own.

"You're up early, too," he told Amanda.

"This isn't early—at home I'm out of bed by five."

Just the mention of her and a bed threatened to overset his control. Determinedly, he glanced at her mother. "You, too, Mrs. Keane?"

"Oh, I never rise before ten. But then, I don't run the mills. Amanda insists upon being there as early as her workers."

The mills. Right. He should focus on that.

Wait, she went in at the same time as her workers? How odd. Few mill owners did *that*. Of course, few were women, either. Amanda seemed to be extraordinary in many respects.

Like the fact that she ate a robust breakfast more suitable to a farmer's daughter. And that she—like her mother—was dressed soberly this morning. Like him, they wore no expensive linens, no rich silks, no lace, as if somehow they'd known that serviceable wool gowns and cheap cotton fichus would be more suitable for today's foray into town.

"So where exactly are we going this morning?" Mrs. Keane asked.

Stephen glanced at Amanda. "Didn't you tell her?"

"Not the specifics. You didn't mention them when we discussed it. You were too busy making bargains." She cast him a secretive little smirk that tightened every muscle in his body. He could practically see the look on her face last night as she'd blown him that kiss.

"Ah, yes." Let her smirk. He'd have the last laugh. "You

said you wanted to speak to my sources. I thought we'd start in town with Mrs. Chapel."

"And what does Mrs. Chapel do at the mill?"

"Nothing."

"Then why are we visiting her?"

"You'll see."

Last night he'd decided there was only one way to decipher the real Amanda Keane—put her in certain situations and watch her react. Because he had to know where she stood. He owed it to himself . . . and to the girl whose memory he honored. To all the children who deserved better than a wretched existence as pauper apprentices.

After they finished breakfast, they headed into the foyer. Amanda donned a somber blue cloak and bonnet very different from her festive green yesterday, yet they didn't keep him from itching to kiss her as she passed under the bough.

He scowled. Why the hell must she do this to him? He'd kissed plenty of women in his day. While at Oxford, he'd even joined Warren on a few expeditions to the stews of London. Yet nothing had ever affected him as profoundly as the simple pleasure of having Amanda in his arms. Indeed, it was all he could do not to drag her back into them as he helped her into the carriage.

While the women settled against the squabs, he leapt in to take his seat opposite them and ordered the driver to go on. Then he leaned back to fix Amanda with an even look. "You mentioned touring some English mills. Which ones?"

"Henley in Manchester. Wright's in Liverpool. And of course, the most important one and the one I primarily wished to see—New Lanark."

"Ah, yes," he said cynically, "everyone's favorite model cotton mill."

"We were very impressed," Mrs. Keane gushed. "I've never seen a mill town built from the ground up, with decent lodgings for the workers and schools for their children."

But Amanda had caught Stephen's sarcasm. "I take it you are *not* so impressed, my lord."

He sighed. "Don't misunderstand me. I admire what Robert Owen has done. I merely wish he wasn't the *only* forward-thinking fellow. It took him years to make enough profit to please his investors, and even then, he had to buy some of them out before he found men willing to see his vision. Sadly, no one else wants to follow his stellar example."

"I do," Amanda said stoutly. "I hope to model my own factories after New Lanark."

"*Hope* to? So that's a new endeavor?"

She glanced out at the snowy fields they were passing. "For me, yes."

Mrs. Keane smiled thinly. "My late husband and daughter didn't always see eye to eye on the running of our mills. Now that he's gone, Amanda wants to make improvements." Before he could remark that *wanting* and *doing* were very different things, Mrs. Keane added, "And speaking of family disagreements, is it true that you and your brother, the marquess, are at odds?"

The abrupt change of subject, not to mention the highly personal nature of the question, threw him entirely off guard.

"Mama," Amanda chided, "that's his lordship's private business."

"It can't be all *that* private," her mother said with a sniff. "Everyone heard him and his brother arguing in the drawing room last night."

He burst into laughter. Mrs. Keane was apparently as forthright as her daughter. "Warren was merely trying to convince me in his usual autocratic fashion to move back home, where he can keep me under his thumb." His brother hadn't admitted that was his intention, but Stephen suspected it was.

"You don't live at home?" Amanda asked, bracing herself in a turn.

"No. If I did, it would make it harder for me to convince the workers that I'm their champion. This may surprise you, but some of us 'whose idea of hard work is writing an article' have the courage of our convictions."

Amanda winced. "I . . . er . . . suppose I should apologize for that particular remark. I know that you do more than write—that you give speeches about reform and take great care with your research."

"Do you?"

"I'm well aware of your reputation," she said defensively. "And I laud your efforts. I just hate your assumption that all mill owners are alike, that the perfidy of the ones you *haven't* destroyed with your pen merely hasn't yet been revealed."

He resisted the impulse to squirm under that rather harsh assessment. He focused on the bad ones because he wanted to shut them down. That didn't mean he hated all mill owners.

"So if you don't live at home, Lord Stephen," Mrs. Keane said, clearly trying to steer the discussion into safer waters, "where do you live?"

He tore his gaze from Amanda to smile genially at her mother. "I have modest lodgings in Chelsea, but I'm seldom there since I travel so much."

Mrs. Keane arched an eyebrow. "And how does your wife feel about that?"

He stifled a smile. Apparently matchmaking mothers were the same the world over. "I'm not married, madam."

"Why not?" the woman pressed. "You seem old enough."

"Mama!" Amanda said with more force this time . . . and a decided blush.

Absurdly, that blush pleased him. It reminded him that beneath her fierce mill-owner exterior was a warm woman with a penchant for hot, intimate kisses.

He flashed Mrs. Keane his most ingratiating smile. "Few Englishwomen are interested in marrying a lord who eschews the trappings of his rank, especially a younger son."

That seemed to catch Amanda's interest. "I thought younger sons in England usually became clergymen or barristers or soldiers."

"They do. Sadly, I'm not terribly religious, wigs make me itch, and by the time I was old enough to consider becoming a soldier, England had stopped fighting Boney."

It was a flip response. But telling the truth—that he was too wary of all such institutions to join them—would only rouse more questions. "So there you have it. Instead, I write. And no woman wants to marry a writer with only a bit of money left to him by his mother, and no land at all. Land is everything in England."

"*Money* is everything in America," Mrs. Keane said.

"So I hear. But my inheritance is hardly enough to tempt anyone, English or American." It was the truth . . . and also a warning, if she wanted her daughter to set her cap for him. "And despite my brother's wishes to bring me back into the fold, I'm not interested in giving up my ideals to return to a world where I'm neither comfortable nor welcome."

"I see." Mrs. Keane smoothed her skirts. "In other words, you aren't married because your wife would have to join you in being an outcast from society."

"Oh, heavens," Amanda muttered.

He chuckled. "You could put it that way."

"Then Englishwomen must be stupid indeed," Mrs. Keane said.

That stymied him. "Because they don't wish to be outcasts?"

"Because they force you to choose between two opposite spheres, when there are many gradations between."

"In America, perhaps," he said dryly. "There aren't many gradations in England."

Mrs. Keane sniffed. "I hardly believe that. I've met several respectable females who are neither outcasts nor ladies of high rank. Surely you could find a woman among them who's willing to compromise for the sake of love."

"You don't understand, Mama." Amanda steadied her gaze on him. "It's not the women who don't want to compromise. It's Lord Stephen."

He met her gaze evenly. "I suppose you consider my refusal to compromise a flaw in my character."

"That's a flaw in anyone's character, young man," Mrs. Keane said. "Especially in a husband. Marriage is all about compromise."

"For the women," Amanda said tartly. "Never for the men."

Her mother stared at her. "That's not true."

"Isn't it?" The resentment festering in Amanda's voice gave him pause. "Papa never compromised with you. Things were always his way."

Was that also true of the man's treatment of his daughter? Was that why Amanda was so quick to take offense when a man with strong opinions started voicing them?

Mrs. Keane sighed. "All right, I'll grant you that." She smiled sadly. "But that's precisely why I know how important compromise is, my dear."

Stephen wanted to hear more about Amanda and her father. About *her*. But just then, they pulled up in front of a shop in the center of town.

Amanda looked out and frowned. "We're going shopping?"

"No, but I want it to appear that way. I'd rather not call attention to Mrs. Chapel's willingness to speak to us by driving right up to her cottage in your brother's impressive carriage."

That sobered both Amanda and her mother, as well it should. Warren hadn't been entirely wrong to worry about the danger of Stephen's activities. But it wasn't dangerous for *Stephen*; it was dangerous for the workers feeding him information.

As soon as they'd disembarked, the coachman handed down the basket Yvette had sent along. Then Stephen ushered his companions through a series of alleys and streets until they were strolling on the outskirts of town.

So far his companions had asked no questions and made no fuss. Had Mrs. Keane known what she was agreeing to when she came along? Or had Amanda pawned it off as some fun excursion? Whatever the case, Mrs. Keane didn't look at all perturbed when he led them up to a tumbledown wattle-and-daub cottage.

He knocked, and Mrs. Chapel answered the door with her babe on one hip. "Milord!" Pleasure wreathed her face in smiles until she spotted his companions. Then she turned wary. With a quick survey of the road behind them, she swung the door wide open. "Quick, come inside, if you please. Before anyone sees."

Neither of his companions questioned her caution, but Amanda did shoot him an odd look as they entered the single room that constituted the entire home.

In the center was a rickety table with four mismatched chairs, and a kettle was on the hob. On one side sat a worn chest of drawers. The other side held a crudely built trundle bed, a basket that served as a crib, and a separate horsehair mattress lacking a bedstead. The beds were neatly made up, though a three-year-old wearing a threadbare cotton dress sat atop the trundle bed banging a pot enthusiastically with a wooden spoon.

Mrs. Keane's eyes lit up as she saw the child, but Amanda turned distant once more, her eyes regarding him with a suspicion that roused guilt in his chest.

He tamped it down ruthlessly. "Mrs. Chapel, I've brought some friends from Walton Hall to visit. This is Mrs.

Keane and her daughter Miss Amanda Keane. They own mills in America."

Mrs. Chapel's wariness turned to confusion. "You mean, *Mr.* Keane owns the mills, don't you?"

Amanda smiled. "Actually, *I* own the mills. They were left to me and my brother by my father. My brother sold his share to me with my mother's blessing."

Something like awe passed over Mrs. Chapel's face. "A woman owner. Who'd have thought it? America must be very different."

"Not as different as we'd like," Mrs. Keane said dryly, "but it's so vast a land that both men *and* women are needed to run things." She stepped forward. "May I hold the babe?"

"Oh! Why, of course, ma'am. Though hand her right back if she turns cross. Wouldn't want her to spit up on you."

As Mrs. Keane took the child and began to coo at it, Stephen handed Mrs. Chapel the basket. "The mistress of Walton Hall asked that I bring you these. Her guests went shooting yesterday and managed to kill more pheasants than anyone at the hall could eat. She said she was sure you could use them."

Mrs. Chapel blinked back tears as she took the birds. "Oh, yes, milord, thank you. Tell her it's most kind of her. The lads will make short work of these."

"How many boys do you have?" Mrs. Keane asked as she jiggled the baby up and down.

"Three, counting the baby, ma'am. And Mary there makes four children altogether."

Mrs. Keane glanced about the small room and frowned, but didn't say anything. He sympathized. He'd long ago become accustomed to seeing whole families crammed into a room the size of a pantry at home, but that didn't mean he liked it.

"Tom and Jimmy are at the mill right now, along with Mr. Chapel," Stephen said.

"I would work there meself," Mrs. Chapel said, "but someone has to tend the little ones."

Mrs. Keane blinked. "Surely you aren't old enough to have lads of an age to work at the mill."

That caught him off guard. Mrs. Chapel looked every bit of her thirty years, even a little older. Mrs. Keane shouldn't be surprised.

Mrs. Chapel preened a bit. "Thank you kindly, ma'am, but my oldest is nearly eleven."

"Eleven is the *oldest*?" Amanda looked shocked, which gave him pause. "How old is the younger one?"

"Seven," Stephen said in a hard voice. "Tom is a mule scavenger."

Amanda fixed him with a horrified look. "Climbing about under the moving parts of the spinning mule for whatever bits of cotton fall," she said, as if to clarify.

"That *is* what a mule scavenger does, isn't it?" he said coldly. "Don't you use them in your own mills?"

Mrs. Keane gaped at him. "Our mule scavengers are fourteen, my lord. My husband used to hire them as young as twelve, but Amanda refuses to hire anyone before the age of fourteen."

"Anyone?" He turned to Amanda. "That's the youngest age of *any* of your workers?"

"Yes. The piecers and tenters are generally older."

Astonishing. There wasn't a mill in England that started their apprentices as old as fourteen. But neither her nor her mother's shock had been feigned. Perhaps Amanda *wasn't* as hard-nosed as he'd assumed.

Then again, he'd been fooled by owners before.

Mrs. Keane now had a martial light in her eyes. "How can they let a seven-year-old work in the mill?"

Mrs. Chapel turned defensive. "We don't have no choice, ma'am. They hired my husband as a mule spinner only because the two boys could work, too. I was agin' it myself, but my husband—"

"Yes, yes, I'm sure he saw no way out," Mrs. Keane said. "I'm not talking about your and your husband's choices, Mrs. Chapel. Sometimes we have to do difficult things to support our families." She glanced at Stephen. "But I was told it was illegal in England for any mill to employ children under the age of nine."

At the word *illegal*, Mrs. Chapel whirled on Stephen in a panic. "You said you wouldn't make trouble for me husband! He needs this post, milord. If they turn him off because you report Mr. Hanson—"

"They won't turn him off," Stephen said. "No one will know who gave me the information."

"Really?" Amanda said. "You can promise her that?"

The hint of accusation in her voice made him bristle. "Why do you think I'm taking these precautions? When I write my article, I won't use the Chapel name. I won't give specifics anyone can tie to her or her husband. Trust me, plenty of other seven-year-olds work in that mill. And six-year-olds and five-year-olds and—"

"Enough," Amanda said, her voice soft with compassion. "I know that your intentions are good, but mill communities are small. You must be careful or you'll endanger the very people you want to help."

"I suppose you think I should look the other way and never try to change things," he snapped. "Let devils like Hanson bully their workers, paying them wages so low that they're practically forced to sell their children in order to eat. Let them put the children in dangerous situations and punish them by—"

"No, of course not," she said, her cheeks now as pale as Mrs. Chapel's.

"I've been doing this awhile. I know how to keep the workers safe." He turned to Mrs. Chapel. "I promise you, nothing will happen except that Hanson will be forced to follow the law of the land and not the law of profit."

"And if something does happen," Amanda told her, "I'm sure my sister-in-law up at Walton Hall can find work for your husband."

He stifled a snort. And she thought *he* was making promises he couldn't keep. Still, her words seemed to calm Mrs. Chapel's fears where his own assertions hadn't.

"Thank you, miss," she said gratefully. "It's much appreciated."

Taking out his notepad and pencil, he licked the tip. "I've been asking everyone certain questions, Mrs. Chapel, so I can get my facts straight. If you don't mind, I'd like to ask you the same ones."

When she glanced to Amanda for reassurance, it annoyed him. *Amanda*, not he, was supposed to be the person no one trusted. It was galling. It had taken him a week to gain Mrs. Chapel's trust, and Amanda had gained it in minutes. He still wasn't entirely sure she deserved it.

Mrs. Chapel seemed to consider a moment longer, then steadied her shoulders. "Things has got bad, real bad, at Hanson Cotton Works of late. If you think you can make them better, milord, I'm willing to tell you what I can."

Chapter Four

On the walk back to the shop where their carriage had been left, Amanda couldn't even bear to look at Stephen for fear she'd fly into a rage. Over the past few hours she'd begun to suspect why he'd brought them to Mrs. Chapel's, and if she was right, then he was the most deceitful, pompous—

"I can't believe they work those poor children so long and hard," Mama said in a hollow voice as they walked down an alley.

Amanda's throat closed up at the thought of everything Mrs. Chapel had revealed. Workers at Hanson Cotton Works endured shifts of at least sixteen hours, which often stretched far into the night, in horrible conditions. Awful punishments were administered to those foolish enough to fall asleep. Accidents were so common, they were scarcely even reported any more.

"And the apprentices are so young, too," Mama said. "It's appalling."

They were called "pauper apprentices"—most of them

orphans taken from the workhouses in London to labor in the mills until they were twenty-one. Some began as young as four—four!—working as mule scavengers. Mr. Hanson and his men ought to be horsewhipped.

"It's appalling indeed," Amanda choked out.

"That's all you have to say?" Stephen snapped.

Oh, that tore it. She halted just as they reached the alley's end. "Mama, I'd like a word alone with his lordship."

Her mother glanced from Amanda's set features to Stephen's narrowed gaze. "I'm not sure that's a good idea."

"I promise to leave him in one piece. That's about all I can promise." When her mother paled, Amanda softened her fierce tone. "Please just go on to the carriage. We won't be long."

Fortunately, Mama knew when to refrain from arguing with her headstrong daughter.

The moment she'd left, Amanda whirled on Stephen. "Why did you bring me to Mrs. Chapel's?"

Something flickered in his eyes. Guilt? She doubted it. He was incapable of *that*.

He crossed his arms over his chest. "You said you wanted to speak to my sources."

"*You* said you wanted to interview me. Except that this *was* the interview, wasn't it? To see how I reacted to the recitation of such horrible, despicable—"

"Yes," he said tightly.

She trembled with a fury she could scarcely contain. "And you thought I would approve of such methods? You thought me such a monster?"

"No!" He raked his hair away from his face. "I merely . . . Other mill owners regard these practices as acceptable, even necessary to their profits. The bastards don't care about the human cost. I can't tell you how many times I've listened to them defend their cruelties in Parliament speeches."

"So you assumed I was as bad as they." Her belly roiled. "You *kissed* me last night—several times—while thinking that I might be—"

"No." He gritted his teeth. "You don't understand." Stepping closer, he lowered his voice. "I had to determine whether you were an ally or an enemy. I think I have good reason for caution."

"Really? Have *I* personally given you any reason?"

"Not yet, but—"

"Not *yet*? Are you waiting for me to show my true colors?"

A distinct unease crossed his face. "Certainly not, but—"

"We're all the same to you, aren't we? All monsters."

"I do not think you a monster," he bit out.

"You could have fooled me." Before he could respond, she said, "Tell me something, my lord. Where do you think your cotton shirt and cravat were made? Or did you personally see to it that they were produced by handloom weavers in a cottage somewhere?"

"Of course not," he said stiffly. "There are scarcely any of those left in England."

"Precisely. Because people need cheaply made cotton goods. So *somebody's* mills have to produce them. Wouldn't it be better to support those mills that follow fair practices, rather than trying to tear down an entire industry?"

"I'm not doing that!"

"No? Without so much as a shred of evidence, you apparently assumed that my mills are as awful as Hanson Cotton Works. Have you ever even been to America?"

"I have not." He drew himself up. "But I have trouble believing that American mills are any better than English ones."

"*My* mills are better!" Amanda cried. "I can only speak for my own. Unlike you, I don't presume to know the practices of every mill in the world. But I should hope that most owners are conscientious enough not to prey on their workers."

"Most? I doubt that, having spent countless hours in research and observation."

"Of the worst mills you can find."

"Yes! The ones that need changing. It makes no sense to look at the good ones."

"Maybe if people were to hear how things *could* be, they might push for change more willingly."

He glared at her. "People only change if you shock them into it."

"Now you sound like a mill owner who justifies his harsh treatment by saying that people only work hard if beaten." Her voice caught. "I suppose you used the same argument to justify your manipulating me so you could find out where I stood on these matters. Instead of *asking* me, like a decent person."

He looked momentarily shaken. Then his eyes hardened. "How could I have been sure you would tell the truth?"

"Why would I lie about practices I thought were, to use your words, 'acceptable' and 'necessary' to my 'profits'? You pointed out last night that I speak my mind. Did you think I wouldn't speak it about this?"

He met her gaze coldly. "And what about your determination to talk to my sources? You had some purpose for that which you didn't bother to share with me."

Drat it all, she wasn't like him. She wasn't! "You never asked my reasons, so I never told you. But they were innocuous enough. I wanted to find out why the English are more successful in their cotton textile production than we Americans."

"Well, if American mills are all as perfect as you claim, then the owners of English mills succeed because they hire children and work them to death!"

"That is not why!" She thrust her face up to his. "I've run

factories long enough to know that horrible conditions lead to accidents and losses. Such practices don't even make good business sense. And when it comes to mistreating children that young . . ."

She choked down bile, unable even to think of a child as young as four in a mill.

Unexpectedly, he pulled her into his arms. "I'm sorry." When she tried to struggle free, he wouldn't let her. "I admit I jumped to conclusions about you." He brushed a kiss to her hair. "I just . . . worried that you were too good to be true. And I stupidly thought this the best way to find out."

Pushing against him, she scowled. "This, and kissing me. Seeing what you could wheedle out of me by flirtation."

"Absolutely not." His eyes burned into hers. "The kisses had naught to do with it."

"Really?" she said bitterly. "They weren't an attempt to soften me up?"

He shook his head. "Perhaps I had some notion along those lines at the beginning." He rubbed his thumb over her lips. "But our kisses rapidly became something else. An unintended complication. An unwise attraction."

"Very unwise," she agreed, only somewhat mollified by his assertion that his flirtations had been honest. Tearing herself from his embrace, she turned toward the end of the alley. "I'm glad to hear that we agree on that."

He blocked her path. "I'm sorry I manipulated you, but as far as I'm concerned, our bargain still holds."

"If you think I am going to—"

"You said I should write about the good mills. Very well, help me do that."

That arrested her. "How?"

"Tell me about *yours*."

"And you'll listen without bias," she said skeptically.

He flashed her a rueful smile. "I promise to try. And in

exchange, I'll see if I can't find people who can tell you more about English mills and how they work."

"The good factories," she prodded. "Not the awful ones who rule their workers by fear and deprivation."

"Yes." He stared at her. "But first I must finish my article. And I'm hoping you can assist me."

She lifted an eyebrow.

He seized her hand. "Help me interview the workers. I can see you have a good heart. What's more, the workers see it, too. They may be even more likely to talk honestly to a female owner who understands their concerns and isn't part of the English system. Working together, you and I could learn a great deal more than I could learn alone; we could put an end to at least one bad owner's reign. That's what you want, isn't it? To force Hanson into cleaning up his mill?"

She sighed, still haunted by the fear in Mrs. Chapel's voice for her family. "I do."

"So, what do you say?" he asked, his gaze intent on her. "It's Christmastide, a time to set things right. Will you help me with my article? Agree to a truce for the sake of the children?"

"I suppose." Her tone hardened. "But only because you need to nail Mr. Hanson and his disgusting compatriots to a wall."

"*We* need to do that." Cocking his head, he smiled faintly. "I had no idea you had such a bloodthirsty streak."

"Luckily for you, I can restrain it when necessary."

"Well, you did promise your mother to leave me in one piece," he teased.

If he thought he could jolly her out of her bad humor, he had another think coming. "That's the only thing that saved you from my wrath," she said, and slid past him.

"I was saved from your wrath?" he called after her. "I think I missed that part."

As she headed down the street, his laughter rang in her ears.

Let him laugh. He would soon find she wasn't the sort to easily give up a grudge. Especially one that involved her being manipulated by some *man*.

Christmastide or no, it would be a long time before she forgave Lord Stephen Corry.

✦ ✦ ✦

Five days had passed since Stephen's argument with Amanda in the alley, and to his irritation, they were once again surrounded by far too many people. Earlier in the day, the servants had brought piles of holly, cedar, and other fragrant greens into the drawing room, and the ladies were now weaving them into garlands and wreaths in preparation for hanging them tomorrow, on Christmas Eve.

"I'm so glad you accepted my husband's invitation to shoot, Mr. Hanson," Yvette said as the mill owner helped himself to some cucumber sandwiches. "We *do* so want to be an important part of the community in our new home. I'm just sorry that the sleet forced all of you gentlemen inside."

"I'm not sorry one bit, with such lovely ladies for company." Hanson glanced over to where Amanda was cutting lengths of wire for the wreaths and flashed her an oily smile. "And such industrious ones, too. I'm rather surprised, my lady, that you didn't leave all this to your servants. I should hate to see Miss Keane cut one of her pretty fingers with those wire cutters."

Amanda's eyes narrowed dangerously before she caught herself and smoothed a smile across her face. "I'd be happy to have *you* cut the wires. It would be *such* a help, a big strong fellow like you."

Stephen nearly choked on his wassail, even though he was perfectly aware that the point of inviting Hanson was for Amanda to have a chance at persuading the man to let her tour his mill.

Keeping an eye on the arse now heading over to help her, Stephen rose to refill his glass with wassail. These past few days, Amanda had seemed perfectly content to go everywhere with him, speak to everyone, find out everything . . . as long as her mother was with them.

Now that he'd come to know her better, he wanted more—private moments with her and a chance to kiss her again. He'd gone to the conservatory every night, but she was never there.

It was driving him insane. And that, too, drove him insane. He had no business wanting a more intimate friendship. How could it work between them?

"You do that so well, Mr. Hanson," Amanda said sweetly. "I would dearly love to see you commanding all those strapping fellows at Hanson Cotton Works. Are you quite certain you won't have a chance to take me about it sometime?"

Hanson ran his gaze down her in a way that made Stephen want to leap across the table and throttle him. "Perhaps on your next visit to Walton Hall, Miss Keane. With the holidays approaching, my workers don't need anyone as beautiful as you distracting them from their labors."

When it looked as if she might throttle the man herself, Stephen said, "How is your mother, Miss Keane? Yvette told me she has a cold."

Amanda drew in a deep breath as she faced him. "I'm afraid so. She has taken to her bed today in hopes that she'll be well rested for the festivities tomorrow, so with any luck we'll see her at breakfast."

"Speaking of Christmas Eve," Blakeborough broke in to ask his sister, "will there be a Yule log?"

"I hope so." Yvette wrapped some ribbon around a giant wreath. "It's still drying out in the stable, but our servants assure me it will burn well enough tomorrow night. Why?"

"You know Edwin," Clarissa said archly. "Everything must be perfect to keep him content."

Blakeborough lifted an eyebrow. "And you know Clarissa. Everything must be chaotic to keep her amused."

When Clarissa glared at him and looked as if she was about to say something cutting, Yvette said, "Edwin, why don't you help Amanda hang this wreath on the front door?"

"I'll help her." Stephen hurried over to pick up the wreath. It would finally give him a few moments alone with Amanda. "I could use some fresh air anyway."

"So could I," Amanda said blithely, looking relieved to leave Hanson's side.

The sleet had stopped, but the cold had not, so as soon as they were out on the portico, she shivered. "When I'd rather be outside in freezing temperatures than inside a warm, cozy room with a certain mill owner, you know I truly detest the man."

He laughed. "I could tell that long before we came out."

She shot him an alarmed look. "Could *he*, do you think?"

"I doubt it." He wrapped some wire around the knocker to support the wreath. "I know you well enough to see it, but he's too full of himself to notice anything but a pretty woman flattering him."

"I hope you're right." She supported the wreath from below while he threaded the wire through the ribbon. "But it worries me that he won't let me tour the mill. I wonder if he's heard about our questioning people."

"No, he's probably just the sort of man who believes that women shouldn't run factories."

"And you?" She toyed with the ribbon. "What do *you* believe?"

"Do you care?"

Her gaze shot to his. "Of course." She forced a smile. "You're writing about me, aren't you? I should hope I care what you write."

But he wasn't fooled. Sometimes when he least expected it, she looked at him as if she cared very much what he thought of her. It was the only thing that gave him hope she might one day forgive him. "I believe any factory would be very lucky to have you for an owner."

The blazing smile she shot him made his heart catch in his throat. God, how he wished he had more time with her. The house party ended on Boxing Day, and she left two weeks later.

He wasn't ready for this . . . whatever it was . . . to end. Which was odd, since he generally had no interest in prolonging a relationship with a woman he merely desired.

But you don't merely desire her. That's the trouble.

He scowled. That couldn't be true. Mustn't be true. She was returning to America, and he couldn't follow. He had too much left to do here in England.

"Well, I hope you're right that Mr. Hanson hasn't guessed what we're up to," Amanda said as he opened the door for her. "He could make matters very difficult for the workers. Have you gathered enough material for your article yet?"

"I believe so, yes." He shut the door behind them. "I was planning on working on it some more in a bit. Would you like to help?"

Pleasure suffused her cheeks a lovely pink before she masked it. "Me? What do I know about writing?"

"You were fairly eloquent when dressing me down in the alley five days ago," he pointed out as they paused just inside the door.

Now her cheeks were positively crimson. "I was maybe . . . a bit too forceful in my opinions."

"No, you weren't. But I hope you've formed a better opinion of me over the past week."

"Maybe a *little* better," she said with a brief, almost teasing smile that sent his pulse galloping.

"So will you help me with the article? Read it over, put in some comments?"

"All right." She glanced back toward the drawing room, and her gaze sharpened. "I'll definitely do whatever I can to make sure that a certain individual gets his just deserts."

A chuckle escaped him. How could he have ever thought her a hard-nosed owner? Beneath that pragmatic exterior beat a heart as wide as the ocean. "Let's meet in the conservatory in half an hour to work on it."

She arched an eyebrow at Stephen. "I think not. The atmosphere in the library is more conducive to writing articles. Right now I'll tell everyone I'm going up to keep Mama company. But I'll just check on her and then sneak back down. After I've been gone a bit, you can make some excuse for leaving the drawing room and meet me in the library."

He forced a look of disappointment to his face, though inside he was doing a little dance. Thanks to her randy brother and sister-in-law, a kissing bough hung in the library, too. She probably hadn't noticed.

"Very well," he said, trying to sound downcast. "If you insist."

For the next half hour, all he could think about was meeting her in private. Holding her. Taking her mouth with his. Caressing her. So when he walked into the library to find her reading a book right under the mistletoe, he exulted.

She was so engrossed in her reading that she didn't even glance up when he entered. Closing the door behind him, he paused to look at her, and something knotted in his chest.

God, she was magnificent, even in that subdued gray wool gown she favored. Her glorious red hair was an upsweep of ravishing curls, and her freckled cheeks shone pink and pretty in the muddy light from the window. It was enough to turn a gentleman into a raving rogue.

But it wasn't just her looks that captivated him. She was the first woman with whom he felt entirely at ease, the first woman who didn't make him impatient to be somewhere else. When he was with her, he found himself yearning for something deeper, something more . . . permanent.

No, that was ridiculous. Right now, he yearned for one thing only—a kiss. More than one, if he could manage it. He started toward her and reached up to pluck a berry from the bough, then froze.

There were none. How could that be?

His disappointment was so acute that he spoke without thinking. "What happened to the mistletoe?"

Startled, she looked up from her book. Then she followed his gaze to the bough and smoothed her expression. "How should I know?"

Remembering what she'd said about why women didn't pluck the bough clean themselves, he scowled at her. "Are you telling me the berries all just disappeared?"

With a shrug, she returned her gaze to her book. "The house party has been going on for days. I can't help it if the men here take every opportunity to blackmail women into kissing them."

"It isn't blackmail," he grumbled. "It's supposed to be fun."

"So I'm told."

But he noticed she fought a smile as she stared down at her book. The little minx had probably plucked them all herself, just to torment him.

Now thoroughly out of sorts, he dropped into a chair across from the settee where she sat. "What are you reading?"

"*Christabel*, by Samuel Taylor Coleridge."

"Poetry? You?"

"I *like* poetry. It has a steady rhythm, like music. Or the machines at the mills. It's quite soothing."

He shook his head. Only Amanda could find poetry in a mill. "You really enjoy running your factories and working in them every day, don't you?"

"I do." She got a faraway look in her eye. "I like seeing something beautiful spun from a piece of nature. I like the whoosh and clack of the flying shuttle, the hum of the spinning mule, and the haze of cotton dust that casts everything in a soft light."

Hearing her speak of it made his gut clench. If he ever did offer marriage to her, she would never accept. Not if it meant staying in England. She too had a mission of sorts, very different from his.

"I'm afraid I can't see them as romantically as you," he said.

"Only because you don't look at them in the proper light." She held out her hand. "So, let's see how you *do* view them. Is that your article?"

"Yes." Handing it over, he sat back and watched as she looked it over.

It was a bit disconcerting. He'd never actually witnessed someone reading his work. He didn't like it. She sighed, she marked things with a pencil, she furrowed her brow. It was enough to drive a man to drink.

When she gasped, he demanded to know why. She merely ordered him to hold his tongue until she was done.

At that point, he couldn't sit there any longer. Rising from the chair, he strode over to gaze out the window at the icicles melting off the eaves. Perhaps this hadn't been such a good idea. Perhaps she would hate how he'd characterized her. When he'd initially written the piece, he'd thought she might approve, but he was beginning to understand that Amanda—

"Very interesting," she mumbled.

He glanced over at her, his blood racing when he saw her set the pages down. "You're done?"

She looked up. "Yes."

"And you found it interesting." His stomach lurched. "In a good way? Or a bad way?"

"A good way, of course." She sounded surprised that he would think otherwise.

He released a breath. "You like it."

"I do. It's much more even-handed than your usual work."

Probably so. The whole time he'd been writing it, he'd heard her voice sounding in his ears, telling him to be fair. "You didn't mind that I contrasted your methods with those of Hanson."

"Of course not." Her cheeks colored. "I'm flattered that you spoke of admiring them."

She'd blushed more today than in the past five days. It brought his desire roaring to life.

Then she tapped the pencil against one sheet of paper and frowned. "But I'm confused about this part concerning a girl piecer. Jimmy Chapel is eleven, and I don't recall our interviewing any eight-year-old piecers."

He tensed. "That's because we didn't. Since you wanted me to be careful about implicating the workers, instead of using Mrs. Chapel's son for my example, I chose to make the piecer a girl."

Her eyes warmed. "You listened to what I said?"

"I'm not immune to criticism, you know," he muttered.

"I see that."

Her soft smile made him want to scoop her up and spend the rest of the afternoon ravishing her. "According to sources, there were several piecers at the mill, so I figured that would make it harder to determine whom I meant."

"Yes, but the way you describe her is so powerful, so true." She searched his face. "She feels very real to me. And not just a female version of Jimmy, either."

How astute of her to notice. He thought about denying it, but he couldn't. Not with Amanda. Not when she'd come to understand so much about him and his quest.

Possessed by an overwhelming urge to explain why this crusade was so important to him, he said, "You're right—

she's not a female version of Jimmy." He dragged in a heavy breath as memories assailed him. "She was a real girl named Peggy, whom I considered a friend. She died in the mills when I was eight, and I never forgot. So I do all of this for *her* . . . and children like her."

Chapter Five

For a moment, Amanda could only stare at him. She'd wondered what drove him, but she hadn't expected this. "How on earth does a marquess's son have a mill girl for a friend?"

"Not easily, I assure you." Glancing away, he speared his fingers through his hair in a gesture she'd come to adore.

But she dared not let him see how she felt, or he would guess that she was falling for him. And that was hopeless.

Even if he were enough of a rebel to consider marrying a woman in trade, she doubted he would move to America. He felt compelled to do what he did *here*, in England.

And did she even *want* him to marry her? What if she let him close, and he turned out to be like Papa, trying to take things over, trying to make *her* mills what he wanted?

He's nothing like Papa. Just look at what he wrote.

Yes. He'd shown he understood her, far more even than she'd guessed. It was gratifying. Intoxicating.

And a little alarming. Though it made her want to understand him, too. "How did you meet Peggy?"

He rose to roam the small sitting area like a caged beast. "My late mother used to help support a school for the children of our local mill workers. She would drag me along when she went to observe. Said it would be good for me, would teach me compassion."

His voice turned self-deprecating. "As you might imagine, I detested going. At eight, I was starting to be rather full of myself, and I hated being forced to deal with grubby urchins whom I considered beneath me. But I was a dutiful son, so I did as I was told, though not happily. Until I met Peggy."

A smile softened his face. "She was my age and the most beautiful girl I'd ever seen—always neat as a pin, with a face like a cherub and a head full of ginger curls. She took a shine to me when she caught me stealing away from Mother one day at the school to read a book. She, too, was a great lover of reading."

"She could read?"

"Oh, yes, she had a gift for it, a thirst for learning. And in her I'd found an ally. At first I lent her books from Father's library. I got in trouble for that, as you might imagine, so then I took to buying her books with my allowance."

"Your mother didn't mind," Amanda said softly.

"She told Father it was good for me to learn kindness to those beneath me." He shook his head. "She never understood—it wasn't about charity or kindness. It was about the books. None of my brothers were keen readers, but Peggy knew at once why Sir Walter Scott transported me, why Shakespeare lifted my heart. We could talk for hours just about that.

"Then one day she wasn't there at the school. When I asked about her, I was told that her father had fallen ill, so all his children had been put to work in the mills to keep the family afloat."

He sank onto the settee beside her, his eyes bleak. "I

made a fuss about it with Father, who said it was none of our concern. Mother said she sympathized, but we couldn't interfere with another family's choices." His voice grew choked. "As if there was a choice. Mill workers don't earn enough to have choices."

She took his hand in hers, but he hardly seemed conscious of it.

"Since I couldn't see her anymore, I wrote her a letter, but I got no answer. For a long time, I wasn't even sure if she'd received it. Then one day her father came to the manor. He said he thought it only right, since I'd been so kind to his girl, that I be told of . . . of . . ."

Sensing what was coming, she clutched his hand to her heart.

"Of her . . . death." A shuddering breath escaped him. "She fell into one of the machines and . . ." He stared blindly past her. "Well, you know what happens."

"I'm so sorry," she whispered, though the words were wholly inadequate. She brushed a kiss over his knuckles. "So very sorry. Eight is far too young to lose a friend."

"Eight is far too young to *die*." His angry gaze shot to hers. "And for what? Commerce? Cheap cotton shirts? It isn't right!"

"No, it's not." She lifted her other hand to cup his taut cheek. "Why do you think I'm so careful with my own factories? I could never bear it if some sleepy child got hurt. It's why I'm helping you with this article. I know how bad things *can* be if an owner is indifferent to the risks."

"The problem is there aren't enough owners like you." He let out a ragged sigh. "Sometimes it feels as if I write and shout and pound the walls and nothing happens."

"That's not true," she said earnestly. "Thanks to you and others, there's the Factory Acts, there's New Lanark . . . there are members of Parliament fighting for better conditions. It just takes time for things to change for the better."

"How can you always be so full of hope? I look and see only hardship and difficulty. You see potential."

"Because I believe most people have good intentions. They want to do the right thing. They want to help, to make improvements."

"But when faced with men like Hanson—"

"I look to people like *you*." She brushed back the lock of his hair falling into his eyes. "You're the ones who give me hope."

His gaze caught hers, fierce and intense and full of longing. It mirrored the longing in her . . . for a connection with him deeper than their platonic friendship of the past few days.

He obviously saw it, too, for hunger leapt in his face.

Suddenly she realized how close they sat, how tightly he gripped her hand . . . how hard she found it to breathe. His eyes deepened until they shone as glossy-dark as holly, and he lowered his head to hers infinitely slowly, as if giving her a chance to stop him.

There wasn't a chance in hell of that. So as her eyes slid closed, he kissed her.

It started tender and soft, the merest press of lips meant to get her attention. But soon it began a slow crescendo. His tongue slid inside to toy with hers. Then his hands clasped her head to hold her still so his mouth could give and take with impudent, hot strokes that made her blood roar and her heart thunder.

Even his kisses shouted.

Ohhhh, how *lovely*! How she'd missed this.

A strange excitement built in her belly and she squirmed, not sure why she felt the urge to press against him . . . everywhere. But he must have felt it, too, for he cupped her breast in an intimate caress.

She froze. She should shove his hand away. Shove *him* away.

There wasn't a chance in hell of that, either. So she pretended not to notice that he was kneading her breast, lightly, carefully, as if afraid she might revolt.

How could she revolt when she'd just been yearning to have his hands on her? When the sheer wonder of his fondling whipped her blood into a frenzy? Giving herself up to his caresses, she looped her hands about his neck and just held on.

His mouth grew wild on hers, and his hand grew bolder. Oh, it felt like heaven, all of it. She wanted more. She wanted everything.

After several moments of hot kisses and hotter caresses, he murmured against her lips, "I've dreamed for days of having you in my arms, putting my hands on you."

"Why didn't you do anything about it?" she whispered, arching into his hand.

"You know why." He planted kisses along the line of her jaw down to her neck. "Your mother was always around." Shooting her a wry glance, he said, "And you wouldn't go to the conservatory."

"Oh. Right." She began to regret her stubborn refusal to forgive him for his earlier manipulations, because this sweet intimacy was incredible. Now it was nearly Christmas Eve, and they had little time left to experience such delicious . . . astonishing . . .

"You did it on purpose," he growled against her throat. "And admit it, you plucked all those berries from the bough, too."

"Not a bit," she said, then betrayed herself with a giddy laugh.

"I *knew* it, you cheater." Even as his hand kept fondling her breast, his eyes gleamed with darker intent. "So now it's *my* turn to cheat."

He tugged her fichu from the neck of her pelisse-robe and tossed it over the back of the settee.

"Stephen!" she gasped, but any further protest died in her throat once he started kissing his way down inside the vee of her bodice. "Ohh, you . . . devilish fellow, what are you doing?"

"Claiming my kisses," he said hoarsely. "All the ones I would have taken if you'd left the berries on the bough."

Her breath came in hard gasps as he unbuttoned her front-opening gown just enough to draw it open and bare her corset and chemise to his gaze.

Oh, help. "You really shouldn't be doing this," she said as her traitorous hands buried themselves in his hair.

He fixed her with a decidedly carnal look. "I really shouldn't." Then he tugged down her corset cup and chemise to reveal one breast, and his gaze dropped unerringly there.

Dear Lord. Who would have thought that having a man look at one's naked breast would be so enthralling? The part of her that would normally urge caution had clearly gone to sleep, because she wouldn't have stopped this for the world.

Especially when he lowered his head, closed his mouth over her breast, and began to suck.

What *bliss*! Her body entirely betrayed her. It pressed into him like that of a dockside tart. Her fingers clutched him tight to her breast, and her lips scattered kisses over his silky locks. He smelled of mint and bergamot, some rich scent that probably only lords used.

But his mouth was just a man's, with a man's boldness, a man's eager hunger. It made her squirm and moan.

As if that encouraged him to recklessness, he eased her back down on the settee until he lay atop her, the strength and power of him surrounding her. That ought to panic her. Instead, it made her feel oddly safe.

This was Stephen, *her* Stephen. She trusted him with her virtue.

He kissed her again, slowly, leisurely, with heart-stopping strokes of his tongue, and it was *perfect*. His hand rubbed her breast while his thumb teased her nipple and his mouth made her eager for more.

Then he settled between her legs, and even through her layers of petticoats and skirts she felt an unmistakable bulge hardening against the tender flesh down there. For a moment, it tempted her to be naughty. For a moment, she relished the way he pushed against her, rousing urges she'd ignored most of her life.

Until he groaned against her lips, and her good sense finally reasserted itself. She was playing with fire. And she was the only one who'd be burned by it.

She tore her mouth from his. "We mustn't," she whispered. "We can't do this."

He froze, then muttered a soft oath, and she had a moment's fear he wouldn't relent.

But he didn't resist when she pressed against his chest to put some space between them. "We have to stop this. Someone could come in any minute."

Bracing himself up on either side of her, he stared down into her face. "So what if they did?"

She could feel the thundering of his heart against her hand. "Then we'd be forced to marry."

At the word *forced*, he narrowed his gaze. "Would it be so terrible? For us to have to marry?"

That made her silly pulse leap. "Are you . . . making an offer? Because this isn't quite how I envisioned that happening."

A rueful laugh escaped him. "No, I would imagine not."

Pushing himself off her, he slid to the end of the settee so she could sit up. For a moment he just sat watching as she restored her clothing. Then she began hunting for her fichu, so he rose to fetch it from behind the settee.

But when she reached for it, he kept hold of one end.

"You didn't answer my question. Would marrying me be so terrible?"

She stared up at the face that was rapidly becoming dear to her. "No."

With a ragged breath, he released the fichu and came around to sit beside her. Unable to look at him, she struggled to repin the scrap of fabric inside her bodice.

"But it wouldn't be what you want," he said tightly. "Living here. With me."

She concentrated on her fichu. "I've worked hard to gain my birthright. I have people depending on me, who need the work that my mills provide. So the 'living here' part wouldn't be what I want." She slanted a shy glance at him. "But the 'with you' part sounds . . . lovely."

A long silence fell between them, punctuated only by the crackling of the fire and their slowing breaths. She could hardly believe they were discussing this. Was he really so taken with her that he would marry her? Or was this just his manly urges prodding him on?

She had to know. Twisting to face him, she said, "You could move to America. With *me*."

"And what would I do there?" he asked warily.

"The same thing you do here. Try to change the world." She seized his hands. "You can help me try to change my little corner of it."

"And abandon all the children who have no one to speak for them?" he said harshly. "The pauper apprentices, the orphans, the lads and lasses whose families can't feed them so they're farmed out to the factories instead?"

She gave him a sad smile. "You wouldn't be abandoning them. There are bad mills in America, too." When he tried to pull his hands free, she gripped them tighter. "You could help *those* workers. You could help me make my own factories better."

"It's not the same," he bit out.

"Why not?" When he had no answer for that, she had to resist the urge to shake him. "You aren't the only person in England who cares about the children, you know. Other people care, too. You don't have to take the weight of the world on your shoulders."

Temper flared in his features. "That's precisely why I want you to stay. So we can do it together. Make a difference together. You say it doesn't matter whether we do it here or there, so why *not* stay here with me?"

"Because my mills aren't here. And England isn't my home." Struggling to conceal her disappointment, she slid her hands from his and rose. "From what I can tell, England hasn't been much of a home to you, either. But if you'd rather live here alone than leave with me, I was obviously wrong about that."

As he shot to his feet with a shuttered expression but said nothing to contradict her assertion, she fought a sudden urge to cry. She should have known better. She should never have tried to alter his rigid principles. They were unalterable, even for her.

"It's odd," she said past the thickening lump in her throat. "That first night in the conservatory, I actually got the insane notion that you might teach me how to have fun." She shook her head. "But all you really know how to teach is guilt and loneliness. And I already have plenty of both."

"Damn it, Amanda—"

"So these are yours." Grabbing his hand, she reached into her apron pocket and pulled out several white berries, which she placed in the center of his palm. She closed his fingers around them. "I believe I've paid my debt in full."

Then she left him standing there under the naked kissing bough.

◆　◆　◆

That evening before dinner Stephen stood in the drawing room, watching as Amanda talked intently with Blakeborough. Was she trying to make him jealous? Or was she simply cutting her losses, now that it was clear he wouldn't come to heel?

Stephen winced. That wasn't fair. She was the least manipulative woman he knew. She hadn't attempted to force him into anything, not with guilt, nor with any other weapon at her disposal. She'd merely stated the obvious—that their lives were in two different places.

And yes, it had been unfair of him to ask her to give up everything for him. But she was asking *him* to give up everything—his work, his home . . .

From what I can tell, England hasn't been much of a home to you, either.

She had a point. He'd made his life here not because he wanted to, or even because he belonged here. He'd done it because he wanted to show them all that he didn't need them. That, younger son or no, he could make a difference in the world without playing by their rules.

"You're an idiot, you know that?"

He jumped, then scowled at Warren, who'd come up to stand beside him. "Why? Because I won't move back home and do your bidding?"

Warren took a sip of his mulled wine. "Because you won't take what you want."

He went rigid. "And what do you think that is?"

His brother nodded at Amanda. "Her."

Bloody hell, the last thing he needed was Warren reading his mind. "What makes you think I want her?" he asked with feigned nonchalance.

Warren snorted. "Right. You only stare at her every chance you get, spend every waking hour with her, and watch her as if she holds the key to your future."

Sometimes he nearly hated his brother. "Has it occurred to you that she might not want *me*?" he said irritably.

"No. I've seen how she looks at *you*, too."

Not anymore. Not after their discussion this afternoon.

His brother lowered his voice. "She's an heiress, you know."

"And I suppose you think I should marry her for that reason alone."

"It's as good a reason as any."

"If I were a fortune hunter—which I'm not."

"True. Her brother may worry about it, but I know you better. You're too full of righteous fervor to be a fortune hunter."

He bristled. "I'm getting damned tired of people accusing me of that." Seizing his brother's glass, he downed the spiced drink, then handed Warren the empty glass. "There's nothing wrong with having a conscience."

"And you wonder why we haven't invited you to join our club," Warren muttered as he waved over a footman carrying a tray of steaming glasses.

"Because I have a *conscience*?"

"Because you can be a dead bore sometimes." When that made Stephen scowl, Warren added hastily, "Don't get me wrong: I'm proud of what you're doing. Your articles are well written, and your speeches inspire people to do the right thing. They've made a stir in Parliament, whether you realize it or not, and that's always good, given how stodgy those Tories can be. I daresay you've influenced more than one MP."

Stephen just gaped at him. Warren was proud of him? He'd *read* the articles, heard about the speeches? He actually thought Stephen had made a difference?

"But you do have a tendency to go on and on." Snagging a glass from the footman, his brother stirred the wine with the cinnamon stick. "You're very single-minded. And sometimes when a man goes to his club, he just wants to relax and enjoy himself, not hear a lecture about the miseries of the world."

I actually got the insane notion that you might teach me how to have fun.

Damn Warren. And damn her, too. Stephen knew perfectly well how to have fun. He just . . . chose not to most of the time.

"Yes," Stephen clipped out, "God forbid you should do anything important at your club, like discuss reform."

"No, we just talk about how to keep our women safe," Warren said dryly.

Belatedly, Stephen remembered the real purpose of St. George's Club—to provide a place where gentlemen could band together to protect their women from men who threatened their future or their virtue.

Stephen arched an eyebrow at him. "Who the hell are *you* protecting? We don't have any sisters."

"I have a ward."

"*Clarissa*?" He rolled his eyes. "That woman can take care of herself."

Warren's expression grew shuttered. "Not always."

The words gave Stephen pause. "Is there something I should know about?"

"Not a bit. I'll look after Clarissa." Warren drank from his glass. "You need to concentrate on looking after Miss Keane. Or doesn't she deserve to have someone care about her, too? Are only pauper apprentices worthy of your concern?"

The rebuke stung. "Don't be absurd."

He wasn't choosing the paupers over Amanda. Well, perhaps he was, a little. But only because they had no one. While she had—

He let out a breath. No one. Not really. Oh, she had her mother, but Mrs. Keane didn't deal with the mills. And

Jeremy Keane had washed his hands of them long ago. So Amanda would be going back to America to run them alone. Because he wouldn't go with her.

Stephen muttered a curse. "Look, I appreciate your concern, but she and I have already decided we wouldn't suit, so that's an end to it."

"You're an idiot."

"Stop saying that! It won't change anything."

"You do tend to be a particularly inflexible idiot."

Inflexible and single-minded and full of righteous fervor. Warren was painting a rather dour picture of him that Stephen wanted to ignore. But Amanda had said much the same. It was harder to dismiss when it came from both of them.

A masculine guffaw from across the room made him look over to see Amanda being teased by another male guest. A handsome one. By all accounts, an *unmarried* one. And as Warren had so helpfully reminded Stephen earlier, she *was* an heiress.

Stephen choked down bile. Judging from the misery on her face, she probably wasn't getting ready to run off with anyone just yet—but one day she would. One day she'd find a husband who *did* care about her. Who knew how to compromise and have a little fun.

And then she'd forget *him*. The thought made Stephen's gut knot.

"Either go after her or put her from your mind," Warren said. "But whatever you do, stop drooling over her. You're making an arse of yourself."

He'd already done that—by hurting her. By ignoring the precious gift she'd offered. By insisting that everything had to be his way, or no way at all.

So perhaps it was time he reconsidered the convictions he'd held so dear. Because if he didn't, he was going to lose the only woman he'd ever wanted to marry.

Chapter Six

Christmas Eve was generally Amanda's favorite day of the year, with all the anticipation of Christmas and none of the tumult. But when she rose early, after a night trying to beat thoughts of Stephen from her head, she was too heartsore to even think of Yule logs and feasts and carols sung by roaring fires.

So with a footman accompanying her, she took her brother's carriage over to Mrs. Chapel's. Maybe giving joy to someone else would help drown out her despair. And considering the nature of her errand, no one would think it amiss this time if she drove right up to the cottage, especially since the sky threatened snow.

Before Amanda could even knock, Mrs. Chapel opened her door and stood beaming at her. "Miss Keane, what a welcome surprise! I couldn't believe it when I saw your carriage coming up the road. After the many visits you've already paid us, I didn't expect you on Christmas Eve."

"I know." She forced a smile to her lips. "But I have some happy news for you, and I just couldn't wait to tell you."

"How very kind of you to come all this way for that, miss." Mrs. Chapel peered beyond her to where the footman stood with the horses. "Where's your mother? And his lordship?"

"I'm afraid Mama has a bit of a cold. And his lordship—" The emotions were still too raw; she couldn't even drum up an excuse. And to her horror, that made tears start in her eyes.

"Oh, my dear Miss Keane." Mrs. Chapel drew her into the cottage and urged her to sit at the table. Then, handing little Mary a doll, the woman checked on the babe sleeping in the crib and then went to fetch the kettle off the hob. "You just tell me all about it while I make you a nice hot cup of tea."

For some reason, that simple kindness started the tears flowing that Amanda had suppressed ever since yesterday's encounter with Stephen. She couldn't speak, much less lay out all the intricacies of her tangled relationship—such as it was—with Stephen. All she seemed able to do was cry.

Mrs. Chapel bore it all with sweet generosity. She urged tea on Amanda and offered her honey for it, a luxury that Amanda knew she could ill afford.

"No, no," Amanda protested. "You keep the honey for your little ones. I won't be the cause of you . . . of you . . ."

Tears burned her eyes again, and she swept them ruthlessly away.

Mrs. Chapel sat down to pat her hand awkwardly. "There, there. Can't be as bad as all that. Surely his lordship weren't so cruel as to break your heart."

Amanda drew out her handkerchief to dab at her eyes and nose. "What makes you think . . . this has to do with his lordship?"

As Mary climbed into her mother's lap, Mrs. Chapel shook her head. "Any fool can see that he's sweet on you."

"I wish you'd tell *him* that." Amanda scowled. "I don't think he knows."

Mrs. Chapel laughed heartily. "Go on with you, of course he knows. But men ain't good at saying such things proper. They like showing it better than saying it."

That was certainly true of Stephen. Amanda stared down at her balled-up handkerchief. "He wants me to stay here and marry him, instead of returning to America."

"Well, that ain't fair. Who's supposed to take care of them mills of yours?"

She blinked at the unexpected support from Mrs. Chapel. "That's what *I* said!"

"But that's how them lords is, you know. Even a nice one like Lord Stephen wants to be in charge. And if he goes off to America with you, he'll have to give that up." Mrs. Chapel bounced Mary on her knee. "He'll have to find his place in *your* world. P'raps that don't sit well with him."

The words gave her pause. She'd been so eager to convince him to go with her that she'd ignored his manly pride, which dictated that he ought to have a purpose, too. Had she been too hasty in brushing off his concerns?

But she couldn't give up her whole life for him. Why couldn't he see that?

A knock came at the door, and they both started. Setting Mary down, Mrs. Chapel rose to peer out the window. "Well, well," she murmured as she headed for the door. "Speak of the devil."

Before Amanda could even react, Mrs. Chapel was opening the door.

"Good morning, Mrs. Chapel," said a painfully familiar male voice. "I understand that Miss Keane is here?"

Oh, Lord. Had Stephen followed her?

"Why, indeed she is," the woman answered.

As Amanda frantically wiped at her eyes and nose, Mrs. Chapel ushered him inside.

Determined to hide that she'd been crying, Amanda rose to face him. "What are you doing here?"

As he looked her over, he paled. "You weren't at breakfast."

"I figured I'd get my errand run early, before all the festivities began. Why do you care, anyway?"

"I was worried about you. No one seemed to know where you'd gone. I had to ask ten servants before I could find out."

"Well, as you can see, I'm perfectly fine."

"All the same, I'm happy to accompany you back to Walton Hall. It's snowing now, so we should probably return." He glanced from her to Mrs. Chapel. "Er . . . what errand are you on, anyway?"

"Miss Keane says she's got good news for me," Mrs. Chapel said. "We was just gettin' to that."

"I came to tell Mrs. Chapel that Lady Yvette wants to hire Tom as a footboy." Amanda turned to Mrs. Chapel, whose mouth had fallen open. "That is, if you can spare him. Yvette says she could really use him at Walton Hall, and he's just the right age to start, since he's nearly eight."

"A footboy?" Mrs. Chapel said. "Oh, *miss.* My boy in service at Walton Hall? I . . . I can't believe it!"

It had taken Amanda a while to learn that being "in service" in England was the holy grail for those without education or birth. Aside from the fact that it paid better than most rural or factory positions, it had a certain cachet.

But Amanda cared less about that than about the fact that little Tom would no longer be risking life and limb as a mule scavenger. The one time she'd met the child, when they'd come here late in the evening to speak to Mr. Chapel himself, Tom had shown them the scars on his hand from where it had gotten caught in one of the machines. That had chilled her to the bone.

"Shall I tell her that you're interested in having Tom take the post?" Amanda asked Mrs. Chapel.

"You bloody well shall!" Mrs. Chapel blushed. "Forgive my language, miss. I'm just so delighted!" Seizing Amanda's hands, she squeezed them hard. "I know this was all your doing, and I'm ever so grateful, I am. My husband will be beside himself. Our Tom, a footboy! Oh, he shall be so grand!"

"He shall indeed," Stephen said, clear emotion in his voice. "I'm very happy for you, Mrs. Chapel."

When Amanda ventured a glance at him, he was watching her with a soft approval that turned her knees to jelly. She steeled herself against the warm emotions threatening to swamp her. She wouldn't let him do this to her again. She wouldn't!

Suddenly they heard a commotion outside. Then the door to the cottage swung open, and young Jimmy dashed inside. "Mother! Mother, you must come! The mill has caught fire! Father is hurt, and Tom . . . Tom's inside."

Mrs. Chapel screamed, and just that quick, they all plummeted from heaven to hell. Amanda knew better than anyone that fire could eat up a cotton mill faster than a glutton at a feast, and the thought of little Tom being trapped made her sick.

The soot-stained Jimmy caught sight of Stephen and grabbed his arm. "You got to help Tom, milord. You got to!"

"Of course." Stephen swung the door open and strode out, with the rest of them hurrying after him. "If you don't mind, Amanda, I'll take the carriage in case we need it to ferry people. You can ride, can't you?"

"I'm going with you," she said stoutly.

"So am I," Mrs. Chapel said, "me and the children. My husband's hurt and my boy's in there!"

Stephen gritted his teeth. "There's no time to argue it."

"Exactly, so we're all going," Amanda said. "We'll walk

if we have to." She turned to the footman. "Take his lord-ship's horse and ride back to Walton Hall. Tell them there's a fire at the mill, and we could use any servants they can spare."

While the footman rode away, Stephen helped Amanda, Mrs. Chapel, and the three children into the carriage. "The folks at Walton aren't going to like that," he said. "Their big Christmas celebration starts tonight, and they'll need the staff."

As they set off, Amanda glared at him. "Well, I don't know about *your* family and friends, but mine will want to help however they can."

"I hope you're right. Because anyone they can send will give us some advantage." Stephen turned to Jimmy. "Where in the mill is the fire?"

"In the picking room, sir. The master there had to go out, so he left a wee lad in charge. I think the boy fell asleep. Must have been a spark or something . . . Oh God, it's spreadin' fast!"

No doubt. The mill wasn't far off, so they could already see the smoke.

"How badly is your father hurt?" Mrs. Chapel asked her son.

"He broke his leg jumping out the piecing room win-dow, but they say he'll be all right. Can't walk on it, though." Jimmy's eyes filled with tears. "Tom was having breakfast in the cellar; nobody saw him come up with the others when the alarm bell was rung."

She and Stephen had learned that half-past nine was generally breakfast for the apprentices, since they came to work at 5:30 A.M.

"I should have gone back inside to look for Tom," Jimmy said, his eyes filling with tears. "But nobody would let me back in!"

"Where's the entrance to the cellar?" Stephen asked.

"It's just inside the front door, sir, to the right of the stairs. A pair of big double doors painted blue."

Jimmy glanced worriedly out of the carriage as they approached and saw flames licking out the windows of the two top floors. Mrs. Chapel paled and Amanda's heart dropped into her stomach.

Thank goodness Hanson and his overseers had brought in the mill fire engine, and men were already using the pumper to attempt to halt the flames. So far, the fire was still confined to the top two floors, but that made it hard for the pumper to reach high enough.

"The snow might help," Stephen said, "as long as the temperature doesn't drop too fast and impede the pumper."

"I don't see Tom." Mrs. Chapel leaned out the still moving carriage to scan the crowd. "I see your father, but I don't see my boy!"

As soon as the carriage shuddered to a halt on the outskirts of the crowd, Stephen leapt out. "You look after your husband and your other children," he told Mrs. Chapel. "I'll go search for Tom."

As he started pushing through the crowd, Amanda jumped out and told Mrs. Chapel, "We'll find him, I promise." Then she set off after Stephen, hoping to God she could keep that promise.

When she caught up to him, he growled, "You should stay in the carriage."

"I know the inner workings of mills better than you. And two of us can find him quicker than one."

Stephen was already vaulting through the crowd so fast that his hat tumbled off. She had to hurry to keep up. She scanned every boy's face she saw, but didn't see Tom anywhere. As soon as they reached the entrance, she broke into a run ahead of Stephen.

"Damn it, Amanda!" Stephen called as he raced after her up the stairs and into the building.

She paused in the entryway to look around. There wasn't much smoke down here yet, thank goodness. She instantly spotted the open blue doors and headed for them.

Stephen caught her by the arm. "You're not going down there. I'll look for him."

"From what I remember the workers saying, it's a large cellar. It will take us both to search it." Wrenching her arm free, she darted through the doorway and down the stairs before he could stop her.

The cellar was only three quarters of the way in the ground, so a short stairway down and they were entering a cool, damp space that stretched the entire width and depth of the building.

At least the walls were stone—those weren't going to burn, but the floor above . . .

She shuddered. As long as they found Tom before the fire engulfed the first floor, they ought to be fine. There wasn't yet a whiff of smoke down here. But if the single fire engine couldn't get it stopped, this would become a tomb, since the only windows were two tiny ones at either end, too small for even her to crawl through.

Fortunately, between the windows and the lantern Stephen had fetched off a hook by the landing on their way down, there was light to see by. Calling Tom's name every few steps, they roamed the tables built to accommodate nearly a hundred apprentices.

At the back of the cellar the walls were lined with old pieces of equipment, thread cabinets, broken spindles. And on one end were stacked several cotton bales, which fell short of the ceiling by a couple of feet.

That would certainly be a place for a boy to hide, wouldn't it? And as she recalled from their interviews, child apprentices were often punished for returning late from meals for work because they were sleeping.

So as Stephen moved swiftly along the tables, she

searched the tops of the bales. She found Tom atop the third stack.

"Tom!" she cried, and he jerked awake.

"What's happened? Where am I?" He leapt off the bale. "Cor, I'm late, ain't I? The master will beat me!"

As Stephen came toward them, she snatched Tom up in her arms. "No one's going to beat you ever again." Tears stung her eyes. "No one!"

"We have to go," Stephen urged.

"Yes, yes, of course."

They headed back toward the entrance just as a sudden rumble sounded somewhere above.

"Damn!" was all Stephen had time to say before something crashed down at the top of the stairs.

Chapter Seven

The dust settled enough for Stephen to look around. At least they still had light coming from the cellar windows and the lantern.

"Is everyone all right?" Amanda asked.

"I am," little Tom said.

"Let me go make sure it's safe before we try to get out." Still carrying the lantern, Stephen climbed the stairs. But as he neared the top and the light fell full on the doorway, his blood chilled. "It looks like the entrance is blocked."

He set down the lantern and shoved against whatever blocked the opening. Made of solid iron, it didn't budge.

This was bad. Very bad.

As Stephen descended the steps, he saw Tom gaze up at Amanda and ask, "Are you sure I won't get beat for being late, miss?"

"I'm sure," she said fiercely and clutched him to her. "I won't let them."

Stephen's heart flipped over in his chest, the way it had when he'd heard her tell Mrs. Chapel about Yvette giving

Tom a position. While he talked about reform, she *did* something about it, even if only to help one little boy. It humbled him.

"I think it's a piece of machinery," he told Amanda. "Bloody thing must have fallen through the second floor and right in front of the doorway. I can't move it."

She swallowed hard and looked about her. "Might Tom be able to get out through a cellar window?"

"It's worth a try." As they approached the nearest one, Stephen removed his cravat and wrapped it about his hand. "Stay back." He pounded on the window until the glass broke, then cleared the glass from the frame.

Amanda lifted Tom in her arms. "Do you think you can get through, my boy?"

"Oh, yes, miss. I've squeezed into spaces smaller'n that."

"Good boy." She pressed a quick kiss to his cheek. "Just be careful of the glass once you get free."

Stephen hoisted the lad up to the window. Young Tom wriggled his arms and half his body through, but it took a shove from Stephen for him to get completely out.

When he scrambled to his feet, he turned and bent to peer down at them. "Now *you*, miss."

Amanda shook her head. "Sorry, but there's no chance of my getting through that window."

Tom looked crestfallen.

"But you can go fetch someone to help clear the door," Stephen said. "Hurry, now!"

As soon as Tom ran off, Stephen turned to Amanda. "It will take him some time to make himself heard in that melee."

Amanda nodded. "In the meantime, we should see if the machine blocking the door can be moved." She took the lantern and rushed up the stairs. Swinging the light over the metal contraption, she released a defeated breath. "It's an iron boiler. Several men and possibly horses will be needed to move *that*."

Slowly she descended the stairs to the landing and set down the lantern, then removed her bonnet and tossed it aside. Her eyes were bleak and lost. "We're going to die here, aren't we?"

Stephen's heart thundered in his chest as he hurried up to the landing to sweep her into his arms. "No," he said fiercely. "Not if I can help it."

"How are you supposed to stop it?" She wrapped her arms about his waist and laid her head against his chest. "The boiler is blocking our only way out. Eventually the fire will burn through the floor above us, and the smoke will kill us before anyone could even get close enough to help us out."

She was only voicing what he knew to be true, but it stabbed him through the heart to hear her lose faith. It wasn't like her. "They might still put it out."

"I doubt that. One of our mills caught fire when I was a little girl." Her breathing grew ragged. "Jeremy and I watched it burn to the ground."

He clutched her to him, his throat closing up. "You have to have hope."

"I'm all out of hope."

Tipping up her chin so he could look into her face, he murmured, "You saved Tom, didn't you? So there's no reason yet to despair. He'll get help."

"Even if he does, there's nothing they can do!"

"You don't know that. Have faith. I swear I'll get us out of this somehow."

She cupped his head in her hands. "Oh, my darling. Even you have your limits."

My darling. The words fell on his parched heart like summer rain, and he couldn't help himself. He kissed her. Hard, with his blood beating a wild staccato.

Then she threw her arms about his neck and kissed him back. There was desperation in their kisses, both of them knowing these might be their last ones. After a few moments, she pulled back to whisper, "Make me yours."

He couldn't have heard her correctly. "What do you mean?"

"You know what I mean." She brushed a kiss to his jaw. "If this is our last chance to be together, I want to *be* together."

"Amanda—"

She cut him off with a kiss, her mouth soft and supple, then eager, opening beneath his. With a groan, he gave in. The landing was far enough up the stairs to be out of sight of the windows, giving them their own private space, and he wanted to be together, too. He *wanted* her, even in this place, in this hour. Because the idea that he might die before ever making her his cut him to the bone.

After that, they moved in a frenzy. She shoved off his coat. He untied her cloak. As he worked her wrapped bodice down to her waist, she unbuttoned his waistcoat and slid her hands inside.

Within moments, he had her undergarments lowered and her soft bare breast in his hand. "My dearest," he murmured in her ear as he rubbed her nipple erect. "I wish we had more time. I would kiss and lick every inch of you. I would make you want me so badly that you never left my side."

Her eyes slid closed and her mouth parted as he fondled her breast. "I already want you . . . more than you could possibly imagine."

"Do you? Let's see." He raised her skirts and felt around beneath until he found the slit in her drawers. Then he cupped her warm flesh, exploring with his finger until he discovered the slick feminine core of her.

"Ohhh . . . *Stephen* . . ." she moaned as he slipped his finger deep.

"So sweet and hot and wet for me," he said, exploring inside her satiny passage. "You're mine."

"Not yet, but I will be, my darling," she whispered, her breathing shallow, panting. "And you'll be mine, too. I'll take however much I can have of you. Now. Here."

She tried unbuttoning his trousers, and he hissed out a breath at just the brush of her hand against his straining cock. Impatient to be inside her, he pushed her hands away so he could get his trousers and drawers open. Shoving both down past his hips, he backed her against the stairwell wall and caught her behind the thighs to lift her so he could fit himself between them.

"Hook your legs behind mine," he ordered. When she did so and he felt the damp silk of her plastered against his aching cock, he nearly lost his mind. "I have to be inside you."

"Yes," she said. "Yes, *please*."

Though she didn't know what she was asking for, he didn't have the strength to resist her. It took some maneuvering to get her positioned, but the minute he was easing inside her, it felt so incredible that he wished he could make the moment last forever.

She tensed, and he murmured, "I can stop."

"No," she said hastily and clutched at his shoulders. "No, don't."

"I swear I will make it good for you, dear heart." He took his time pushing into her, but she only uttered a small mew of complaint at the beginning and then she was opening to him like a fragrant winter rose.

Thank God she was such a slip of a thing. Otherwise, he would never have been able to hold her against the wall and still enter her.

Once he was fully seated, he let out a heavy breath. "If being inside you is the last thing I ever know, I'll be content."

"I won't. I want to know it all." She tightened her grip on his shoulders. "I want to have it all."

He brushed a kiss to her temple. "And I intend to give you what I can while I can."

Amanda meant to hold him to that promise. Already he was exceeding her expectations. She would never have thought she'd relish being pinned against a wall and filled with a man's . . . member. Especially when it was so thick and hard inside her, so embarrassingly intimate. But when Stephen began to move with slow, steady strokes, like a well-oiled piston in perfect rhythm, he roused an odd aching between her thighs . . . and a piercing need in her heart.

His eyes met hers, hard and searching, in the reflected glow of the lantern. It was as if he looked into her very soul and saw what she wanted most. To have more time with him. Nights entwined like this, days spent running her mills together.

Shoving that futile dream from her mind, she threw herself into taking what she could of him now. She kissed his chin, his throat, whatever she could reach. In the little time they had left, she meant to learn every inch of him.

He shifted her higher. The next time he thrust, he hit that aching spot between her legs so perfectly that it sent her into a mad frenzy of squirming and bucking against him for more. "Oh, Lord, that feels . . . oh, Stephen . . . that's . . . *astonishing* . . ."

"Yes . . . it is." His breath came in staggered gasps. "You make it so."

Dragging his shirt up, she worked her hands beneath it to feel the muscles of his chest working and flexing as he held her suspended with such ease. "Goodness, you're . . . strong."

"Not strong enough." He drove harder inside her. "I'd give anything . . . to be able to shove that . . . boiler free."

"So would I."

With a low moan, he quickened his thrusts until he was pounding into her, deeper and hotter and fiercer with every stroke. The force of it sent her careening wildly, as if a wind had caught her and was carrying her up and away, high and fast, until she shot into the pure white air of sky . . . and exploded all over Stephen.

"Yes!" he cried, and drove into her hard, then spilled himself inside her. "Yes . . . my . . . sweet . . . Amanda. My dearest . . . love."

The word *love* sounded like a gong in her ears, and, still quaking from her own release, she cried, "I love you, Stephen. I do."

He bent his head to her ear, his breathing still rough and ragged. "I love you, too."

The words were so sweet she wanted to clutch them to her. But she wasn't sure she trusted them. As he pulled himself from her and she let her feet slide down to the landing, she whispered hesitantly, "You're not just saying that . . . because we're about to die, are you?"

He caught her head in his hands. "I'm saying it because it's true. *And* because we're about to die—I don't want to go to my grave without your knowing that I love you."

This time it was her heart, not her body, that soared. Tears stung her eyes, but before she could even swipe them away, he was kissing her, deeply, warmly, as a man kisses the woman he loves.

"Stephen! Miss Keane!" called a voice. "Are you there?"

Both of them jumped. Thank goodness they couldn't be seen in the stairwell.

"Stay here," Stephen whispered as he hastily did up his drawers and trousers. "I'll be right back."

Then he strode down the steps as if he weren't in only his shirtsleeves, with his waistcoat undone and his cravat missing. "We're here!" he called out. "We've been seeing if we can't move that boiler."

Hastily, she pulled her bodice up and her skirts down. *Stay here,* indeed. She wasn't about to hide like some lily-livered coward. She hurried down the steps to go to Stephen's side.

Lord Knightford's alarmed features filled the cellar window. He glanced from her to Stephen speculatively, but merely asked, "Are you both all right?"

"Except for the fact that we're about to die, we're fine," she snapped. "Please tell me that they've put out the fire."

The look of utter agony on his face gave her the answer even before he said, "I'm afraid not."

Slipping his arm about her waist, Stephen pulled her to him. "Is there any chance that they might?"

"It's not looking good. And it's too hot to go in and move the boiler, even if they could do so in time."

More voices sounded behind Lord Knightford, but she couldn't make out what they were saying. His face disappeared from the window, and she heard a muffled discussion.

When next he peered in the window, he looked decidedly cheerier. "Listen, old boy, the mill chaps here tell me there's another exit. It's boarded up and it's behind equipment and furniture in the back of the cellar, but they're going for the ax to chop the door down, so if you and Miss Keane can start—"

He hadn't even finished the sentence before she and Stephen were racing to the back of the cellar. They couldn't see any door, but there was so much refuse and equipment that it would be impossible to see anything without moving some of it.

"Did they tell you where exactly the exit is?" Stephen called out to his brother as he started yanking pieces of equipment off the pile and tossing or shoving them behind him.

"I'll find out!" Lord Knightford cried, and disappeared.

Meanwhile, she pulled anything she could reach from the tops of bureaus and cabinets and dragged empty barrels back from the mass of refuse.

Wisps of smoke had started to seep through the floor-boards over their heads, lending their efforts more urgency. She kept her head down and took great gulps of air from below to keep from breathing in smoke. All it would take was one spark from the floor above, and half of this, especially the cotton bales in the corner, would go up in flames.

"How deep does this go, anyway?" Stephen wrestled a broken carding machine away from the wall, then paused to wipe sweat from his brow with his shirtsleeve.

"I don't know," she shot back, her hands bleeding from tugging on jagged metal objects. "I didn't get to tour the place, remember?"

Then suddenly they heard it. Chopping. And it didn't sound too far ahead of them either. Heartened by that, they focused their attention on the sound, frenziedly pulling and jerking and tossing refuse behind them. They were about to attempt to move a massive cabinet when it suddenly started moving toward them of its own accord.

They both jumped back just as a soot-blackened head peered around the edge of it. "This way, Miss Keane!" the fellow said and extended his hand.

That was all the invitation she needed to get the hell out of that cellar.

Choking on smoke, they rounded the cabinet and stumbled up an ancient cracked brick stairway overgrown with ivy. When they broke free into the snow-covered lawn behind the mill, she thought she'd never seen a more beautiful sight. Behind them, smoke billowed into the air and fire crackled, but they were safe. Alive. Together.

Once they got free, they were swamped by friends and

family, everyone laughing and crying and congratulating the men who'd rescued them.

Amanda glanced anxiously back at the burning mill. "Is there anyone else in there, do you think?"

Mrs. Chapel pushed to the front of the crowd. "They done a count, miss, and they think everybody got out, thank the good Lord. Though if not for you and his lordship, my Tom—"

She burst into tears, and it was Amanda's turn to soothe the woman who'd become a friend. Next thing she knew, Lord Knightford was drawing Stephen away to consult about something, and Jimmy came running up to tell her that her mother was out front looking for her.

And she was engulfed in chaos.

Chapter Eight

Several hours later, night was falling when Stephen drove back from the Chapels' cottage to the now smoldering mill. He'd just ferried Mr. Chapel home after the lone village doctor had seen to setting the man's leg. The poor physician had been sorely taxed all day, but fortunately, though nearly fifty workers had suffered burns and some had broken limbs from trying to escape the fire, everyone was expected to recover.

Still, as the carriage approached what had once been the main building of Hanson Cotton Works, Stephen thought again that it looked like the scene of a battle—smoke still rose from the blackened shell and twisted hunks of metal lay in the ashes.

A shudder wracked him. He and Amanda had nearly been entombed there. He prayed he never came that close to death again. They had been very, very lucky.

As he got out of the rig, he glanced about for her. The last time he'd seen her, she'd been helping the townspeople in the makeshift tents erected for those injured who couldn't be moved until the doctor saw them. But those tents were rapidly emptying and he saw no sign of her.

So he scanned the area where Yvette's servants were scurrying about at her command, spooning bowls of soup from vats that she'd had brought from Walton Hall. He didn't see Amanda there, either, though he caught sight of her brother speaking to the magistrate, and Hanson being forced to answer what were probably some very pointed questions.

"If you're looking for Miss Keane," Warren said from behind him, "she took her mother back to Walton Hall. Mrs. Keane is still suffering the effects of her terrible cold, and the day wore sorely on her. Besides, most everyone has been taken care of, so I believe even Yvette and her husband are heading back shortly."

Stephen released a frustrated breath. He'd tried to get Amanda alone ever since they'd escaped the cellar, but they'd all been drawn into helping the mill workers.

Glancing over at Yvette, Warren smiled ruefully. "I'm told that she invited the pauper apprentices to sleep at the hall tonight and eat Christmas dinner there tomorrow, since they have nowhere else to go. They were all housed in the mill."

Stephen chuckled. "Does she have any idea what she's getting herself into? I think Hanson Cotton Works has something like twenty pauper apprentices."

"You know Yvette. She has a big heart."

Just like Amanda. And like Mrs. Keane, judging from what he'd seen of Amanda's mother today. Not to mention Yvette's husband.

He frowned. Come to think of it, every single guest at Walton Hall had been at the mill, dishing up soup or allowing their carriages to be used to ferry food and servants, or sitting with those waiting in the tents for their burns to be tended. He'd even seen Blakeborough helping a little girl find her mother.

A lump clogged his throat. What had Amanda said yesterday? *You don't have to take the weight of the world on your shoulders.*

She was right. He chose to take that weight, and he chose to take it here. But there were other mills, other workers. Other possibilities. And even if Yvette and Keane were more altruistic than most, he *had* met other good people of their rank. He just chose to dwell on the worst ones.

A half smile tipped up his lips. Just as Amanda had accused him of doing with the mills. And if he were to marry her . . .

He turned to his brother. "Why did you never consider marrying Yvette? I used to think you might, before she ended up with Keane."

Warren shrugged. "She's a fine woman, but I've always seen her as rather more of a sister than anything. I've known her too long, I suppose."

Stephen nodded. He'd felt much the same about her, even though he hadn't been as close to her and Blakeborough as Warren had been.

"What are you going to do about Miss Keane?" Warren asked.

He gazed over to where Blakeborough and Clarissa were attempting to drink wassail while they pulled a succession of small boys about on sleds. His heart thumped in his chest as he remembered something else Amanda had said: *You aren't the only person in England who cares about the children, you know. Other people care, too.*

Perhaps it was time he let them. "I'm going to marry her, of course."

Warren let out a long breath. "Thank God. In that case, I have a proposition for you . . ."

❖ ❖ ❖

Amanda awoke on Christmas Day feeling as if she'd been pummeled. Every inch of her hurt, and her throat still felt raw from the smoke. Thank goodness she'd been able to have a nice long bath last night.

She'd intended to join everyone for the hanging of the greens and the burning of the Yule log and the singing of carols, but she'd fallen asleep in the tub and then had crawled into bed.

Besides, she'd been afraid to see Stephen in a crowd when she didn't yet know what he intended. He'd said he loved her, but that was when they'd both thought they were about to die. Since then, she'd had no chance to talk to him privately.

Did he still want to marry her? And if he did, would he only do it if she stayed here? Because now more than ever, she wanted to go home. She wanted to make changes in her own mills, to do more to help workers there. And she wanted him to do it with her.

Mama came into the room and frowned. "Good heavens, girl, are you still abed?"

The look of disapproval on her face was so comical, Amanda couldn't help but laugh. "What happened to, 'I would have died if I'd lost you'?"

"That was yesterday," Mama said. "Today is Christmas, and Yvette has planned a big breakfast for her guests and all those children. I don't intend to be late to anything my daughter-in-law has planned, and neither should you."

Then Mama called for their lady's maid, and that was that. Amanda could no longer put off seeing Stephen.

A short while later, dressed in a new gown of green silk, Amanda nervously descended the stairs with her mother. As they passed under the kissing bough, she noticed all the berries were gone. The last time she'd checked, there had been a good dozen left, so the gentlemen must have been quite busy last night.

A footman redirected them from the breakfast room to the ballroom, where several tables had been set up, including a long one for the children. Each place was set with little treats, and the apprentices were all huddled in a group in one corner, gawking at the decorations and the tables groaning with food.

Someone came up behind her to murmur, "I suspect there will be more than one pauper apprentice who finds a position in Yvette's stables or kitchens."

With pulse stammering, she faced Stephen. "You look well this morning."

And oh, he did. His beautiful hair fell recklessly about his collar, and he was dressed in a suit of dark green wool that brought out the emerald lights in his eyes.

"You look beautiful." His gaze played over her with a hunger that roused her own.

Her cheeks flamed, and she knew everyone would notice. But right now she didn't care.

He offered her his arm. "Let me escort you to your seat, Miss Keane."

As she let him lead her to the table, she noticed that everyone—*everyone*—was observing her furtively while heading for their own seats. Even the apprentices seemed to be watching and whispering as they sat down with a scraping of chairs. What the devil?

Stephen brought her to a chair and pulled it out for her. It was only after she sat that she noticed the bowl in the center of her plate.

It was filled with mistletoe berries. He must have stripped every bough in the house.

With her blood pounding, she looked up at him as he took the seat next to her. But before she could say a word, his brother rose across the table and tapped his glass with a knife to gain everyone's attention.

Beneath the table, Stephen clasped her hand.

"As some of you have already heard," Lord Knightford began, "I have bought what's left of Hanson Cotton Works."

Amanda's mouth dropped open. Thank goodness someone had finally taken action! Hanson could no longer torment his workers.

"Hope you got a good price for it!" Lord Blakeborough called out, and everyone laughed.

"A very good price indeed." Lord Knightford scowled at Lord Blakeborough. "Now stop interrupting, or I'll convince you to invest."

That got another laugh.

Lord Knightford shifted his gaze to Stephen and Amanda. "I asked my brother to run the place since he seems to have a fondness for mills—"

Everyone laughed again, but Amanda's stomach sank. This was what happened when you trusted a man. He did things behind your back without consulting you. Like Papa, and every man she'd ever known.

She tried to tug her hand from Stephen's, but he wouldn't let her.

Lord Knightford went on. "It seems he has other plans, though. So he recommended some competent people to serve as managers, and I will soon be interviewing them."

And just like that her heart went from sore to soaring. Her gaze flew to Stephen. He was smiling softly at her, giving her hope, making her blood quicken.

"In the meantime," his lordship said, "it appears that I have become the owner of a cotton mill."

"Better you than me!" Jeremy cried and gave her a sly wink.

With another squeeze of her hand, Stephen rose and held up his glass. "To the new owner of Hanson Cotton Works!"

Everyone stood and toasted Lord Knightford, who was now wearing his usual world-weary expression. But after seeing how he'd fought to save her and Stephen from the fire, after watching him purchase a whole mill on his brother's behalf, she knew it to be a facade.

As she drank from her glass, Stephen used his knife to clink *his* glass, and every eye turned toward him.

With an uncertain smile, he took her hand. "Miss Keane, while we were in the cellar yesterday, you said that even I have my limits. You were speaking of my rather pompous tendency to believe I can save the world single-handedly."

She was finding it hard to breathe, hard to do anything but hope.

"While I admit that a self-righteous fervor is a particular flaw of mine, I've recently learned that there is one person who understands it for what it is: a fear of losing what I love most . . . a world of decency and honor . . . good people . . . and *you*. As it happens, what I love *most* of all is you. So would you possibly consider doing me the honor of becoming my wife?"

The word *yes* was on the tip of her tongue, but she still needed to be sure. "Before I can answer, I have to know—"

"Where we will live, yes." He cast her a tender smile that made her throat tighten. "That's up to you. Because I am perfectly willing to follow you to the ends of the earth."

As tears stung her eyes, she whispered, "Even if the end of the earth is in America?"

"*Especially* if the end of the earth is in America. That's where the love of my life resides, and I cannot live without her."

There wasn't a sound in the room as everyone waited for her answer. Normally she would hate being the center of attention like this. But normally, the only man she'd ever loved wasn't proposing.

"In that case," she said, "of course I will marry you. Yes."

Cheers went up around them, and no one made a single

protest as he pulled her into his arms and kissed her soundly on the lips.

When at last they broke apart, Yvette gave a signal and the servants started serving. But as Amanda sat down at her place with her cheeks on fire from all the jokes and well wishes, she caught sight of the bowl of berries.

Leaning over to Stephen, she whispered, "What were these for?"

With a grin, he plucked one from the bowl. "These were in case you refused me." His eyes gleamed at her. "That way I could have kissed you as many times as it took to get you to accept."

And as he kissed her again, she realized that she'd been right, after all. He *did* know how to have fun.

TWELVE KISSES
TO MIDNIGHT

Karen Hawkins

Blessed is the
season which engages
the whole world in
a conspiracy of love!

—Hamilton Wright Mabie

Chapter One

"Och, what is *she* doing here?" Marcus Sutherland, the fourth Duke of Rothesay, narrowed his gaze on a lone female who stood to the side of the sitting room.

Nikolai Romanovin, the Crown Prince of Oxenburg, turned a mildly curious glance at the other guests waiting for supper to be announced. "Which 'she'? There are too many 'shes' to count."

"That one." Marcus nodded toward the petite brunette who stood near the terrace doors, under a long bough of evergreen and mistletoe. Dressed in gray, as befitted her widowed station, she stood alone, her gloved hands clutched awkwardly before her, a huge reticule hanging from her elbow.

Nik's grandmother, Grand Duchess Natasha Nikolaevna, peered past them from where she sat on a gold settee. Dressed in black, stiff backed and regal, her hand clutched about her cane as if it were a scepter, she looked like an elderly queen holding court. She eyed the woman and snorted. "That reticule is the size of a portmanteau. What on earth could she be carrying in that thing? A whole cake? A child?"

"A book," Marcus answered. "Perhaps two. She's never withoot one."

Nik's brows rose. "I don't suppose you know the topic of these tomes?"

"Either history, horses, or some sort of romantic novel."

"You know her well, then." Nik eyed her as if she were an especially sweet pastry. "You must tell me about her. She is quite lovely."

Marcus's jaw tightened. The last thing he wanted to do was talk, think, or in any way remember Kenna Stuart. Just seeing her stirred memories he had hoped were dead. He had to fight an instant vision of full, lush breasts, of a trim waist that swelled into voluptuous hips, of thickly lashed eyes, slumberous after hours of lovemaking—

He clenched his jaw and turned away. At one time, he'd worshipped her and thought no other woman could compare. *But she's far, far from perfect. I've tasted the bitter cut of that icy heart.*

Of course, all Nik saw was a pretty young woman, looking lost even while surrounded by boughs of holly and festive Christmas candles. Marcus refused to allow that to affect him. "I used to know her," he said shortly. "But nae more."

"Who is she?" Nik's gaze slid back to the woman, approval on his face. "She is the most beautiful woman here."

It was true. The soft gray of her gown enhanced the flush of her creamy skin, while her dark ringlets, artfully arranged around her heart-shaped face, made her brown eyes seem even larger. Had she smiled, Marcus knew they'd have been treated to a pair of dimples that could melt a man's heart.

But no more. "She is Lady Montrose, widow of the late earl."

"Such dark eyes," Nik murmured. "They speak to you."

"That woman is nothing to look at," Nik's grandmother announced. "*Bidnyahshka!* She is short and plump, her eyes too large for her face, and that hair—pah! Ringlets are out of fashion. She looks like a ruffled kitten."

Marcus noted that Kenna's mouth tightened as the duchess spoke. *Can she hear us? Surely not. She is too far away.* Realizing he was staring and in danger of being caught, he shifted so that she was no longer in his line of vision.

"Tata Natasha, *please*." Nik sighed. "If you cannot say anything nice, then do not speak."

Her grace snorted, but didn't offer another word.

"Forgive my grandmother. She is in a foul mood because her friend Lord Lyons did not join us here at Stormont's estate, even though she specifically invited the gentleman."

The grand duchess muttered something under her breath about men and empty promises.

"Soured milk," Nik announced. "So, Marcus, this woman with the beautiful eyes and the mouth like a kissed rose. You said she was the widow of the late Earl of Montrose?"

"Nikolai likes widows," the grand duchess announced loudly. "But only the pretty ones."

"Pretty ones are the best." Nik's gaze lingered on Kenna in a way that burned Marcus's soul. "Tell me more. I would know everything about her."

Marcus realized his hands were curled into fists, and he forced them to open. *Damn it, I should feel nothing for her. I do feel nothing for her.*

But perhaps it was normal for a man to feel possessive of what was once his. Male pride was blind and foolish. Everyone knew that. Marcus removed a piece of lint from his coat sleeve. "When I knew her she was Lady Kenna Stuart, daughter of the Earl of Galloway. Six months after I left England, she married the Earl of Montrose, a man nineteen years her senior."

"And now he is gone, which is to my benefit. How did you come to know her, my friend?"

"At one time, she was my fiancée."

Nik couldn't have looked more astounded. "I've known you for over ten years and never once have you mentioned an engagement, broken or otherwise."

"It happened shortly before you and I met. As my pride was sorely wounded at the time, I had nae wish to mention it. Later, it dinna seem to matter."

Nik's gaze returned to Lady Kenna. "How did this engagement end?"

"We discovered we dinna suit. And just in time, for the wedding was but a month away."

"That didn't cause a scandal?"

"Some, but I dinna stay to enjoy it. I accepted a post as attaché under Lord Wellmont and traveled to the Oxenburg court, where I met you."

"And glad I was, to have you there. It's cursed boring at court; you were a godsend." Nik crossed his arms and rocked back on his heels, his lively gaze on Marcus's face. "I must say, you don't seem overly despondent about this woman."

"'Tis auld news." Now. At the time, though . . . Those had been dark days indeed. *Days best left in the past.*

"So you do not care for Lady Montrose any longer, then. Which means you would not mind if I dance with her at the ball this evening."

Marcus shrugged. "Do as you wish, although you should know this: for all that she looks like a ruffled kitten, Lady Montrose has claws. And she doesna hesitate to use them."

To Marcus's chagrin, Nik brightened, his interest piqued yet more. "I like spirited women, and I have a predilection for . . . how do you say, women with dark hair?"

"Brunettes," Marcus answered shortly. *Kenna would laugh to hear one of my friends admire her so.* He remembered that laugh, low and husky, almost promising in its tone. He stirred restlessly and wished he had a drink.

"Pah!" her grace said. "Nikolai also likes women with

blond hair, *and* women with red hair, *and* women with brown hair. You should just say you like women with hair."

Nik sighed. "Tata Natasha, you are too harsh."

Her grace thumped her cane on the floor. "Marcus, tell him he is getting too old for flirting. He is to be king, so he must marry a noble young woman able to give him many strong sons. Neither a worn-out widow nor a *vishnha v tsvetu* will do for his wife."

Marcus sent Nik a questioning look.

"It means 'cherry blossom.'" Nik lowered his voice. "In my country, it signifies a woman of low moral character, much like your term 'soiled dove.' I'm sure that, no matter her faults, Lady Montrose is not a soiled dove."

"Bloody hell, nae." Honesty made him add, "I've never heard a breath of scandal aboot her."

Her grace sent him a hard look. "Even after her husband died?"

"Nae even then."

"Hmm. She is no *vishnha v tsvetu*, then. But she is still not good enough for my Nikolai. She is a widow. He needs a youthful woman, one who has not already been dragged through another man's marriage."

Nik gave his grandmother a droll look. "Fortunately for us all, I will not be king for a very, very long time. Father is healthy and strong, and I am in no hurry to see him otherwise."

She sniffed. "One never knows, Nikolai. It is best to be prepared for the worst."

Nik grimaced. "The Romany way. Always so negative."

"Always so practical."

"Always so depressing." His gaze returned to Kenna. "Marcus, pray introduce me to Lady Montrose. She's not the usual piece of fluff one finds at Stormont's fetes, and I would enjoy a conversation about something other than the weather. I've had to talk about last week's rain four times already this evening."

The grand duchess puffed out a sigh. "How do you know Lady Montrose is not 'a piece of fluff?'"

"Two reasons. One, she is carrying books, which leads me to believe she has put more into her head than fashion and weather. And two, she was once engaged to the most intelligent man of my acquaintance. Marcus would never offer for a woman who couldn't carry her half of the conversation. So I must meet this Lady Montrose. Will you do the honors, my friend?"

Marcus found his feet welded to the spot. There were plenty of women in the room; why in hell did Nik find Kenna the most interesting? The man could have his choice—he was a prince, for God's sake, six foot three, wealthy, athletic, and handsome, and women flocked to him. But that was Nik for you—always wanting the one woman who wasn't interested in him, scarce as they were. Perhaps it was the challenge.

Well, if any woman was a challenge, it was Kenna Stuart Graham. The problem was, Marcus didn't relish Kenna becoming Nik's particular challenge. Though they were close friends and Nik was an honorable man, the grand duchess was right: he was a profligate when it came to women. It was all about the chase, not the catch.

Normally Marcus found that to be one of Nik's more humanizing traits, but for some reason, now it irked him like the sound of fingernails upon a blackboard. For no reason at all, he found himself turning so that Kenna was once again in his line of sight. She was now standing on the near side of the doors, looking at a bust of Socrates someone had draped with festive ivy. She flicked at the ivy with one finger in a desultory manner, as if the sight of it irritated her, but not enough to do something about it. She used to make that exact face when they'd been forced by politeness to listen to someone play wretched piano pieces during social visits. *She never had patience with silliness.*

He realized he was smiling, and shook the smile away. *If I am to sink into old memories, I should remember the day she sent me away, refusing to listen to a word I had to say, and—* No. The past was best left in the past. His jaw ached a bit from unconsciously tightening it.

Still . . . she looked so young. Even dressed in widow's weeds, she didn't appear to be a day over eighteen, the age she'd been when he'd last seen her ten years ago. She was still young, a mere twenty-eight, although to society that was well over the hill.

Over the hill—he almost laughed. But his humor dissipated as his gaze traced over her heart-shaped face, then lingered on the delicate arch of her dark brows. Her large, velvet-brown eyes were framed with a thick sweep of lashes that made them seem mysterious and sensual, while her mouth was rosebud pink and deliciously plump. *And at one time, she was mine.*

He gritted his teeth at the thought. *Aye, but less than six months after I left, she'd entered into an engagement with Montrose, and less than a year later, she married him.*

With a mental shrug, he turned back to Nik. "If you must have an introduction, then I will—"

"Rothesay! I've been looking for you." The Countess of Perth, Marcus's current mistress, approached. Lila Drummund was a seductive blonde who knew the power of her figure and face. Dressed in an icy blue silk gown, she looked exactly what she was—beautiful, witty, and (most importantly) discreet. Marcus had enjoyed her company for several years now, although lately Lila had been hinting that once Perth escaped his earthly bonds, she expected Marcus to make their relationship more formal. Thus far, Marcus had found it convenient to pretend he didn't understand Lila's many, many hints.

"Lady Perth." He took her proffered hand and bowed over it. "You look lovely, as ever."

"Thank you." She slipped him a glance under her lashes

that promised much, then turned to curtsy to Nik. "Your highness! How good to see you again."

Nik bowed in return. "Lady Perth. It has been awhile."

"Since Lord MacDonald's rout, I believe. Two—nay, three months ago."

"Indeed. And how is your husband?"

She waved a hand. "The same as ever. He swears he is on his last leg and far too fragile to travel. Yet no matter how ill he claims to be, he still manages to totter down to the sitting room every night and play whist with his particular friends. He never misses a game."

"Ah yes. His lordship is rather, er . . . *stayryj*?"

She blinked. "Sta—?"

"Old," the grand duchess replied from her gold settee.

Lila instantly curtsied. "Your grace. I didn't see you hiding there."

"I'm not hiding; I like this settee," her grace announced. "I have a bony arse and the deep cushions are a comfort."

Lila's lips twitched. "It looks very comfortable."

"So it is." The older woman fixed her black gimlet gaze on Lila. "Tell me, *is* he old, this husband of yours who is too fragile to travel?"

"He just turned eighty-four."

"Pah. Some of my people are twenty years past that and do not fear travel." Her grace sent Lila a hard look. "Of course, you're a child compared to him. What are you? Thirty-five? Thirty-six?"

Lila's smile froze on her face, and Nik coughed to hide a laugh.

"I am twenty-nine, your grace," Lila said in a faintly chilly voice.

Her grace snorted in disbelief and Marcus hurried to intercede. "I'm nae surprised Perth no longer travels. He was a friend of my father's and was never healthy, even when he was younger."

Lila sent him a thankful look. "He has always eschewed any sort of physical activity and keeps himself locked in closed rooms. It's sad, as fresh air can cure many ailments. For myself, I ride to the hounds whenever the opportunity presents itself." She caught Marcus's gaze and smiled. "I wish you'd joined the hunt today. It was quite invigorating."

"I dinna enjoy chasing hapless animals that are running in terror for their lives. Besides, I had a meeting with Lord Selfridge aboot the coming treaty with Germany."

Nik's brows rose. "You must work even when enjoying a holiday house party? Lord Wellmont is a cruel taskmaster, and so I shall tell him when next I see him."

"We've worked for two years on that blasted treaty, and I willna have it falter merely because I am on holiday." He turned toward Lila. "I noticed that *some* of the hunting party dinna return until quite late."

She smiled. "You needn't have feared; I wasn't about to miss supper or this evening's masquerade. I shall be a black and silver swan. I have a black wig and a silver gown—it's quite dashing!"

The grand duchess squinted at Lila. "Lady Perth, why are you wearing only one earring?"

Lila touched her ears, a look of dismay in her blue eyes when she found no earring in her left earlobe. "Oh no! How did that happen?"

Marcus recognized the earring that was left; he'd given her the gold and ruby pair for her birthday not four months ago. They'd been damned expensive, too. "I hope you find it."

"I'm sure I will. It must have fallen off when I was dressing, and that stupid maid almost smothered me while helping me into my gown. I— Oh! Stormont is waving at me. He mentioned earlier he wished my opinion on the music to be played this evening." She made a droll face as she offered her hand to Marcus.

"You must go, of course." Marcus bowed over her hand

as she curtsied. "If I dinna sit near you at dinner, I will find you at the ball. A black and silver swan."

"Under the mistletoe." She smiled. "And what will you be?"

"I shall be dressed as the Crown Prince of Oxenburg."

Nik, who'd been watching Kenna, turned back to them at this sally. "*Nyet*. You do not have the air of a prince."

"That's true," the grand duchess chimed in from her settee throne. "You're a handsome man, Rothesay, if one likes the dark and athletic type, but there's nothing regal about you."

"Oh, I think Rothesay quite regal." With a playful smile, Lady Perth dipped a curtsy. "Your highness. Your grace. I hope to see you both at the masquerade." With a final smile, she left, her silk gown swishing with each step.

Marcus watched as Viscount Stormont approached Lila, a cat-with-the-cream smile on his smooth visage. "Stormont seems to have taken a particular interest in Lila."

Nik shrugged. "The viscount is a sad flirt, and I've never seen Lady Perth turn up her nose at a compliment. But enough about her. You said Lady Montrose's books might be about horses, so I take it she's an aficionado. Do you think she'd like to ride the new bay I just purchased?"

"You'd allow a woman you will have just met to ride your bay? You wouldna let me ride it, and I've asked numerous times."

"There's no benefit in letting you ride my bay." The prince grinned. "Only Lady Montrose will be allowed. It will be a privilege and she will be honored to know that."

"You're out if you think that will impress her. She's the only daughter of a prudish, better-than-thou earl, and she's already spoiled beyond belief."

"Perhaps she is worth spoiling. Or at least"—Nik added, a wolfish sparkle in his eyes—"*be*spoiling."

Her grace sputtered. "Do you forget I am here?"

He sighed. "I had indeed. And a glorious, lovely moment it was, too."

"Pah!" She rose to her feet, her black shawl fluttering. "I am leaving. Do not try to stop me, because I wish for pleasanter company, or at least someone with some good gossip." With a sniff the grand duchess hobbled off, her cane thumping with each step.

Nik said, "Good. Now we are free to speak to the intriguing Lady Montrose and— *Chyort*, she is gone!"

Marcus looked around. Kenna was nowhere to be seen. A pang of regret pressed against his chest, one so deep that it surprised him and made his heart sink yet more. *Damn it, it's too late for regrets. Ten years too late.*

"Where did she go?" Nik said. "I must find her."

The supper gong sounded, and the assemblage began to move toward the door.

Nik sighed. "I suppose we will find her at the masquerade later this evening, *nyet?*"

Marcus smiled politely, though he had no intention of looking for Kenna Stuart. She belonged in his past, and he was determined that was where she'd stay.

◆ ◆ ◆

"That is nae a costume," Marcus announced.

Nik looked down at the gold sash and dozens of colorful medals that hung across his red military-style coat, which complemented his black breeches and shiny boots. "This is a very fine costume."

"You wear that coat and that sash and those medals to every formal event in Oxenburg. 'Tisna a costume if you wear it all the time."

"Perhaps, but beside you, who wear no costume at all, I'm as dressed as a peacock." Nik captured two flutes of champagne from a servant walking past with a tray and handed a glass to Marcus before peering around the room at the bejeweled and bedecked guests. "Have you seen the lovely Lady Montrose? I cannot locate her in this madness.

There's scarcely any light—bloody hell, can the man not afford more candles?"

"Stormont thinks the dimness adds to the intrigue." Marcus grimaced. "What it does is make the room as dark as a bloody cavern."

"We'll never find Lady Montrose," Nik said mournfully.

"Nay," Marcus said baldly. "We dinna know what costume she's wearing, so 'tis unlikely we'd recognize her even if we could see through this gloom."

Which was far better for them all. Despite his best intentions, Marcus had found himself looking for Kenna throughout supper. It should have been an easy task, for there were fewer than fifty people in the dining room, but Stormont had packed the guests so closely that they could barely bend their arms to eat, much less lean out to see down the long table. It hadn't been until the fifth course that, by chance, the line of people had moved as if one, and Marcus had finally caught sight of the gentle curve of Kenna's cheek as she turned to say something to her companion.

It had been but a glance, and the only one he'd been allowed during the entire two-hour-long supper, but for some reason that lone sighting had left him pestered with yet more unsettling memories.

After supper the women had all moved to the sitting room, where after-dinner refreshments were to be served, while the men had joined Stormont in his study for cigars and whiskey. The two companies wouldn't reassemble until the masquerade at ten, so Marcus was left on his own to fight off the old, irksome memories as best as he could.

Later, while dressing for the ball and half listening to his valet repeat the gossip heard belowstairs, Marcus had decided that his curiosity—for it was no more than that—was totally normal. He and Kenna had been close once, and they hadn't seen each other in years. It was only natural that he was curious about her. And the best way to end his curiosity would be to speak to her for a few moments, to free himself from any lingering thoughts about what used to be. Then he would finally be free from this irritating tendency to dwell on things he hadn't thought about in years.

That decided, he'd made his way to the ballroom. But as Marcus stepped through the festively decorated doorway, he'd found himself facing hordes of mysterious masked women, none—and all—of which looked like Kenna.

He said in a sullen tone to Nik, "Och, we'll never recognize anyone in this mess."

"It's impossible," Nik agreed. As he spoke, several costumed women sauntered past, arms linked as they sent Nik and Marcus sultry smiles, protected from discovery by their glittering masks.

Marcus blew out his breath in irritation. "Bloody hell, why must Stormont throw a masquerade ball every blasted Christmas? 'Tis in poor taste."

"Perhaps he likes the drama. These masks and the lack of light—he is setting the stage for debauchery."

"He is a fool."

"*Da.* At supper, he could not stop talking about the pleasures he'd gotten from the hunt today. He was so obnoxious that I wondered if he was actually talking about the hunt, or something else."

A woman dressed in a Greek goddess costume floated past and eyed Nik seductively. He glanced at her blond hair and offered her nothing more than a vague nod before looking over her head at the others in the room. Her smile faltered and, with narrowed eyes, she left.

Nik didn't seem to notice as he scowled at the room. "I cannot find Lady Montrose and you cannot find Lady Perth. Neither of us can be with the women of our dreams, which is an insufferable state of affairs."

"They are all dressed alike, too. From where I stand,

I can count nae fewer than nine Greek goddesses, twelve Egyptian priestesses, and fourteen befeathered swans."

Nik sighed. "At least with Lady Perth, you have a clue. She was to be in a silver gown and wait beneath some mistletoe, correct? I have seen two dozen swans, but none dressed in silver and— Oh! The one by the fireplace. Is that your Lila?"

Marcus shook his head. "The gown is silver, but that swan has light brown hair. Lila was to wear a black wig. Even knowing she will be standing under mistletoe is of nae help as every bloody door in this house has been decorated with the stuff."

Besides, he'd rather find Kenna first. He'd keep his tone casual, ask her a polite question or two—perhaps about the health of her father and if she were enjoying the house party; the types of questions faint acquaintances burdened one another with. She would answer in the like, polite and distant, chilly and disdainful—he remembered her expressions far too well—and those few sentences would confirm what he already knew: that there was nothing more between them. Not one spark, not one flicker, not one hope.

"Silver dress, black wig, and mistletoe," Nik murmured as he leaned to one side, then the other, peering over the heads of the guests. "I do not see Lady Perth at al— Wait. In the doorway to the sitting room."

Marcus turned to look. The woman standing beneath a wide swath of mistletoe faced away from them, but he could see black curls that fell to one side, and a trim figure enclosed in a silver-gray gown. She turned her head, and her black and silver swan mask came into view. "That must be her."

Nik nodded thoughtfully. "That gown . . . I approve."

Marcus had to agree. Lila wore a gown from an earlier era, when the female form was more on display than today's draped fashions allowed. The silver-gray material clung low on her shoulders and hugged her full breasts to her corseted waist, before spilling across two side panniers and falling to the floor in a dramatic flow. The long black curls cascading down her bared shoulders complemented her creamy skin, and she looked deliciously decadent, the feathers of her mask brushing her delicate neck every time she moved her head. *Perhaps I am a fool to be thinking of Kenna when Lila is here.*

"Go to her," Nik advised. "Stormont is trying to make his way to her side. I must admit, I dislike our host more and more. It is only his lavish entertaining that makes him palatable."

"That, and he possesses some of the finest hunting lands in England." Marcus finished his champagne. "If nae for that, I doubt anyone would attend his house parties at all."

"Then go rescue your lady. I shall wait and see if I can spy Lady Montrose. But if you see her first—"

"I'll bring her here for an introduction. Of course." *Of course not.* Marcus placed his empty champagne flute on a nearby table and, with a bow, left to join Lila.

As he approached her he caught sight of Stormont, whose progress had been halted by a pair of determined women who, judging from their black wigs and the heavy kohl lining their eyes, were dressed as Egyptian priestesses.

Excellent. One less obstacle. Marcus reached the doorway just as Lila moved to the side, half hidden now among large pots of palm fronds hung with holly and festive red bows. It seemed as if she had no desire to mingle with the other guests, but he knew her too well to believe that. Lila was many things, but shy was not one of them. *She must have seen me coming and thought to give us some privacy.*

He came up behind her, stepping between her and a broad potted palm, and slipped an arm about her waist. With an insistent move, he pulled her against him and then moved deeper into the privacy afforded by the palm pots. With a few steps they were completely hidden from sight.

Marcus murmured in her ear, "There you are, under the mistletoe, just as you promised."

She held still, though her breath quickened visibly, the feather near her mouth fluttering. "Rothesay?" she whispered.

"Who else?" He chuckled and slipped his hands from her waist up her front, finding her full breasts.

Her hands closed over his and she gasped, shivering in delight.

"Mmmm, I have been thinking of this—of you—all evening," he murmured into her delicate neck and increased his ministrations.

A deep sigh shuddered through her and she pressed back against him, tilting her head to give his lips better access to her neck. Her scent tempted and teased him.

"A new perfume," he whispered. "From an admirer? Should I be jealous, my lovely swan?"

In answer, she quickly turned in his arms, slipped her arms about his neck and pulled his mouth down to hers. The second his lips touched hers, a wild, savage heat raced through him and his heart thundered in his ears in a reaction so swift, so furious, his breath disappeared. *Damn, I haven't felt this since—*

He opened his eyes. Instead of Lila's light blue eyes, smoky brown ones met his. *Can it be—?*

He broke the kiss, tightened his arm about her waist, and lifted her off her feet, holding her prisoner against his chest while he yanked free the bow tied behind her ear. With a twist of his wrist, he jerked the mask free.

And there she was, bare-faced, her body held to his, her thickly lashed eyes wide with fear and something else, her lips but an inch from his. *"Kenna!."* It was more a moan than her name, for even as he was furious at her deception, his body ached to taste her again. *Damn it, damn it, damn it!*

"Marcus, I—I didn't realize you were—" She grasped his

hands where they held her and tugged futilely. "You must release me or—"

"*Damn* you! What in the hell do you think you're doing?"

She cast a glance behind him and hissed, "Shush! People will hear—"

He kissed her. It was the last thing he should have done, for he didn't wish anyone to see them. But she was *here*, in *his* arms, and all of his fury and pain from years long gone burst to the surface and would not be assuaged with anything less than possessing her, tasting her, silencing her every word with firm, possessive kisses.

For a startled moment she was still beneath his onslaught, but then her arms slid once again about his neck and she curved into him, her face tilting to his as she opened her mouth to him. His body exploded into passion as pure desire engulfed him and he, trying so hard to be the master, became the slave to her soft lips, her intoxicating scent, her slender arms that held him so tight. He deepened the kiss, taking a small step back to steady himself—

A pot met the back of his knees.

He staggered.

Kenna's eyes flew open and she instinctively tightened her grip about his neck, throwing him even more off-balance.

He twisted, trying to regain his footing, but it was too late—with a muffled curse he fell backward over the huge pot, through the palm fronds, to land on the ballroom floor, scattering the dancers and causing an instant outcry. Kenna, pulled with him, was splayed over his chest, her voluminous skirts flipped over their heads. Yet though their faces were shielded from sight, someone recognized them, for somewhere in the darkness a man's deep voice boomed over the orchestra's fading notes, "My God, Rothesay has seduced Lady Montrose!"

Chapter Two

"Lord love ye, lass, ye've done it now." MacCready shook her head, her mobcap fluttering as she handed Kenna a fur-lined bonnet. "Ye're in the suds guid and weel, ye are."

"Nonsense. I shall come about." Kenna smiled at her maid, though she felt like doing anything but. "Father will help." *I hope.* She instantly chided herself for doubting. *Of course he will.* "He will join us here at Stormont's and act as if last night's unfortunate incident doesn't deserve any attention. If anything will silence the gossips, it is Father's disregard." Which was why she was going to ride out to his home now to ask him to help.

Such was the power of her father, the stern, unyielding, always correct, and often chilly-toned Earl of Galloway. Father was known far and wide for his rigid standards, lauded for his self-control, and held up as an example for his perfect sense of decorum.

"I dinna know," MacCready said in a doubtful tone. "Yer father isna one to take oop a cause, and ye're askin' him to just tha'."

"I'm not a 'cause'; I'm his daughter. And I'm only asking him to join me here this morning and remain a day or two. Besides, he likes Lord Stormont and will be eager to assist."

Truth be told, Father liked the earl far more than she did. Lately Father had been demanding she accept Stormont's repeated offers of marriage, which she'd been steadily rebuffing over the last year.

Father seemed to think this was her last opportunity to marry well, and perhaps it was. Fortunately for her (according to Father), Stormont already had several sons by his late wife and had no interest in having more. All he wanted was a well-bred lady to serve as a hostess and give him access to a considerable dowry, and Kenna met both of those requirements.

Stifling a sigh, she hooked the loop of her riding-habit skirt over her wrist and shook out the long skirts. "I hope this coat and cloak will be warm enough. 'Tis icy this morning. The windows were frosted when I arose."

"Aye. Cook says there's a snowstorm brewing, but hopefully 'twill nae come fer a day or two."

"Good, for I've no wish to get caught in it." She smoothed the sleeves of the fitted coat. "Please have a gown ready when I return. If all goes well, I'll be taking lunch with both Father and Lord Stormont."

"Aye, yer ladyship." MacCready gathered Kenna's reticule, grimacing at the weight. "Are ye certain you want to take this? 'Tis heavy."

"I'll need it. Father will only travel in a coach, and I'll wish for something to read on the ride back." She was fairly certain he'd be too angry to speak. Father loathed scandals and she was neck deep in one. She could already imagine his icy stare, and she absently rubbed her chest, where a familiar sense of dread pressed. It seemed she'd spent her entire life avoiding that stare.

Catching MacCready's concerned gaze, Kenna forced a quick smile. "I'm reading a very good book right now. 'Tis about a lass who is kidnapped by pirates and goes upon a grand adventure. I'll read some to you tonight before bed, if you'd like."

The maid beamed as she handed the reticule to Kenna. "Och, yer ladyship, I would like tha' verrah much indeed."

Kenna hung the reticule on her arm, the weight of the book affording her some comfort. If Father assisted her, he would expect a payment of some sort. That was how he did things—nothing was free. She could only hope Stormont was so disgusted with her oh-so-public fall from grace that he would refuse to reopen his offer for her hand.

Which is highly unlikely. Before last night's embarrassment, she'd overheard various people whispering that Stormont was deeply in debt and could no longer hide it. If that was true, there was little chance he'd walk away from aligning himself with her. Not only did she have a handsome jointure from her mother's estate, but her late husband had left her several properties as well as a large per annum for her expenses. On top of that, Father had "sweetened the pot," as he'd called it, by offering the earl some of the rich pastureland that resided between their conjoining estates as a bridal gift.

All in all, their marriage would be a fiscal relief for the expense-laden Earl of Stormont, and a pragmatic move for her. *But I've been pragmatic before. This time I want more. Much more.*

Right now, though, she had to rescue herself and Rothesay from this mess. "Thank you, MacCready. That is all for now." Kenna threw a thick cloak over her arm and removed her fur-lined gloves from the pocket of her heavy pelisse.

"Verrah guid, my lady. I'll have the blue silk gown ready on yer return. Yer father has always been partial to tha' one."

"Thank you." Kenna smiled and then left, hurrying down the hallway to the grand staircase, the thick rug masking the clip of her booted feet.

It was only seven in the morning, far too early for the masquerade revelers to be up and about, for which she was thankful. The person she most wished to avoid was Rothesay. After their disastrous fall, she'd been too embarrassed to look at him. It wasn't until later in the evening, when he'd caught her gaze from across the room, that she'd realized the extent of his fury.

She couldn't blame him. The situation was untenable, which was why she'd decided to ask for Father's help. *Of course he'll help. How could he say no? He will be as desirous to avoid a scandal as I am.* Still, her stomach ached with uncertainty as she hurried down the main stairs into the empty foyer. *Damn my impulsive nature for this mess. I can't seem to think straight, especially where Rothesay is concerned. He always muddled my sense of decorum and prudence, ever since—*

"You, there! Stop!"

Startled, Kenna whirled to see who'd called out.

The Grand Duchess Nikolaevna sat in a decorative side chair beside a large suit of armor outside the main sitting room. The old woman was dressed head to toe in black, a gold-knobbed cane clutched in her veined hands as she looked Kenna up and down. "Come, girl. I would speak with you."

When Kenna didn't move, the old lady scowled and tapped the cane on the marble floor. "*Ti smatri!* Did you not hear me? I said I would speak with you."

Kenna hid a grimace and walked to the duchess, bobbing a quick curtsy. "I would be delighted for a tête-à-tête. Perhaps when I return, we can—"

"*Nyet.* I would talk now." The old woman's gaze narrowed on Kenna's habit. "I do not recommend riding in this weather. It will snow."

Kenna forced herself not to glance longingly at the door, and instead offered a tight smile. "Thank you for the warning, but the weather should hold off for another hour, which is all I require. I beg your pardon, but I'm surprised to find you—or anyone—up so early."

"Old women never sleep. Besides—" The duchess's black eyes traveled over Kenna. "—I have much curiosity about you."

"About me? May I ask why?"

"Lord Rothesay is my grandson's closest friend. I would not have him injured; it would upset my grandson greatly."

Kenna stiffened. "I would never knowingly injure anyone, least of all Lord Rothesay."

The old woman's expression grew shrewd. "Ah. There is that word, *nyet*? 'Knowingly.' That's what happened last night, isn't it? You did not mean to, but you pinched Rothesay's pride."

Kenna's face heated and she hurriedly dipped a curtsy. "Pardon me, your grace, but I must go." She turned back toward the door.

She'd just reached it when the duchess called out, "Rothesay is waiting for you outside."

Kenna looked down where her gloved hand rested on the large brass knob. *He cannot be waiting; no one knew of my plans this morning.* But it was obvious the duchess knew, so . . .

Kenna stifled a sigh and peered out the tall windows beside the huge oaken door, moving the thick curtain to one side. Outside, wearing a heavy wool coat and cloak to ward off the cold, Rothesay stood talking to the prince. Her gaze flickered over the prince, his classical handsomeness complemented by the military cut of his black coat, tight breeches, and shiny boots. He was the embodiment of male beauty.

Most women would never look past him, but her gaze was irrevocably drawn back to the duke, and there it lingered. Tall, dark, broad-shouldered, his hair ruffled by the wind, Rothesay managed to appear to advantage even beside the prince. The duke's face was deeply lined, less refined, his nose bolder, his brow wider, but he exuded confidence and power.

"See?" the duchess asked. "He is waiting to escort you to your father's."

Kenna released the curtain. "How did you know I'd decided to visit my father? I didn't tell a soul, except for my maid this morning."

"Last night, I came downstairs and requested a glass of warm milk." The duchess made a face. "That shilly-shally they call a maid was to bring me one after the ball, but she left it too early and when I reached my room, the milk was cold and disgusting. I brought it down and made one of the footmen bring me a warm glass. While I was waiting in the sitting room, I heard you come downstairs and order your horse to be waiting at seven."

"And you mentioned it to Rothesay."

"Perhaps. He came with my grandson to escort me back to my chamber. I may have mentioned it . . . I cannot remember."

Kenna vaguely remembered that the door to the small sitting room had been open, but it had been so late, she'd assumed it was empty. "I see."

The duchess sniffed. "People don't think I notice things, being older than most mountains, but I'm not dead yet."

"I never thought you to be dead, your grace. Far from it." Sighing, she turned from the window and took a few steps into the center of the huge foyer. Perhaps she could leave through the kitchens and make her way to the stables and have another horse saddled to—

"*Bidnyahshaka*. You didn't expect to see him this morning, did you?" The shrewd black eyes locked on Kenna's face. "When he discovered you'd asked for a horse to be saddled, he thought you were going to visit your father."

"So I am," Kenna answered honestly. "But I must go alone. Father . . . he is not an easy man."

"Rothesay said much the same. It is why he was determined to go with you."

Irritation simmered through Kenna. Rothesay had said very little to her last night, merely helping her to her feet after their fall and then giving her a curt bow before striding in the opposite direction.

She supposed he thought he was being noble. Had he stayed by her side, the wags would have wagged harder. But *still* . . . He'd just walked away. Left her as if it were easy. *Left me as if he couldn't wait to be free from my presence.*

The memory stung, salt in a very real wound.

She tugged her cloak about her shoulders and fastened it under her chin. It was better to face the duke; avoiding him would only mean another meeting later. "Rothesay will not be escorting me."

The old woman cackled. "Send him back inside, then. I've a mind to speak to him myself."

"I'm sure he'd have more to say to you than to me, your grace. If you will excuse me, I must go."

The black eyes narrowed. "You must, eh? Humph. I wonder if Rothesay would like to know that embrace was not a mistake? That you planned to be mistaken for Lady Perth all along?"

Kenna froze, her heart pounding in her ears. After a long moment, she said calmly, "I'm sure you are mistaken. Good morning, your grace."

With that, she turned on her heel and went outside.

❖ ❖ ❖

Nik rubbed his arms and settled his chin deeper into his muffler. "Even by hell-iced-over standards, it's cold. Scotland makes snowy Oxenburg seem warm."

A stiff wind swirled into the courtyard and Marcus held his hat in place and hunched against the gust, his breath puffing white in the cold air. He glanced sourly at the sky. "It's going to snow. I can taste it. This whole thing is a bloody mess. Why, oh why, dinna I wait for her to speak before I kissed her?"

Nik shrugged. "It was an understandable mistake. Both Lady Montrose and Lady Perth were wearing similar costumes—it could have happened to anyone."

"It could have, but it dinna," Marcus returned glumly. "It happened to me."

"*Da.* But *bozhy moj,* the room was so dark! It's a wonder you didn't kiss old Lady Durham as well, for she was dressed as a swan, too."

Truthfully, what irked Marcus the most was his reaction. The second his lips had touched Kenna's, he'd known who she was. He should have never kissed her that second—or third—time, but he hadn't been able to stop himself. *Why?* Why hadn't he turned on his heel and left her standing where he'd found her? Instead, he'd yanked her to him like a drowning man would clutch a rope.

"What has the lovely Lady Montrose to say about the incident?" Nik asked.

"Nothing." Which worried him. Of course, they'd scarcely had a moment to speak, as they'd been surrounded by people every second since the incident. It was one reason he'd decided to ride with her to her father's, even though he was certain she was on a fool's errand. The Earl of Galloway was a coldhearted stickler and would rather burn at the stake than unbend himself to help another person, even his only daughter. But perhaps Marcus wasn't giving the old man his due; perhaps the earl cared more about Kenna than he showed.

Nik shook his head and sighed, his breath puffing white. "All of this over a simple kiss. I find the rules of your country archaic."

"So do I, but there is nae changing them. Lady Montrose and I were caught in a compromising position, which could lead to talk. Once such talk begins, if it is nae silenced quickly it could cause her ruin, or at least much embarrassment."

"And you?"

Marcus shrugged. "I would be looked at with a disapproving eye for a while, and some mothers might hide their daughters, but nae for long. I've a title and some wealth. Society is lenient on well off, unmarried men and unrelenting on similarly placed females."

"So this effort is for her sake." Nik shook his head. "In Oxenburg, if this were to happen, you would pay a bride price to Lady Montrose and her honor would be restored, your penance accepted, and the event quickly forgotten."

"I hope Scotland becomes so enlightened. But until then, I must do what I can to alleviate this wretched error."

"I hope Lady Montrose's father will help."

"So does she," Marcus said. Galloway had never approved of him, which still rankled after all these years. Now that Marcus had some distance from the painful events that had led up to his and Kenna's broken engagement, he placed some of the blame squarely on the earl's narrow shoulders.

The door opened and Kenna appeared. Her formfitting habit accentuated her curvaceous figure, a long cape fluttering from her shoulders as she marched down the steps as if ready for battle. Her cheeks were rapidly pinkening from the cold, her dark brown hair pinned to no avail against the wind, as already several curls had escaped and now caressed her neck and forehead.

Marcus found himself fighting a twinge of regret. For what, he didn't know. *Even after all these years, she looks as young and innocent as the day I met her.*

"So, so lovely," Nik breathed.

Marcus forced himself not to glare at Nik. "She's well enough."

Nik laughed and sent him a side-glance. "Every time you look at her, you appear irritated."

"Because I am," he replied sourly. "Just look at this situation I'm in now, because of her." *And my own damned reactions.* He had to shoulder some of the blame, if not most of it.

"Hmm. I wonder if there is another cause for your irritation. Something you don't wish to face. Say, for example, the loss of a betrothed that has caused deep, grievous wounds to your heart and—"

"Och, dinna romanticize a long-dead relationship. Kenna and I said our good-byes years ago. Neither of us wishes to return to that path."

Though, to be fair, he supposed that there was some truth to what Nik said: no one could leave an engagement without feeling something. It was only normal to carry a scar. After all, they'd been at an impressionable and romantic age when they'd parted. But his angst had been due to his youth and impressionability rather than real love. *Real love doesn't stop existing when faced with a hurdle, so it was never true love.*

When he saw Kenna now he felt something, of course, but it was no longer agony. Now he felt only a faint, persistent . . . pinch. *And love is not just a "pinch."*

As Kenna drew near, Marcus could tell from the set of her mouth and her exasperated look that she was displeased to find them there.

Unaware of the telltale signs, Nik stepped into Kenna's path and bowed. "Lady Montrose, it is a pleasure to finally meet you."

Kenna looked anything but pleased as she slid to a halt but, after a brief pause, she dipped an abrupt curtsy. "Thank you, your highness. I already know of you from the gossips. I believe you are a friend of his grace's." Her gaze flickered to Marcus and then away.

"I do not listen to the gossips." Nik's bold gaze swept her from head to toe. "Lady Montrose, may I say you look lovely today?"

Marcus fought an absurd desire to tell Nik to stop making a fool of himself. *Nik will flirt; it is his way. But he never means anything by it. Or hasn't so far.*

Kenna had flushed at Nik's obvious admiration, a feat indeed, as the cold had already brightened her cheeks to a cheery pink. "Thank you, your highness. It was kind of you both to come to see me off, although"—her voice was stiff, challenging—"it was *most* unnecessary."

"I dinna come to see you off," Marcus said bluntly. "My horse is saddled and standing beside yours. I'm coming with you."

"You will do no such thing." Kenna's feet were now planted a bit apart, one hand resting on her hip, as if she stood in a strong wind. "I'm perfectly able to ride by myself a bare half hour."

Och, I know what that pugnacious stance means. I know all too well. He crossed his arms and rocked back on his heels. "Withoot a groom, I noticed."

Her lips thinned. "Neither you nor a groom are needed. I'm going to see my father. 'Tis better I do so alone."

"Fine. Go visit your father, but I am traveling with you. 'Tis nae a safe trail."

She stiffened. "You don't know which trail I was planning on taking."

"The one by the mill, which is shorter. 'Twould be safer if you took the main road."

Her brows snapped low with irritation. "And longer! Almost twice the length of time."

"But safer," he repeated stubbornly.

After a frustrated silence, she shrugged. "Fine. I agree: the main road is the safest route."

The wind buffeted them anew, sending skirts and cloaks and coattails alike flapping wildly in the cold. Kenna shivered and burrowed her chin, tugging her cloak more tightly about her.

Marcus noted the firm set of her chin and he swallowed

a sigh. "Fine, fine. Will you promise to use caution and avoid dangers?"

"Of course," she snapped, irritation clear in her stiff form. "I'm a cautious person."

"If it were warmer, I'd debate that with you, but 'tis cold through and through, so off with you."

She eyed him suspiciously. "And what will you do while I'm gone?"

"Have breakfast. Play billiards with the prince, perhaps. We might even sample Stormont's whiskey. And we will await your return."

"Very good." She inclined her head, as unthinkingly dismissive as a queen, and then turned toward her horse.

Nik stepped forward, his hands raised to help her onto the horse. Yet somehow, without even realizing he was going to do it, Marcus reached her first. His hands sank through her thick cloak and tightened about her waist as, with an effortless lift, he set her into the saddle.

Kenna's eyes widened in surprise as she gripped his shoulders for balance until the pommel was close enough to grab. The second she was seated, he withdrew his hands and stepped away.

Although Kenna was covered in layers and layers of clothing and his hands were covered in thick, fur-lined gloves, that touch hummed through him, warming him despite the frosty air. *Bloody hell, what is it about her?*

She turned the horse toward the drive. "Good day, then. I will see you both when I return." With that, she touched her heels to her horse's sides and rode down the long drive, her cape fluttering about her, the long skirts of her riding habit flowing.

Nik came to stand beside Marcus. "It's a long ride."

"Aye."

They were quiet another moment before Nik asked, "Does it truly take twice as long if she takes the main road?"

"'Tis ten miles and then some. The mill path follows the river and is only two miles." A snowflake landed on his sleeve. "She willna take the road."

Nik turned a surprised glanced to Marcus. "But she promised."

"This is Lady Montrose. She only said 'twould be the wiser route; she never agreed to take it."

The prince blinked. "She didn't, did she? And yet you didn't challenge her about it."

Marcus shrugged. "I dinna wish to stand here in the icy cold and argue for naught. She will do what she will do."

Nik watched Kenna for a long moment. "I like this woman more for her spirit."

Marcus sent his friend a hard look. "'Tis dangerous to take an auld trail one hasn't ridden upon in years, especially alone, and in the face of possible snow. She is foolish to even—Ah! There she goes."

He and Nik watched as Kenna turned off the drive well before the main road and set her horse into a trot. Soon she was loping out of sight, lost among the trees.

Nik broke the silence. "I don't think she can see you now."

Marcus nodded to a groomsman. "My horse, please." A moment later, he was in the saddle. "I shall return in a few hours."

"I hope your journey is successful and that you meet your destiny. Or rather, that she meets you."

"'Tis nae destiny I'm chasing, but a woman too stubborn for her own good. One you go toward, the other you run from."

"And when they are the same?"

"In this instance, they are nae. Rest assured, I will see you by lunch." Marcus turned his horse and galloped away.

Nik watched as he disappeared into the woods where Lady Montrose had last been seen. "*Da*, my friend, but whether you wish to admit it or not, she may be your destiny yet."

Chapter Three

Snow began falling before Kenna was even five minutes down the trail. The small flakes melted as soon as they hit her cheeks and chin, dripping down her face and dampening the neck of her heavy wool cloak. She wiped her face with the end of her muffler but it didn't help, for the wool was already icy and wet. Shivering, she wished she dared go faster, but it would be madness to do so. Marcus had been right about the trail, blast it all. It was in sad shape indeed. Here and there large branches blocked the way, while thick shrubberies hid the less rocky portions until the path was almost impossible to follow. She had to pick along, careful that her horse, a restive and prancy animal, didn't step into a hidden hole and send them both tumbling.

She hated it when she was wrong. But she really, really hated it when Marcus was right.

Scowling, she pressed on, her nose, fingers, and toes already so numb that she could barely feel them. She could taste the clean flavor of the snow in each biting breath and it worried her. *There is more coming. But surely I'll be at Calz-*

eane Castle in another half hour or so, and before a warm fire. She was just glad Father had chosen to winter at the castle this year, as he didn't trust his man of business to oversee the long list of improvements he'd ordered for the new wing. Father never trusted anyone with important decisions.

The trail made a sharp right bend and as she came around the corner, she pulled her horse to a stop. A huge fallen oak tree blocked the path. Even on its side, it was taller than she was on horseback. Grimacing at the inconvenience, she turned her nervous horse so they could pick their way through the dense forest to the other side of the felled tree.

The whicker of another horse stopped her, and Marcus appeared on the path, his large bay blowing steam from its nose.

"What are you doing here?" She almost winced at the ungracious note in her voice.

"I'm riding. Nothing more."

"You followed me here."

"I followed the trail here. *You*, my dear, were nae supposed to be upon it. Remember?" His gaze flickered past her to the tree, and then back. "So what have we here?"

Blast it, why did he have to always be so right? This particular trait had annoyed her before, although not as much as it seemed to irk her now. She scowled at him. "It's not a problem. I'll ride around."

"Through the shrubberies? With a nervous mount?"

As if it understood Marcus, at that very moment her horse began to shy away from the tree. She tightened her hold on the reins, quickly bringing her mount under control.

"This trail will take you just as long, perhaps longer than the main road, but it's nae safe," he pointed out annoyingly. "I daresay this isna the only tree that's fallen." His stern gaze pinned her in place. "That's a problem. And 'tis already snowing."

It was indeed, the flakes falling faster and beginning to

stick to the browned leaves and iced stones alike. "This tree is not a problem," she insisted. "I'll just ride around it."

"And the next one? And the one after that?" He pulled his horse beside hers and sent her a flat look before standing in his stirrups to see over the fallen trunk.

She watched him out of the corner of her eye, noting the differences between this Rothesay and the one she used to know. They were far more different than she'd originally realized. The Rothesay she used to know wasn't as muscular, his face unlined, his expression less dark. The years had strengthened him; experiences had hardened him.

There was yet another change: he used to smile more. He used to tease and laugh, and when he wasn't talking, he'd always had a faint smile resting on his lips. Now, he seemed to scowl all of the time.

She didn't like that particular change, and she couldn't help but wonder if it had come from his past. *Their* past.

She sent him a look from under her lashes, saddened by the thought. How had they come to hurt each other so much? At one time, she'd thought no one could be as in love as they'd been. But then that illusion—for what else could it have been?—had shattered, slicing them both deeply, and altering everything. It was so tragic, so foolish, and so . . . wasted.

He settled back into his saddle. "There's no clear path around this tree. We'll have to lead the horses, rather than ride."

What a bother! But looking at the tangle of broken branches and the heaviness of the surrounding shrubbery, she had to admit he was right. The ground was too uneven, filled with holes from the tree's fall. "Fine. We'll walk." She glanced up at the sky, and grimaced when the snow hit her cheeks but didn't melt so quickly. *Perhaps I should have taken the main road, after all.*

The thought soured her mood as she hurried to dismount. Her horse, free of her controlling touch, instantly began to back up, snorting nervously. Kenna grasped the reins tightly and held him in place. "Easy."

Marcus, who'd already dismounted, frowned at her horse. "The groom should be shot for giving you such a nervy beast. It's obvious it hasna been properly exercised."

"So I've been thinking the last ten minutes. He's been well enough, but I can tell he'd like to run, with me or without me."

"Here, I'll lead him. You take my mount. He's large, but he's steady." Marcus held out his reins.

"That's kind of you, but I can handle my own horse. I've ridden my entire life and—"

"Stop arguing." He took her reins. "We havena time to argue. The snow is coming faster."

It was. The flakes were larger now, too. She swallowed the impulse to argue and took the reins of his mount.

Marcus turned and led her horse down the side of the felled tree, carefully picking his way, Kenna behind him.

They walked in silence, their feet crunching on the dead, frozen leaves. At one point, Kenna's horse shied away from a looming branch, but Marcus held the horse firm and calmed the beast with a stern command.

They were just rounding the top of the tree when the horse Kenna led stepped on a rock that rolled beneath its hoof, throwing it off balance. The horse whinnied and backed up. Though Kenna clung to the reins and held him in check, the noise and confusion set off the mount Marcus was leading, and it reared up.

Kenna's heart thudded to a halt as Marcus struggled to control the horse. It bucked, then bucked again, yanking its head this way and that. Finally it reared wildly, lashing the air with sharp hooves.

"Marcus!" she gasped.

He turned in surprise just as the horse reared again. Before Kenna's horrified gaze, one of the horse's hooves glanced off the side of Marcus's head and he fell to the icy ground, deathly still.

Chapter Four

Marcus awoke slowly, roused from the deepest of sleeps by a sharp pain in his forehead. He clenched his eyes tightly, his head aching like Satan's swordfire. *Bloody hell, how much whiskey did I drink last night?*

He reached up to press his fingertips to his forehead and unexpectedly encountered a bandage. He cracked his eyes open. *What's this? How did I—* Memory flooded back.

Kenna. The horse rearing. And then . . . nothing more. He carefully looked around and realized he was lying on his side on the floor, facing a fireplace. The fire danced, warming him, but the light worsened his headache. *Why am I not in a bed? At least someone gave me a pillow.*

Then he became aware of a warm body curled against his back, an arm thrown over his waist, the faint scent of vanilla and rose. *Kenna.*

Her deep breathing told him she was asleep, so he cautiously looked over his shoulder to find her dark head pressed snugly against his shoulder. She was still dressed in her riding habit, her heavy skirt and cloak draped over them both. They obviously hadn't made it to her father's home, nor were they at Stormont's. *So where are we?*

Ignoring the stabbing pain behind his eyes, he glanced about the room. It was a smallish room with one sitting area around the fire and another near two windows. The curtains were tightly drawn, most likely to keep in the heat, since the room was chilly despite the blazing fire.

He carefully lifted Kenna's arm from his waist and she sighed in her sleep, her warm breath teasing him. Grateful his headache put such wasted thoughts to rest, he carefully arose, fighting a wave of dizziness that made him seek the closest chair.

From there, he looked at Kenna, who was now huddling into herself, obviously cold. He looked around for a blanket. Finding none, he arose, took off his coat, and placed it over her. A faint smile curved her lips as she rubbed her cheek against the wool and then fell back into a deep sleep.

Marcus looked around the small room. Though the house appeared smallish, it was luxuriously appointed. The curtains were of thick, rich velvet; the floor covered with high-quality Persian rugs; the furnishings fine enough for a royal palace; the walls hung with paintings in large gilt frames.

His stomach growled and he rubbed it absently as he went toward the drawn curtains. Turning his head so he wouldn't look directly into the light, he twitched back the curtain and let the sunlight spill into the room. Then, squinting, he steeled himself and peered outside. A heavy snow fell silently, and he was surprised at how much had already fallen. Two, perhaps three feet of the stuff had piled up, bending the smaller trees and weighing down shrubs. A brutal wind blasted the snow into swirls, depositing it against the house, and he looked down to see a drift so deep that it had already reached the bottom of the window and was threatening to begin covering it. It had to have taken hours for the snow to fall so deep.

A noise behind him made him drop the curtain and turn around. Kenna had just arisen from the floor. She was sleep-mussed, her thick brown hair falling about her face, her cheeks pink from sleep. Her gaze flickered to him as she hooked the loop of her riding skirt over her wrist. "Good morning. How do you feel?"

"I have a headache, but nae more."

"Good. I hoped you'd feel more the thing when you awoke." She started to pick up a pillow from the floor but winced and put her hands on her back. "I'm so *stiff*." She stretched, her arms twined over her head, her now-wrinkled riding habit pulling tightly across her breasts. "What time is it?"

The clock on the mantel chimed as if in answer. He glanced it, more to look away from Kenna than to check the time. "A quarter after nine." Even focusing on the clock made his eyes ache, and he pressed his fingers to the side of his head.

Her gaze darkened. "You should sit."

"I'm fine. How did we get here?"

She bent down again to collect the pillows from the floor. "You don't remember?"

"Nay. I remember the horse rearing, but that's all."

She tossed the pillows onto a chair and then picked up his coat, carefully folding it before she placed it across the back of the settee. "We walked here. I helped you, because you were dizzy."

"I— Nay. That canna be right."

Her brows arched.

"I could nae have walked here," he insisted. "I dinna remember anything."

"Well, I couldn't have carried you. And the trail isn't close."

"The horses?"

"They ran away."

"*Both* horses ran? My mount is not usually so jittery."

"Aye, but the beast I was riding took off and charged your mount, spooking him. I tried to hold him but couldn't. I had hoped the horses would run back to Stormont's and alert the grooms that we needed assistance, but no one has come."

"Give them time. If the horses ran straight for the barn, they would have just arrived. A hue and cry will be raised and then they will send a search party."

"Marcus."

He glanced back at her, surprised to find her gaze filled with concern. "Aye?"

"We arrived here more than a few hours ago."

"Oh?"

"Yes. Much longer."

Something in her voice made him look at her. *Really* look at her. "But it's only nine in the morning, so how—" He stopped, his gaze flickering back to the clock. "Bloody hell. I was unconscious for a full day?"

"And night," she affirmed. "I was beginning to wonder if you'd ever wake up."

He pressed his fingertips to his temple, trying to accept the astonishing fact. *An entire day. I suppose that explains the deep snow, but . . .* He raised his gaze to hers. "Damn it, what will everyone think?" Lila would be furious, although at the moment he didn't really care.

"You know exactly what everyone will think." Kenna's voice cracked on the last word, and she turned away.

Years ago, he'd admired the control she always had over herself. But since he'd first caught sight of her in Stormont's ballroom, he'd seen a difference in her—an air of vulnerability, of uncertainty, the suggestion that she'd lost some of the cool, calm composure that used to be such an integral part of her.

What caused her to lose her confidence in such a way? Was it Montrose? Had their marriage been difficult for her?

In the past, when Marcus had thought of her marriage, he'd felt nothing but fury. Now he found himself wondering what the cost had been.

She caught his gaze and lifted her chin. "Just so you don't

worry too much over this, even if we are found here and there's a scandal, I've no desire to marry again. Especially not you."

He raised his brows.

She flushed. "I'm sorry; that sounded ungracious. I only meant that we already know we don't suit, so I've no wish to stir that pot again."

Which was what he wanted to hear. Until she said it aloud. Then his pride began to sting, as if she'd slapped him. "That's fine. I've nae desire to wed, either." He didn't add "especially not you," but he was certain by the way her lips thinned that she knew he thought it.

"Good." Kenna turned away to the mirror and attempted to put her hair into a semblance of order, doing more harm than good.

She's never been without a lady's maid for a day in her life. He'd traveled, often to faraway reaches, and over the years he'd learned to do without the help of a servant. But Kenna had stayed here, cosseted and protected.

She gave her hair an impatient glance before turning away from the mirror, but not before he caught her expression—worry over their predicament, concern about the reactions they might face, and something else . . . a deep sadness that turned down the corners of her mouth and shadowed her brown eyes. And he wondered about that sadness, even as he reminded himself he shouldn't care.

And he *didn't* care. Not at all.

Suddenly as restless as a wolf in a cage, he walked to the fireplace and regarded the fire. "Where are we?"

"A cottage deep in the woods. We stumbled on it by accident."

He pinged his finger against an ornate silver candelabra that decorated the mantel. "It's certainly luxurious. Tell me more aboot our walk here. Maybe it will help me regain my memory."

"A little while after the horses ran off, I was finally able to rouse you. But you were pale and shaking, and you weren't making sense." Kenna shot Marcus a glance from under her lashes.

"Delirious, was I?"

She nodded, remembering those long, frightening moments. Then the long walk here, trying to keep him upright as they trudged through the snow. And the tense hours with Marcus unconscious by the fire, while she had nothing to do but worry whether he'd ever awaken again, as the snow sealed them into the house as surely as boards and nails.

When she'd awoken this morning, she'd been so happy to see him standing by the window that her heart still ached with the bittersweetness of that relief, even as she cautioned herself not to put too much store in it. It was only natural she was glad to have some company while they awaited rescue. It kept her from thinking about other things—Father's fury, Stormont's disappointment. Things she had no wish to remember, much less examine.

Marcus broke the silence. "When I was suffering from delirium . . . what did I say?"

"You thought we were in a battle. The one at Salamanca."

Marcus's thick lashes dropped low, his mouth tightening. "Indeed."

She waited, but he offered nothing more. *Secretive as always.* Well, she was no longer a young innocent who would allow questions to go unanswered. "You were there, weren't you?"

Marcus turned, walked back to the window, and tied open the curtains. Though the sky was gray, the room brightened in the white light. He stood for a long moment, watching snow drift down.

Perhaps he didn't need to answer, though, for she'd never been so certain of anything in her life. It explained the differences she had begun to notice. *He's harder, and more arrogant.* "Your cousin Robert was at Salamanca, wasn't he? It was where he was wounded."

A long, deep sigh tore through Marcus. After an obvious struggle, he said, "Aye. I was with him, at the battle. What . . . what did I say?"

"So it wasn't delirium, but a memory. You thought we were there, that we were on the move during the battle. You kept saying we had to find shelter, to fall back and find a better position from which to fight." She noted his expression growing grim and she tentatively added, "I'm sorry about Robert's injuries. I know they were severe."

"He lost his leg, but he's doing better than expected." Marcus placed his hand on the window frame and then rested his bandaged head against his fist, looking out at the snow. "It seems like a lifetime ago."

She moved to the side of the settee so she could see his profile. "How did you come to be at Salamanca?"

"I'd been assigned to deliver a missive to Wellington from the Oxenburg king—a promise of their best troops and the use of their general, Nik's brother Max."

"I've heard of Nik's brother. He just married into the Muir family."

Marcus nodded. "When I arrived at Wellington's camp, I dinna realize the battle was aboot to begin. I could have delivered my message and left, but when I met the general, he was with his brigade leaders." Marcus gazed out the window, as if he could see what he saw that day. "I knew them all. Campbell, Pakenham, Hope, Alten—they were each leading a brigade. My cousin Robert was Pakenham's aide de camp. So young and so excited. He had no idea what he was aboot to face."

"But you did."

"I'd been traveling throughoot Europe for months, gathering information and sending it to Wellington and back home to the Foreign Office. And where Napoleon's armies had marched, there were miles and miles of nothing but smoke and bodies. It was . . ." He shook his head.

"When I saw Robert and his blind enthusiasm, I knew I had to stay."

"The two of you were always close."

"He is like a brother to me." Marcus smiled tightly. "I convinced Pakenham to let me join his forces so I could fight beside Robert. It dinna take much persuasion; they were short on men and I had a horse and weapons. So, I loaded my pistols and joined in. I was there for the charge, at Robert's side. We won, but it was a costly battle. Thousands killed, injured, and maimed. And Robert—" His voice thickened. "His horse fell on his leg and crushed it. I knew the second I saw it that he wouldna be able to keep it, but he kept hoping . . ."

Kenna noted the shadow in Marcus's eyes, the deep lines that ran from his nose to the corners of his mouth. *So much pain.* She wondered if he'd spoken about it to anyone else, and decided it was unlikely. Never had she met a man more given to holding himself away from others.

What should she say in this rare moment where he shared something he cared about? While she was struggling to find the words, Marcus's stomach rumbled.

"I'm famished," he said shortly. "I dinna suppose there's food in this empty house?"

And just like that, the rare moment was over. It was probably for the best; she couldn't afford any additional emotions when it came to this man. *Naturally I'm intrigued by his noble actions, and admire him for them. But that doesn't change anything.*

She picked up her cloak from the floor and shook it out. "The larder is well stocked, so we should be able to find some breakfast." She put on the cloak for warmth and glanced at his bandage. It was still in place, and only a small stain of blood had seeped through. Other than looking pale, he was almost back to normal—which in his case meant dark, restless, and achingly handsome.

It really wasn't fair. After all these years, he still had the power to make her skin warm with just a glance. No other man had ever made her feel that way.

"Since you put on your cloak, I take it this is the only room with a fire."

"Yes. And I'm very proud of that fire. It took me almost an hour to light it."

Amusement warmed his gray eyes. "In other words, it took you an hour to find the flint box. If there is food in the larder, then the fire was likely already laid."

She smiled. "Yes, but I've had to keep it going."

"You did verrah well. The room is decently warm, considering the temperature it must be outside." His gaze brushed over her. "Thank you."

"For?"

"Everything—finding this cottage, walking me here, bandaging my head, starting the fire. All of it."

He had the longest lashes of any man she knew, and they emphasized the hard line of his nose and mouth. She sighed as she looked at his mouth. Even when he was asleep, it had seemed bold and uncompromising. And he was both.

He picked up his coat from the settee and shrugged into it. "Where is this kitchen?"

"This way." She led the way through a door at one end of the room, carefully closing it behind them. She shivered in the cold hall and led the way to a set of stone stairs. "Careful," she called over her shoulder. "The ceiling is low."

He ducked under the low doorframe and followed her down the narrow steps into the kitchen.

"It's small, but there's every kind of food imaginable," she said.

There were apples in a wooden bowl on a low table, and he took one and polished it on his sleeve. "Would you like one?"

"No, thank you."

He took a bite, his gaze flickering about the room. "I see no dust, but no one was here when we arrived?"

"It was empty."

"And the door? Was it locked?"

She shrugged. "Yes, but I was able to undo it with a hairpin. It only took a moment."

He sent her an amused glance. "Remind me to install extra padlocks on my house."

"I can open those, too. You wouldn't believe how much damage a woman with a strong hairpin can do."

He laughed, and the low, deep sound curled around her and banished some of the chill. "This is quite a neat little residence," she said, looking around. "There is a larder and a pantry as well, which surprised me, given the small size of the cottage."

"Someone has a cook." He eyed the shiny line of pots and pans that hung along one wall. "This must be Stormont's hunting box."

She shook her head. "I've been to Stormont's hunting box. It's quite large, and he always has servants stationed there during hunting season. But we're still on Stormont's land, so . . ." She looked around. "I just don't know what this is."

"Whatever it is, I'm glad you found it."

"It was sheer luck," she admitted. "As I was helping you to your feet after the accident, I noticed a path leading off the trail. We followed it here and I was never more glad to see a cottage in my life." She went into the larder and began peering at the full shelves, selecting a pot of jam, a loaf of bread wrapped in waxed paper, and a tin of tea. She carried the goods back into the kitchen and placed them on a long table.

Marcus was lighting a fire in the large wood stove and she tried not to be irritated that, after just a few moments of effort, flames were already licking at the wood.

He picked up the kettle and filled it at a pump, then carried it back to the stove.

She looked about for a knife and saw one in a bowl. As she reached for it, her heavy skirts tugged at her wrist, so she removed the loop and let her skirts fall to the floor.

His dark gaze flickered over her. "We must find you more comfortable clothes."

She grimaced. "The long skirt is annoying, but hopefully I won't be wearing it much longer. Surely someone will find us today."

He glanced out the window, where the snow was piled halfway up the glass, but said nothing.

She fought a sigh, turning her attention to the task at hand. She unwrapped the bread, the crusty scent rising through the air. "At least we won't starve to death."

"Thank goodness." The kettle on the budding fire, Marcus returned to the table, where she was preparing to cut the loaf into slices.

"It's odd that Stormont's never mentioned this cottage," she said idly, pulling her cloak closer about her to ward off the chill.

Marcus looked at her. "Why would Stormont bother to tell you aboot this house or any other?"

Because he wishes to marry me. There was no reason she shouldn't say the words, yet she knew instinctively that Marcus didn't like the viscount, and for some reason, that mattered. "The viscount is a friend of my father's. I've grown to know him over the last year."

Marcus's gaze flickered to her and she thought he was about to say something, but he just opened the pot of jam and placed a spoon beside it. "Were there any cheeses in the pantry?"

"I think so, yes. On a shelf by the door."

He disappeared into the small room, and she cut the bread as well as she could. When Marcus returned, he looked at the hunks of bread and stifled a laugh.

Her cheeks heated. "The knife is dull."

He set the cloth bag containing cheese on the table and held out a hand. "Give me that knife."

She bit back a sigh but gave it to him. "You'll see what I mean. The blade is—"

He cut a perfect slice of bread, placed it on a small plate, and shoved it toward her. "Eat. I dinna suppose you know how to cook."

"Of course I don't know how to cook. Do you?" she threw out in challenge.

To her surprise, he smirked. "Aye. I'd make us some stew for our supper, but I doubt there will be a need. Someone will come before that."

"You can cook?"

"A few things. I've traveled a lot, and it wasna always Grillon's Hotel."

At the mention of one of the best hotels in London, she found herself hungrier than ever. "I ate there once," she said. "The chef . . . oh my, such glorious pork roast." She looked down at her bread and jam. "Perhaps we should talk about something else."

"Like how we're going to handle the scandal of being alone overnight in this cottage?"

Stormont must be furious, she decided, a flicker of hope warming her. Now, not even Father could save that proposal—and she couldn't be sorry. Yes, people would talk, and some would drop her from their invitation list, but she really didn't care. This would stop Father's pressure to accept the viscount's unwelcome offer, too.

Marcus was watching her, a question in his eyes.

She shrugged. "It'll be fine, whatever happens."

"You'll be ruined."

"I'm almost thirty and a widow. I wouldn't mind receiving fewer invitations. I find it more and more onerous to go into public, anyway."

He looked surprised. "You used to enjoy plays and such. At least, you did when nae enthralled with a new book."

"I used to play with dolls, too," she replied dryly. "I would be quite happy to be left alone with my garden, books, and friends."

"You could lose some friends from this."

"Not real ones." She watched him take a bite, his even teeth closing over the jam-slathered bread. Instantly, she had a memory from long ago when, in the heat of passion, he'd gently raked his teeth over her nipples, driving her mad with desire and—

She put down her bread, her heart pounding against her throat. "I'll see if the water is ready." She hurried to the stove and pretended to check the heat.

"It will take a while," he warned. "The water from the pump was icy cold. I'm surprised it hadna frozen."

"Of course." With nothing left to do, she returned to the table.

Marcus picked up a small towel hanging from the side of the table and handed it to her. "You have jam on your chin."

She swiped at it. *Wonderful. I'm remembering times I shouldn't be, and he's thinking about what a mess I look. And he's right; my clothes are horribly wrinkled, my hair is falling down, and now there's jam smeared on my—*

"You missed it."

She wiped her chin again and the towel came away sticky. "There. Thank you."

He shook his head. "There's still a smudge left. Give me the towel."

"No, no. I can—"

"Bloody hell, can you nae let me even wipe off some jam withoot arguing? You are the most contentious woman I've ever met."

She had to swallow a heated retort. Perhaps he was right. He was just trying to help. With her lips folded tightly over her own protests, she handed him the towel.

He took her arm and pulled her closer, and then wiped her chin. As he did, his eyes met hers, and time froze.

She'd always loved his eyes. Almost slumberous in heaviness, they seduced with each glance. A deep gray like a stormy ocean, his emotions lurked in their depths. It took a cautious fisherwoman to extract their secrets, and at one time, Kenna had been able to do that. Now, though, she knew him so little that she didn't even dare guess what he felt.

"The towel isna removing the jam." Marcus's voice had deepened.

She couldn't look away. "No?"

"Nae. Shall I find something that will?"

Did he mean . . . She couldn't even finish the thought. Instead, she nodded mutely.

He dropped the towel and slipped an arm about her waist, pulling her to him. Her body fit his as if she'd never left him, softening to fit his harder planes.

With his free hand he tilted her face to his, and then he bent to place a kiss on her chin.

Tremors of awareness crashed through her as his warm lips touched her chin . . . and all thought fled.

She slipped her arms about his neck and drew his mouth to hers, seeking and desiring. She wanted him; she'd always wanted him. And now she had him here, alone, no one watching, no one condemning. She kissed him deeply, opening to him, teasing his tongue with hers.

His hands tightened about her and with a single move, he lifted her to the table, pushing her legs apart with his knee even as he moved his kisses from her lips to her chin, lingering where the jam had been. Every touch of his lips sent her senses careening madly, made her shiver with need, with desire. It had been so long. Too long. She had wanted this since she first saw him in Stormont's sitting room.

But there will be consequences, some uncooperative part of her whispered. *Dire ones.*

I don't care, she responded fiercely, as she gripped Marcus's coat and pulled him closer. *I want this. Now. While I can.*

She tightened her knees about his hips and arched against him, welcoming him, urging him forward, begging for more.

Chapter Five

Marcus deepened the kiss, reveling in the feelings of both the familiar and the new, of Kenna's rounder curves sliding under his seeking hands; of her scent, the memory of which had teased him mercilessly in the years since they'd parted ways; of the taste of her lips, which were softer and yet more demanding than any others. He slid his hand down her hips to her knee, and on to her boot-covered ankle, pushing aside her light wool chemise so that he could cup her bare calf in his palm. Her calf just fit his hand and he reveled in the warmth of her skin under his fingertips.

She was succulent, delicious, making him hungry for more even as he greedily tasted. Kenna stirred against him, restless and urging. He slid his hand higher up her leg, curving his fingers about her knee as he trailed a line of kisses from her jaw to the delicate hollows of her neck.

Shivering, Kenna shifted to grasp his arm, and as she did so, the long skirt of her riding habit tugged under his foot. It was a faint tug, barely distracting. But it acted like cold water upon his reactions. They hadn't come to this cottage to enjoy a flirtation. No, they'd been madly dashing to her father's house, hoping for assistance to rectify an error—an error he was responsible for, one that could impact her life in the worst of ways.

It could impact his, as well, if he made the error of caring for her again. She had walked away from their love and never once looked back. And if there was one thing Marcus didn't wish to repeat, it was being the one who loved the most. It would be sheer madness to torment himself so again.

But here they were, alone together, protected from the curious gazes of society, friends, and families, and once again irresistibly drawn into one another's arms. *But it's not real,* he told himself. *What happens here, in this isolated cottage, far away from our responsibilities and concerns, is far from reality. It is illusion, fragile and unreal, and it will end just as painfully as the last time.*

Unless . . . unless he could find a way to kiss her, yet keep from falling in love with her again. He pulled back and cupped her face, looking into her eyes. Deep brown and slumberous with sensuality, they held secrets he ached to know.

Could he be with this woman and still protect his heart?

It wasn't impossible. He'd done it before with many other women. He could do it now.

Couldn't he?

No.

The word whispered deep in his mind, as loud as a shout. *Not with Kenna.*

Heart burning, he dropped his hands and stepped back, away from temptation, away from madness. "Kenna, this canna be." He shook his head. "Nae again."

She blinked, obviously stunned, her skirts draped over her spread knees, her lips damp and swollen from his kisses, her hair yet more disordered. The coat of her riding habit hung partially off one shoulder, and she looked like what she was—an almost ravished woman. Her gaze was hazy, as if passion still muddled her thinking, disbelieving that he'd left her.

He'd never seen a more beautiful woman. One step, and he'd be back in her arms. *One. Step.* As if to rescue him from the inevitable, the kettle whistled loudly, its sound discordant and shrill. His hands ached from emptiness, so he curled them into fists and turned to the demanding kettle. "I'll make the tea."

Bemused at Marcus's sudden abandonment, his words as cold as ice water, Kenna found herself alone, her heated skin rapidly chilling, especially the burning trail left by his lips.

Feeling almost ill, she straightened her cloak and tugged her skirts back into place, then slid off the table and moved to the other side. She rubbed her arms, aware anew of the chilliness that permeated the room. What had just happened? She'd opened to him, shared with him, offered herself freely, and he'd walked away.

Again.

She pressed her lips into a tight line, fighting hot tears. In her entire life, she'd never felt so achingly alone. It was as if she'd been given a glimpse of something special, something to be treasured, something that lifted her soul . . . only to have it ripped out of her arms with neither warning nor care.

Marcus placed two mugs near the kettle, the crockery rattling on the small slate-topped table. Without sparing her so much as a glance, he opened the tin holding the tea. Soon, the fragrant scent of bergamot lifted through the air. "I dinna suppose you saw any milk in the larder?"

Ah yes, he always took his tea with milk. She'd almost forgotten that. Glad he hadn't looked at her, she swiped her eyes with her sleeve. "No, although I daresay there's an icehouse out back. If it's halfway as well stocked as the larder, there should be milk."

"I'll be damned if I traipse into that snow for nae more than a splash of milk; I'll do withoot."

She nodded, wondering miserably what she should say to make it seem as if their kiss had held no meaning for her, either. But no words came, because the kiss had meant something to her . . . She only wished she knew what.

Marcus searched through the line of tins sitting upon a shelf until he found the sugar. He carried the tin and the two mugs to the table, where Kenna leaned. "Here." He dipped a spoon inside the tin of sugar and placed a heaping spoonful into her mug, stirring it once before he slid it across the table in her direction.

He remembers how I take my tea. It was a small thing. Tiny, really. But the fact that he'd remembered, added to the fact that his hand shook the faintest bit and caused him to spill some of the sugar beside the mug, soothed her embarrassment. She wasn't the only one affected by their embrace.

The realization made her sigh in deep, sudden relief. *He is affected just as much as I am; he just hides it better.*

She wasn't sure why it mattered, but it did. A lot. Now able to breathe more normally, she picked up her mug of tea and held it in both hands, hoping her face wasn't as red as it felt. "Thank you for the tea." Her voice was husky even to her own ears.

Marcus gave her a dark, searching glance that made her tingle all over again.

The tea was so hot, she could barely hold the mug. Marcus must have felt the same, for he lifted the mug and blew upon the curls of steam. They danced away, disappearing in the sunlight, his lips damp.

She watched, mesmerized, longing. She could stay here, silent and miserable, or take a chance and speak her mind. *If I don't say something, this moment will be gone. And we've allowed so many such moments to disappear already.*

Kenna placed the mug back on the table with a thunk. "Marcus."

His gaze flickered to her. "Aye?" There was caution in that word, and distrust.

"That kiss. It was—"

"—a mistake." He said it firmly, as if in doing so, he could make it true. "It willna happen again." His gaze met hers. "I promise."

Disappointment rippled through her and she curled her fingers into her palms in frustration. In the past, she would have swallowed her true feelings and avoided a potentially embarrassing confrontation. *But I'm no longer that girl. I am older now, and changed by my mistakes and triumphs.* "'Twas no mistake." She met his gaze boldly. "Mistakes don't make my knees weak."

Marcus's mug was halfway to his lips, but now he lowered it. "Perhaps 'mistake' was the wrong word. You and I . . . we are like a spark to tinder."

"We have passion." She leaned toward him. "That's good, isn't it?"

"As strong as our passion is, 'tis nae enough. Ye canna build a true relationship upon it, for it crumbles like ash in the wind whenever there's a problem or an argument. 'Twill nae bear the weight."

"But—"

"Nae. We canna make that same mistake again. This time we must fight that passion and win over it, instead of the other way around."

"And if we don't?"

His cool gray gaze locked with hers. "Then we face the pain of yet another parting."

"You don't know that. This time, it could work. We could—"

"But I do know. And so do you. We dinna work well together, you and I. We are both stubborn and headstrong, we both have tempers that flash and flare, and neither of us is willing to give the other an inch."

She shoved a loose curl from her cheek. "You make us sound wretched together. That's not a complete picture. We had more than mere passion, Marcus. We laughed together, you and I. We loved and lived and fulfilled one another."

"You are remembering only the good times."

"And you're only remembering the bad!"

"If our relationship was so much more, then why did we part after only one argument? *One*, Kenna. That is nae love."

He waited, but she had no answer.

His expression softened. "We canna repeat auld mistakes. 'Twould be madness."

Her heart sank with each word. He might have only felt passion for her, but she'd felt much more for him. She'd been devastated when they'd ended their relationship. *More than devastated. The wounds pain me still, even after all these years, so it was definitely more than mere passion. But perhaps it wasn't the same for him. Perhaps that was all the feeling he had for me.* The thought lowered her spirits yet more.

Marcus watched the emotions play across Kenna's face, and it took all his strength not to reach for her and pull her into his arms. *She is facing the truth for the first time; a truth I knew years ago.* " 'Tis good we are discussing this now, before we make another error."

She stiffened, the flash in her eyes reassuring him. "Kissing me was an 'error'?"

"Or a fool's impulse. Call it what you will; it willna happen again. I willna *allow* it to happen again." There. That made sense. Calm, cool, dispassionate sense.

She picked up her mug and took a sip, a pensive look in her warm brown eyes. "Fortunately for us both, I am not as afraid of my passions as you are."

"Afraid?" he sputtered. "I'm nae afraid of anything!"

She shrugged. "Then what's a kiss or two?"

"Your reputation—"

"The damage to my reputation has already been done, so there's no fixing that, at least not now. And no one would know what happened here, unless we told them—which I would never do." Her gaze locked with his. "Would you?"

"That is nae the point. It's aboot stopping before—" He pressed his lips together. "We're playing with fire, Kenna. We were burned before and I, for one, willna be burned again." He picked up his mug, the steam wisping before him. "I owe you an apology for this mess. That kiss at the masquerade ball caused this entire situation. The fault was mine."

Her brows lowered. "If it was anyone's fault, it was mine."

"As soon as I kissed you, I knew who you were. I should have stopped there, when no one was the wiser, and we were undiscovered. But I lost my temper." He shook his head. "I'm sorry, Kenna. It was childish of me and—"

"Marcus, please. That kiss at the masquerade ball, I . . ." She wet her lips, and his gaze instantly locked upon her moist mouth. "It was my fault."

"Nonsense. I knew who you were and I kissed you again. When it comes to kissing you, I canna seem to stop when the time comes."

"But I—"

"Och, lass, say no more. I've apologized and we'll leave it at that." He finished his tea and placed the mug back on the table, glancing out the window. "If help does nae come soon, I'll walk to the nearest road and flag doon a passing coach."

"Walk? In this weather?"

"It canna last forever."

Sighing, Kenna cupped her mug between her hands, her gaze following his to the window. "I wonder why no one has yet come for us."

"Perhaps they canna find us. You said the cottage is some distance off the trail."

"Aye, but not that far."

"The prince knew what path we took, and he would have told Stormont as soon as we were discovered missing. It's just a matter of combing the woods near the path, which is the first thing I'd do, if I were searching for a lost party. We will be rescued today, I'm certain of it." He glanced at her and caught a flicker of concern crossing her face. "What's wrong?"

"'Tis naught."

She smiled but it wasn't a genuine smile, for her dimples remained in hiding. It dawned on him that she often did that—turning her smile on and off as if it were a lamp rather than a true reaction. *Does she hide her feelings behind those smiles? Did she do this before?*

He placed his hands flat on the table and leveled his gaze with hers. "'Tis nae naught if it keeps you from smiling. What is it?"

The false smile disappeared and she sighed, a deep, long sigh that said more than words could. "If you must know, I was hoping no one had sent notice to my father that I've been missing."

"Ah. You dinna wish him to come swooping down from his high perch and sprinkle you with his rancorous judgments."

"Something like that, yes. 'Tis to his benefit to pretend all is well in public, but in private—" She curled her nose. "He'll swoop to his heart's content, claws bared. He's not an easy man to deal with in the best of circumstances, but when he feels his good name has been threatened . . . you don't want to know him then."

"I'm well aware of your father's hawkish tendencies. He never liked me."

She stifled a laugh. "And you returned the favor, if I recall."

His lips twitched. "Perhaps."

"You should have seen him after we ended our engagement. He was furious."

His smile slipped. "I knew he'd be angry with me, but surely nae with you."

"Oh, he was angry with both of us. As you weren't nearby to listen to his fuming, I had to listen to enough of it for two."

Marcus caught the darkening of her gaze. "I never meant that to happen. I left the country to make things easier, nae to leave you to deal with your father's wrath alone."

"His wrath consists only of sharp words, but he knows how to cut with them." She took a sip of tea that dampened her bottom lip. He had to fight the urge to draw her close and taste her yet again. Her lips would be warm from the tea, and slightly sweet, too. His groin ached anew and he bit the inside of his lip. *Stop that*, he admonished his too-vivid imagination, and forced himself to focus on something less tempting than her lips.

He turned away, looking back out the window. "Bloody hell, it's a blizzard out there." The wind blew the snow in white waves against the window, pelting the glass with tiny, icy flakes.

"It was snowing like that when we reached this cottage yesterday." She shivered. "I'd never been so cold."

"We should take our tea back to the sitting room where it's warmer, although . . . I suppose you explored the rest of the cottage while I was unconscious?"

"Me, leave a cupboard unopened? Perish the thought." She managed a smile, an honest, genuine smile that crinkled her eyes and made her dimples appear. And oh, how he wished he could kiss those dimples.

Irritated at himself, he pushed away from the table. "We should explore the rest of the house."

She placed her mug on the table. "I didn't have time to examine the rooms in detail, as I was afraid you'd wake up while I was wandering around, and not know where you were."

"Thank you for your forbearance. How many bedchambers are there?"

"Only one master chamber. There are two servants' quarters in the attic."

"Hm." He brushed a hand over his chin, the scrape of his whiskers audible. "I dinna suppose you saw a razor when you were peeking aboot?"

"I didn't pay attention, although I did see some clothes in one of the wardrobes."

"Men's? Or women's?"

"Both."

"Interesting. Perhaps we can find something more comfortable for you to wear than that riding habit."

"I'd like that," she replied honestly. "There is a copper tub in the master bedchamber, too. Perhaps we could warm water so we can bathe—" *"We"? I meant to say "I"! Why did I say that?*

And yet now that the words were said, Kenna couldn't seem to make her lips take them back. Instead, she met his gaze and this time she couldn't hide the smoky truth his presence had stirred to life. She wanted him. She wanted his kisses and his touch. She wanted to taste him and feel him and be with him. She wanted more than that, too. She wanted this: to talk to him, to find out what he thought, and why he'd acted as he had, and why he was here now, talking to her in this way, *listening* to her and—

He straightened, his mug thumping heavily on the table as he pushed it away. "I should make sure there is more firewood in case we've need of it."

"There's a large stack by the front door and—"

"It may nae be enough."

"It's huge—we could never burn through the lot of it, were we stuck here a month."

"Still, I should make sure we've extra wood before the weather worsens even more." He was already out the kitchen door, striding to the steps that led back upstairs, his boot heels ringing with each step.

"But it's still snowing," she called after him. "And you'll get cold and could catch an ague and—"

"I'll wear my coat." His voice drifted back down the stairs. "Enjoy your tea until I return."

She went to the bottom of the stairs. "I thought you wished to look through the house?"

But he was already out of earshot and in the sitting room; his footsteps sounding on the ceiling above her. Just as she decided to go back upstairs, she heard the front door open and then close so rapidly that she had to believe he almost ran from the cottage.

All of that, to protect himself from one look.

She sighed. She should have known better than expose her feelings in such a way. He'd warned her that he thought there was no future for them, but she'd ignored his words.

Her heart aching, she picked up her mug—but the tea suddenly tasted unbearably bland.

Chapter Six

An hour and a half later, chilled to the bone and thoroughly caked with snow, Marcus entered the cottage, his arms filled with firewood. He stomped the loose snow from his boots, set the stack on the foyer floor, and took off his coat. He hung the wet coat on a peg by the door beside Kenna's cloak and winced as his exhausted muscles complained. He ached from splitting so many logs into firewood. He'd already made several trips inside, and the brass rack by the fireplace was overflowing. He'd gone on to add several rows of split wood to the stack beside the kitchen door, too, enough wood to last this small cottage the rest of the winter.

Swinging the ax in the biting wind had cleared his mind, in addition to leaving him blissfully tired, both good remedies against the unruly passion Kenna stirred within him.

Pleased with himself, he gathered the firewood from the floor, and opened the door to the sitting room.

Kenna was on the settee beside the crackling fire, and he was surprised to see an embroidery basket at her elbow. She'd apparently found a brush too, for her dark brown hair was now smooth, and her clothing, though still wrinkled, seemed more orderly as well. She held a small hoop in one hand and a threaded needle in the other. She eyed the load of firewood in his arms before looking pointedly at the overflowing bin by the fireplace. "You've certainly made yourself useful."

He carried the wood to the bin, and—unable to fit even one more log in it—placed the wood on the floor beside it, then dusted the loose bark from his sleeves into the fire. "The wind is picking up."

Her gaze flickered to the rattling window. "I noticed." She was silent a moment. "It looks brutal out there. I wonder if—"

A crack sounded from outside, followed by a thud that shook the small cottage.

Kenna's wide gaze met his.

"A broken tree limb. The snow is heavy and wet, and there are broken limbs everywhere. It's only getting worse." It was why he'd decided to return to the cottage when he did; a huge limb had come perilously close to landing on his already bruised head.

She looked worried. "It's almost noon and no one has come. Do you think this wet snow and the falling tree limbs will put them off?"

I hope not. He pulled off his gloves and placed them over the fire screen to dry. "It may be too risky to the horses. We may be stuck here another night, or they may press through. I dinna know."

She looked at her embroidery and sighed. "I finished the book I bought, but then found this basket so at least I have something to do. I also started a stew. It was very quiet after you left, and I wished to keep busy."

"That was verrah industrious of you."

"It was very desperate of me. I've never cooked before; I don't know if it will be worth eating or not."

"How can you ruin stew?"

"That's what I thought. 'Tis why we're having it." She glanced at the table beside a display cabinet, which she'd set with fine china and silver for their luncheon. "I thought we'd eat in here, where it's warm."

"That is verrah kind of you."

"I could do no less, what with you cutting down the entire forest for heat."

He found himself smiling at the wry twinkle in her eyes. "I dinna cut down a single tree; I only split the wood already cut and drying in the shed."

"All of it?"

"Almost," he lied. He nodded to her embroidery basket. "Where did you find the basket?"

She patted it as if it were a cat. "In one of the servant's rooms. I daresay the housekeeper kept it handy for when she wasn't needed."

Marcus held his hands to the flames. "I dinna suppose you found any books? This house seems strangely empty of them."

"Not a one." Disapproval folded her lips. "Who can live in a house with no books?"

"Nae one I would call a friend."

"Nor I. I brought one with me, but 'tis a novel and I know you prefer histories, so . . ."

"So I do."

She replaced her embroidery hoop back in the basket and stood. "I daresay you're hungry. I'll see if the stew is ready."

"Has it been cooking long enough?"

She smoothed her skirts. "Oh, yes. I wasn't exactly sure how long stew should take, but I wanted it ready for luncheon, so I made sure the fire was high."

He raised his brows at this startling news, but she was already leaving the room, closing the door behind her.

Marcus looked down at his hands and decided to wash for lunch. He went back to the foyer and pulled on his coat and then hurried outside. There, he used the pump to wash his hands, the water so cold his hands ached, but at least he was clean.

He'd just returned and left his coat back in the foyer when Kenna appeared carrying a tray, the stew in a fanciful soup tureen, a pitcher of water balanced precariously beside it.

He stepped forward and rescued the pitcher as it slid to one side, and then filled both of their glasses. Afterward, he took his seat while Kenna dished the stew into his bowl.

He looked at the stew, the smell instantly choking him. Pepper, garlic, and other scents he couldn't quite identify seemed to fight for attention. "I can see you seasoned it well."

She took her seat, confessing with touching candor, "I wasn't certain what went into stew, so I put in a little of everything I could find. You can't have too much flavor, can you?"

"Nae." That explained that. He poked at the stew, which had the consistency of water, dotted with floating gray lumps. "I've never seen stew of this consistency—" At her concerned look, he hurried to add, "—but there are many types of stews."

As he spoke a carrot floated to the top and slowly, ever so slowly, rolled over to reveal that it was half burned. He tapped it with his spoon and discovered that the half that wasn't burned was uncooked.

He noted that Kenna was staring at a piece of a turnip that sat in her spoon, cooked much like his carrot. She tried to bite it, but it was impossible, and the flavor made her choke. Face pink, she dropped the turnip back into her bowl, her shoulders sagging. "It's wretched."

Marcus's first impulse was to agree with her. Yet he heard himself murmur, "I'm sure 'tis verrah tasty."

"It's not. I didn't put enough water in it at first, which burned the vegetables, so then I added more water, thinking to thin out the stew, but I must have added too much, and the spices . . . I should have been more cautious with them."

"I'm sure it's fine." He took a bold sip of the watery, lumpy gravy. It was horrid, the spices clumped, burned pieces of various vegetables floating about.

Realizing her gaze was locked on him, he forced a smile. "Quite tasty." He reached for his glass of water and drained it.

She dropped her spoon in her bowl, where it landed on a large hunk of onion that sat half submerged like the back of a turtle at low tide. "It's wretched."

He watched, wondering if there would be any tears, but she just sighed and said, "Well, I tried. That's all I can say."

"All it needs is a little something more. After all, what's stew without a nice crust of bread?" He placed his napkin on the table and arose. "I'll be back in a moment."

When he returned, he carried a tray that held a plate of crusty bread, two kinds of cheese, a pot of jam, and thick slices of a ham he'd found hanging in the back of the pantry. He placed the tray on the table. "The perfect side dishes to our stew."

"Side dishes? That's an entire meal."

"Nonsense," he said firmly. "They're just side dishes. Nae more."

A smile quivered on her lips, but she joined in. "The ham will make our meal especially appetizing, especially if I eat it between the slices of bread and *without* the stew."

They ate quickly after that, and Marcus realized he was indeed famished. When the meal was over, they collected the dishes and returned them to the kitchen. The fire in the stove had heated the small kitchen, so they washed the dishes and left them on a dish towel to dry, before returning to the sitting room.

"An excellent lunch," he declared as Kenna dropped onto the settee with her embroidery.

She sent him a shy smile. "Yes, it was."

"I find I quite like our small cottage." Marcus looked about the room. Perhaps there was a chessboard or a backgammon game to be found, something a bit boring that would cool his ardor. His gaze moved over the decorative vases, candelabras, and a small painting of a couple by a river—

He looked at the painting more closely. He'd thought it was of a knight and a lady washing in the river, but now he realized they were— *Bloody hell!* He glanced at Kenna, who was rethreading her needle.

He clasped his hands behind his back and casually strolled toward the painting, pausing to examine a glass dish here, a vase there. He kept an eye on her bent head as he progressed across the room. Just as he reached his goal she looked up, and he stepped between her and the painting.

Her brows knit. "What are you doing?"

"I'm . . . looking out the window to see if any more branches are falling— Ah! There goes one now."

She turned toward the window.

He grabbed the painting off the wall, then slid it facedown under a chair.

He'd just straightened up when Kenna turned back to him "I didn't see anything—"

A thud on the roof answered her, and she looked up with concern. "Could that harm the roof?"

"I doubt it; the trees hanging over the house are nae large." As he spoke, he glanced at the other paintings in the room. The first one seemed fine; an idyllic village sitting on a hill surrounded by flowers. He moved a bit closer. In one of the fields, near the stream . . . could that be a man and woman— *What in the hell is going on?*

He pointed out the window. "Is that a deer?"

Brightening, she turned to look.

He grabbed the painting, staring wildly about the room for a hiding place. Before he found one, she said, "I think you must be mistaken," and turned back around.

He held the painting behind his back, glad it was so small. "I know I saw a deer; it must have run away."

She sent him a concerned look. "Is everything well?"

No, everything wasn't well. He'd just realized that every picture in this room—all five of them, were bawdy representations unfit for her eyes. He supposed he was being a prude, which was a new hat for him to wear, but he'd be damned if he'd expose her to such tawdriness. *We've stumbled upon a damned love nest.*

"Marcus, what's wrong? You're scowling as if you'd like to murder someone."

He forced a smile. "I was only thinking that I would like to see the rest of the cottage. I may walk aboot for a bit."

She put down her embroidery. "I'll come with y—"

"Nae! There's no need." God only knew what awaited them beyond the doorway. "I'll look myself."

"Don't be ridiculous." She stood. "I've already been in the rest of the house. I can lead you through it."

Which could only mean that the tawdry touches were subtle, or she would have noticed them. He supposed he should allow her to go with him; to do otherwise would just raise her suspicions. He would take a mental inventory, and then later, perhaps when she was asleep, hide whatever needed hidden. "Fine. We'll go together. Are you certain you wouldna rather stay here, where it's warm, and enjoy your embroidery?"

"It'll wait." She glanced back at the embroidery hoop and frowned. "It's a complex pattern of some sort; I'm not really sure what it is."

Good lord, not the embroidery, too. He walked behind a chair, leaning the picture he held against the back, and then stepped out from behind it. "Let me see the pattern. Perhaps I can decipher it."

Her brows rose. "I've had more practice deciphering embroidery patterns than you."

"Perhaps. Perhaps nae."

She blinked and then gave a surprised laugh. "If you insist . . ."

"I do."

She picked up the hoop and handed it to him. "What do you think it might be?"

While he looked at the pattern, Kenna put away the extra thread and tucked away her scissors. The pattern looked innocent enough, a series of circles and swirls. They seemed random, though he was certain there must be something lascivious to it.

Jaw set, he placed the hoop facedown on a table near the fire.

She put the basket aside, her bright gaze on him. "Well? Do you know what it is?"

" 'Tis an animal," he announced. "One from Africa, I believe. I canna remember the name of it, but it'll come to me." He gestured to the doorway. "Shall we?"

"Of course." She led the way to the door.

He took advantage of her back being turned away to toss the embroidery hoop into the fire, along with one of the pictures hanging nearby, before following her into the hallway. He'd make certain they stayed away long enough for them to burn completely.

Kenna was already opening the door to a small dining room. They looked about, and he instantly noted three glass figurines that needed to be consigned to a cupboard at the first opportunity, and one painting of a drunken Bacchanalian feast that was so large he'd be hard-pressed to hide it. Fortunately, Kenna didn't seem to notice anything amiss, merely commenting on the fine furnishings and the light spilling in from the windows. Afterward, they made their way to a small, neat den where he found much the same.

"Shall we look upstairs?" Kenna led the way from the den to the stairwell. "The bedchamber is quite large. Wait until you see it." When she reached the small landing, she opened a large oak door.

As soon as Marcus crossed the threshold, he halted dead in his tracks. If he'd had any questions as to the purpose of the cottage, they were permanently laid to rest.

Most hunting boxes were used to provide guests with a place to stop for rest and refreshments during a hunt. They were usually decorated with a hunting theme, the walls containing paintings of men and women riding to the hounds, displays of ancient firearms, and the occasional mounted animal trophy. In every hunting box Marcus had ever visited, there was usually one large room for gathering and an assortment of smallish bedchambers for the guests should they need a rest.

This cottage only had enough room for one couple and their personal servants. The stable only had room for two, perhaps three horses, and hidden behind that was a shed where a coach could park under a covering, well away from the main road. There were no large rooms for gathering; just small, intimate chambers.

And this room proved beyond all doubt that he and Kenna had stumbled onto someone's luxurious and well-hidden love nest. A huge, ornate bed sat in the middle of the room, hung with thick red curtains and adorned on each post with huge cupids, their arrows all pointing at the mattress as if ready to skewer the inhabitants with love arrows.

The huge picture over the fireplace showed a pair of lovers lounging under a tree, the gentleman partially disrobed as he cupped his companion's exposed breast, her low-cut gown hanging off her shoulder and baring her to all. A fat red velvet settee, the back of it shaped like a heart, sat before a huge fireplace adorned with red and blue Chinese tiles that, on closer inspection, illustrated various lovemaking positions. And in one corner, half hidden by a screen, was a decent-size brass tub with feet of gold, each shaped like a statue of Aphrodite he'd seen in the British Museum.

But the grand mural on the ceiling exceeded everything else. Zeus lounged boldly naked, surrounded by a bevy of maidens, each one plumper and more lascivious than the next, while a horde of fat, goat-footed men danced around, leering.

Marcus rubbed a hand over his eyes. "Bloody hell."

Kenna's low, throaty chuckle surprised him as she came to his side. She looked up at the mural, crossing her arms against the chill. "It's a bit much, isn't it?"

He glanced down at her, surprised to see her grinning as she looked about the room. "I laughed so hard when I first saw it," she admitted. "There's something to be said for a bold picture now and then such as those hanging downstairs, for the human body is lovely, but this—" She glanced up at the ceiling and laughed. "None of them look very happy. I don't know if they've come to seduce him, or to smack him. Honestly, either could happen."

He had to smile. "The paintings in the living room are risqué, too, though nae in such an obvious manner."

"Oh, I noticed." She turned an amused glance his way. "I must protest your use of the fire. The walls will be bare if you assign every naughty painting in this house to the flames."

"You saw that, did you?"

"I did. And my embroidery with it." Laughter bubbled from her lips, her eyes warm and bold. "I can assure you there is no hidden picture in that pattern. I specifically looked."

"I'm glad to hear it. I would hate for shock to damage to your delicate sensibilities."

"Sadly, I have none, as my father frequently reminds me." She walked farther into the room, rubbing her arms.

He moved past her to the fireplace. "I'll start the fire to warm the room."

She sent him a surprised look. "Why?"

"I am nae sleeping upon the floor another night. My back is still stiff. We'll sleep here tonight."

She blinked. "*Both* of us?"

"I'll sleep upon the settee. Even that will be better than the floor."

The fire was already laid, the tinder in place, and he found a flint box on the mantel and lit the wood. The first puff of smoke roiled up the chimney, but then puffed back down into the room. "Ah. The vent is closed." It took three good hard pulls, but he managed to get it open, the fire flaring to life at the rush of air.

Soon, Kenna came to stand with her hands toward the crackling flames. "That's much better. I hope we have enough firewood. We have so little . . ." She slanted him a mischievous look, which instantly made him wish all sorts of carnal things.

That wretched mural does nothing for me, yet one smile from her and I can think of nothing but the softness of her under me, of the scent of her hair and the—

"I will search the wardrobes and see what clothes we can borrow," she announced. "I looked earlier, but didn't do an inventory."

He nodded. "And I'll look in the trunk at the foot of the bed. Perhaps there are extra blankets."

"Very good." As she walked to the wardrobe, she passed an elaborate washstand. "There's a straight razor here, and clean towels. We'll have to carry water from the kitchen, though."

He rubbed his chin. "Is that a hint?"

Her gaze flickered to his chin and she smiled. "Not at all. If you like being unshaven, by all means stay so for I have no complaint." She opened the large wardrobe and disappeared from sight.

She likes me unshaven. It makes me think what the feel of my chin might feel like against her thighs—

No. He couldn't think about such things. And neither should she.

He opened the trunk and shifted through it. "There are extra blankets and some riding boots, but little else. What did you find?"

Kenna's muffled voice drifted from the wardrobe. "There are some very nice shirts, although the arms might be a little short. The breeches are all too short and won't do at all."

"You said before that there are ladies' gowns as well?"

She pulled a blue silk gown from the wardrobe. "Many." She held it before her and looked in the mirror. "Sadly, they are too long—I would fall down with every step. They would fit fairly well, otherwise."

He watched as she turned this way and that, letting the skirt flow around her. It was an unconsciously feminine gesture, and made him want to wrap his arms around her and buy her a hundred such gowns. Instead, he said, "Here. Let me see it."

She tilted her head to one side as she held out the gown. "What are you going to do?"

"You'll see." He took the gown and placed it upon the bed and spread out the skirts. Then he turned to look at her legs, then back at the gown, measuring silently. "It is aboot four inches too long."

"At least that."

He picked up the razor from where it sat near the washbasin, slipped it from its sheath, and held up the skirt—

She caught his hand. "You can't do that!"

"Why nae?"

She dropped her hand from his. "It's not mine."

He shrugged. "I'll leave some coins to replace it. It's

highly unlikely we'll be rescued until morning, nae with tree limbs dropping all aboot. Do you wish to wear that riding habit yet another day?"

She looked down at her wrinkled habit. "No. To be honest, I'm beginning to hate it."

"Then I will do this. When the time comes, we'll purchase the owner a new gown." When she hesitated, he added, " 'Tis an emergency, true?"

Kenna looked wistfully at the gown. It was so beautiful, the watered silk the exact shade of blue she loved, the neckline adorned with tiny pink roses. It would look so much better on her than her tired riding habit, and would be far more comfortable. "Very well."

Marcus nodded his satisfaction.

She watched as he marked the gown in one place with the point of the razor, and then repeated the marks around the rest of the skirt, using his hand as a measurement.

"Whoever owns it has excellent taste in both gowns and jewelry." Kenna reached over to the washstand and picked up an earring. "I found this yesterday. It's beautiful, isn't it?" She held the earring up so the light caught the large ruby that dangled from it.

At the sight of the earring, Marcus paused in cutting the gown. His brows lowered. "Where did you find that?"

Something about his voice gave her pause, and she said cautiously, "On the rug in front of the settee."

His gaze flickered to the settee, and though his expression didn't change, she was certain he was irritated.

She held out the earring. "Perhaps you should keep it. I'd hate for something this valuable to go missing while we're here."

He hesitated, but then reached for the earring and tucked it away in his pocket before returning to his task, slicing the flowing skirt in smooth, long strokes. Finally, he finished and handed her the gown.

She took it with both hands, letting the silk sink between her fingers, soft as air. Grateful, she smiled at him. "Thank you. You should try on some of the shirts." She carefully placed the gown over a cushioned chair and then looked through the shirts hanging in the wardrobe. He could roll up the short sleeves, but if his broad chest and muscled arms were too big, there was nothing to be done. She'd just pulled out a shirt when the red silk robe that had been hanging on a hook by the door fell to the floor. As she bent to pick it up, the crest on the front pocket caught her gaze.

She straightened and smoothed a finger over the gold and purple embroidery. She knew this crest, of a lion holding a blazing sword. And it confirmed what she'd suspected.

Marcus moved so he could look over her shoulder. "Whose is it?" he asked.

"Stormont's."

"I suspected as much. You did say this is his land."

"I wondered if this house was his as well, but—" She shook her head. "Stormont seemed too bound in propriety to use such a place. I suppose I was wrong to think that."

"Some people are very different in public than they are in private."

She couldn't argue with that. She waited for a feeling to hit her: jealousy, concern, worry . . . anything. But nothing happened. Nothing at all.

She hung the robe back on the hook and removed the shirt she'd spied earlier. "See if this will fit. It's a bit larger than the others."

He tossed the shirt over the back of the settee, then undid the simple knot of his cravat. That gone, he took off his coat, revealing a white linen shirt underneath.

She watched as he reached up to pull the shirt over his head, his muscles flexing with each move. He was more muscled than he used to be, his shoulder and arms especially. He was also more tanned, which gave him a faintly exotic look when paired with his dark hair and gray eyes. All in all, he was a handsome, devilishly intriguing man.

He tossed his shirt aside, and her breath left her in a whoosh as she saw his broad shoulders and the muscled lines of his broad chest. But even more intriguing was his stomach, rock hard and flat, with the crisp curls that covered his chest narrowing to a thin trail that thinned down his stomach and disappeared under the band of his breeches.

The coolness of the room faded, replaced with an inner heat that stole her breath and muddled her thinking. She wanted him so badly, her body ached with need. *But he's made it plain he does not wish to tread that path.*

Afraid she might reveal herself should he look her way, she turned and hurried to the door. "I must go."

"Go?" Marcus's voice deepened with surprise. "Where?"

"Downstairs." *Now. Before I do or say something I shouldn't.*

"Nonsense. Stay here and try on the gown. I will leave and you can have the room to—"

"I'll try it later. I-I-I'll wish to bathe first, which will take more time than I have now."

"Time? We have plenty of that. I'll—"

"Perhaps later, thank you. Now, if you'll excuse me, I'll see you downstairs." She hurried out to the landing, dashed down the stairs, threw open the door to the sitting room, and then closed it behind her. Leaning against the door, she pressed her cheek to the cool panel and waited for her breath to slow.

Chapter Seven

An hour and a half later, Kenna stabbed the needle into the embroidery pattern. She'd been fortunate to find both another hoop and several other patterns in the basket; otherwise she'd have had nothing to do.

Marcus hadn't returned to the sitting room since her awkward flight, and she was glad. It gave her time to think of a reason to explain her actions: she'd tell him she'd felt ill from the stew. That was certainly believable. She even practiced the telling of it, looking at herself in the mirror to make sure she appeared sufficiently distressed.

But Marcus hadn't granted her the opportunity to perform; he'd left her alone as the sun outside slowly slid out of sight.

What is he doing? She eyed the closed door curiously. Immediately after she'd retreated to the sitting room, she'd heard him make his way to the kitchen, where he'd stayed for almost half an hour. After that, she heard him walking back up the steps, and then—a very short time later—back down to the kitchen. That had happened a dozen times or more. What was he up to? Perhaps he was avoiding her, too?

She frowned, a bit miffed. Should she find out what he was doing? Join him in the kitchen, under the pretense of wanting something to eat? But no, that might seem as if she were trying to woo him. She wasn't, of course. Their relationship was over; he'd made that abundantly clear. She was just . . . curious. Yes, curious.

She sighed, her breath fluttering the thread in her unused needle. Perhaps he merely wished for some time alone. *Perhaps he finds the situation as difficult as I do. It's so awkward.*

She stabbed at her embroidery as she heard his tread upon the stairs yet again. It was truly an agony, being so close to him but separated. He was a man made for touching, and she was realizing how, over the years, she'd missed that aspect of their relationship. Her lips still tingled at the thought of tracing his jaw with kisses, of sliding her hands over his flat, firm stomach, of the heat of his skin against hers—*None of which will happen if I sit here like a lump on a log and wait. I must make an effort if I wish this relationship to*—She wasn't sure what she wished their relationship to do. Certainly she'd like to be friends. But if she were honest, she wanted more, too. She wanted to move past this frosted, awkward friendship (if it could be called that) and rekindle the passion they'd always had. *Marcus said passion isn't enough, but it's a beginning. And perhaps all we need is another one of those.*

She put down her embroidery and stood just as the door opened, and Marcus strolled in. His coat was gone, his fresh shirt unlaced to reveal his throat, the sleeves rolled to his elbows, revealing his powerful forearms.

She hurried to sit back down, snatching up her embroidery and pretended great interest in the stitches, few as they were.

He walked to the fire, clasping his hands behind him as

he faced her, his gray eyes shadowed by his lashes. "I see you found another embroidery hoop."

"There were several in the basket, as well as more patterns."

"I'm glad I dinna deprive you of your needlework."

"No, I have plenty to do." *I just wish I were kissing you instead of embroidering.* "I heard you go to the kitchen. Did you have supper?"

"Nae. I ate an apple, but I was too busy to eat more."

"Busy doing what?"

"I was heating water. You said you wished for a bath, so I drew one for you."

"You . . . for me?" She blinked. "All those trips up and down the stairs . . . you were carrying heated water." She was so surprised, her voice squeaked on the last word.

Marcus decided to ignore her obvious shock. He sat in a chair by the fire, stretching his legs out toward the warmth, feeling oddly pleased with himself.

"You heated the water and filled the tub all by yourself?"

She still looked astonished, and some of his delight diminished. "Of course I did it by myself. Who else is here?"

"I know, I just . . . I didn't imagine you'd—" She caught his scowl and flushed. "I'm sorry. It was very kind of you. Thank you."

"It was, wasna it?" he agreed, trying not to feel slighted. *Did our previous relationship so marr her opinion of me that she doesn't believe me capable of even a small show of good will? Bloody hell, I hope not.* "Your bath is ready, so go and use it. It willna stay warm for long."

"A warm bath . . . I—I—Thank you."

Her voice was warm with gratitude and his earlier pleasure returned. "You're welcome."

She put her embroidery away, her face aglow with anticipation. She stood and moved to the door. She'd just placed her hand on the knob, when she stopped and stood still. After a second's hesitation, she looked back. "You have been very thoughtful. I—I—" She wet her lips. "I don't suppose you'd care to join me?"

He went still, his ears unwilling to accept what he'd just heard.

She flushed, smoothing the palm of her hand on her skirt. "It . . . it is a large tub."

He managed a nod. It *was* a large tub.

"If we wished, we could easily fit in it together." She peeped at him through her lashes, uncertainty and hope mingled on her face. "You and I."

Dear God, I'm so tempted. Every fiber of him hummed with yearning and desire. The image of the two of them in the tub burned through his mind, a vision of wet skin and her full breasts rising from the steaming water. His hands sliding across her lush hips and more.

He was clasping the arms of his chair so tightly, his fingers were growing numb. *This is how it began before—a glance and a smile, a suggestion followed by a touch, fueling a desire that became impossible to quench. If I go with her we will consummate our relationship again—and when we part this time, what will be the cost?*

For part they would. They had spent two days together, snowbound in this small cottage, and still they hadn't fully addressed their past. Either he was unwilling, or she was. *We avoid what we know will pain us. What we know is unanswerable.*

She'd changed, yes, but not enough. She still looked anxious when she mentioned her father, still ran from honest discussion. Worse, he himself was guilty of the same. *Neither of us is capable of following this to a good conclusion. We are both too flawed.*

He met her gaze and saw her longing and the faintest flicker of hope. Drawing strength from the simple knowledge that he was right, he yanked his gaze from her and turned them instead to his boots. "Nay, lass. 'Tis best if you bathe alone."

Even to him, who burned with his own desire, the words sounded cold and disinterested.

He heard her swallow, and then there was a click as she opened the door, pausing in the doorway. "Thank you for the bath." She shut the door behind her.

He listened as she climbed the stairs, holding his breath until he heard the bedchamber door close. "You're welcome," he whispered back, his heart aching anew.

✦ ✦ ✦

An hour later, washed and wearing the altered gown, Kenna descended the stairs. The blue gown was almost the right length, but the bodice was a touch tight across her breasts. She'd combed her hair beside the fire in the bedchamber for the better part of half an hour, but she'd grown bored before it had dried, so it hung damp about her shoulders, loosened from its pins, a chestnut brown mass of curls.

The bath had been heavenly; the hot water had soothed her pained soul. She would never understand Marcus. One moment, he looked at her as if he would devour her whole. The next, he rejected her without a bit of care.

Her face burned to think of it. She was done hoping, wishing, wanting, and not succeeding. He'd managed to make her realize the hopelessness of their situation, and for that she could only be grateful. Still, they must talk. And in that talk, they had to face their histories, their faults, and their shortcomings. It would not solve anything, it was too late for that; it might even make things worse. But it had to be done. Once they were gone from this place, they would melt back into the patterns of their lives and might never cross paths again.

She paused outside the sitting-room door, her hand resting on the knob. What would she say? Would he even listen?

She dropped her hand to her side. It was one thing to know an unpleasant task was at hand, and another to gather the courage and face it. *Just get it over with. March inside and tell him it is time to put our ghosts to rest.* And yet the door remained closed.

When her stomach rumbled noisily, she almost sighed with relief. Of *course* they needed supper first; neither of them could discuss anything while hungry and ill-tempered. Filled with purpose, she turned on her heel and hurried to the kitchen.

A half hour later, she returned with a repast. It took all of her balancing skill to open the door while carrying the heavy tray, but she managed, shoving it closed with her hip.

Still in his chair, Marcus made no move upon her entry. She carried the tray to the small table where they'd had lunch and, fixing a pleasant smile on her face, turned to him. "Marcus, come and e—"

He was asleep, his head resting against the high back of the chair, his legs still stretched to the fire. He looked so peaceful, his thick lashes resting on the crests of his cheeks, his hands open and relaxed on the chair arms. Between chopping wood and fetching water up and down the stairs, he'd had an exhausting day.

She crossed to where he sat and watched as the firelight caressed the planes of his face and the strong brown column of his neck. A dark bruise could barely be seen under the fall of his hair over his temple, a remanent of the accident that had stranded him here.

Her fingers itched to smooth his hair from his brow, but she curled her fingers closed and kept her distance. She'd leave him to rest. Unwilling to examine the emotions roiling through her heart and mind, she turned away, went to the table, and sat down to eat. She'd brought more of the ham and bread they'd had for their luncheon. For variety, she'd sliced some of the small apples, obviously a recent gift from someone's greenhouse. She'd also made tea, so she filled her teacup with the steaming brew. She ate quietly, watching Marcus as she did so. She'd just finished and had reached for the teapot when—*thump!*—a branch landed on the roof.

Marcus sat straight up, his gaze locked on the ceiling.

Kenna poured her tea, her cup rattling against the saucer.

Marcus turned her way, blinking. His gaze flickered to her damp hair, and down to her mouth, her shoulders, and finally to where the blue gown stretched across her breasts.

She held her breath, waiting, hoping.

He flushed and looked away. "Damn tree limbs." He rubbed his eyes. "That was startling." He gazed past her to the table. "It seems I missed supper."

"Your plate is here." She pointed to it. "Should I pour you some tea?"

"Nae, thank you. But I will have some ham." He stood and stretched, rubbing his shoulder before he came to sit at the table. Soon he was eating, his gray gaze flickering over her and then away, only to return a moment later.

She sipped her tea, trying to think of a way to start a conversation, but none came. He was quiet this evening, and because of that, so was she.

He finished his supper and then stood, wincing.

"You are sore from all of your tasks," she said.

"Verrah." He collected the dishes and placed them on the tray, then threw his napkin over them. "'Tis time for bed."

She put down her cup. "I'll sleep here, on the settee."

"We canna keep a fire burning in two rooms—nae withoot one of us losing sleep. We will sleep in the master bedchamber. I will take the settee, and you will have the bed."

"You won't fit on that settee. It's half the size of this one."

"It'll be better than the floor, which is what I had last night."

"Hm. We'll see." She put down her teacup, wiped her hands on her napkin, and picked up the tray.

He frowned. "Leave that until morning."

"I'd rather do it now." She carried the tray to the door. "We will need extra blankets; 'tis blowing icy cold and the windows leak cold air with each rattle."

"There were some blankets in the trunk at the foot of the bed. I'll set them oot." He opened the door for her, his gaze dark and questioning.

She wished she knew how to answer that look. She was the one with questions, not him. She'd put all of her wants and desires upon the table, and he'd rejected them, and her. If anyone had the right to toss out questioning looks, it wasn't Marcus.

Muttering to herself, she returned to the kitchen. It took her longer to wash and put away their dishes than she expected, so when she finally made her way to the bedchamber, almost forty minutes had passed.

She entered the room, where the crackling fire provided the only light. There were extra blankets piled upon the bed, but there would be no further discussions, for Marcus was already asleep, draped over the settee, his boots sitting side by side before the fire.

She tiptoed past him, pausing to look at his sleeping face. He'd taken off his shirt but had left on his breeches. A blanket covered his chest but left his broad shoulders and muscular arms exposed, his tanned skin warmed by the flickering firelight. One leg was draped over the end of the small settee, while the other was stretched out straight, his stockinged heel upon the floor.

A log in the fire fell to one side, pulling her gaze away from Marcus. The fire would die down over the night, but he'd stoked it enough that there would still be coals when they awoke in the morning. Still, as the fire diminished the room would cool, and he'd given himself only one blanket.

She crossed to the bed and picked up two more blankets. She carried them to the settee, unfolded them, and covered him from neck to feet. As she did, her knuckles brushed the stubble on his chin, a hot tingle shooting up her arm.

She yanked her hand away, her heart careening wildly at the innocent touch as she stared at him. She'd once loved this man and had planned to include him in every aspect of her life. What had happened to them? What had gone so awry that they'd stormed away, neither willing to admit their fault? Perhaps they'd just been too young, too foolish? Or had it been pride?

Kenna slowly reached out and brushed her fingers over his firm jaw.

He murmured in his sleep, his lips parting, though he didn't move.

Encouraged, she did it again, letting his whiskers tickle her fingertips before she slid them along his jaw to his neck where his damp hair curled. He must have washed before going to sleep, for she caught the the fresh scent of soap. Even though he'd made it abundantly clear that there was no room for her in his life, had the settee been large enough, she'd have crawled onto it and wrapped herself around him.

Sadly, the settee was barely large enough for Marcus, much less the two of them. Sighing, she straightened and went to the wardrobe, where she collected a night rail of fine lawn and went behind the screen to dress. Then, with a final glance at Marcus, she made her way to the huge empty bed, shivering as she climbed between the cold sheets, dismally aware of the emptiness that surrounded her.

❖ ❖ ❖

The piercing light of the morning sun pulled Marcus from a deep sleep. He frowned and tried to turn over, almost falling off the settee in the process. He caught himself in the nick of time, planting a foot firmly on the floor to maintain his balance, tangled in an amazing number of blankets.

Muttering curses under his breath, he kicked off the

blankets, grasped the back of the settee, and pulled himself upright, assailed with sore muscles, a stiff back, and a stomach that growled hungrily. He couldn't have felt worse if he'd drunk himself blind the night before.

Tick. Tick. Tick. He scowled at the clock on the mantel, but it had stopped. *Where's that sound coming from?* He glared around the room, his gaze finally finding the window. A large icicle hung outside, water dripping from its tip. *The snow is melting. And quickly, from the looks of it.* He leaned back against the settee, feeling like a sail that had lost the wind.

They would be rescued soon. Certainly sometime today. *That should cheer me up, shouldn't it?* But it didn't. Instead, he found himself gritting his teeth as, with a kick at the blanket about his feet, he stood.

His back protested the movement. Kenna had been right; he didn't fit on the settee. He turned to look at the bed, but it was empty, a small indention showing where she had slept. She was so tiny and the bed so big. *She was lost in that huge bed. And I let her be.*

Irritated anew, he crossed to the washstand and splashed cold water on his face, then met his gaze in the mirror. His face was shadowed with the beginning of a beard, and he rubbed his chin with a sigh. *Back to civilization.*

He found the razor he'd used to cut Kenna's gown and tested the blade. It had dulled some, but it would have to do. After digging in the drawer, he discovered a block of shaving soap and went to work.

Chapter Eight

Kenna knelt on a chair set by the front window in the sitting room and used the edge of her shawl to wipe a circle in the condensation on the glass. The morning sun glittered across the blanket of snow that covered the forest, pure white against the brown and green. Heavy and wet, the snow bent branches and weighed down the shrubs as if intent on pressing the world flat. Clumps of melting snow fell as she watched.

Her time with Marcus was nearly over. *I'll have to face Father soon, and Stormont as well.*

She waited to feel the usual dread, but instead all she found was a hollow emptiness and a faint sense of disappointment. *I'd hoped Marcus and I might find some closure to our past travails, but all we've done is dance about one another as if on eggshells.*

Sighing, she turned and sat in the chair, irritation settling between her shoulders.

Footsteps sounded in the stairwell and she straightened, smoothing her skirts and patting her hair. She'd lost most of her pins, her hair barely held in place by those left.

The door swung open and Marcus entered, dressed except for his neckcloth and coat, which hung over his arm. The small room instantly seemed half its size. She eyed him up and down. "You shaved."

He sent her a sour glance, turning his head to look out the window.

She frowned at a spot of blood on his chin. "Oh no, you nicked yourself."

"The blade was dull." His gaze flickered over the hem of her gown before he tossed his neckcloth and coat over the back of a chair, and then turned to the fireplace. "Bloody hell, it's cold in here."

Like a grumbling bear, he began fussing with the fire, adding wood and stirring the logs to life. "Why dinna you stoke it when you arose?"

She frowned at the accusation in his voice. He was in a hell of a mood this morning. Well, so was she. In fact, just seeing him fanned the flames of her ire.

She lifted her chin. "Of course I stirred the fire. Who do you think put in the fresh wood?"

He didn't answer but sent her a black look before returning to his efforts, clanging the fire iron noisily.

Kenna scowled at his broad back. She wished he didn't look so blasted handsome when he frowned. How could she carry on a decent argument when he looked like *that*? It didn't help that his borrowed shirt was rather tight, clinging lovingly to his strong chest.

She shifted restlessly. "Someone will find us today. The weather is better."

Marcus didn't even look up from adding wood to the fire. "If they dinna come to us by noon, I will go to them."

She frowned. "How? You cannot walk in such deep snow with only riding boots. You'll freeze."

He turned his gaze on her and she could see his temper

simmering behind his thoughts. "I'm nae staying here another day. It is a waste of our time."

She thought she could detect a note of blame in his voice. "Waste of—But I—How can you—" She stood. "*Fine!* You're right. It *is* a waste of our time. Perhaps you shouldn't wait but should go now."

Marcus straightened. "I havena had my breakfast yet."

"I brought it up an hour ago." She nodded to the tray on the small table. "The tea is probably cold by now."

He eyed the tray with distaste. "Let me guess—ham and bread and cheese. Again." He dropped the fire iron noisily into its holder, then stood with his head bent, his jaw set as he stared moodily into the fire.

"What's wrong with you this morning?" she demanded.

"I'm tired. I'm tired of this place. Of this situation. Of this blasted snow. Of the food. But mostly—" He looked up, and the heat in his gaze shocked her. "Mostly I'm tired of wanting you and never having you."

Kenna's breath caught. She was tired, too, and of the same things. But . . . and there it was yet again—the "but" that kept her from acting. *But it might not work. But I might get hurt again. But he might laugh or leave or reject me. But it won't last.*

He must have read her expression, for his face hardened. "Of course I dinna expect you to take a chance on anything, especially something not sanctioned by your father."

She stiffened. "That's unfair."

"Is it?" He pushed away from the fireplace and came to stand before her, towering and furious. "Had it nae been for your father, would we still be together?" He saw the hurt flicker in her eyes, but he refused to back down. By God, he was due this conversation. Due it, and then some.

"This has nothing to do with him."

"It has everything to do with him. He hated that you chose me, because he wasna given a say in the matter. From the moment we made our intentions known to him, he spent every waking moment trying to tear us apart. And you let him do it."

"I did no such thing!"

"Oh? What was our last argument aboot? The *only* serious argument we ever had?"

She pressed her lips together. "We argued about why you'd been spending time with Lady Cardross. I'd heard rumors, and I'd seen you at Vauxhall with her the night before. But when I asked you to explain it, to tell me why you were with her, you wouldn't. You—you just looked at me as if I disgusted you, and then you walked away."

"You chased me down quick enough, and told me what you thought of me in no uncertain terms."

"I'm glad I did!" She stepped so close that her toes touched his. "We were engaged to be married, yet you couldn't come off your high horse long enough to answer one simple, important question."

"If all it took was for one person to whisper a falsehood in your ear for you to distrust me, then you never truly trusted me to begin with. Lady Cardross was nae one, a person I spoke to only because she spoke to me first."

"Why didn't you just tell me that?"

"Why did you ask me aboot her as if you already knew the answer and thought anything I said to the contrary would be a lie? You were willing to listen to everyone but me."

Her eyes grew damp, but her chin stayed high. "Perhaps if you'd included me more in your life, then I wouldn't have had to rely on others to tell me of your actions and whereabouts!"

"Who told you I'd been spending time with Lady Cardross?"

She fisted her hands at her sides, but didn't answer.

"Your father."

"Perhaps. It was a foolish argument, and I know that now. Actually, I knew it then. But I never had a chance to tell you that; before morning, you'd packed your things and left—not just the city we lived in, but the entire country!" She poked a finger in his chest. "You left, Marcus. Without a word! How do you think I felt?"

"How do you think I felt to be charged and convicted of cheating when nothing could be farther from the truth?"

"I was wrong, and I would have told you, but you were nowhere to be found. How do you expect anyone to repair a relationship under those circumstances? You *can't*."

"There is nothing to repair if there's nae trust."

"You— That's just— What a blind-arse way to see things! It leaves no room for— Oh, damn you and your stubborn pride! *That* is what sent you racing to the Continent: not your belief that a lack of trust had doomed us, but your pigheaded pride."

"I'm nae the only one who suffers from pigheadedness," he replied grimly.

"I can see how it is; you'll never admit you were just as at fault as I was. Fine. But I'll be damned if I let you mar my last peaceful moment in this charming cottage." She marched to the fireplace, bent down, and grabbed a piece of charcoal from the hearth.

Marcus watched from beneath his lowered brows. "What are you doing?"

"I'm making a line of demarcation."

"Demar— You mean the type they use in war?"

"We're at war, are we not?" Her chin still in the air, she gave him a displeased look. She bent down at the center of the fireplace, and started to draw a line on the floor.

He should have been furious with her for her accusations, but two things held him back. First, a nagging suspicion that she was right—at least partially. His pride had ever been at fault for the pains in his life. And second, the sight of her sweetly rounded behind as she walked backward, bent over, drawing her blasted line across the floor. Damn, but even when he was furious with her, he couldn't stop thinking of touching her.

She came close to where he stood, but he didn't move from her path. Other than sending him a scowl, she didn't let it deter her as she arced the line around him, her skirt brushing his legs. Reaching the other side of the room, she dropped the charcoal on the table and dusted her fingers on a napkin. "There."

He looked at the thick black line that bisected the room, and raised his brows. "Care to explain the purpose of that?"

"That"—she pointed to his side of the room—"is your side. And this"—she gestured from the line to behind her— "is my side. We will not cross that line until someone comes for us."

"You're joking."

"Not at all. You stay there. I will stay here. Then there will be no more arguments."

"Do you really believe that?"

"Aye." She sat primly on one of the two chairs in her half of the small room.

Marcus considered ignoring the line, but he couldn't shake the humor of the situation, which went a long way to erasing his earlier irritation. He walked along the line, his foot brushing against it. Finally, he stopped. "Fine. We'll do it this way. It'll be a relief nae having to share every square foot of this matchbox."

"I feel the same way." Her voice crackled with irritation.

His lips quirked, though he hid his grin. So much passion, and in such a small package. Somehow over the years, he'd only allowed himself to remember her passion between the sheets. He'd forgotten she was just as passionate in her beliefs, her opinions, and, apparently, her desire to make a point.

Marcus went to the settee, which she usually occupied, and made a great presentation of moving her embroidery basket to one side.

Kenna winced, then pressed her lips together and looked away.

Hiding his smile, Marcus stretched out, put his hands behind his head, and stretched his feet toward the fire. "This isna so bad."

Kenna bit her lip. "It's fine."

The fire crackled and the silence lengthened. Outside, icicles dripped on the windowsill.

Kenna sighed. "I don't suppose you'd allow me to have my embroidery basket?"

"I would, but sadly it's on my side of the room."

"Yes, but you might wish for some breakfast, and both the table and the door to the kitchen are on my side of the room."

She had him there. He'd mocked the ham before, but now it sounded rather appealing. He reached out with his foot and scooted the basket over the charcoal line.

She jumped up to collect the basket, setting it beside her chair before she prepared him a plate of food, placed it on the floor, and then pushed it over the line. "There."

He arose and collected the plate, nodding in thanks as he sat and began to eat.

She settled into her chair and pulled out the embroidery piece she'd been working on. He watched her as he wolfed down his breakfast. When he was done, he placed his silverware on the plate and slid it back across the line.

When her brows lowered, he spread his hands. "As you so rightly pointed out, the kitchen door is on your side."

She sent him an exasperated look but arose and collected the plate, putting it back on the table before she returned to her chair.

Quiet reigned and he watched as she stitched, her fingers nimble and light. "How long have you been embroidering?"

The words seemed to surprise her as much as they surprised him. "A few years now. I took it up when Montrose fell ill during the final two years of our marriage."

"Montrose was ill before he died? I heard it was sudden."

"He kept his illness a secret. He had a slew of relatives—'buzzards' he called them. In the end, only his son was at his side when he passed away. That made him very happy."

She continued on, her voice softer, as if she were speaking more to herself. "He was kind to me. Perhaps more than I deserved. I was so young when I married him, barely nineteen. He was a man of the world, sophisticated and experienced in all manner of things. He'd traveled almost everywhere, even China."

She grimaced as she took another stitch. "Before I met him, I'd never left our borough except to go to Edinburgh to see a dressmaker, or to London for my season. And neither of them count as a true adventure, as I was accompanied by my father and a swarm of servants intent on making our travels as comfortable and unexciting as possible."

Marcus stared at the flame of the fire. He'd been upon the Continent when word reached him that Kenna had married the Earl of Montrose. It had been a bitter pill indeed. As a young man Marcus had admired Montrose, who was fourteen years older than he and a well-respected member of the sporting set. A Corinthian of the first water, Montrose had inherited a fortune at an early age, and had surprised everyone when he'd turned that fortune into an even larger one, investing in sugar plantations and gem mines.

It was difficult to find fault with Kenna's selection of a husband, though Marcus had fumed with a rage that had taken months to overcome. "You were happy, then."

"Content, yes. He loved me, but . . . I could never love him the way he wished. We both knew it, too. In the end, he became a very dear friend. I still miss him."

She was silent a moment. "What about you? Did you enjoy traveling?"

"Some of it, aye." Nothing had been enjoyable after he'd learned of Kenna's marriage. Still, as time passed, he'd come to relish the challenges. "It was fascinating. I learned a lot, nae just aboot other people, but also aboot myself. But then there was Salamanca." He put a pillow under his head, watching her. "I returned home after that. Robert and his family needed help."

She bent her head over the hoop. "And now, here we are. I'm a widow. You're a former attaché."

"And both victims of a masquerade party gone awry."

"I hate masquerade parties. It's a pity they've become so popular simply because Princess Charlotte favored them."

"I will never attend another."

"Nor I." Kenna snorted dismissively, stabbing the needle into the fabric. "I vow, but there was not an original thought in the entire room. Nothing but swans and priestesses and goddesses."

"You were dressed like a swan," Marcus pointed out.

"I was going to be an angel, not a swan, but then I overheard—" Her gaze met his and she closed her lips over the rest of her sentence.

He sat up, unable to believe what he'd just heard. "You were never going to dress as a swan."

She closed her eyes. "No."

"Until you heard Lady Perth mention what she would be wearing and that she would meet me under the mistletoe."

Kenna wet her lips, her heart thudding sickly. "Yes. I borrowed the mask from Lady MacLeith. I overheard her saying how she wished she'd brought something more original than a swan costume, as there were so many. So . . . I traded my angel's mask with her." She peeped under her lashes at Marcus.

His mouth was thinned into a straight line, the corners white. "You knew it was me all along. You *planned* that kiss."

She closed her eyes and nodded.

He stood and walked to the line. "You tricked me, made me a fool in front of everyone."

"No, no! Marcus, I—" She dropped her embroidery hoop on her seat and hurried to meet him. "I wasn't trying to trick you. I was just—" Her cheeks heated and she blurted, "I was curious!"

"Aboot what?"

"Whether we were still attracted to each other."

"Bloody hell! Of course we were! You played me for a *fool*. I daresay getting stuck here was another stratagem of yours."

"What? No, no. I didn't even know this place existed."

"I'm supposed to believe you now? You've been lying to me."

"I never lied about that!" Kenna pressed her hands to her hot cheeks. "As soon as I could, I tried to apologize, but you wouldn't let me."

"Only because I dinna realize you had anything to apologize for! You, my lady, are a manipulating liar."

"Oh! You—you—" She couldn't get the words out. They stood, toe-to-toe, the charcoal line smudged under the toes of their shoes. "You think I planned the nervous horse and the *snowstorm*? You *are* a fool! And I damn well wouldn't have wanted to be locked in Stormont's love nest. I'm supposed to *marry* him!"

As soon as the words were out, she regretted them.

Marcus's eyes blazed. "You're to marry Stormont? Since when?"

"No, no. I'm not *going* to marry him. I'm *supposed* to. My father wishes it, and so does Stormont. He's deeply in debt, so . . ." She waved a hand. "But I haven't agreed."

"You will, though."

"I will not."

"With both your father and Stormont pressuring you? Ha! You'll fold like a wet sheet."

She stiffened, leaning over the line to poke him in the chest. "Listen to me, Rothesay! I'll not have you telling me what I will or will not do. You don't know me anymore—any more than I know you."

"I dinna know you? Then how do I know you like *this*?" He swept her into his arms, lifting her feet from the ground as he kissed her.

It was masterful and wild, consuming and fiery. And she loved it, kissing him back with every bit of the wild passion he'd stirred.

One moment they were kissing, and then they were on the floor, tugging and pulling at each other's clothing, furiously struggling to get closer, to feed the passion that threatened to consume them.

Never breaking the kiss, Marcus tugged the neckline of her gown aside, slipping a hand inside her chemise to cup her breast. He kneaded it, and as he ran his thumb over her peaked nipple, she gasped against his mouth. He gently nipped her lip, rocking against her, his hard cock pressed to her hip.

Her skirts rustled as he lifted them with his other hand, sliding his seeking fingers up her leg, to her thigh, to her very core. There he stroked her tight curls, increasing the rhythm, urging her on with every stroke, every movement.

Kenna's nerves pulled tight, her expectation stretching. Heat flushed her skin as her passion swelled, a fire rising in her veins, pooling in her belly and lower as she rocked up to meet his stroking fingers, moaning his name against his kisses.

Passion threatened to overwhelm her and, throwing her leg over him, she rose onto her knees and straddled him, reaching for the buttons on his breeches. Before Marcus realized what she'd intended, his breeches were opened and she was atop him, sliding down on his turgid member with her velvet-hot grip.

He gasped, grasping her hips and guiding her further down. But she grabbed his wrists and, with a twist, pinned them over his head.

Shocked and excited beyond belief, he met her gaze as she slowly, ever so slowly, raised herself on his shaft, and then just as slowly lowered herself. Each stroke was madness, driving him to the edge of reason, his body aching with growing need as she enclosed him over and over in slick, tight heat. His desperate breath mingled with her furious panting. When she lowered herself the next time, he leaned up to catch her nipple with his lips, flicking his tongue over it as she slid down his cock.

When he closed his teeth lightly on her nipple, she let out a moan and arched, her eyes closed in glorious pleasure, her sheath closing tightly over him. He tore his wrists from her grasp and encircled her waist, holding her in place as he thrust up into her. Over and over, he took her, owned her, gave himself to her.

Just as he thought he could withhold himself no longer, she cried his name and bucked wildly, her heat igniting his own—and, holding her tight, he fell over the edge of passion and into her open arms.

Afterward, they lay entwined as thought and feeling slowly returned. Kenna's head rested on Marcus's shoulder, fitting as snugly as if it had been made for her alone. Knowing that was a delicious illusion, she sighed and rubbed her cheek against him.

She smiled as he threaded his fingers through her hair, untangling her curls. There was so much in her heart, so much to be said, she couldn't decide where to begin.

She spread her hand over his chest, her finger sliding through his crisp hair. His shirt had gotten torn in the their furor, and she wondered if her borrowed gown was the same.

Not that it mattered. The only thing that mattered was that she was finally back in Marcus's arms. She didn't know for how long, but right now she didn't care.

She sighed, her breath stirring the torn edge of his shirt. "I don't want to move."

He tightened his hold on her, his large hands warm and firm. "Neither do I." His breath stirred her hair.

She smiled against his chest. The crackle of the fire filled the quiet room, broken only by the tick-tick drip of melting icicles on the windowsill, and the distant sound of a horse's neigh . . .

She blinked and then sat up, her startled glance going to the window. A group of horsemen rode toward the house across the snow, and in the front, looking stern and implacable was her father.

Chapter Nine

Marcus swiftly lifted her to her feet. "Straighten your clothes and see to your hair." He tucked in his shirt and grabbed his coat and neckcloth from the back of the chair.

Kenna hurried to the mirror, tugging her gown down and tying the ties. She combed her fingers through the worst tangles in her hair, then wove the strands into a hasty braid. She didn't have enough time to do more before a demanding knock sounded on the door.

"That's Father." Her voice quavered, and she bit the inside of her lip to hold her calm.

"I'll let him in." Marcus paused to tilt her face to his, a serious look in his gray eyes. "Dinna look so worried, lass. He canna bite you. Nae while I'm here." He bent and kissed the corner of her mouth, and then went into the foyer.

Kenna pressed her fingers to that tiny kiss, aware of the rising tide of butterflies in her stomach.

Male voices could be heard, some strident, some calm, and then the door flew open and Father strode in, followed closely by Marcus, Stormont, and the prince.

"Kenna!" Father's voice dripped with disappointment. A short man with grizzled hair and a military bearing, he was dressed with the utmost propriety, his riding boots agleam, his coat of dull buff, his waistcoat a solid, deep blue. He looked Kenna up and down. "Your hair and that gown—Bloody hell, what's the reason for this?"

Marcus made a move as if to come between her and Father, but the prince shook his head.

Grateful for that little interference, she smiled tightly. "I can explain everything."

"You damn well better!" He turned his glare from her to Marcus. "And you, you jackanapes. I've half a mind to call you out!"

She saw Marcus stiffen and she hurried to Father's side. "Father, no. Lord Rothesay did nothing wrong. We were—"

Outside, there was the noise of horses and the jangling of traces.

Marcus frowned. "Is that a carriage?"

The prince sighed. "Tata Natasha had to come. She said it was too cold to ride a horse, so, the carriage."

"I saw no road wide enough for a carriage," Marcus said.

Stormont, who'd hung back, took the opportunity to step a bit closer to Kenna. "A small road splits from the main drive of my house. I daresay you couldn't see it for the snow." He took Kenna's hand between his and patted it awkwardly. "I trust you are not injured, my dear. We have been so worried about you."

"Look at her!" Father snapped. "She is a disgrace, and I know who to blame!"

Kenna's throat tightened but she kept her head high, the pressure of Marcus's kiss still on the corner of her mouth as she tugged her hand free from Stormont's grasp. "There is no one to blame here."

"Ha!" Father replied, his face a dull red, his mouth thinned.

Stormont pasted on a fake smile. "Now, now, Lord Galloway. Your daughter has been trapped in this cottage without a maid or else for two days. Naturally, her clothes and hair are not as neat as usual." He turned a smile her way, though it didn't reach his eyes. "I think she looks lovely."

She'd so hoped Stormont would take her impending scandal as a reason to break off his courtship, but he was clearly too desperate for funds.

She managed a smile. "Thank you, my lord. You are too kind." *And a liar, as well.*

Father opened his mouth to reply when the door was opened by a liveried footman, and the grand duchess entered. Dressed in a heavy fur-lined cape, her black eyes bright with curiosity, she made her way into the room, the thick rug muffling the thump of her cane. The footman closed the door, leaving them alone. "So!" she said, her black gaze bright and direct. "We have found them, have we?"

"No thanks to you," the prince answered.

Marcus frowned. "What do you mean?"

The prince fixed a hard gaze on his grandmother. "Well, Tata Natasha? Will you tell them, or will I?"

The duchess sniffed. "I do not know what you are talking about."

The prince turned to Marcus. "The morning you disappeared, my grandmother saw your riderless horses gallop up the front drive. She paid one of the footmen to catch them and told him that they'd been spooked, but not to worry, that you had both returned unharmed."

Stormont looked earnestly at Kenna. "Thus we were led to believe you were home safely. It wasn't until supper that it became clear neither of you were there. By then, the weather was too bad to risk a rescue."

"Ah." Marcus crossed his arms over his chest and leaned against the fireplace. "So that's what happened."

Stormont kept his gaze on Kenna. "We were desperate with worry once we knew you were both stranded."

"Hm. I must say, we've found these accommodations

quite interesting." Marcus's voice warmed with amusement as he idly reached over to straighten one of the pictures still on the wall. "Stormont, I must ask the name of your decorator for this . . . what is this, anyway? A guest house? A love ne—"

"No!" The viscount sent a quick look at Kenna's father before forcing a smile. "It's nothing, really. A cottage for friends who do not like to stay in the main house."

"I don't give a damn what this house is for," Galloway snapped. "I will not have my daughter stay a moment longer."

"But it is not so ill furnished." The duchess looked around, curiosity plain on her wrinkled face. "It is small. Like for a doll." She tapped her cane on the floor. "What is this line? Who drew this?"

Kenna's face heated. "I did. Lord Rothesay and I had an argument. I divided the room in two. You are standing on his side."

"Ridiculous!" Galloway snapped.

The duchess looked around the room. "You gave him the side with the settee? That was an error."

"The door to the kitchen is on mine."

"Ah. Then it was a good choice. This dollhouse might have been useful, if it kept you safe from the storm."

The prince sent her a hard look. "We are lucky they found shelter. You put them in grave danger with your games."

"Nonsense. Look at them. They are healthy, well fed, perhaps not so well dressed, but—" She squinted at a painting by the fireplace. "Is that a—"

"The artwork is very stylistic," Kenna said hastily.

Stormont had the grace to flush.

"Stormont?" Marcus asked. When the viscount turned his way, Marcus added, "I believe this is yours as well." He reached into his pocket and withdrew the ruby earring Kenna had found in the bedchamber.

Stormont's expression froze. "I've never seen that before. I have no idea whose it is."

"I know whose it is—and why it is here," Marcus said quietly. He tossed the earring to the viscount, who caught it automatically. "When you return home, pray tell Lady Perth she is to move her things from my town home before I return to Edinburgh."

"Lady Perth?" Lord Galloway looked from Marcus to Stormont, and then back. "What does she have to do with anything?"

"Ask Lord Stormont," Marcus said.

"I will not," the earl said testily. "She is a harlot. Everyone knows it. Kenna, come. I will take you home, where you will stay until all talk of this unfortunate event has died down. If you are fortunate, Lord Stormont will restore your good name."

"I would like that very much," the viscount said eagerly.

"No." Kenna shook her head, her thick braid swinging against her shoulder. "Father, it would be best for me to—"

"You don't know what's best. You never have. You will go with me, but for the love of God, put something over that mussed gown. You look like a milkmaid."

The duchess thumped her cane. "Nik! Give the gel your cloak!" As she spoke, she cast a warning glance at Marcus.

Marcus frowned, wondering what the old woman was about. But just then, in the mirror over the fireplace, he caught sight of the back of Kenna's gown. A thick black charcoal stripe went straight down the back of the blue silk. His shirt was probably similarly marked. He cleared his throat. "Nik, your grandmother is right. Please allow Kenna to use your cloak."

It was obvious Nik had no idea what was going on, but he obediently undid his cloak and swung it about Kenna's shoulders, hiding the telltale stripe from sight.

"Enough of this." Father walked toward the door. "Come, Kenna."

She didn't move.

He continued on, only pausing when he realized she was not following. "Did you hear me?"

"I did. And I'm not coming."

His mouth turned white. "If you know what's good for you, you'll do as I tell you."

Kenna's jaw firmed. "No."

A startled silence settled over the room, and then Stormont laughed nervously. "Kenna—Lady Montrose, please. Go with your father. I'll come and visit first thing in the morning, so you won't be left alone."

"No. I'm through, Father. Until you can speak to me without ordering me about like a dog that needs to be brought to heel, we will be polite but distant strangers."

"Do you know what you are saying?"

"I know exactly what I am saying."

"I will disinherit you!"

"Then do so. I never wished for your properties, anyway. I've plenty on my own."

Stormont made a whimpering sound, while Galloway's face went from red to white. "You ungrateful, irreverent, pathetic—"

Marcus started forward, but Nik grabbed his shoulder. "Let her handle this," the prince murmured.

Kenna was already speaking. "It would be best if you returned home, Father."

"You'll—"

"Now."

Silence filled the room. Marcus had to curl his hands into fists to keep from reaching for her, this proud woman. She had changed since he knew her and he was only now realizing how much.

Stormont gave a nervous laugh. "It— This is such an awkward moment, isn't it? I— We should— Kenna, ride with me, and we'll take your things to your father's later on, when you are less—"

"No. I will not ride with you."

Lord Galloway's gaze narrowed, though Lord Stormont merely blinked. "But . . . I'm willing to marry you!"

"But I don't wish to marry you," she replied baldly.

The viscount looked astonished. "But Lady Montrose, your father and I have spoken and—"

"You may speak to him all you wish, but he does not speak for me. You have asked me to marry you a dozen times, and a dozen times I've said no. I'm tired of repeating myself. In fact, if you ask me again, I will cut off both of your ears and stuff them in your mouth."

Stormont paled.

The duchess nodded thoughtfully. "You cut his ears off because he will not listen, *nyet*? That is a good retribution. I approve."

"Thank you, your grace. If you could spare me a seat in your carriage, I will return to Stormont's—"

"We can talk there—" he began eagerly.

"—where I will pack my things, and leave."

The viscount's shoulders sagged. "I don't understand."

"I do," Galloway said grimly, with a venomous look at Marcus. "Kenna, if you've thrown yourself in this man's path again, I will—"

"I don't want to hear it, Father. Do what you will—but do it in quiet."

She turned to Marcus, who had never seen her so stern. "As for you, I am returning to my home in Edinburgh. I think we have a future, if we but have the patience and courage to pursue it. I will wait two days for you to make up your mind. After that, I am leaving. I don't know where. Perhaps Italy. Maybe Greece. But it's my turn to enjoy myself."

"Kenna!" Lord Galloway snapped. "You are making a fool of yourself! This is unmaidenly—"

"Good-bye, Father." Kenna turned and left the room, the prince's cloak swirling about her blue gown, the duchess's footman closing the door behind her.

Marcus had never been prouder of her.

The duchess chuckled. "This is a good day, *nyet*? I think

I will have something to remember it by." She walked to the wall, took a picture from its nail, and tucked it under her arm. "This will do."

Marcus stifled a laugh as she limped from the room, her footman hurrying to close the door.

In the foyer, Kenna turned as the duchess joined her. "Thank you for your kind assistance, your grace."

"Pah! You stick a finger in all their eyes. They deserve it. I will take you home, and we will have some vodka while your maid packs your bags."

"Vodka?"

"It is like lemonade, only better for your blood. Hmm. Now that I think about it, I have some in the carriage. I will share some with you on the way home. It will cool those hot cheeks of yours."

"Thank you. That is very kind."

They walked outside, the bright sun almost blinding on the snow. The footman took the duchess's arm and helped her walk down a narrow path that had been stomped into the snow on her arrival, Kenna following.

Her heart ached, even as she reveled in the freedom she'd just declared for herself. Father would not bother her now; she'd never again succumb to his bullying. And she'd never again allow Stormont to even speak to her. Now, all she had to do was make her way to Edinburgh and await Marcus.

If he comes. Her heart ached at the thought. *He has to,* she told herself. *We still have much to talk about, adventures to have, perhaps even lives to share. Only time will tell. Will he take the chance?*

She'd been bold in giving him an ultimatum, and perhaps Father was right about her being unmaidenly. But she was tired of being the one left behind. Tired of waiting for happiness.

They reached the carriage, where more footmen met them, opening the door and pulling down the steps. Just as the duchess was handed inside, Marcus strode around the corner of the cottage.

He walked straight to Kenna, never hesitating, dark and powerful. "Leave us," he ordered the footman who stood ready to assist her into the coach. "I would speak with Lady Montrose."

The footman looked at her grace, who gestured for him to stand at the ready by the coach door. Then she leaned out the window as if watching a sporting event.

Kenna's throat was so tight, she could barely breathe. *Perhaps he will tell me not to wait the two days. That I have made assumptions I had no right to. He might say I am forward and demanding—*

"You have been bold this morning. Bold in many ways." His deep, rich voice flooded her with warmth from head to toe, thawing the tears she'd held back.

Her grace leaned close to the footman who stood at attention by the door. "This is a good beginning."

He stared straight ahead, although a small smile curved his mouth.

Marcus ignored them. "Kenna, these last few days reminded me of all the reasons I used to love you."

Used to. Her heart sank.

"I was too prideful, and too immature to fight for you then." He took her hand between his. "But I'm older now, and far, far more intelligent."

The duchess cackled. "Men need to age, like good wine. I know this."

Marcus sent her a hard look. "Your grace, if you dinna mind?"

"What? Oh. Of course. Continue." She waved her hand as if conferring a great honor on him.

Marcus turned back to Kenna. "I came to tell you one thing and one thing only; I dinna need two days. I need only one second to tell you how much I love you and that I will never, ever let you go again."

"You . . . love me."

"I never stopped loving you, lass. I was just too proud and too foolish to admit it. You called me pigheaded earlier and you were nae wrong." His hands tightened over hers. "I'm still pigheaded, but I'm smart enough to know it, and auld enough to keep it from ruining us both. Will you have me, Kenna? Will you give me—us—one more chance?"

She sniffed as tears threatened. "I can't promise it will be easy."

"I know; we're strong people, the two of us. There will be many arguments." His expression softened as he lifted her hand and kissed her fingers, one by one. "But just as much lovemaking, passionate and fulfilling."

"We will have to talk through our problems, work with each other, trust one another—"

"Good God!" the duchess said. "Are you trying to talk him into it, or out of it?"

Marcus pressed Kenna's hand to his cheek, his eyes dark and serious. "Arguments, difficult times, interference from your father or the world in general—none of it will matter. If I have a question, I'll come to you. If I need an opinion, I'll come to you. If I need a woman's touch or a friend to listen, I will come to you. Because you are my soul, my heartbeat, my breath. And withoot you, there is no reason to live."

The tears now rolled freely down Kenna's cheeks.

Behind her, Tata Natasha told the footman, "Face the coach."

There was a rustle as he did so.

"Rothesay," she called, "you may kiss the chit if you wish. The servants will not be watching."

Marcus tugged Kenna closer, smiling into her eyes. "Thank you, your grace."

"It is my pleasure. Now, kiss this woman and put her out of her misery. Lord knows she's waited long enough. And I'm too old to stay out in the cold much longer—"

Marcus swept Kenna into his arms and kissed her deeply and passionately, as if they were indeed alone. And Kenna, unable to hold back her love any longer, threw her arms around his neck and kissed him back.

"That's a good kiss," her grace said approvingly, many long moments later. "Footman, fetch vodka and glasses. We've a toast to make."

Kenna laughed against Marcus's mouth, and he pulled away to smile at her, love in his eyes. "We've an elopement to plan."

"Oh no," Kenna said. "There will be no elopement. I've dreamed about walking down the aisle to you for far too long."

"Fine. A wedding, then. But a small one."

"A large one." She traced his bottom lip with one finger. "And I want flowers. Lots of them."

He captured her hand and pressed a kiss to her palm, sighing as he did so. "A large wedding with flowers it will be. And then we'll go to my home and—"

"After our honeymoon."

"Honeymoon?"

"To Italy. For a month, at least. And *then* we will go to your home."

He chuckled softly. "If we must have all of this, then I will insist that the wedding be soon."

"But of course, my love." She rested her forehead to his and grinned widely. "You may have whatever you want."

He laughed and knew that with her, even when he lost, he won. As long as he had her by his side, the world was his for the taking. With a grin, he swept her into his arms and, with her arms snugly about his neck, carried her to the waiting coach.

BY ANY OTHER NAME

Candace Camp

Love was born at Christmas.

—Christina Rossetti

Chapter One

Edinburgh, 1807

Rylla Campbell had long ago prepared her escape from the house in the middle of the night, but she had never before had occasion to use her plan. Quietly she shut her door behind her and went on stocking feet to the stairs, her heart pounding all out of proportion to the risk she was taking.

Truthfully, it would have been an easy matter if only her friend Eleanor had not been staying with them until Christmas. Her parents, at the back of the house, were unlikely to hear her above her father's snoring. But Eleanor was a light sleeper and her room lay between Rylla's and the stairs. Though Elly was a dear friend, she was depressingly *inflexible* in her standards. She was the daughter of a minister in a small town, and worse, she seemed to have little taste for adventure. If she caught Rylla sneaking out of the house dressed in her brother's old clothes, Elly would feel dutybound to stop her.

Fortunately, Rylla made it to the bottom of the stairs without Eleanor popping out of her room. She eased open the front door and stepped into the dark night. Remnants of yesterday's snow lingered near the base of the houses, but it was not falling tonight. Instead, fog hung in wisps and patches and the cobblestoned streets glistened wetly from the dampness in the cold air. Rylla shivered. It was just the cold, she thought. It was not because she was scared of being alone outside so late at night. She could not allow herself to be frightened. She had to find her brother. It was almost Christmas, and she had to bring him home.

Rylla went down the steps and started up the street. It was a trifle strange to walk alone like this in the hushed night. Strange, too, not to feel the movement of skirts around her legs as she walked. But she rather liked it. There was a freedom in wearing masculine attire—not just the ability to stride along at a rapid pace in breeches but the knowledge that no one would expect her to be shy or soft-spoken or sweetly dependent. Besides, though it was odd, even a little scary, there was a tingle of excitement, too, at the risk she was taking.

It would be a scandal if she were caught—and then there were the lurking dangers people whispered about. But Rylla was certain she could pull it off. As long as she convinced everyone she was a man, she need not worry about the horrors that awaited a lone female. In fact, she quite looked forward to entering the mysterious world that only men were allowed to know.

She was proud of the costume she had scavenged from a trunk in the attic. One of her brother's old suits had to be altered only a trifle to fit her. The bulk of shirt, waistcoat, and jacket were enough to conceal the curves underneath. Thanks to the addition of a warm greatcoat, a hat, and a pair of Daniel's old shoes stuffed with a sock in each toe, no one would suspect that this slender gentleman of medium height was in reality a woman. Rylla did wish she had thought to bring a fashionable cane to complete her costume, but it was not worth going back for it.

It was fortunate that they had cut off her hair this fall

when she had caught a fever, so she did not have to wear a wig. Her froth of golden curls gave her a decidedly effeminate look, but she had managed to smooth her hair back and straighten it with pomade. That had had the added advantage of darkening the color. Her voice was naturally husky, so she need only lower her tone a bit more. She had practiced her gestures and walk in front of the mirror half the afternoon.

Rylla made her way toward the area below the castle, where she knew several of the gambling clubs Daniel frequented were located. They were not the staid gentlemen's clubs where her father and his friends might go, but neither were they gambling hells of the sort springing up around the Grassmarket. She would be all right as long as she kept to games she knew and avoided deep play. She and Daniel had played cards for matchsticks many a winter evening. Having saved a good amount of her pin money, she could afford to lose a little.

She started at Faraday's, standing behind the tables and idly watching the play. There was no sign of Daniel or any of his friends. Of course, she did not know many of his new friends—the 'bad lot' that had been the subject of that last terrible row between her brother and her father.

"First time here?" a pleasant male voice inquired.

Rylla turned, taken aback at being addressed by a stranger. She recovered quickly, adopting the careless, bored air of a fashionable young gentleman. "Yes. I've been told it's deuced fine play."

"Quite right. Name's Harry Lindsay." Her newfound friend gave her a nod.

"Rolly Campbell." Rylla supplied the alias she had chosen for its similarity to her own name. "Perhaps you know my cousin, Daniel."

"Daniel Campbell?" Harry Lindsay shook his head regretfully. "No, can't say as I do."

"He's the chap who recommended it. Thought I might run into him."

"He may come in if you stay. Say, there's a table opening up. Shall we join it?"

Rylla strolled over to the table with him. She was hesitant to play, but she could hardly stand about all evening doing nothing. As they sat down, Harry made a joke that she did not understand, but since he and the man on her other side laughed, Rylla laughed as well.

One of the players at the table beside theirs glanced around at the sound of their laughter, and his gaze fell on Rylla. A curious feeling flickered through her. She looked away quickly. However, a moment later her eyes returned to the man. Even though he was lounging carelessly in his chair, it was easy to see that he was tall and lithely built. A sconce on the wall directly behind him gleamed on his gold hair, warming it with tones of red.

Rylla pulled her attention back to the game. Harry ordered a bottle of port, and "Rolly" could hardly refuse a convivial glass. She took a drink and struggled to conceal the fact that it burned all the way down to her stomach, where it exploded. She managed not to cough, though her eyes watered a bit. She turned aside to conceal her reaction and saw that the man at the other table was watching her again.

Rylla had a sudden fear that he had seen through her disguise. One of the other men at his table said something to him and he turned, smiling, and answered. His smile, she realized, warmed her insides as much as the liquor had, though fortunately not so explosively. She glanced back at him from time to time as they began to play.

She wasn't sure why she felt compelled to look at him. He was attractive enough, though not astoundingly so. But there was something about his slightly tousled hair that made her want to reach out and smooth it into place. Her nerves danced when she looked at his long narrow fingers, adorned with a plain gold and onyx ring on one hand. Absently he turned the ring with his thumb now and then, and that, too, stirred an odd sensation in the pit of her stomach.

It was the liquor, she decided. She was doing her best to appear to drink it while only sipping, even going so far as to surreptitiously dump half a glass on the floor at her feet. Still, she could not avoid drinking entirely, especially since Harry filled up her glass every time it was low.

She listened for any mention of her brother or his friends and tried to work Daniel's name unobtrusively into the conversation. It soon became clear that none of these men were going to be of any help. She wondered what the etiquette was for leaving a game. At least she had not lost all her money; indeed, she was a trifle ahead.

One of the men pulled out a cigar and offered her one from his case. She took it with what she hoped was an appearance of ease, covertly watching the others and copying their actions. The cigar, she discovered, was even fouler tasting than the port. It also made her cough. She downed the remainder of her glass just to remove the taste of the tobacco. After a couple of puffs, she mostly held the thing and knocked off the ash periodically. Now and again she would raise it to her lips without pulling the smoke into her mouth.

Rylla was beginning to wonder if men had any sense of taste, given the things they were willing to put in their mouths. It was time to move on, but when she made to leave, Harry protested and poured yet more port in her glass. She glanced over at the table where the man with the red-blonde hair had sat and felt some disappointment in seeing that he was gone. It took her a moment to find him standing against the wall, chatting. He used his hands as he talked, and his face lit up expressively. He smiled, and once again that odd buoyant sensation bloomed in her chest.

Next to her, Harry puffed out a stream of smoke, clouding the air, and Rylla's stomach lurched. She was, she realized, feeling rather queasy. She remembered once when Daniel had been ill, he had told her privately that it was only from drinking so much the night before. Surely she had not drunk that much. She felt a trifle muddleheaded, but it wasn't as if she was inebriated.

Suddenly the combination of liquor and cigar smoke was more than she could stand. It was far too warm in here, as well. She knew that if she did not leave immediately, she would embarrass herself by casting up her accounts in front of everyone. Rylla shoved back her chair and stood up. She sent her tablemates a smile that was more a grimace. Grabbing her hat and coat, she made for the door.

A man stepped back, knocking into her, and she stumbled. A hand lashed out and caught her arm, keeping her upright. Rylla turned her head and found herself looking up into the face of the man at whom she had been sneaking glances all evening.

"Steady on." His teeth flashed in a smile, and she saw that his merry eyes were a bright blue. "Are you all right?"

"Yes! Oh, yes!" Her mind was a blank and her cheeks burned. She pasted on a bright smile. No, that was probably too girlish a thing to do. Rylla pulled away and rushed out the door.

The night air cooled her cheeks, and her stomach quieted. She shoved the hat onto her head and strode away. To her dismay she wobbled. Oddly, her brain seemed foggier now—though at least her stomach was no longer rolling. She had planned to visit another club, but she thought perhaps she should go home.

She started up the steep slope, her feet slipping on the damp cobblestones. The fog had grown thicker. Suddenly a figure stepped out of a doorway in front of her. He held something in his hand and he reached out, grabbing her wrist.

"Give me your money. Now!"

Chapter Two

Gregory Rose frowned slightly as he watched the young man hurry toward the door. He had noticed the fellow earlier, when he had heard that odd throaty laugh that affected him like a fingernail running up his spine. Gregory had almost expected to see a woman. Instead, there was only a table of men, one of them a lad of medium height wearing a too-large greatcoat. His dark blond hair was slicked back, and he had the sort of large-eyed, pretty features that guaranteed he had been the victim of upper-form bullies.

It was easy to see that the youngster was a lamb in the company of wolves. Gregory had kept an eye on the boy, suspecting that the young man's companion was a sharp. There was something else about the lad that bothered him, though he could not determine what. Gregory had smothered a smile at the expression on the boy's face when he downed his first drink. A cigar later had turned him a mite green, but at least his stack of coins hadn't dropped.

When he left the table, the young man had staggered and Gregory had had to catch him to keep him from falling.

He had realized then that the boy was not only inebriated but even slighter than he'd thought.

Back at the table, the boy's former companion gave a sharp upward nod with his chin. Gregory turned and saw a rough-looking fellow lever away from the wall and walk out the door. Frowning, Gregory grabbed up his coat and followed.

Outside, he spotted the slender young gentleman heading up the hill. The other man followed quickly. Both men disappeared into the fog. Gregory hurried after them. He heard a shout ahead of him and broke into a run.

"Hey!" Two figures struggled in the fog. The larger man glanced back at Gregory's shout. He shoved the smaller one to the cobblestones and took off running. Gregory reached the boy. "Are you all right?"

The lad nodded, gasping for air, his hand to his stomach.

"Can you stand?" Gregory took his arm, pulling him up. When he released him, the young man swayed. Gregory grabbed his arm again. "Here, don't pass out on me now."

"No, no, I won't. I'm all right." His voice was breathless and high with fright, but it had the same throaty rasp Gregory had heard in his laugh earlier. The sound skittered across Gregory's nerve endings in a decidedly unsettling way.

Gregory started up the street, his hand under the young man's arm, trying not to think about the effect the stranger's voice had on him.

"He hit me!" The young man sounded more indignant than frightened now, but his steps were unsteady. He sagged against Gregory's supporting hand.

"My rooms are just ahead." Gregory tightened his grip. "You can rest there a bit."

"What? No! No, I cannot." Despite his words, he leaned more heavily against Gregory. Gregory was beginning to wonder if the lad would be able to make it to his building.

"It's fine." Gregory was not sure what he was reassuring the boy about. "What's your name?"

"My name?" His tone was vague.

"Yes. I am Gregory Rose." When his companion made no reply, Gregory said encouragingly, "And your name is . . ."

"Oh! Rolly. My name is Rolly." He perked up at this feat of memory, but soon he was sagging again.

Gregory plowed up the hill, taking more and more of the other man's weight, though the difference in their heights made it difficult. They were almost to his door when Rolly stopped.

"I—I feel odd."

Gregory eyed him suspiciously. "You're not about to be sick, are you?"

"I'm—I'm—" Rolly's eyes rolled back, and he went limp.

"Bloody hell!" Gregory wrapped his arm around Rolly tightly, holding him up. What the hell was he supposed to do with him now? Half carrying, half dragging the boy the last few feet, Gregory opened the door to his building and pulled him inside.

It would be easier to drape Rolly over one shoulder and haul him up the stairs that way. However, Gregory was afraid Rolly really would empty the contents of his stomach if he did that. With a sigh, Gregory picked him up in his arms as though he were a child and began to climb the stairs. Thank goodness the chap was small.

He propped Rolly up with one arm as he unlocked the door, then propelled him inside and over to the sofa. Rolly's head lolled back, his arms falling to his sides.

"Rolly?" Gregory patted his cheek. "Wake up, lad." He lit a lamp and closed the door. Returning to the sofa, he gave the boy a more stinging pat.

Rolly's eyes flew open. He started to stand, but flopped back against the sofa, blinking. "Who are you?"

"Gregory Rose. Remember?"

"Oh. Of course."

"You look deuced uncomfortable. Here, let's get your coat off." Gregory tugged him forward, grappling with one arm to remove the greatcoat.

Rolly managed to sit up and help pull off his coat before he sank back against the cushion. There was a tear across the front of his jacket.

"Good God!" Gregory leaned forward. It was no rip, but a clean slash. "He stabbed you!"

"What!" Rolly sat up and fumbled at his jacket.

Gregory helped him remove it. The waistcoat beneath held a similar slash on the front right side. Gregory let out a curse. He knelt on the floor in front of the sofa to unbutton Rolly's waistcoat.

"No, wait." The young man stirred and shoved feebly at Gregory's hands. "I can—"

"Hush. He cut right through your clothes. I don't see any blood, but we have to take a look."

With the waistcoat open, Gregory unknotted the lad's neckcloth and started on the ties of his shirt. Annoyingly, Rolly squirmed, pushing ineffectually at Gregory's hands.

"Holy hell, stop twitching about like a blushing virgin." Ties undone, Gregory grasped the sides of both shirt and waistcoat and shoved them apart.

He stopped short, gaping. "You have breasts!"

"Ohhhh . . ." The girl moaned, covering her face with her hands. "I'm sorry."

"Don't be sorry." Gregory grinned, sitting back on his heels. "They are lovely breasts."

❖ ❖ ❖

Rylla had never in her life been so thoroughly embarrassed. She let out a mortified groan and jerked the sides of her shirt together. Gregory was watching her with an amused grin on his face. His long masculine form was suggestively positioned between her legs. To make the situation even more humiliating, the sight of him there set up a strange heavy heat low in her abdomen. Whatever was the matter with her?

"So you were masquerading as a man tonight—or a lad, I should say," Gregory said.

"A lad! I am fully twenty-two years old." It occurred to Rylla that out of all this, she had seized on a peculiar thing to be indignant about.

"A very ripe old age, indeed." His blue eyes twinkled. "You must admit, though, you are the size of a stripling."

"There are any number of men my height. It is simply that you are abnormally tall."

"Ah, of course." Annoyingly, his grin grew even wider. "I stand corrected."

"You aren't standing at all," she pointed out sourly, and he laughed. "Really, sir, please move. This is not at all proper."

"And you are such a pillar of propriety."

Rylla glared. "You are in the way. I cannot get up with you crouched there."

"That, I think, is for the best. You're in no condition to be walking about."

"I'm fine. I was simply dizzy for a moment."

"Mm. No doubt the impropriety of being attacked outside a gambling hell turned you quite faint."

Rylla swallowed a bubble of laughter. "You are most annoying."

"So I've been told." He moved, no longer sitting back on his heels, but coming up so that he was once again kneeling at the edge of the sofa, unnervingly close. "Still, I need to check your wound."

He reached out to grasp the sides of her shirt, and Rylla jerked back, squeezing into the sofa cushion as far as she could go. She clutched the garment even more tightly to her. "You don't need to do any such thing! I'm perfectly all right."

His hands dropped. "You don't know that. The knife went through your clothes."

Holding her shirt together at the top with one hand, Rylla carefully lifted the bottom of her shirt. She peered at her stomach. "It's only a scratch."

"'Tis a pity to mar such beauty." Gregory was studying her skin as if it held great secrets. His face was flushed, his blue eyes glittering, his mouth soft and full. She had never seen such a look on a man's face before. It shot a strange leaping excitement all through her. He had lowered his hands, but now they rested on her thighs, warm and heavy. It was thoroughly indecent—and even more indecently, Rylla liked the way they felt on her.

He smiled at her, more with invitation than amusement. "What were you doing at that gambling den, I wonder? A romantic assignation?"

Rylla's jaw dropped. "I beg your pardon!"

"But surely no man is so foolish as to leave you waiting. He would arrive early and wait any length of time." He went on musingly, "No, I think more likely you were spying on a lover."

"A lover!" Indignation surged through her. "You think I am a . . . a hussy!"

"Nae, I would never use such a term for you."

"Oh!" Rylla jumped up, shoving him back with both hands. Irritatingly, he only laughed and rose lithely to his feet. "You are rude! Insufferable!" She rushed to refasten her clothes, her fingers trembling and clumsy with fury. In her agitation, she fumbled at both shirt and waistcoat, succeeding with neither.

"Wait, here, you are doing them up all wrong." Gregory's expression was indulgent as he reached out to help her. His action only served to fuel the fires of her anger.

Rylla slapped his hands away. "Don't touch me! You are no gentleman. You're a . . . a perfect beast. A scoundrel." She drew herself up to her fullest height and lifted her chin haughtily. The pose was somewhat spoiled by the fact that she wobbled and Gregory had to grab her elbow to steady her.

"I did come to your rescue," he pointed out mildly.

"My rescue! Hah!" She shrugged off his hand. "You were probably in league with him."

Gregory's brows popped up. "I like that. I chase off a thief who is attacking you, and now I'm a villain."

"You took advantage of me." Rylla had managed to get her shirt fastened, even if the buttons were a trifle askew. She decided to abandon the attempt on her waistcoat.

"Took advantage of you! You are drunk as a wheelbarrow and running about dressed in men's clothes, visiting gambling hells. And *I* took advantage of you?"

"I am not drunk as a wheelbarrow! Nor am I a woman of loose morals." She fisted her hands on her hips and glared at him. "I, Mr. Rose, am a lady."

He stared at her for a moment, then let out a long breath. "Devil take it. You really are a blushing virgin, aren't you?"

Chapter Three

"Yes, if you must put it in such a crude manner."

"I believe I must." Gregory shoved one hand back into his hair and sighed. "What am I to do with you?"

"You don't have to 'do' anything with me," Rylla said loftily. "I am perfectly capable of doing it myself."

"Indeed. And what is it you are so capable of doing?"

Rylla scowled. "Of . . . of whatever needs to be done." She swept her hand out in a vague, all-encompassing gesture and lost her balance.

Gregory grabbed her arm again to keep her from falling. His lips twitched. "I think you better sit down." When Rylla tried to pull away, he gave her a sharp tug—rather more forcefully than necessary, Rylla thought—and put her back down on the sofa. "You're in no shape to go anywhere. Stay there. I'll make you some coffee."

He strode off. Rylla sent a baleful glance at his back before she flopped back against the couch and closed her eyes. Everything tilted, then settled back into place. Maybe she was a trifle foxed, at that. How else could she explain the peculiar sensations she'd she felt this evening? The way her stomach flip-flopped when she looked into Gregory's blue eyes. Or the warmth that had blossomed deep inside her when she saw him kneeling between her legs. The way her pulse speeded up every time his hand closed around her arm—even though she hadn't wanted him to touch her. She hadn't wanted it at all. She listened to Gregory clattering about and muttering curses. Rylla had the suspicion that he was not entirely sober himself. She smiled faintly, thinking of the blank astonishment on his face when he realized she was a woman. He'd been nice, really, coming to her rescue like that, helping her to safety. And his concern that she might have been cut was rather touching.

"I can only hope that smile is for me."

Rylla scowled at Gregory. She had no intention of telling him any of the things she'd just been thinking. "It isn't."

"Here. Drink this." He handed her a cup and sat down on the footstool in front of her.

She took a sip. The liquid burned her tongue and tasted bitter. "This is awful."

"It is rather," he agreed amiably. "Well, it's the first time I've made coffee."

"Are you sure you did it correctly?" Rylla looked dubiously into the cup. "I don't think it should have all those grains floating about."

"You may be right." He peered into his own cup, then took another sip. "It doesn't taste like the coffee the housekeeper makes. Still, best drink it down like the man you are not. Maybe it will counter whatever you were drinking."

"It was port. I can't imagine why men like to ruin a good meal with that. And smoking cigars! Ugh."

Gregory laughed. "You turned a bit green after you took a puff."

He was quite close to her, his position on the stool making his face nearly level with hers. Rylla could see each line, each curve of his face. Looking at him made her feel edgy and restless . . . and daring.

His bright blue eyes were lined with brown lashes, darker than the color of his hair. His eyebrows were reddish-brown, as well, and they had a sharp downward slant at the ends that added to the hint of perpetual mischief in his expression. She could see the shadow of his beard, and somehow that sight made her abdomen tighten and twist. His lips were full and soft, his mouth wide. And she had the most startling desire to press her own lips against his. What, she wondered, would he taste like?

"I think it's most unfair," she said.

"What is?"

"No one thinks anything of it if a man goes about kissing anyone he wants."

He let out a startled laugh but did not question her sudden change of topic. "I think some people might object."

"You know what I mean. Everyone excuses men when they have affairs. They say, 'Oh, he's a man and everyone knows that men are given to lewd behavior.'"

"Is that what they say? Perhaps I have been behaving too circumspectly."

She ignored his remark. "But if a woman wants to kiss a man, she is adjudged wanton. A hussy. Scorned by society." She swept her arm out grandly. "Why should a man have pleasure and a woman only duty?"

"Why indeed?" His blue eyes danced. "Tell me, do you plan to kiss someone? I'd be happy to volunteer. Purely to right an injustice, of course."

"You are an exceedingly foolish man."

"You are an exceedingly tempting woman." His gaze dropped to her mouth.

Warmth flared inside her. Rylla knew her reaction was wrong. The way he looked at her should make her indignant, not strangely eager. There was none of the respect a gentleman should have for a lady. But what else was he to think, given the boldness of her words just now? No lady would have brought up such a topic. "I'm sorry. I should not have said that. I am not usually so improper."

"Are you not? I confess, I'm disappointed."

"Perhaps you are right. I may be somewhat inebriated. I have not behaved well. Indeed, I've been quite shocking."

"I'm not easily shocked."

"I think that says something more about you than it does about me," she retorted. That brought another laugh out of him. The sound made her chest lighter.

"You wound me." He laid his open palm against his chest.

"I doubt that very much." Rylla picked at an invisible piece of lint on her trousers. "I can't imagine why you're being so nice."

"Can't you?" He studied her for a moment. "Who are you? For I am sure you are not Rolly."

Rylla said nothing. She could not tell him. She had thoroughly compromised herself this evening, but as long as he did not know who she was, there could be no scandal.

"Why were you in Faraday's this evening?" he went on when she did not answer.

"It was nothing to do with you." Rylla stood up. "I must go." She pulled on her jacket.

"Who did it have to do with?" He rose with her.

"No one. It had nothing to do with anyone but me. I wanted to see the inside of a gentleman's club. That's all." Seeing the skeptical look on his face, she decided to turn their conversation down a different path. "No doubt you are appalled at such unladylike curiosity."

Irritation flashed in his eyes. "You certainly assume you know a great deal about me."

"I know you are a gentleman."

"And that means I'm a prig?"

"It means you prefer ladies remain unknowledgeable about . . . lower sorts of activities."

"Indeed?" The light in his eyes was different now, and the smile that touched his lips was slow and inviting. "I think I might prefer a lady to be knowledgeable about some 'lower' activities." He leaned a little closer, his voice as soft and beckoning as his smile. "I fear I rarely do what I ought. The truth is, I think you are a refreshing, delightful, and thoroughly intriguing woman. Will you not even tell me your name?"

Rylla shook her head, unable to meet his gaze. "No. You ask too much."

"I will not reveal anything that happened tonight," Gregory said. "I swear it."

"I cannot take that chance." She grabbed her greatcoat. "Where is my hat? Oh, drat, I have lost it. He won't be happy."

"Who won't be happy?" He stiffened slightly. "Do you have a husband?" She shook her head. "A fiancé?"

"No. No one. Mr. Rose, please stop."

"Gregory," he corrected. "If you will not tell me your whole name, your first would do. Tell me if you are Anne or Mary or Katherine. Sybil, perhaps?"

"Sybil!" Rylla laughed. "No, my name is not Sybil. Or any of those. Please stop asking me."

"But how will I see you again if you don't tell me your name?"

"You won't." She took a step away from him, surprised by the sting of regret.

"Why will you not tell me?" His voice was tight with frustration. "You must realize you can trust me. I came to your aid. Hell, I carried you up a flight of stairs."

"Which proves you are brave and have a strong back. One could also say you abducted me and carried me off to your rooms."

"You fainted!"

"Good-bye, Mr. Rose," she said firmly and turned once more to the door.

He heaved a sigh and followed her, reaching out with ingrained courtesy to open the door. "We may have difficulty finding a hack this late. If we go a street over, one should come by before too long."

"I am sure I will find one. Thank you for all you've done." She walked away, but he caught up with her on the stairs. "Mr. Rose, really . . ."

"I thought we had established that you would call me Gregory."

"Your memory is clearly faulty. And you do not need to accompany me."

"I could not allow a lady to go home unescorted."

"But tonight I am not a lady." She swept her hand down at her male attire. "I went to the club unescorted."

"Yes, and look what happened to you."

Rylla would have liked to protest, but she could hardly dispute the attack. And she had to admit that she would feel safer with Gregory by her side. Stepping out the front door only made her even more sure of that. The street was dark and cold, made even eerier by the wisps of fog trailing across it.

However, if Gregory saw where she lived, it would be an easy enough matter to establish who she was. Even though she was tempted to trust him, she couldn't put her family's name at risk. "I am grateful to you, but I doubt I will be attacked twice in one evening."

"One never knows what might happen," he told her darkly, still walking at her side.

"Gregory . . ."

"Why are you being so unreasonable? What is wrong with me seeing you home?"

"I am determined to keep what I have done tonight a secret."

"But—"

"My father is a very strict man." That was not entirely true. He was no more rigid than most, certainly not as stuffy as Eleanor's father. Inspired, she added, "He is a minister." It would do no harm to borrow a bit of Eleanor's life story as long as she did not give him Eleanor's name. "He would be disgraced if word of my escapade got out."

"I told you, I won't reveal anything. I want only to see you again."

"I cannot count on that. I scarcely know you. And how would you see me again? You can't simply come to the house unknown."

"I will think of a way." He grinned. "I can be quite inventive."

She ignored the appeal of his smile. "In any case, there is no point. I will soon be gone." She might as well continue with her adoption of Eleanor's background.

"Gone? You do not live in Edinburgh?"

"No, I live in a small village."

"Really? I do as well. Obviously we have a great deal in common."

"Many people come from the country."

"True. But how many of them frequent the same club? On the same night?"

She laughed. "You are absurd."

"So I've been told. If you do not live here, then I suppose your family must be renting a house?" She shook her head, and he ventured, "Staying at an inn?"

"I am staying with a friend." That was almost true, only a bit reversed. "We went to a ladies' academy together."

"Really? Which one?" When she merely sent him a repressive look, he sighed. "You are as secretive as the grave." They walked on in silence for a moment, then he said, "I'm from the Highlands. I'm visiting my cousin Andrew."

"Sir Andrew Rose?"

He narrowed his eyes. "Yes. Do you know him?"

She shook her head. "No. How could I? I do not live in Edinburgh."

"I remember." His voice was dry. "You see how freely I have told you about me. It seems only fair that you reciprocate."

Her laughter tumbled out, and she turned toward him. The look in Gregory's eyes took her breath away.

"Your laughter bewitches a man," he told her, his voice husky.

Rylla stopped, astonished. "What?"

"I heard you laugh tonight, and it sent shivers through me. I can tell you, it gave me a peculiar feeling to think you were a man." He curved his hand along her cheek. "Tell me your name." He bent and brushed his lips against hers.

A quiver ran through Rylla, and she had a sudden, urgent desire to wrap her arms around him and burrow into his warmth, to raise her lips to his. He dug his fingers into the sides of her coat, holding her in place without touching her. He did not need to; Rylla was certain she could not move. She did not want to. Slowly he lowered his head.

Then his lips were on hers, soft and seeking, drawing vivid, unfamiliar sensations from her. He did not press, did not seize, but beckoned her to further pleasures. His tongue slipped along the line separating her lips, startling a gasp from her. He apparently took this as an invitation, for his tongue stole into her mouth, exploring and awakening an absolute maelstrom of feelings.

Rylla was intensely aware of her body—of the pounding of her heart, the heat that flickered along her skin, the bizarrely melting, shivery state of her insides. Gregory cupped her face between his hands. She felt the touch of his ring, cool against her cheek, and remembered how the look of it had drawn her earlier tonight.

He lifted his mouth from hers. His breath shuddered out against her cheek. "I have to know you."

Rylla was certain that her knees were about to give way. She struggled to pull together the pieces of her will and stepped back. "If anyone comes along, you will present a most shocking image, sir."

Gregory glanced down at her male attire and ground his teeth. "The devil." He turned away.

Rylla glanced up the street and saw a hack pull into view at the corner, stopping to let his fare alight. She took off at a run, waving to the driver. Behind her, she heard Gregory let out a curse and come after her. She knew she could not hope to outrun him for long, but it was a short distance and she had a head start. And it was wonderfully easy to run without skirts hampering her.

Luck was with her, for she heard Gregory's footsteps skid to a stop, followed by a man's irritated exclamation and Gregory's hasty "sorry." She reached the hack and, tossing the driver the name of a church near her home, jumped into the vehicle. The hack pulled away just as Gregory reached it.

Rylla stuck her head out the window, calling back to him, "Thank you!"

"Blast it. Stop!"

But her carriage rumbled off down the street. Rylla sank back against the seat with a sigh. It was silly to be downcast about the matter; she scarcely knew the man. But she could taste him on her lips, feel his heat as he pulled her to him.

The thought that she would never see Gregory Rose again was a cold ache in her chest.

Chapter Four

Gregory trotted up the steps of the graceful Queen Anne house where his cousin lived. He had wasted the morning in a frustrating and fruitless search for his mystery woman.

How the devil had he let her slip away? At least he had overheard her give the driver the name of a church. Certain that his lovely deceiver either lived there or was visiting a friend who lived there, he had set out this morning for St. David's, only to discover that the pastor was a childless widower without a houseguest. After tramping up and down several of the nearby streets, Gregory had to admit that there was little possibility of coming upon "Rolly" by simply wandering around the area. That left him with only one slim chance: Cousin Andrew.

Despite "Rolly's" disavowal, Gregory was certain she had recognized the name Sir Andrew Rose. Andrew was Gregory's cousin and lifelong friend, and he moved in the best circles of society. He might know the woman's name. Moreover, he was someone Gregory could talk to freely and whose curiosity would be minimal. It was a pleasant benefit of dealing with a man who was largely self-absorbed.

Unfortunately, he was not a man Gregory felt comfortable pinning all his hopes on.

Sir Andrew's valet showed Gregory into his bedroom. His cousin, still clad in his dressing gown, was contemplating the clothes his valet had laid out on the bed before him.

"Gregory!" Andrew had a winning smile. "Didn't know you were in Edinburgh."

"I haven't been here long. Had to make duty calls on my mother's sisters first."

"I'm sure we can find more interesting places to visit."

"No doubt." And no doubt they would be the sort of places Andrew should avoid. Gregory had deliberately not invited his cousin to accompany him to Faraday's last night. The less Andrew saw of gambling dens, the better. "I am surprised to find you here. I thought you might go to Baillannan for Christmas."

"Thought I'd let the newlyweds have their first Christmas alone." Andrew shrugged. There was little love lost between Andrew and his new brother-in-law. In fact, both Andrew's sister Isobel and her husband Jack had suggested that Andrew leave their house last summer.

"I didn't feel much like Christmas at home, either," Gregory admitted. "I thought Edinburgh would be a nice change from Kinclannoch."

"Purgatory would be a nice change from Kinclannoch."

"Isobel tells me you've joined the social whirl here."

Andrew snorted. "If you could call it that. Aunt Adelaide has decided it's her duty to marry me off to a wealthy girl now that I've managed to lose the estate. She insists on dragging me to every bloody party she can find."

"You're thinking of marriage?" Gregory looked at him in surprise.

"I suppose I must at some point. It would be more pleasant to have a wealthy wife than a poor one. But the present hunt is all Aunt Adelaide's idea." He gave Gregory a pained look. "I used to think my aunt was a sweet, harmless female, but the woman is relentless."

"It's probably wise to assume that no female is harmless. I need your help, Andrew."

"You do?" His cousin's eyebrows lifted. "Whatever for?"

"I'm looking for a girl."

"Will any girl do, or are you searching for a particular one?"

"A very particular one. I don't know her name. But I know she is a lady, and I think she lives relatively close to St. David's church."

Andrew gazed at him blankly.

"A sort of grayish stone church," Gregory offered. "Has one of those pie-crust arches over the doorway. A few blocks north of here."

"Oh, yes, I think I recall seeing it."

"She told me a few other things, but I'm not sure they're accurate."

"You think she lied to you?" Andrew's brows soared higher.

"It's a distinct possibility. She's twenty-two years old. And she said her father was a clergyman in some small town."

"Good Gad!" Now Andrew's eyebrows were in danger of reaching his hairline. "A yellow-headed termagant?"

"She is blond," Gregory admitted, startled by the description. "Though I wouldn't call her a termagant."

"If it's the clergyman's blond daughter I know, she certainly is. Her name is Eleanor McIntyre, but I would not advise finding her, Greg. You'll be disappointed."

"I'm willing to risk it."

"It's clear you haven't spent much time in her company. I'll grant you, she's a handsome female, but about as sweet an armful as a bouquet of thistles."

"You seem to have a decided opinion about her."

"I should say so. I've danced with her. The dancing was nice enough. But when I asked her to promenade around the room afterward, she spent the entire time lecturing me."

"Lecturing! About what?"

"Easier to say what she *didn't* lecture me about. The evils of gambling. The demons of alcohol. The plight of the poor. At another party, I made the mistake of asking her if she'd care to take a stroll along the gallery. She acted as though I'd proposed to seduce her. She went on about the wickedness of men scattering their illegitimate progeny all over. As if I'd ever produced a by-blow! She is the most rigid, straitlaced, rule-abiding, prudish woman it has ever been my misfortune to meet."

"Perhaps we are talking about a different lady." Gregory thought about the object of his pursuit and the way her mouth had yielded beneath his the night before. "I would not term her prudish."

"I hope it *is* a different girl. Miss McIntyre is not the sort of woman any man would want to attach his affections to."

"Still . . . I should like to meet her, just to make sure."

Andrew stared at him. "Are you serious?"

"Yes. Can you introduce us?"

"I could. But that would mean I'd have to talk to her."

Gregory chuckled. "Come, Andy, surely she cannot be that fearsome."

"She scares the devil out of me." Andrew heaved a great sigh. "But if you are determined to throw yourself into the fire, I imagine she'll be at Lady Stewart's Christmas ball this evening. It's an enormous affair. I have an invitation."

"Cousin, you are a true friend."

"Hmph. Best save your thanks until after you've talked to her."

Gregory left his cousin's home in a far better mood than the one in which he had arrived. However little Andrew's description matched the adventurous young woman Gregory had met, it seemed likely they were the same person. How many blond, twenty-two-year-old daughters of a country parson could be visiting Edinburgh?

Gregory ignored his cousin's martyred air when he insisted on arriving at the party that evening at an unfashionably early time. The ball was, as Andrew had predicted, a crush. While Christmas remained an austere celebration in much of Scotland, Lady Stewart clearly had adopted a more English style. Boughs of fir decorated banisters and mantels, and fat red candles ringed by holly glowed on every available surface. Mistletoe dangled in doorways, ready to ensnare the unwary. Gregory thought of catching the girl he sought under one of the mistletoe balls, and he smiled.

Andrew announced his intention to seek the comforts of the host's smoking room and the bowl of wassail that awaited there. Gregory, however, insisted on a tour of the party in search of Miss McIntyre. There was no sign of "Rolly."

"She probably had enough sense not to come early," Andrew opined. "I say we visit the wassail bowl. Everything will look brighter afterward."

Gregory sighed and turned for a last look at the entrance to the ballroom. A woman and man had just stepped into the room. As they moved forward, the two young women behind them were framed in the wide doorway.

Gregory scarcely noticed one of the ladies, for his eyes were focused solely on the tall girl beside her. The high waist of her white gown emphasized pert breasts, their rounded tops enticingly skimmed by a wide neckline. A blue patterned shawl was draped around her arms, bared by short puffed sleeves. A cameo necklace was her only adornment.

Her hair, shorter than the style worn by most ladies present, was not the dark blond it had appeared the night before, but a riot of fluffy golden curls, wound through with blue ribbon.

Gregory stiffened. "There she is."

Andrew followed his gaze. "The devil! That *is* Eleanor McIntyre."

His cousin continued to talk, but Gregory did not hear him. He was already making his way toward the doorway, all his attention focused on Miss McIntyre. As if she had felt his gaze, she glanced in his direction. Her eyes widened in shock, and she bolted from the room.

Gregory started after her.

Chapter Five

"Amaryllis, that is the third time you've yawned since we left the carriage," Rylla's mother said to her as they walked into the crowded ballroom. "Did you stay up late reading again last night?"

"No, Mama." It was more boredom that afflicted her than lack of sleep. The Stewarts' Christmas ball seemed flat in comparison to her adventure last night.

Eleanor cast a quick, sharp glance at Rylla. "I heard you up and about very early this morning. Were you all right?"

"Mm. I had a bit of trouble sleeping."

It made Rylla uncomfortable to lie to Eleanor. More than that, she would have liked very much to tell her friend about the evening before. Not just about the freedom of walking about town or the strangeness of the gambling club or even the frightening robbery. Rylla ached to spill out everything that had happened afterward in Gregory Rose's rooms. The only thing that kept her silent was the strong suspicion that such confidences would fill Eleanor with a horrified concern for Rylla's soul.

She followed her parents into the ballroom, pausing on the threshold to survey the room. And there, across the crowded ballroom, stood Gregory Rose. His eyes locked on her. Rylla froze, panic shooting through her.

"Pardon me. I left something in my cloak," she murmured to Eleanor, then whirled and hurried off.

Rylla wove through the new arrivals behind her with no thought to where she was going, driven only by the need to get away. She hurried down a nearly empty hall that led toward the back of the house. Glancing back over her shoulder, she saw Gregory shove his way through the crowd at the door. Tall as he was, it took him only a sweeping look to locate her. He sidestepped a clot of people and strode down the hallway after her, his long strides eating up the distance.

She spotted a small door tucked under the staircase. She suspected it opened into an oddly shaped storage closet much like the one they had beneath the staircase in her own home. Her first thought was to slip inside it to hide from Gregory, but she knew he would see her and follow. She had to face him.

She turned, waiting. When Gregory reached her, she grabbed his wrist and pulled him into the closet with her. As she closed the door, darkness swallowed them. The only light was a glow at the bottom of the door.

"Well." There was something very much like a purr in his low voice. "What a welcome surprise." His hands went to her waist as he stepped closer. "I wouldn't have guessed you'd be so eager to be alone with me."

"I'm not," Rylla replied crossly, putting her hands on his chest to shove him back. He was rock solid beneath her palms. And warm. His masculine scent filled her nostrils, and she felt curiously light-headed.

"No? Then why, I wonder, did you pull me into this room?" Gregory's teeth gleamed in the near darkness of the small space.

"It's not a room. It's a closet."

"I know." He lowered his head. "A very small . . . very dark . . ." She could feel the brush of his breath on her face as he came closer and closer until his lips hovered over her mouth, a mere inch away. "Very intimate closet."

His lips settled on hers, a gossamer touch that deepened as his arms slid around her. His kiss was warm and soft and damp, both invitation and demand. Rylla felt the same swift spear of heat rush through her as it had last night when Gregory had kissed her. Unconsciously she curled her hands into his lapels, seeking balance now instead of pushing him away. For a moment, she clung, her mouth answering his, before reason finally returned to her.

Rylla jerked away, pulling out of his arms. "Stop. We—we must talk." She was appalled by the shakiness in her voice.

"Must we?" He moved forward, his hands going to her waist again. "This is much more entertaining. You know, until last night I'd never kissed a lass who tasted of cigars."

Rylla frowned. "If it was so terrible, one can only wonder why you kept at it so long."

He chuckled. "I didn't say it was terrible. Just . . . exotic."

"Perhaps you should find a cigar smoker to kiss."

"Ah, but that would not be nearly as enjoyable as kissing you." His lips curved seductively.

She took another step back, coming up against a stack of boxes. "Stop. We have to talk. No one can know of—of what I did last night. My reputation is in your hands."

"It is safe there, I assure you. No one will hear any of it from me . . . Eleanor."

"What!" Rylla's eyes widened in shock. Good heavens, what a coil! Now she had managed to embroil her friend in it, as well. "How did you—"

"What? Did you think I would not pursue you? You gave me a few hints. It was enough."

"They weren't hints," Rylla protested. "You make it sound as if I wanted you to find me."

"Didn't you?" There was a certain smug male satisfaction in his tone. It was, she decided, extremely annoying.

"Of course not! The last thing I wanted was for you to search for me."

"I think perhaps you did." His thumbs began a slow, enticing circling. "Makes one wonder whether you wanted to see if I would follow. If I wanted you enough."

"Don't be absurd."

"I don't think I am." He drew closer, so that only a fraction of an inch lay between their bodies all the way up and down. Somehow that infinitesimal space separating them was more stirring than if he had actually touched her.

There was a crack, loud in the silence of their hideaway, as the handle of the door turned. Rylla felt the reaction go through Gregory like a shot even before the meaning of the noise registered. He pivoted, pulling her farther back.

The newcomer paused after opening the door, admitting a slender shaft of light. Rylla could now see the stacks of boxes, trunks, and other articles stored in the small room. The space formed by the staircase above was long, the ceiling slanting downward to the rear. A narrow central passageway ran through the middle of the trunks and boxes. Gregory whisked Rylla up the aisle into the deepest recesses of the closet, bending down to avoid knocking his head on the sloping ceiling.

As a footman stepped into the closet, Gregory ducked behind a pile of boxes and sat down on a trunk, pulling Rylla into his lap. They were hidden by the stack in front of them . . . as long as the servant didn't go any deeper. Rylla wriggled back as far as she could. She felt Gregory jerk at her movement, and his arms tightened around her waist.

They waited, trapped, as the footman searched the high shelf on the side wall of the closet, muttering beneath his breath. With each passing moment, the intimacy of their situation grew. Encompassed by the darkness, Rylla was intensely aware of her other senses.

Gregory had curled his body protectively around her, so that she seemed surrounded by him—the heat and scent of his warm male body, the thud of his heart and the rise and fall of his chest beneath her ear, the strength of his arms, the stirring of his breath upon her hair. That pulse of hard flesh beneath her.

His body grew tauter, every muscle and sinew hardening. Rylla heard the beat of his heart increase, felt his chest rise and fall more rapidly. A soft insistent ache began to blossom between her legs. She shifted her position, and Gregory's hand clenched convulsively in her skirts. The footman edged toward them. Rylla's nerves were stretched to the snapping point.

"Ha!" The footman slid something from the shelf. A moment later the door opened, then closed, and they were once more alone in the room. Rylla went limp with relief. Gregory, too, relaxed, his arms slowly sliding from her body.

He let out a long sigh, his breath ruffling her hair. He curved one hand around her throat and slid it up to cup her chin. He turned Rylla's face to him, and his mouth fastened on hers. This kiss was not the soft coaxing of his earlier kisses, but urgent and demanding. Curving one arm around her back, he let his other hand drift down her throat and onto her chest. Rylla jerked in surprise as he cupped her breast. But it was, she discovered, a delightful sensation. She made no protest, letting the pleasure wash through her.

Gregory's mouth roamed over her throat. Rylla's head fell back, offering the vulnerable flesh to his touch. She could hear the harsh rasp of his breath. He mumbled something unintelligible against her skin. His hand left her breast, sliding lower. "Eleanor . . ."

The name jarred Rylla out her pleasure-drenched daze. "No!" She jumped off his lap and staggered back, holding her hand out in front of her as if to ward him off. "Stop."

Chapter Six

Gregory jerked forward as she left his lap, his hand lashing out and grabbing her skirts. He hung there for a charged moment, his eyes locked on hers, the only sound in the room the harsh in-and-out of his breath. He closed his eyes and opened his hand, letting her dress fall free.

"You must stop calling me that." Rylla edged out of the piles of storage. "I am *not* Eleanor McIntyre."

"Is that so?" He leaned forward, elbows resting on his knees. "I don't believe I mentioned your last name." His eyes gleamed in the dim light.

Clearly, she had only increased his conviction that she was Eleanor. Rylla gazed at him in frustration. Even if she told him her real name now, she had the feeling he wouldn't believe her. But she had to convince him not to reveal anything. Eleanor's reputation was at stake, as well as her own.

"Please. I beg of you. Don't speak of me or try to find me again. Don't tell anyone I am Eleanor. If word of what I have done got out, it would ruin me. I know I have given you no reason to believe my reputation deserves guarding, but—"

"You think I would damage your reputation?" He was on his feet and coming after her, his jaw set grimly. "I would never—"

"Kiss me? Manhandle me in a dark closet?"

His brows snapped together. "*You* were the one who pulled *me* into the closet! And I did not manhandle you."

"You scarcely behaved like a gentleman."

"You scarcely behaved like a lady."

"I know I did not!" Rylla snapped back. "That is precisely why I did not tell you my name."

"It's not as if I'm going to bruit your name about town."

"Of course not—until you are drinking one night with your gentlemen friends and bragging about your conquests."

"What conquest? I assure you, I do not feel as if I have won anything here."

"An entertaining story, then. I know how gentlemen would view my actions last night. Or this evening. Boldness is not a trait valued in a lady. Nor is curiosity or a sense of adventure."

"So now I am lumped in with every other 'gentleman' in the world. How do you know what I would or would not do? What have I done that would lead you to believe I am a censorious prig?"

"You are saying you approve of a woman who ventures out in gentleman's dress? Who kisses strangers in closets?"

"I suppose I must, since I approve of you," he shot back. He relaxed, his ready humor lighting again in his eyes. "As long, of course, as the stranger you are kissing is me."

Rylla could not hold back a little laugh. "Gregory . . ." She shook her head. "I don't know what to make of you." She reached out and took his hand between both of hers. "Will you give me your word? Promise you will not say I am Eleanor McIntyre. You can tell everyone the whole sorry story if only you don't say it was Eleanor McIntyre who acted so."

"I will not." He gazed steadily into her eyes. "I give you

my word as a gentleman. As a Rose of Loch Baille. I will not speak of you to anyone. I have never been introduced to Eleanor McIntyre. And I most certainly did not spend the Stewarts' Christmas ball in a deep dark closet with her." He raised her hand to his lips and pressed a kiss upon her palm. "I want only to see you again." He kissed the inside of her wrist. "Let me call on you."

"No! You must not. Please stop trying to see me."

"I cannot." He stepped closer. "You bewitch me. Beguile me." He raised a hand, curving it against the side of her face. "Please. Don't run from me."

Rylla trembled beneath his touch. She knew that running was precisely what she should do, but her feet stubbornly refused to move. He lowered his head toward her. And instead of pulling away, she closed her eyes. Surely it would not matter if she let herself have one more taste of him.

Then his mouth was on hers, so warm, so sweet, so seductive, she almost could not bear it. If it was wicked to feel the way she did, she must be steeped in sin indeed. All she wanted was to be in his arms, to have his mouth on hers, to feel this urgent heat inside. A tiny moan escaped her, and she felt his response.

With great effort of will, Rylla pulled away. "I must go." She stepped back, opening the door to peer out into the hallway.

"No, stay with me." His hands were on her waist, but their hold was light.

She gazed up into his face, taking in the hunger stamped upon it, his eyes hazy with desire, his mouth soft and dark from their kisses, and she wanted nothing more than to stay here and lose herself in his embrace.

"I cannot. They will be looking for me. Please, don't walk out with me. It would mean the death of my reputation if anyone saw us."

"I won't." He leaned down, resting his forehead on hers, his breath coming out in a little laugh. "Indeed, I think it will be some time before I am fit to be seen in polite company."

Rylla tore herself away and opened the door. She looked back at him. "Remember your promise."

"I will not speak of you."

She closed the door and hurried away. Unable to face the other guests, Rylla turned and retreated to the cloakroom. Perhaps she could just sit there for a few minutes and recover her equanimity. As she started along the hall, she spotted Eleanor coming out of the cloakroom, frowning. Her friend glanced up and saw her.

"Rylla! Where have you been? I've searched all over for you."

"I am sorry. I—um—"

Eleanor reached out, taking her hand. "Are you all right? You look flushed."

"Yes!" Rylla seized upon the excuse Eleanor had offered. "I mean, no, I am not all right. I'm not feeling well. That is why I came here. I thought if I rested a bit—"

"I think you may have a fever." Eleanor took her arm. "We should leave."

"You're right. I should return home. But you must stay. I'll send the carriage back for you and my parents."

"Nonsense. I'll go with you. We'll just get our cloaks, and I will tell your parents we're leaving."

Eleanor was her usual efficient self, and in only a few minutes, she and Rylla were bundled up against the cold and climbing into their waiting carriage. Rylla turned to her friend. "I am so sorry to take you away from the ball."

"Nonsense. I don't care about the party. I've already managed to offend Sir Andrew Rose. No doubt if I stayed, I would simply irritate someone else."

"You talked with Sir Andrew? What did he say?"

"A lot of frippery and foolishness. What else does he ever say? He thinks that charm will get him anywhere and that moral convictions are nonsense. Do you know that he as much as told me I was sanctimonious?"

"Well, I suppose you must seem so to someone like him."

Eleanor was silent for a moment. She smoothed her gloves over her hands, keeping her eyes on them. "Is Sir Andrew really—I mean, do you think he is a wicked person?"

"Wicked?" Rylla glanced at her, startled. "I wouldn't think so. I have never heard of him doing anything evil. He is like many young gentlemen and spends much of his time on frivolous things. Daniel once said his 'dibs weren't in tune.'"

"What does that mean?"

"I'm not sure. I think perhaps his finances are not in order. Not that Daniel is anyone to talk," she added darkly.

"I've heard Andrew is looking for a wealthy wife." Eleanor was still engrossed in the fit of her gloves.

"I don't think he is looking very hard. I haven't seen him dangling after anyone in particular. Eleanor . . . do you *like* Sir Andrew?"

"Good heavens, no." Eleanor raised her head at last, her tone indignant. "He is not at all the sort of man I admire. I couldn't even think of— And, anyway, as I said, he finds me a great trial."

"I have seen him at more parties recently," Rylla mused.

"No doubt because it is a festive season. He is clearly a man who enjoys . . . enjoying himself." She glanced over at Rylla, and they both laughed. "I do find Sir Andrew handsome, I admit. But looks do not matter. It's a man's character that's important. And I fear he is lacking in that. He lost his home, he told me, playing cards."

"Perhaps he has changed. People do not always act in an upright manner. It doesn't make them bad, really. I mean, sometimes it's necessary to do something that's wrong or might appear a bit scandalous, but surely that doesn't mean one's a bad person."

"Rylla, what are you talking about?" Eleanor looked at her narrowly. "Is this something to do with Daniel?"

"No. I mean, not entirely." Rylla sighed. "No doubt you heard that great row he and Papa had the other night."

"It was hard to miss," Eleanor admitted. "But surely Daniel is not in any sort of trouble."

"No. No, of course not. I am sure he and Papa will get over their disagreement. Daniel will be here for Christmas." Rylla pasted on a smile. "He has to be."

✦ ✦ ✦

"Where the devil did you run off to?" Sir Andrew said in an aggrieved tone when Gregory approached him.

"I was, um, around." Gregory could hardly tell him that he had spent a good portion of his evening in a closet under the stairs kissing Eleanor McIntyre. And waiting for his fevered blood to calm down.

"You said you wanted to be introduced to Miss McIntyre. Then you took off. She disappeared as well. When I finally found her, you never appeared. I felt a proper nodcock, I can tell you. And I was trapped talking to Miss McIntyre for God only knows how long."

"Yes, well . . . I was, um, otherwise occupied."

"Otherwise occupied! Doing what?"

"Walking about. Talking to people." Andrew would think him totally mad if he said he had spent the time since he left the stairway closet searching for Eleanor all over again. How the devil had Andrew managed to stand about chatting with her without Gregory seeing them? "I, ah, couldn't find you, and I thought I might come across her."

Andrew sent him a peculiar look. "Too late now. She already left. Headache or some such thing."

Such as a desire to avoid *him*. Gregory clenched his teeth.

"I say, cuz, are you all right? You've been acting strangely."

Gregory shrugged. He couldn't explain his actions to his cousin. He couldn't even explain them to himself. It was not like him to pursue any woman with such zeal. Nor had he ever been so consumed by lust that he'd thought of pulling a woman down on the floor of a closet and taking her right there—with scores of other people around, no less.

He had always enjoyed the company of women, flirting with ladies and taking his pleasure with women who were not. But he could never remember being so . . . eager. When she had fled the ballroom, he had taken off after her like a hound who had spotted the fox. Every nerve in his body had been alert, his blood pumping through his veins, his only thought to chase down his quarry.

And he hardly knew the woman.

Eleanor McIntyre clearly did not want him to find her. A gentleman would not continue to pursue her against her wishes. But Gregory had no intention of stopping. He could not.

"I'm fine," he told Sir Andrew. "Just regretting that I was not here to meet the lady."

"You really are taken with Miss McIntyre, aren't you?" Andrew stared at him in some astonishment.

"Yes, I am."

His cousin let out a martyred sigh. "She told me she was going to some lecture tomorrow evening. About the culture and customs of the Highlands. She said she thought I might want to attend. I ask you. As if I hadn't spent my life try-ing to get away from the dashed culture and customs of the Highlands!"

"Now, Andrew, laddie, dinna say you dinna want some Lowlander telling you all about yourself." Gregory grinned. "I think this lecture would be the perfect place to introduce me to Miss McIntyre."

"Perfect place to nap, you mean. Very well. I will take you to the bloody thing and introduce you. But I'm warning you: you better not take to your heels again."

Gregory had another restless night, followed by a seemingly unending day, but his spirits were high the next evening when he set forth with Andrew for the lecture. Sir Andrew sent a frown in his direction as they strolled along. Gregory realized he had been whistling under his breath. He swallowed a smile and discontinued his whistling, contenting himself with imagining the look on Eleanor's face when he walked in with Andrew.

Only a few people had gathered for the lecture, and Gregory could see instantly that none of them was the woman he sought. Andrew started purposefully toward a small blond woman who stood near the front. Gregory trailed after him, glancing around in the hopes Eleanor would appear.

The blond woman turned, and her eyes widened. "Sir Andrew. I am surprised to see you."

"Always a student of history," Andrew replied airily. "Pray allow me to introduce my cousin, Mr. Gregory Rose. He has been most anxious to meet you. Gregory . . . Miss Eleanor McIntyre."

For a long moment, Gregory simply stood, staring at the woman. Color flared along his cheekbones and his eyes flashed in a way that made Miss McIntyre's brows rise. She had done it to him again!

"Miss McIntyre. Pleasure to meet you," he said tightly. "Pardon me." He swung on his heel and stalked off, leaving Eleanor and Andrew goggling after him.

❖   ❖   ❖

Gregory strode blindly down the street. He knew he had been abrupt and rude, not normal behavior for him. No doubt his cousin, as well as the perfectly blameless Miss McIntyre, would never forgive him. But he could not bring himself to care. All he could think about was that *she*— whoever she was, blast it—had once more slipped out of his grasp.

She had deceived him. Lied to him. Well, to be fair about it, she had not actually told him she was Eleanor McIntyre. Indeed, she had said she was not Eleanor McIntyre. But still, his belief that she was Miss McIntyre was based upon the tissue of lies she *had* told him. The daughter of a clergyman—hah! He should have known that was a falsehood. A woman who visited gambling clubs dressed up as a male, who looked as she did, acted as she did, who, dammit all, kissed as she did, was no minister's daughter.

It was frustrating. Infuriating. Unbearable.

Why had she lied to him? Why did she want so much for him not to know who she was? He had helped her. He had not scolded or been censorious. He had not told anyone what had gone on between them. Yet she refused to give him even so much as her name.

The answer, of course, was obvious, and it was enough to drop him right where he stood. She simply did not want to see him again. She had no feelings for him.

It began to snow, but Gregory was oblivious to it. He continued to tramp along, mired in his thoughts. His best course of action would be to forget her. He should find some party or other to attend this evening—one where he did not spend his time searching for her. The idea had little appeal. But the thought of going back to his rooms and sitting in front of the fire drinking brandy was even grimmer.

Eventually his aimless wandering brought him to Faraday's. Irritated, he swung around to leave, but he reconsidered. Perhaps a convivial night at a club was the best way to get one's mind off a woman. Unlike at a party, there would be little chance of running into her at Faraday's. She would not visit a club in disguise now that she knew the risks involved. Cardsharps, footpads, drunken youths looking for a fight. What might have happened if anyone discovered she was actually a woman was enough to chill his blood.

A quick look around Faraday's told him "Rolly" was not there. Just what he wanted. But the place seemed flat, and before long he moved on. Despite the falling snow, he tromped from one gambling den to another. The woman he had known as first Rolly, then Eleanor, was in none of them. Perversely, instead of bringing him relief, that fact only put him more on edge. He should, he thought, go home. At that moment, he glanced up and saw a young man walk into the club. The collar of his greatcoat was turned up, his hat pulled low on his forehead, so that only a narrow slice of his face showed.

Gregory shot forward and clamped his hand around the young man's narrow wrist. "You are coming with me."

Not waiting for an answer, he strode out the door, pulling the youngster after him.

Chapter Seven

"Let go of me!" Rylla tugged uselessly against the manacle hold of Gregory's hand. "Stop! You have no right."

He paid no attention. She tried to plant her feet, but they skidded along on the cobblestones, made slick by snow. Realizing that her efforts were useless, Rylla finally went along with him, keeping what she hoped was a disdainful silence. By the time he had hauled her up the hill at his rapid pace, she didn't have enough air to rail at him, anyway.

Gregory clearly didn't have that problem, for as soon as he whisked her into his parlor, he rounded on her, thundering, "What the hell do you think you're doing? Have you gone mad?"

Rylla lifted her chin, too out of breath to speak.

"Do you not remember you were attacked the last time you went masquerading? Robbed? Knocked down? Are you *trying* to get injured?"

"No! Of course not! Stop shouting at me."

"I'm not shouting!" Gregory lowered his voice to a fierce, determinedly controlled level. "Even if I was, who could blame me? Do you realize what could have happened to you tonight if someone had seen through your disguise? What a man might have done?" He grabbed her shoulders, his fingers digging into her.

"You mean, the same thing you did?" She knotted her fists on her hips, glaring back at him.

A wild light flared in his eyes. Rylla had the uneasy feeling she had pushed him too far. With a low growl, he pulled her to him and his mouth came down on hers, hard and demanding.

Everything inside Rylla melted. Irritation, anger, distrust all slipped away in a rush of heat. She did not pull back from the ferocity of his mouth, but instead pressed up into it. Her hands stole beneath his unbuttoned coat and slid around his waist. She felt the involuntary jerk of surprise in his body at her touch. He moved into her, his knee edging between her legs until his thigh was flush against her.

His kiss went on forever, and she softened with each passing second, the ache between her legs swelling and throbbing. He slid his hands down her body, pressing her even more firmly against his leg.

A shudder ran through him. He tore his mouth from hers, burying his face against her neck as his arms clenched around her.

"No." The low, harsh word seemed ripped from him. "I will not do this again." He stepped back, holding her away from him. He was flushed, his breath rasping, but his face was set in determination. "I'll not play the randy fool again for you. This time I will have answers." He drew a steadying breath. "Who are you, and what mad game are you playing?"

Rylla stared at him, rigid with frustration. Her body wanted nothing but to feel his hands and mouth on her again. Her spirit was equally bent on not bending to his demands. Her mind—well, she was not sure what her mind wanted, since it did not seem to be present at the moment.

She sighed, finally giving in. "I am Amaryllis Campbell. I am ruined if you speak of this to anyone."

"I shall not." He, too, visibly relaxed, his face softening. "Amaryllis . . ." He lingered over the name, savoring it. "A lovely name. Almost as lovely as you."

"It's too long and flowery." She made a face. "Everyone calls me Rylla."

"Rylla, then." Gregory shrugged out of his coat and eased hers off as well. He led her to the sofa. Taking both her hands between his own, he said, "Now. Tell me what you are doing."

Rylla looked at his long, capable hands encasing hers. His fingers were slender, the bony knuckles prominent. The sight of them was somehow reassuring—and at the same time did peculiar things to her insides.

"I am trying to find my brother." She raised her eyes to his. Both anger and male hunger drained from his face, replaced by warmth and concern. Tears sprang into her eyes. "Oh, Gregory, Daniel has been gone for four days, and no one knows where he is."

He curled an arm around her shoulders, cradling her to him. "Don't worry. We'll find him. You think something has happened to him?"

"I don't know!" She swallowed hard. "He had a terrible row with our father. Daniel chafes under Papa's restrictions. He is at university now, and he regards himself a man. But he is only eighteen, and Papa controls his allowance. Daniel has taken to drinking and gambling. I am sure it is only high spirits. He is eager to kick over the traces. But it makes Papa tighten the reins. Papa dislikes his new companions." She paused and looked earnestly at Gregory. "I fear our father is right; they are not nice men."

"You have met these friends?"

"A man named Kerns came to the house looking for Daniel. He frightened me."

"Did he threaten you?" His fingers tightened on her shoulder.

"No. It was Daniel that he threatened. He told me Daniel was getting himself into trouble and that he'd better pay his debts. He didn't actually say something bad would happen to Daniel, but he implied it. Finally I gave him my brooch in payment."

"Your brooch! He took your jewelry?" Gregory scowled.

"He said it would cancel Daniel's debt. I didn't really want to. My grandmother gave it to me. If she asks about it when I see her on Christmas, I shall have to say I lost it. But I couldn't let Daniel be harmed."

"Kerns was a cur to put you in that position. What did your brother say?"

She sighed. "I didn't tell him. It was only a day or two before Daniel and Papa argued and Daniel left. The brooch is not the problem. What worries me is that Daniel stormed out of the house after their argument, and he has not returned. It's been four days. I have no idea where he is."

"I know how your brother feels. I chafed for years under my father's restrictions. More than once, I hared off after an argument. It didn't mean I was in any danger."

"Without even telling your sister?"

"I don't have a sister. Nor a brother, either." He paused, looking thoughtful. "My cousins knew—Andrew and Isobel." He smiled faintly. "Of course, it was usually their house where I went after an argument with Father. Or Coll and Meg's."

"More cousins?"

He shook his head. "Not exactly. It's complicated. Andrew's nurse was Coll and Meg's mother. They were raised with Andrew and Isobel at Baillannan, the Rose estate. My father was a military man, and when he was away, my mother and I lived at Baillannan as well. After she died, I continued to live there."

"I'm sorry." Rylla slipped her hand into his. "I can't imagine what it must be like to lose your mother. With your father frequently gone, you must have felt quite alone."

"You're kind." He linked his fingers with hers and lifted her hand to press a brief kiss upon it. "I missed my mother. But it probably saved both my father and me much grief that we did not live together. I was happy at Baillannan. They were my family more than my father. Andrew and I went off to school, then London. It has only been in the last year or two that I've spent much time at home."

"Is your father there? Has he retired?"

"Yes, he retired. He is . . . not entirely well." Gregory's open face grew shuttered. "But my point is that your brother's being absent for a few days doesn't mean something terrible befell him. He has probably gone to stay with a friend or another member of your family."

"But that's just it. He might not think to write us, but any relative would have sent my mother a note saying he was there. His friends don't know where he is, either. I must find Daniel and talk to him."

"Is that why you went to Faraday's?"

"Yes. It was all I could think to do. I can't bear for him and Papa to be at odds. If he's not home for Christmas, Papa will be furious. I dread to think how upset our mother will be."

"Surely his friends will tell him you're looking for him."

"I fear he may not visit them either. It's been so long now. It's as if he is avoiding everyone. It's not like Daniel to be so careless. He knows we would worry. What if he has been hurt?"

"I'll ask around, see if I can locate him for you."

"Would you? Truly?" Rylla beamed.

"Yes, of course. But you must promise you won't go searching for him yourself. Your brother would not want you to. It's dangerous."

"I won't go by myself." She smiled. "I'll go with you."

Gregory's eyes widened. A smile twitched at the corner of his mouth, but he shook his head. "No. I can't take you with me. I'll have to visit some rough places, and you can't go to a gambling hell. There are other places that—" He paused, looking embarrassed. "Well, trust me, it would be impossible for you to go there."

Rylla studied him. "Do you mean bordellos?" It occurred to her that she did not want Gregory visiting a brothel even if he was looking for her brother.

Gregory's brows shot up. Something hot and dark flared in his eyes before he dropped his head and began to laugh. "Don't you know you shouldn't talk about such things?"

"What fustian!" She rolled her eyes. "As if women weren't aware of their existence. If it's not too shocking for a man to visit such a place, how can it be shocking for a lady to have heard about them?"

His laughter increased. Gregory leaned back and regarded her with gleaming eyes. "Amaryllis Campbell . . . you must be a sore trial to your mother."

"Yes," she admitted. "I fear I am. No doubt you are appalled, too, and wish me at the devil."

Gregory gave her that slow, enticing smile. "Nae. I wish you no place else but here. With me."

"You do not find me scandalous? Shameful?"

He reached out and took her hand, lifting it to his lips to kiss each finger. "I find you utterly beguiling."

"Then surely you would enjoy taking me with you to clubs and taverns and such."

"I would." His eyes sparked with light. "Truth is, I would enjoy taking you anywhere. Or nowhere." He sighed and laid her hand back on the sofa. "But I cannot. No doubt it would astound my family, but I am going to be mature and responsible. It would be wrong of me to expose you to such places."

"But you need me." Gregory's eyes flew to her face. Rylla felt the blood rushing up her throat. "To find Daniel, I mean."

"Rylla . . ." Gregory pushed up to his feet and began to pace the room. "I can find him."

"I know what Daniel looks like. You could be in the same room with him and not have any idea who he was. I can also recognize his friend Kerns."

"The lout who took your pin? I'd like to get my hands on him." Gregory looked intrigued but shook his head. "No, it would put you too much at risk."

"You will be with me." Rylla rose to face him. "What could happen to me?"

"Pleasant as it is to know you think me invincible, I must point out that I am not."

"A robber would be less inclined to approach two men. And if I did something out of character, you could give me a nudge."

He snorted. "As if you would pay attention."

"Of course I would." She gave him a wide-eyed look. "I'm not shatter-brained, Gregory, however low an opinion you have of me."

"I do not have a low opinion of you," he said through gritted teeth. "How many times must I tell you?"

"You asked if I was insane!"

"Given what you've been up to, it was a legitimate question."

"That's unfair. I couldn't help being robbed. Besides, he didn't see through my disguise. *You* did not realize I was a woman until you tried to take off my shirt."

"I thought you were injured," he said stiffly.

"Mm. The point is, you thought I was a man. I am tall, and my voice is low and—"

"I know what your voice is like." He stopped pacing and faced her, his eyes glittering. "I hear it every night in my—"

"What does that mean?" She put her hands on her hips pugnaciously.

"Never mind. The point is, your voice does *not* sound like that of a man."

"No? What does it sound like, then? Sandpaper?"

"No." His eyes drifted down to her lips, and his own mouth softened. "It sounds like smoke." He moved closer. "Brandy." He raised his hand to her jaw, thumb catching beneath her chin and tilting her face up to his. His lips hovered above hers. "A warm bed on a long, cold night."

Rylla found it suddenly hard to breathe. She should step back. If she did, Gregory would act like a gentleman. But that was the last thing she wanted.

Chapter Eight

Rylla stretched up to kiss him. A shudder went through Gregory. His mouth turned hot and avid. He kissed her again and again, his hands slipping beneath her jacket to explore her body. He fumbled to undo her waistcoat and shirt.

"You have entirely too many fastenings," he murmured against her lips.

He kissed along the line of her jaw and down to her throat, stopping at the obstruction of the neckcloth. Letting out a low noise of frustration, he tugged at the cravat, pulling it free and dropping it at their feet. Rylla's shirt hung open now, and Gregory's gaze fastened on her exposed breasts. Like a man exploring a treasure, he curved his hands over her, hungrily watching as he stroked her flesh.

Embarrassed by her nakedness before him, yet even more aroused by it, she let her eyes flutter closed. Gregory bent to place his lips against the soft curve of her breast, and she shivered, heat flowering between her legs. He moved to the taut rosebud of her nipple, his tongue teasing. Rylla dug her fingers into his hair, the coil of sensation tightening deep within her.

His fingers slipped over her stomach and into the crevice between her legs. She jerked in surprise at the touch, but she could not keep from moving against his agile fingers, the ache inside her growing. His breath was hot against her skin, and he mumbled something unintelligible as his mouth came up to take hers again. A staccato rapping at the door broke through the haze of desire. Gregory's head snapped up.

The door behind them opened and Andrew stepped into the room, saying, "Why the hell did you—" His jaw dropped, the words dying on his lips.

Gregory cursed, instinctively curling his hand up over Rylla's head, pressing her face into his chest, and he wrapped his other arm around her. "Devil take it, Andy!"

In the next instant, Gregory remembered that the woman he cradled to him was dressed in men's clothing. He froze, staring at his cousin, who gaped back at him.

Andrew's mouth opened and closed like a fish. "I say . . . dreadfully sorry . . . um . . ."

"Stay here," Gregory murmured to Rylla and stepped around her, blocking her from Andrew's vision. He strode forward. "Out."

"Wha— Oh . . . yes, of course." Andrew backed out and moved down the hall. "Sorry. I didn't realize . . . I, uh . . ."

Gregory swept his hands over his face, struggling to make his brain work. "I know this looks . . . odd."

"No. No." Andrew waved his hand. "Just gave me a bit of a start. I perfectly understand."

"You do?" Gregory gaped at him.

"Yes, yes. Did it myself a few times at Oxford."

"You did?"

"Don't you remember when I got sent down? Don't

smuggle them in now, of course—no need. No headmaster. But I suppose your landlady might object, eh, to your having a doxy in your room." He nodded sagely.

"What? Oh!" It dawned on Gregory that Andrew had concluded that the "man" he had just seen in his cousin's embrace was in reality a prostitute whom he had slipped into his rooms in disguise. "No!" Gregory started to hotly deny Andrew's assumption, but at the last moment he retained enough sense to put a curb on his tongue. "I mean, well . . . yes. What the hell do you want, anyway?"

"I must say, that's the outside of enough! I apologize— didn't mean to send your ladybird flying." He gestured vaguely behind Gregory. "But after—"

Gregory whirled. Rylla, coat wrapped around her and hat pulled low on her head, was slipping down the stairs behind him. "Blast!" He ran after her. "Ry—wait!"

Pelting down the stairs, he burst out the front door just in time to see Rylla dart across the street and climb into a waiting hack. "No! Stop!" He watched in disgust as the carriage rattled off down the street.

"I say. Your ladybird took my hack," Andrew said as he strolled up behind Gregory.

"She is the most damnably headstrong, stubborn . . ." Gregory stalked back into his building and up the stairs, Andrew following him. He turned at the top of the stairs and shot a dark look at his cousin. "What are you doing here, anyway?"

"I came to find out what you think *you're* doing," Andrew shot back. "Why did you run off this afternoon? First you tell me you have to meet Eleanor, then every time I try to introduce you, you take off like the hounds of hell are after you."

Gregory sighed. "I'm sorry, Andy. It was rude of me. I shall apologize profusely to your Miss McIntyre."

"She's not *my* Miss McIntyre. And she thinks you're mad

as a hatter—which was no surprise to her, considering you're my cousin. It's me you should apologize to. I was the one who got trapped listening to that fellow drone on for hours."

"Drone on about what?"

"How should I know? I wasn't listening."

Gregory began to chuckle.

"I don't know what you're laughing about," Andrew said with considerable bitterness. "I had the devil of a time trying to stay awake."

"I *am* sorry, cuz. I promise I'll not ask you again to introduce me to Miss McIntyre. As it turns out, she was not the one I was looking for." He strolled into his apartment, Andrew on his heels.

"I haven't the faintest notion what you're talking about. Who are you looking for? And why?"

"The why is easy—she's the most fascinating girl I've ever met."

"Who is?"

"Miss Amaryllis Campbell." Gregory saw that the neckcloth he had taken off her lay on the floor in front of the sofa. He swooped down to pick it up, crumpling it in his hand.

"That girl Eleanor's staying with? You want to meet Rylla?"

"I have already met Rylla." Gregory brought the white stock up to his face, inhaling her scent. "I just haven't been introduced." He dropped his hand and turned to his cousin, a smile beginning on his lips. "You know, Andrew, I think that a formal apology to Miss McIntyre is required. You and I are going to pay them a call tomorrow."

✦ ✦ ✦

Rylla kept a smile firmly plastered on her lips and wondered if their visitors would ever depart. They had been here the polite twenty-minute interval already—Rylla knew, for she had been keeping an eye on the clock—but they showed no sign of leaving. Mrs. Fraser was a gossip of the first order. Rylla had the uneasy feeling that the woman had some inkling of her brother Daniel's disappearance and was here to nose out the news. Her companion, Lady Stewart, had come simply to soak up more praise for the elegance of her ball the other night.

"Of course, there are some who will find fault with my little Christmas celebration," Lady Stewart was now saying.

"Oh, no, my dear, no," Mrs. Fraser hastened to reassure her, as was Lady Stewart's intent, Rylla was sure. "We are long past the time of banning Yule cakes, I should hope."

"Yes, well, it's not the common thing here, of course. But being reared in England as I was"—she offered a smile of benign condescension—"I quite miss the charming customs."

"I am sure no one disapproves. Why, I have put up a mistletoe ball myself," Rylla's mother said soothingly, pointing to the decoration hanging in the doorway.

Mrs. Fraser added, "Quite so. Perfectly suitable. And mistletoe adds just that little spice of naughtiness." She tittered.

Rylla glanced at Eleanor, seated beside her on the couch. Her friend's face was perfectly straight, but laughter brimmed in her eyes. Rylla had to press her lips tightly together to keep from grinning back at her. Eleanor might have a strict moral standard, but thank heavens she also had a ready sense of humor.

At that moment, the butler appeared in the doorway of the drawing room. The conversation paused as they turned toward him. "Sir Andrew Rose," he intoned.

"Sir Andrew!" Eleanor murmured, an odd note in her voice that caused Rylla to turn toward her friend again. It struck her that Eleanor was in her best looks this afternoon, despite the tedium of the ladies' visit. Her cheeks were tinged with a becoming pink.

"And Mr. Gregory Rose," the butler went on.

Rylla snapped back around. Her chest was suddenly tight. She wished she had a fan to occupy her hands. She dared not look Gregory in the eyes, yet she could not keep from watching him, either, as he and Andrew crossed the room to bow to her mother.

Her mind was filled with visions of the night before. It struck her suddenly how very far she had deviated from what was normal and expected. At the time, it had been exciting. Daring. And oh, so pleasurable. Now it occurred to her that she must have been mad to do the things she had.

"Allow me to introduce you to my daughter, Miss Amaryllis Campbell," her mother was saying. "Amaryllis, dear, Mr. Gregory Rose. He is Sir Andrew's cousin, visiting him for Christmas. Isn't that nice?"

Rylla had to look at him then. Gregory bowed to her, his blue eyes dancing with mischief. Her breath caught in her throat, and Rylla knew that, given the chance to do it all over, she would choose to do exactly what she had.

"Miss Campbell, it is a pleasure to meet you. Had I known Edinburgh offered such beauty, I would have come long before this."

"And this is my daughter's friend, who is staying with us for a few weeks, Miss Eleanor McIntyre," Mrs. Campbell went on. Gregory turned to Eleanor, greeting her smoothly.

Given the arrival of new blood, it was clear that Lady Stewart and Mrs. Fraser had no intention of leaving anytime soon. Lady Stewart launched immediately into the subject dearest to her heart. "I do hope Sir Andrew brought you with him to my little party, Mr. Rose."

"Indeed he did, and I was honored to attend. The hostesses of London could take lessons from you, my lady." He turned to the sofa where Rylla and Eleanor sat. "My only regret is that I did not have the opportunity to dance with Miss Campbell or Miss McIntyre."

Rylla's heart tripped as he smiled into her eyes, and for once in her life, she was utterly tongue-tied.

Mrs. Fraser filled the silence, saying archly, "I am sure you will have the opportunity to dance with many young ladies on Twelfth Night, Mr. Rose."

"I hope you are enjoying Edinburgh, Mr. Rose," Rylla's mother said. "But surely your parents must miss you at such a season."

"My mother departed this world some years ago, I'm afraid. My father lives in seclusion in Orkney."

"Ah, I see. I am sorry. Then you live alone?" Rylla's mother continued her delicate probing, soon establishing that Gregory had no wife, fiancée, or any dependent, that his father was some sort of invalid, and that Gregory was in charge of all the man's affairs.

As her mother turned to the subject of Gregory's Edinburgh relatives, Rylla stifled a groan. Whatever was her mother doing? She was acting as if Gregory had come courting. What would Gregory think? And what was he doing here, anyway? It was irritating to be mired in this social chitchat, unable to ask a direct question about anything she actually wanted to know. It was also rather annoying that Gregory seemed perfectly at ease.

But as Gregory turned politely to reply to a comment from Lady Stewart, the frustrated glance he sent toward Rylla told her that he was chafing at the restrictions as much as she was. The knowledge made her inexplicably happier.

"Perhaps you will decide to stay in our fair city a little longer," Mrs. Fraser told Gregory coyly.

"Yes, you should." Lady Stewart nodded her head. "Edinburgh is lovely this time of year. Much more civilized than the Highlands." She gave a little shudder.

"Yes, it is lovely." Gregory smiled. "Sir Andrew and I were admiring the view as we walked over here. We intend to take a stroll through the park up the street."

Andrew's startled glance told Rylla that this intention was news to him.

"Perhaps Miss Campbell and Miss McIntyre would care to join us," Gregory went on.

Andrew looked at his cousin as if he'd grown an extra head. "It's snowing."

"Exactly. So picturesque." Gregory gave the other man a hard look. "The trees frosted with snow. Icicles dangling from tree limbs."

Sir Andrew seemed momentarily bereft of speech. Before he could gather himself enough to reply, Rylla said brightly, "That sounds lovely! Doesn't it, Eleanor?"

Eleanor, swifter of understanding than Sir Andrew, said, "Why, yes, I do love a walk in the snow." She smiled at the two men. "I am so glad you thought of it, Sir Andrew. Mr. Rose."

"Er, quite." Sir Andrew adjusted his cuffs. "Wasn't sure you'd like it, you see. Trudging through the damp. The cold and all."

"Oh, no, we'd quite enjoy it." Rylla sprang to her feet, followed by Eleanor.

The two girls escaped to don their boots and cloaks before Mrs. Campbell could decide to object to the outing. As they climbed the stairs, Eleanor commented, "I was rather surprised by Mr. Rose today. I had the impression he was shy."

Rylla gaped at her. "Gregory? Shy?"

"He bolted yesterday as soon as Sir Andrew introduced us. Missed the entire lecture."

"He was at a lecture? With Sir Andrew?"

"Yes. You can imagine my surprise." Eleanor's cheeks colored prettily. "Sir Andrew stayed for the talk."

Rylla's jaw dropped. "I would never have guessed that Sir Andrew had any interest in—well, in anything one might give a lecture on."

"Oh, I don't think he was *interested* in it." Eleanor chuckled. "I suspect Andrew had trouble keeping his eyes open. Frankly, even I was a bit bored. But it was nice of him to stay to keep me company, don't you think?"

"Yes, it was." Rylla tilted her head a little, considering. "I am inclined to wonder if Sir Andrew has developed a tendre for you."

"I would not think so." Eleanor's blush deepened. "I am sure he finds me terribly straitlaced. He is very undisciplined, so of course we should not suit."

Rylla shrugged. "Unfortunately, it seems to me that what we *should* feel is not at all the same thing as what we *do* feel."

❖ ❖ ❖

"Well, you certainly seem to have charmed my mother," Rylla told Gregory as they set off down the street toward the small park. Andrew and Eleanor strolled a few feet ahead of them.

"I have a way with mothers. They are rarely as elusive as their daughters." Rylla rolled her eyes in response, and Gregory grinned. "Though I was afraid she might balk at the idea of a stroll through the blizzard."

Rylla laughed. "It's not snowing *that* hard."

"Fortunately, you look delightful with snowflakes on your lashes."

"Flatterer. Well, I will not quibble. I am far too grateful to have escaped that drawing room."

"I don't know how you ladies bear it."

"You seemed to manage well enough."

"Yes, well . . ." He shrugged. "I wanted to see you."

"Why? Do you have news about Daniel?"

"Not much," Gregory admitted. "I wanted to see you

because . . . I like looking at you. Talking to you." He cut his eyes toward her. "But I find I much prefer being with you as we were last night."

"With me wearing men's clothes?"

He chuckled. "I don't think it's the clothes." After a moment, he said more seriously, "It's the freedom to actually be with you. I never realized before how bloody unsatisfying it is to talk to someone with four other ladies listening in."

"It's a dead bore," Rylla agreed.

"I wish I could take your hand right now." Rylla glanced up at him. Gregory was looking straight ahead, his jaw rigid. "I wish a lot more than that, truth be told. But it's the very devil not even to be able to touch you or look at you or let my face show what I'm feeling. Society's restrictions are"— he let out an explosive sigh—"a dead bore."

Rylla tucked her hand in his arm. "I'm glad you came to call."

"I plan to go out tonight to visit a few gambling dens that are known to prey on gullible young men."

"Really?" Rylla began to frame her argument to go along on the adventure.

"Yes." He slanted a look down at her, a faint smile on his lips. "Would you care to join me?"

Chapter Nine

Gregory crossed his arms and leaned against the stone wall, waiting for Rylla to emerge from the dark house across the street. He was on edge. On edge had, it seemed, become his permanent state.

They had spent the last two days trying to discover Daniel's whereabouts. Tomorrow was Christmas Eve, and Gregory still had not the slightest idea where Daniel Campbell had gone. He was beginning to acquire Rylla's uneasy feeling about the young man.

Gregory was living on little sleep. He spent half the night tromping about the gambling haunts of Edinburgh and most of the day looking for Daniel. However, the search was not the real reason behind his weariness. No, both insomnia and frayed nerves were due to one thing: Rylla Campbell.

The woman tormented him. He had sworn not to take advantage of her. Each night she gave her safety and her reputation into his hands; he could not betray that trust by luring her into his bed. He had not kissed her or caressed her or taken her into his arms—even when they ended their evenings in front of his fireplace, discussing their investigation. But as a result of his chivalrous behavior, he spent all his time with her balanced on a knife-edge of desire.

He should not take her to his rooms to talk after they left the gambling dens. Being alone with her, only feet from his bedroom, was far too tempting. But he hadn't the strength to deny himself. This slice of time was all he could have of her. During his afternoon calls at her house, they were in the company of Andrew and Eleanor and Rylla's mother, unable to speak except in the most stilted and commonplace of ways.

Only alone in his rooms could he revel in talking to her, being with her, able to watch her smile and the animation in her face as she talked. During those quiet moments, everything inside him rushed out to her. He found himself telling her about himself, his father, his house, his family, his doubts and hopes, even his darkest secrets. He was even more eager to hear everything about her.

But those precious hours were also the most tantalizing, restless, unfulfilled, nerve-wracking times he could imagine. He seemed a stranger to himself. He was filled with conflicting desires to take Rylla to his bed and satisfy the profound lust that surged in him, yet at the same time he wanted to protect her and please her. To know her.

Gregory straightened now as he caught sight of Rylla slipping from the shadows around her house. Happiness and a certain pride of possession surged in him as she strode toward him, smiling. She was without equal. And she was *his*.

He went forward to meet her, careful not to touch her. Even offering her his arm would look odd, given her disguise. Gregory had discovered these past days how many small things could reveal that Rylla was a woman beneath those clothes. He had taken to keeping his hands thrust into his pockets whenever he was around her, just to make sure he did not touch her. The most difficult thing to control was the way he looked at her—to hide the delight, the desire, the affection that he suspected shone from his eyes.

They chatted as they walked, but Gregory kept alert. They had already made the rounds of the better places young men went to gamble. Tonight would be a long step down, one he was reluctant to make with Rylla along. He was glad she had brought her brother's cane with her. It would at least give her a weapon should they run into trouble. Gregory had enough of the Highlander in him that he had shoved his *sgian dubh* into the top of his boot for their expedition.

They went from one club to another, each one seedier than the last, and Gregory grew increasingly more concerned. When they stepped into another smoke-filled room, Gregory took one look around and shook his head.

"We should leave." He turned, but Rylla grabbed his arm.

"Gregory!" she hissed. "What are you doing? This is precisely the sort of place we should look."

"If we want to get taken up by a press gang, perhaps."

"You can't expect to find sharps and ivory turners in the finest establishments." Rylla adopted her young-man-about-town stance, feet planted sturdily apart and arms crossed. Deepening her voice and raising the volume, she tossed out cant in a bored, world-weary drawl. "I've a taste tonight for a bit of blue ruin."

Looking at her, Gregory wanted to laugh, pull her into his arms for a kiss, and shake her, all at the same time. None of them would be a wise thing to do. "This isn't even a club. It's a tavern."

"That may be, but I'd guess those chaps over there are casting dice."

He leaned closer, whispering, "This is not the sort of place you should be."

She sent him a flashing look. "Don't tell me you're going to become a prig now."

"I'm not being a prig. But I am not certain I could adequately keep you safe. I'll warrant that fellow just rode in from stopping mail coaches. And what about the one in that red cap? He looks like he's sizing up where to put the knife in his companion."

Rylla glanced over. "You might have a point. Look, there's a little table in the corner. It's dark and protected on two sides. We could easily sit there and watch without getting into any trouble. I promise I won't even talk to anyone. You can get our drinks, and I'll stay right there. Word of a gentleman."

Gregory had to chuckle. "Oh, devil take it, very well. Follow me. And don't look anyone in the face. You are far too pretty, even as a lad."

He led her to the table in question, and Rylla sat down, wedging her stool into the corner. Gregory cast a look back at her, then made his way through the crowded room to the bar. He waited for his glasses of ale and pondered whether he should transfer his *sgian dubh* from his boot top to one of the pockets of his greatcoat. Just as he picked up the filled mugs, all hell broke loose behind him.

✦ ✦ ✦

Rylla had every intention of remaining quietly in the corner, observing the patrons of the tavern. She had enjoyed the past evenings far too much to endanger their easy camaraderie. Gregory was so pleasant and easy to be with, seemingly entertained by her independent attitude and unconventional ways instead of annoyed and restrictive. Even as worried as she was about her brother, she had thoroughly enjoyed their outings.

It would all have been almost perfect, really, if only Gregory had given the slightest indication that he wanted to kiss her again as he had the other night. Why, she wondered, did he not make even the slightest advances toward her? Had her free and easy ways killed his desire for her?

With a sigh, Rylla pulled her mind back from those unladylike thoughts and returned to studying the other patrons of the tavern. They were indeed a rough-looking lot. Even without Gregory's insistence that she stay in the corner, she would not have wanted to venture from this sheltered spot. She liked a little adventure in her life, but she was no fool.

Rylla stiffened suddenly and peered through the smoky haze at a customer sitting a few tables over. He lifted a large mug to his mouth and drank deeply, then thunked it back down onto the table and wiped his mouth. She watched as he talked to the man across from him. When he laughed, Rylla was certain. It was Kerns, the man who had come to their house looking for Daniel.

She turned toward the long bar where Gregory stood. He was scanning the room, watching for possible dangers. She fixed her gaze on him, willing him to look at her, but he swung back to the barkeep, reaching into one of his pockets to pay the man.

Kerns stood up, shoving back his stool, and nodded to his companion. He started for the door. He was leaving!

Rylla jumped to her feet, picking up her cane, and hurried toward Gregory. Just as she edged around a table, a large man staggered into her, knocking her into one of the men seated at the table. The top of the cane she carried struck the man smartly atop the head. He bellowed and jumped up, shoving Rylla away. She stumbled back, falling into another man behind her. Feeling rather like a ball that was being bounced around, Rylla straightened just as a meaty fist came flying at her nose.

She ducked, and the fist thudded into the face of the man behind her. With an inarticulate roar, the two men crashed together like two rams at mating season. They lurched about, flailing and striking, feet tangling up with chairs and other legs. Rylla, who had wound up on the floor, knew her best course was to get out of their path. She crawled speedily away on her hands and knees, still clutching her cane, and dove under the nearest table.

Amazingly, over the shouts and crashing of chairs and the squeals of table legs dragging across the floor, Rylla heard Gregory's voice calling her name. She peered out from under her sheltering table and saw him shoving men aside, struggling toward the center of the fight.

"Gregory!" She leapt out, grabbing at the skirt of his greatcoat, and he whirled.

"Rylla! Thank God!" Gregory's face was stark white. He wrapped his hand around her arm, nearly lifting her off the floor as he propelled her toward the door.

"It wasn't my fault!" She told him as they made their way through the tumultuous crowd.

He pulled her behind a post as a man slammed into it from the other side. "Still, I'd prefer not to have to explain to your mother how you came by a black eye and bloodied nose."

They kept moving toward the door, skirting a pair of combatants rolling around on the floor. Gregory dodged a fist and rammed a chair into another man who charged at them. He did not see the man come up behind him, wielding a thick-glassed bottle, but Rylla did. She brought her cane up sharply, the metal knob on top catching the attacker on the point of his chin. His teeth clacked together, and he wavered, the bottle tumbling out of his hand. It smashed into his foot.

Leaving the attacker hobbling and cursing and wiping his bloody chin, Gregory and Rylla ran for the exit. They were trapped for an instant in a clog at the doorway, then popped through into the street. Gregory took Rylla's arm and pulled her up the street, but she hung back, looking all around her.

"Rylla! Bloody hell, come on. What are you doing?"

"I saw him! He's here!"

"Who?" Gregory stopped, pulling her back against the building. "Daniel?"

"No. Kerns."

"The man who took your brooch? Where?" Gregory swiveled, looking up and down the street.

"I'm not sure. I can't see him. No, wait, up there!" She pointed up the street, which climbed steeply. At the very top, a man was weaving along. He passed under a streetlamp. "I think that's him!"

She started off at a run, Gregory right behind her. His long legs quickly outstripped her, but he slowed down, waiting for her.

"Go on! Go on!" she hissed. "I'll catch up."

"I'm not leaving you." He adjusted to a loping pace alongside her.

As they neared the top of the hill, there was no sight of the figure. Pulling to a stop at the cross street, they peered around the corner.

"There!" Gregory started after the dark figure. Their quarry glanced back, saw them, and took to his heels. Gregory charged after him. With a flying leap, Gregory slammed into the man, and the pair crashed to the ground.

Chapter Ten

The two men rolled across the street, grappling, as Rylla ran up behind them. Rylla raised her cane to strike, but she could not get a clear shot at Kerns. He slashed at Gregory with a knife, ripping his coat. Gregory grabbed the man's wrist and slammed it into the cobblestones.

The man let out a howl, kicking and punching with his free arm, but Gregory ignored his blows and smashed Kerns's arm to the ground again. The knife skittered across the cobblestones. Gregory pinned him to the ground.

"Is this him?" he panted. "Is it Kerns?"

"Yes, that's him."

"Who the devil are you?" Kerns demanded.

"That's not important." Gregory hauled the man to his feet and twisted his arm up behind his back. "We have a few questions for you."

"Questions?" The man gaped at him.

"Yes." Rylla stepped forward. "We're looking for Daniel Campbell. Do you know where he is? Have you seen him?"

"Nae. How should I know? "

"Because you're the sharp who swindled him," Gregory answered, giving him a shake. "You're not the kind to lose sight of one of your flats."

"I never swindled him. Anyway, I hae no' seen him since he got up on his high ropes about his sister paying me for— Say!" He stopped and looked Rylla up and down. "You're her, ain't you?" He laughed. "Well, well, now . . . I'd be happy to play a few hands with you. Ow!" His face contorted and he rolled his eyes toward Gregory. "Hae a care; you'll break my arm."

"I'll break both of them if you continue in that vein."

"I dinna mean anything."

"Never mind that," Rylla said impatiently. "When and where did you last see Daniel?"

"I dinna watch the lad's comings and goings. Six days ago, maybe seven. He came tae ask for more time tae pay. I told him you'd taken care of it. He flew up into the boughs about me talking to his sister. Went storming off. I hae no' seen him since."

"Where did he go? He wouldn't have just disappeared."

"My guess? He's gang tae the moneylenders."

Tears sprang into Rylla's eyes, and she turned away. Behind her, Gregory pulled the other man away, bending down to talk to him in low, fierce tones. Rylla paid them no attention. All she could think of was the disappointment crushing her chest. She had been so hopeful when she'd spotted Kerns a few minutes earlier, so certain that he would be able to lead them to Daniel.

But they were no farther along than they had been. Christmas was the day after tomorrow. How could they find her brother before then? It was becoming clearer and clearer that Daniel did not plan to join the family. How could she and her family celebrate Christmas, not knowing if Daniel was well . . . or even alive?

✦ ✦ ✦

"I'm sure your brother is fine," Gregory told Rylla, taking her arm and pulling her closer to the fire. She had been quiet all the way back to his home. He knew her thoughts had been on her brother. It amazed him how much he wished he could give her what she wanted.

"How can you know?" Rylla held her hands out to the warmth of the fire, not looking at him. She was so lovely, it brought a pain to his chest. Gregory's eyes drifted over her pale, delicate skin, cheeks and lips reddened by the cold. She had taken off the hat she'd worn and combed her hands through her curls, giving her blond hair a charmingly tousled look.

"I can't, of course, not for certain. But I do know young men. I know what it's like to feel foolish and sorry and ashamed of something you've done. That is what is keeping him away. If something had happened to him, if he had been hurt, you would have heard."

"That's what I keep telling myself." She gave him a small smile and turned away, slipping out of her coat and jacket. "What did you say to Kerns there at the end? I saw you looking fierce and talking to him quietly so I wouldn't hear."

Gregory shrugged, propping his elbow on the mantel and watching her. Her breeches curved over her rounded derriere and hugged the contours of her legs. A sweet ache settled low in his abdomen. "I just reminded him it was in his best interests to keep his mouth shut and stay away from your brother. I don't think he'll bother you again."

"Thank you." Rylla looked up at him with lambent eyes.

He could get lost in those eyes, Gregory thought. His fingers itched to reach out to her. He swung away sharply and picked up his greatcoat, searching the pockets. "I got this from him." He extended his hand, palm open.

"My brooch!" Rylla drew in a sharp breath, picking up

the piece of jewelry almost reverently. "But how—I would have thought he'd sold it already!"

"Apparently he hasn't been able to get as much as he wanted for it."

"But Gregory—I did owe him the money. I mean, Daniel did."

He smiled. "Now you're worried about Kerns getting swindled? Don't be. I paid him for it."

"Gregory! No, you shouldn't. I can't accept this from you." She stroked her fingers over the brooch in her palm. "It's too much."

"Nonsense. It's yours." Gregory pulled his eyes from the sight of her fingers caressing the piece of jewelry. He cleared his throat. "Consider it a Christmas present."

Rylla smiled. "I am not noble enough to refuse it." She went up on tiptoe, placing her hand on his shoulder to steady herself, and brushed her lips against his. "Thank you."

Heat surged in Gregory. "I don't ask for your gratitude." His voice was thick, his mind heavy and slow, as if mired in a bog. Only his senses were alive, excruciatingly so.

"I know. But you have it, nevertheless. You are most kind."

"I'm not. Sweet heaven, I am not." Unconsciously he leaned toward her. He must not touch her. He was sure he would be lost if he did. But she was so achingly close, so warm and soft. So desirable.

"You have not kissed me these three days. Not even once." Rylla continued to gaze at him, her eyes wide and limpid. He could not look away.

"No." He sounded rusty as an old gate.

"Why?" The word was deceptively simple. He had no idea how to answer it. After a moment of silence, she added, "Do you not want to kiss me anymore?"

"Rylla . . ." The word came out a groan. His hands came

up to frame her face. "Of course I want to kiss you. I can think of nothing else. But you must know I cannot. I would be a scoundrel to take advantage of you that way. Here, under my roof."

"You mean you were a scoundrel when you kissed me here the other day?"

"No doubt. But at least then I did not know you."

"It's worse to kiss someone you know?" Her voice was lightly teasing. The treacherous tautness deep within him grew worse.

"You are playing with me." He knew she must feel the rush of heat in his hands, hear the unevenness of his voice as restraint warred with passion.

"And you no longer wish to play with me?"

"There is nothing I would like more." It was becoming exceedingly hard to think.

She laid her hands flat on his chest, sliding them up him as she rose onto her toes again, stretching up until her lips were perilously close to his. "Then why don't you?"

"You have given me your trust. You're in my care. I should protect you."

"From yourself?" Rylla's hands slipped over his shoulders and around to the nape of his neck. Her fingers glided up his neck and into his hair, sending shivers down his spine.

"Especially from me." He could not keep from tasting her lips. Just one small kiss would not matter, surely. He knew as soon as his mouth touched hers that that was a lie. It was all he could do to pull away.

There was a wicked glint in her eye. "But who shall protect you from me?" Rylla tugged his head down to hers.

All resistance fled him. Gregory kissed her deeply and at length, savoring the pleasure of her soft mouth, exploring its welcoming heat. He let his hands glide over her, caressing her neck and breasts and sides. The journey was sweet, but he was too eager to reach his goal to linger on the way.

He curved over her buttocks as he had been imagining all evening, fingertips digging in and lifting the firm mounds, pressing her into his body, imprinting her softness with the full hard evidence of his desire.

Rylla threw her arms around his neck, clinging tightly, hooking her leg around his, as if she would climb straight up his body. He lifted her from the ground and turned, reeling, until he came up hard against the wall. He was on fire now, desire pounding through him.

One arm braced against the wall beside her head, he pinned her there, kissing her as if his life depended upon it. His other hand slid over her body, impatiently opening her waistcoat and shirt and slipping beneath them. He roamed over her breasts, enticing the nipples into hard points of desire. His fingers moved down to the place between her legs that he had ached to touch for hours. For days. She was hot and tight, and it made him shudder to find the material already damp.

"Rylla . . ." Her name was like a prayer on his lips as his mouth roamed down her neck. His fingers moved insistently against her. She separated her legs, opening herself to him. "Rylla . . . no . . . tell me to stop. Else soon I will not be able to."

Her answer was a little moan, and she arched up against his hand. "I don't want you to stop."

And he was lost.

◆　◆　◆

Rylla had been thinking of this, dreaming of this, for days. She had not known exactly what she wanted other than a recurrence of the pleasure she had felt at his hands before, but she understood now that this frantic, desperate need that pulsed in Gregory was exactly what she hungered for.

He swept her up in his arms, carrying her to his bed, kicking the bedroom door closed behind them, as though to shut them away from the world even more deeply. Gregory laid her down on the bed, treating her as gently as porcelain despite the taut hunger that limned every inch of him. His eyes on her, he disrobed swiftly, and Rylla watched with fascination. He was so new, so different, to her eyes, his long torso and limbs captivating her, as his fingers had, with their combination of strength and lean grace. The sight of his naked maleness brought a moment's trepidation, but it was more excitement and eagerness than fear that welled up in her. Rylla fumbled at her own neckcloth, fingers clumsy on the unfamiliar clothes.

"Here, I'll do it." Gregory sat down beside her on the bed, expertly going to work on the neckcloth and the buttons of her waistcoat. She sat up and let him pull the garments from her and toss them aside, leaving her upper body naked to his eyes.

He drank her in, his face turning heavy and slack with passion as he reached out to cover her breasts. The look in his eyes made the low, hot ache in her throb more fiercely, and as he caressed her, she stretched beneath his hands like a cat, whatever embarrassment and shyness she had felt at her nakedness swept away by the pleasure of his touch.

Gregory reached down to pull off her shoes and stockings, pausing to caress each narrow foot and slide up her calf to the hem of her breeches. Then he went to the buttons at the top of her breeches, taking his time and sliding his hand inside to stroke and tease her. Rylla gasped at the intense pleasure and moved restlessly beneath his fingers, seeking more.

He stripped off the breeches impatiently, and she thought he would come into her then, but instead his hand returned to tempt and delight her, and he lowered his mouth to her breast. Rylla let out a low moan at the twin pleasures, and she twined her fingers through his hair, holding him to her.

An impatient need built inside her, and just when she thought she could not bear the exquisite pleasure any longer, he parted her legs and moved in between them. He slid up her body, his flesh probing delicately at her tight entrance. Her breath caught in her throat, and she knew with a burst of loss and confusion that this simply would not work, and then he was pushing into her, slow and steady. She started instinctively to pull back, but his hands went to her hips, holding her in place, and then, with a flash of pain, he was inside her.

He went still, and she could see the fierce concentration in his face as he waited. His voice was hoarse as he said, "Look at me, Rylla."

She did as he said, gazing up into his glittering blue eyes, and let herself relax. He bent, taking her lips in a slow, deep kiss. Rylla curled her arms around him, giving herself up to the pleasure of his mouth. He slid into her, inch by slow inch, as he kissed her face and neck. He filled her, bringing her a satisfaction she had never imagined, and as he stroked in and out, she felt need knotting in her.

Rylla dug her fingers into his back, aching for something she could not name, knowing only that the tension in her was almost unbearable. His hand moved down between them, his thumb finding the sensitive bud of flesh between her legs, and she drew in her breath sharply. She tightened all over, digging in her heels, as he drove into her harder and faster. Suddenly the tangle of tension exploded, pleasure washing out through her in deep, strong waves. Gregory shuddered violently, a low cry torn from his throat, and collapsed against her. Rylla wrapped her arms and legs around him, clinging, as she gave herself up to the sweet ecstasy.

Chapter Eleven

Gregory turned onto Rylla's street, his head lowered in thought. He was unaccustomedly nervous. The timing was wrong. He should probably wait until after the holidays. Moreover, Rylla was distraught over their failure to find her brother. Which brought to mind the fact that Gregory had failed at the only thing he could do for her. Not to mention the fact that he had behaved like an utter bounder last night.

He frowned, his steps slowing. Today was possibly the worst day he could choose. Yet he could not turn back. He had to see her. Lifting his head, he looked down the street at the Campbell house and came to an abrupt halt.

A post chaise sat in front of the house. And his cousin was climbing down from it.

"Andrew?"

Sir Andrew swung round. His face lightened. "Gregory!"

"What are you doing here? Are you headed to Baillannan, after all?"

"No. No." Andrew shook his head, tugging at his

waistcoat and checking his neckcloth, then toying with the gold top of his fashionable cane. "Not Baillannan. No."

When Andrew said nothing further, Gregory said, "Then . . . why are you in a post chaise?"

"What? Oh." Sir Andrew glanced over at the yellow conveyance as if surprised to find it there. "Yes, well, fact is . . . I'm escorting Eleanor home. I mean, Miss McIntyre."

"I didn't know she was leaving."

"Mm. Just here for a fortnight, you know. Her father wants her home for Christmas. He's a clergyman."

"Yes. I've heard." Gregory frowned. "Andy . . . are you unwell?"

"Yes. I mean, no, I'm perfectly well. Quite, um . . . Devil take it, Greg! I think I may cast up my accounts right here."

"Are you foxed?"

"No!" Andrew gave him an affronted look. "In front of Eleanor? I mean, Miss McIntyre?"

"Then why are you acting so peculiar?"

"That's the thing. Have to be normal. Proper. Though I dare swear he'll still dislike me."

"Who? What are you talking about?"

"No need to shout. I'm talking about her father. Thing is . . . you see . . . I'm going to ask him . . . for her hand."

"Miss McIntyre?" Gregory's eyebrows sailed upward. "You're proposing to her? Marriage?"

"Yes, of course, marriage," Andrew replied testily. "Really, Greg, what else have we been talking about?"

"I'm not sure." He regarded his cousin for a moment. "Andrew, are you certain?"

"Positive. He's bound to dislike me. He's a clergyman."

"I meant, are you certain you want to marry Miss McIntyre? You told me she was rigid and prudish and rule-abiding."

"Yes, um, perhaps I should not have said prudish." A

faint bit of color tinged his cheeks. "Anyway, one rather wants a wife who abides by the rules, doesn't one?"

"Not always." A faint smile touched Gregory's lips. "I thought you were determined not to marry."

"I was. But . . ." He shrugged. "Things happen."

"Yes, they do, don't they?"

"When she said she was going home today . . . well, I didn't want her to. She's—" Andrew screwed up his face, as if thinking were a painful process. "She *is* very different from me. But, thing is—I don't want to marry someone like me. And I thought I'd like to see her sitting across from me at the breakfast table each morning. Everything's . . . flat without her." He looked at Gregory. "Do you know what I mean?"

"Yes." Gregory smiled. "I believe I do."

◆ ◆ ◆

Rylla leaned her forehead against the windowpane, gazing down at the street below. She sat curled up on the window seat of Eleanor's room, and behind her, Eleanor was packing the last of her clothes into a trunk. Eleanor was talking, but Rylla found it difficult to keep her mind on her friend's words. She hadn't been able to keep her mind on much of anything all morning.

Except, of course, Gregory. And the night before. What would happen now? She thought of the gossip she had heard over the years—how this girl or that was "ruined." How men were no longer interested in a woman once they'd obtained the prize they sought.

What would she do when she saw Gregory again? Or perhaps she would not even see him. Perhaps he no longer desired her. He might now consider her lewd and licentious. It was said men were like that.

But not Gregory. He understood her desire to do things, see things. Indeed, he seemed to enjoy her nature.

He never looked grim or disapproving over something she said. At times he objected, saying something was too dangerous, but he never told her she was too unladylike or acting like a romp. No, Gregory was different. He would not turn from her. Her heart clenched inside her chest. She didn't know how she could bear it if he did.

"I am sorry to go home before Daniel returns," Eleanor told her. "I know you are worried about him."

"Yes." Rylla pulled her thoughts away from their unproductive course. "But it's Christmas Eve. You will want to spend it with your family." She straightened and leaned closer to the window. "There's Gre—Mr. Rose. And Sir Andrew. I wasn't sure—I mean, I wasn't expecting them." She jumped up, shaking out her skirts and checking her image in the mirror.

Eleanor joined her at the window. "Sir Andrew is escorting me home today."

"He is?" Rylla stared.

"Yes." A secretive smile played at the corners of Eleanor's mouth.

Rylla's jaw dropped. "Eleanor! What are you saying? Is he—are you—"

Eleanor laughed. "I will let you know after our journey."

Stunned into silence, Rylla followed Eleanor down the stairs. When she stepped into the drawing room, her eyes went immediately to Gregory. He was sitting on the sofa, talking stiltedly with Rylla's parents and Sir Andrew. Both the young men popped to their feet, looking vastly relieved, when Eleanor and Rylla entered.

Rylla blushed. She could not see Gregory without thinking how he had looked last night, deep in the throes of passion. She wondered what he thought when he gazed at her.

After a few minutes, Eleanor and Sir Andrew took their leave. Gregory and the Campbells stood on their front stoop, waving good-bye until the post chaise turned the corner. Rylla's father retired to his study, and Mrs. Campbell walked back to the drawing room. Rylla started to follow her mother, but Gregory reached out a hand to stop her.

"Rylla. I want to talk to you."

Rylla turned to him, her heart beating painfully hard. Gregory's face was unaccustomedly serious. Her spirits plummeted. She had been wrong. His feelings had changed. He was about to tell her he was returning home to the Highlands. Or he would say he didn't think they would suit.

"Rylla, dear?" Her mother paused in the doorway of the drawing room.

"Yes, Mama." Rylla ducked her head, avoiding Gregory's gaze, and hurried after her. She could not bear to talk to him today. She could not manage a calm, collected front with him.

Rylla avoided Gregory's eyes as she chattered gaily about Christmas and Twelfth Night parties. They were interrupted by the sound of the front door closing, followed by footsteps in the hall. As Rylla looked toward the doorway, a young man walked into the room. He was travel-stained and weary, but he smiled at the two women.

"Daniel!" Rylla popped up and ran to her brother. "I'm so glad to see you!"

"Here now, Ryl, careful, I'll get you dirty."

The next few minutes were filled with excited babble. Finally Mrs. Campbell, dabbing at her eyes with her handkerchief, hurried off down the hall to inform her husband of the news. Rylla waited until she was gone, then swung on her brother.

"Daniel! Where have you been? I was certain something terrible had happened to you. Gregory and I have—"

"What? Who is Gregory?"

"I'm sorry. You don't know Mr. Rose." Gregory had become so much a part of her life that it seemed absurd that her brother had not even met him. Quickly Rylla ran through the introductions of the two men, then returned to her topic. "What happened to you, Daniel? Why didn't you tell us where you were going?"

"I didn't expect to be gone so long," Daniel protested. "After Papa and I, well—" He glanced uncertainly at Gregory.

"Do not stand on ceremony with Gregory," Rylla told him. "He knows all about it. He has been helping me search for you."

"Search for me! But, Rylla, how . . . where . . ."

"Never mind that. Tell me where you went."

Daniel sighed. "I was furious at Papa, but I knew he was right. I had to set everything straight. I went to arrange to pay my gambling debt. And Kerns showed me your brooch!" An aggrieved light shone in his eyes. "Rylla, why did you give that blackguard your pin?"

"I was trying to save you," Rylla retorted. "He said you were in dire straits."

"I would have come about. But when I saw he had your brooch, I knew I must get it back immediately. I couldn't pay it over time. So I went to Ramsey."

"Ramsey! Who is that?"

"A chap I know at school. Only it turned out he had gone home for Christmas. I had to go all the way to Aberdeen. I didn't think to leave you a note. Once I was on the road, there wasn't any use writing you. I'd be home by the time you got a letter. But when I got there, it turned out Ramsey was sick. I had to cool my heels for days, waiting to see him."

"But why did you have to see him? I don't understand."

"To sell him my brace of dueling pistols."

"The ones with the silver chasing?" Rylla stared.

"Yes. He's wanted to buy them for months."

"But you love those pistols!"

"I know." He shrugged. "But I couldn't let Kerns keep

your brooch, now could I? And then, when I get back here, Kerns tells me you've already gotten the thing! Rylla, you shouldn't have gone to see him."

"I was fine. I was with Gregory. It's Gregory you owe. He bought my brooch back for me last night." Rylla could not control the softening of her voice as she turned toward Gregory.

"Mr. Rose, I am deeply in your debt," Daniel began manfully. "It was very good of you to help my sister, and—"

"Daniel." Mrs. Campbell appeared in the doorway, smiling. "Dear boy, do come and speak to your father. He is so relieved and happy to have you home again."

"Yes, of course." Daniel turned toward Gregory apologetically, but Gregory waved him on.

"Go and see your father. Plenty of time to discuss this later."

Gregory watched Daniel and his mother leave the room, then swung around. "Rylla . . ."

"Daniel will be able to pay you back. That will make everything all right."

"The devil with the money," Gregory said impatiently. "Rylla, I must talk to you."

"No, really, there is no need. I knew what I was doing last night. I will not hold you to account for—"

"Bloody hell, what are you talking about? Rylla—" He grabbed her hands between his. "Look at me."

She lifted her chin pugnaciously, though she suspected the look was spoiled by the tears in her eyes.

"Rylla! Are you crying?" Gregory stared at her, aghast. "Please . . . I realize that I acted like an utter cad. But I could not bear it if you hate me."

"Of course I don't hate you." She feared that in a moment she would be in sobs. Rylla tried to tug her hand free, to no avail.

"Then tell me that I still have a chance. That you are not tossing me out on my ear."

"Have a chance? A chance for what?"

"To win your heart. I was too rash, too forceful, I know. But I love you with all my heart, and if you will only let me, I shall prove that I am worthy of you."

"You love me?" Rylla seized on the only words that were important to her. "Do you mean it?"

"Of course I do." Gregory looked surprised. "I will do everything I can to make you feel the same way about me. I will woo you as you should be wooed. No doubt you are angry at me, but I—"

"I'm not angry." Rylla smiled tremulously. "I could not be angry at you."

"Oh, I am sure you could be," he replied candidly, adding, "Probably will be, too."

Rylla laughed and blinked away her tears. "Well, I am not angry with you now."

"I'm very glad to hear it." Gregory grinned. "I thought—you would not look at me, and then you wanted to talk about that blasted brooch. You were crying!"

"Not because I was angry. I thought you were here to tell me good-bye."

"Good-bye! Good Gad, no. Why would I say a thing like that? I came to ask you to marry me. I intended to go to your father, but I wanted to ask you first. I thought he might say it was far too soon, but I don't want to wait."

"Nor do I. He may say it's too soon, but I don't care. He will come around." She grinned. "It's better to start wearing him down as soon as possible."

"I am good at wearing people down," Gregory assured her.

She laughed. "Do you mean it? Do you truly love me? You are not just asking me because you feel obligated?"

"I truly love you," he told her solemnly. "I would marry you today, this moment, if I could."

"Oh, Gregory." She let out a sigh of happiness. "I love you, too."

He raised her hand to his lips and kissed it, then glanced around. "Ah, there it is."

"There what is? Gregory, where are you going?" Rylla laughed as Gregory pulled her over to the doorway.

"Looking for a sprig of mistletoe." He pointed up to the pale white berries hanging in the doorway. "So that it is acceptable for me to do this."

He bent to kiss her. With a long sigh of happiness, Rylla curled her arms around his neck and kissed him back.

It was going to be a wonderful Christmas.

SWEETEST REGRET

Meredith Duran

Moonless darkness stands between.
Past, the Past, no more be seen!
But the Bethlehem-star may lead me
To the sight of Him Who freed me
From the self that I have been.

—Gerard Manley Hopkins

Chapter One

December 22, 1885

The crowd was rowdy; only eight of them, but they managed to make a ruckus better suited to undergraduates on holiday. The noise spilled from the drawing room all the way down the hall to the grand staircase, where Georgie paused to take it in: laughter, clapping, a slurred yell, the ring of champagne glasses knocked carelessly together. Some untalented pianist was mangling "Hark! The Herald Angels Sing."

Foreign diplomats: scallywags by profession. And one among them was evidently a thief to boot. *This* was the crowd her father had left her to host for Christmas.

It will be very easy, he had assured her while hastily packing his things. An international crisis had called him away to Constantinople—some fracas that could only be resolved by the great Sir Philip, hero of British diplomacy.

Georgie was accustomed to her father's abrupt departures. But the house was full of his friends! Worse, one of them had broken into his study and stolen a letter of exceeding political sensitivity. *You can't mean to leave me with them,* she'd protested. *How am I to search their rooms for the letter if I'm the one hosting them?*

Her father had seemed unconcerned. Cheerful, even. *You'll think of something,* he'd told her. *And they'll only stay till Boxing Day. Show them our holiday customs. I promised them a proper English Christmas. Feed them mince pies, keep them drunk. Very easy, Georgiana.*

Easy, was it? Today, from off the coast of Marseilles, he'd cabled a new set of instructions. *Never fret,* he'd written. *I have ordered Lucas Godwin to join the party. He will find the letter.*

Lucas Godwin! Georgie had goggled at the page for long minutes. On no account—not even for peace everlasting— would she endure the presence of that silver-tongued snake in her house!

But an hour ago, his coach had rolled up her drive.

The sight had driven Georgie out of the drawing room. Panic urged her toward the kitchens. There was nowhere she felt safer, nobody's counsel she trusted more than Cook's.

But halfway down the hall, she'd changed course. The staff could not save her from her father's plots. Instead, she had flown up the stairs, bursting into the von Bittners' suite to make a hasty search of two valises, praying to find the letter so she could send Godwin packing.

She'd not found it, though.

Another round of laughter floated to her ears. She took a strangling hold on the ivy-wrapped banister. Did the voices include Godwin's?

Of course they did.

She should march into the drawing room and slap his face!

The thought made her sigh. Some other woman might have done it. Alas, she was Georgiana Trent, daughter of

England's finest diplomat, schooled from childhood in the art of restraint. She was scholarly, politic, retiring. The worst anyone could call her was a spinster. She would not let an old wound drive her to fresh disgrace.

Moreover, if she *did* slap Godwin, he would probably think her mad. He had no idea that he had broken her heart, two years ago. That month in Munich had only been a flirtation for him, one among dozens. Everybody fawned over him—even the great beauties. He had that kind of charm.

Yet for a month, in Munich, Godwin had ignored the beauties. He had looked only at Georgie—laughing at her jokes, praising her insights, gazing at her across crowded rooms as though she were some kind of miracle. One glance in the mirror might have proved otherwise; she was plain and brown-eyed, with ashen hair too frizzy ever to shine. Her perfectly round face had never caused anybody to gape, much less to think of miracles.

But even spinsters could lose their good sense. Godwin's respect for her learning, his interest in her opinions, had touched her deepest, most secret hopes. She had wondered if they might be falling in love.

They weren't. *That* had become clear the morning she'd read of his departure in the diplomatic circular. He'd left! Without a word of farewell, without even a note, he had packed his bags and departed for a new post in Paris!

He'd forgotten her as easily as he'd noticed her. That was the way of the flirt.

Well, *hers* was the way of the civilized. She would abide by her father's instructions. She would allow Godwin into her home, even have a Christmas stocking knit for him. Not by a single look or word would she reveal how he'd wounded her. But she did not mean to go lightly on him, oh no. If he took it upon himself to "charm" her again, she would show him what she thought of cads who built their careers on shallow charisma. She had more weapons at her disposal than a mere slap. She had *erudition*. She had substance and dignity and *pride*.

Resolved, she marched down the stairs, then cut through the entry hall toward the drawing room. The clamor had assumed a wild edge; ragged shouts of laughter drew her to a halt at the door. Her heart skipped a beat.

Godwin stood blindfolded amidst a ring of laughing guests. She'd fantasized, once or twice, that Parisian cooking had turned him into a round-bellied, gout-ridden glutton. Alas, his tall frame remained lean—displayed to very good advantage by his formalwear, black tails and a starched white necktie. He could not have been in company above half an hour, for he had made time to change his suit. But already he'd become the center of attention. *Typical.*

He thrust out one gloved hand, and Countess Obolenskaya, a willowy blonde well accustomed to men's attentions, sidestepped with expert ease. "What is this called?" she giggled to the man at her side—Lord von Bittner, a gruff, silver-bearded German.

"The blindman's bluff," von Bittner informed her. He gave a grand sloshing wave of his wineglass. The Axminster carpet might not survive this party. "English traditions!"

Georgie crossed her arms. Here stood the crème de la crème of European diplomacy, upon whose shoulders rested the future of nations, the fate of politics and continent-defiling wars. And how did they entertain themselves? With a children's game!

Somebody noticed her—Mr. Lipscomb, from the Home Office. "Oh, look," he cried, and then stepped forward to seize Godwin's shoulders, giving him a shove in Georgie's direction. "Better luck that way!"

Godwin grinned, teeth startlingly white against his

tanned face. He had the coloring of a farmhand. Did he never wear a hat? Too late, Georgie stepped back. His grip closed on her arms, startlingly firm. "At last," he said. "My first victory of the evening."

His voice was low and rich, like sunlight through honey. It sent a startling stab through her chest. *You are a wonder, Miss Trent.* So he had told her once.

A wondrous idiot, more like. A man always at the center of parties would never lose his heart to a wallflower.

She tried to jerk free, but his grip tightened. "Who could it be?" he asked, teasing. He'd mistaken her resistance for part of the game. "A lady, to turn so bashful. To say nothing of these elegant hands." His fingers flexed around hers, his thumbs stroking her wrists.

She swallowed. The blindfold obscured the azure brilliance of his eyes and the sharp planes of his cheekbones, but it made a becoming frame for the strong square of his jaw. She would not blame herself for having lost her head to him in Munich; he was quite the most handsome man in the diplomatic corps. But Paris had brought out his raffish side: he wore his black hair long now, with no pomade to tame it. It hardly suited him.

He leaned close—close enough to breathe deeply of her. He still wore the same scent, a faint trace of bergamot that made her stomach clutch. "No perfume," he murmured. "Not Lady von Bittner, then."

"You noticed my perfume, did you?" The German lady sounded pleased about this. Her husband looked less gratified.

This was absurd. Georgie opened her mouth, but the other guests shushed her. "Don't spoil the fun," Lipscomb said, as the rest of them gathered around to watch. Meanwhile, Godwin eased his hands up her arms.

She gritted her teeth. These casual touches were the very reason adults played such games. They gave license to misbehave—and made spoilsports of anyone who preferred to remain aloof.

She would *not* be called a spoilsport. But as Godwin's hand brushed the patch of skin bared between her glove and sleeve, some stalwart place inside her came violently unseated. She felt unbalanced, a little dizzy. The shape of his mouth, that long lower lip . . . She had dreamed of his mouth, but she had never kissed it.

She bit down hard on her cheek. She must mask her inward turmoil, so the others did not remark on it. Godwin had forgotten all about that month in Munich; he would not expect her to remember it, either. How humiliating if he found out the truth!

His hand closed with a testing gentleness on her shoulder. "Well, now," he murmured. His smile settled into a gentler curve, drawing out the dimple in his cheek.

She felt struck through by the sight of it. Two years might as well have been two weeks. She remembered *everything*.

Recognize me. The thought sang through her brain, clear as ringing crystal. God help her, she had not forgotten the least detail of their time together. The conversations they had shared, their easy laughter and instant rapport—she had looked for that kind of kinship elsewhere and never found it. *Remember me, Lucas.* It felt like a prayer. *Say my name! Give me an explanation for why you left*—

"Too petite to be Countess Obolenskaya," he said in a friendly voice. "Mrs. Sobieska, then?"

The breath left her in a sigh. Of course he did not remember.

Anger pricked her. It had meant *nothing*. A fleeting flirtation: why could she not accept that?

"Wrong," cried Lipscomb, "but not all is lost. You're standing beneath the mistletoe—see if you can figure out *that* way."

Everybody laughed delightedly. Aghast, Georgie looked up. What rascal had tacked that sprig above the doorway? "No," she said, but it was too late—Godwin was leaning down. He had the instinct of a rake born rotten: despite the blindfold, his mouth found hers.

Chapter Two

I t did seem a bit odd to Lucas, as he leaned down under the mistletoe, that Mr. Lipscomb would egg him into a kiss—for by Lucas's count, Mrs. Lipscomb was the only woman remaining whose name he hadn't guessed. Or perhaps he'd lost track of the ladies in the room? He was exhausted to the bone.

Four days ago, he'd been shaken awake by the British ambassador to Paris. The sight of Viscount Lyons hanging over his bed had been bewildering enough; Lucas had wondered for a moment if the Queen had been assassinated, war declared. Surely nothing short of disaster could move such a lofty personage to steal into Lucas's apartment in the middle of the night.

But Lyons's news had proved stranger yet. Lucas's uncle was dead. That man's widow, Lady Lilleston, was due to give birth at any moment. But all of Lilleston's children, to date, had been girls.

"In short," Viscount Lyons had told him, "you're on *disponibilité* until the child is born. Get to England; you will want to pay your respects to the countess, of course. If she gives birth to a boy, you'll return to your post after Christmas. But if it's a girl, well . . ."

Here Lyons had let his pause speak for him. If Lilleston's last child was born female, Lucas would inherit his uncle's honors. *He* would be the new Earl of Lilleston.

A fine piece of irony. Lucas had never met Lilleston, nor any of the Godwin family. Given a chance, they would have cut him dead in the street. But if the newest Godwin was born with the wrong bits, Lucas would soon be their patriarch.

Moreover, he would be retired from the diplomatic service. It was one thing to have clawed his way up the ranks, despite being the son of an outcast. But the Foreign Office would never keep him on if he were made nobility. The British government did not employ earls as midgrade flunkies.

Ten hours by the tidal express to Charing Cross, then—not counting the two hours Lucas had spent hanging over a bucket on the winter-tossed seas of the Channel. A night in flea-ridden lodgings, then a long trip by rail to Harlboro Grange, where he had tendered his card to the Lillestons' butler, then cooled his heels beneath a mirror draped in mourning crepe.

Harlboro Grange had felt like a dream. The only thing Lucas's father had ever mentioned of the manor was how cold it had grown in wintertime. He'd claimed to prefer the two-room flat in which he'd raised Lucas. Strange, then, to think that Father had grown up here, a beloved son; had played, perhaps, in this very room, a domed hall some three stories high; and had slipped out through that very door to Lucas's left, to elope with Lucas's mother one night.

That elopement would never be forgiven. The butler, returning, told Lucas he was not welcome. Very well; Lucas caught the next train back to London, where he promptly booked himself into a hotel far too expensive for his salary, determined on getting some rest. Before he could fall asleep, however, a knock came: a clerk with a letter from Sir Philip Trent.

The sight of Sir Philip's scrawl had set Lucas's blood boiling. How had the old devil tracked him down?

Godwin—

Understand you are in London. Require your aid. Was forced to abandon my guests at Brisbon Hall in order to mediate a quarrel between Russia and Bulgaria. One of the guests, probably von Bittner, has broken into my study and stolen correspondence that must remain private. Get to Brisbon Hall. Find the letter (details enclosed). Do not let it leave the premises. Would ruin my negotiations.

A dozen curses, a rage so livid that it hazed Lucas's vision—no use. Lucas could not afford to cross a superior.

And so—to Brisbon Hall for the holidays. Delightful! Had Philip Trent ordered him to hell, Lucas might have felt more cheerful.

At least the hostess was nowhere in evidence; Miss Trent had retired early, no doubt as unhappy with his visit as he was. After all, Brisbon Hall was not accustomed to receiving mongrels, and Miss Trent's pride must prick keenly at the prospect of Lucas soiling her purebred circles.

Do the job. Find the letter. Leave. His aim was plain.

A game of blindman's bluff, greased by copious champagne, seemed a good strategy for putting the guests into an oblivious mood. Lucas gamely leaned down toward Mrs. Lipscomb. Her mouth briefly startled him; it was surprisingly soft, for all that she walked about so purse-lipped. But she kissed woodenly.

On the other hand, that seemed about right for a woman being mauled at her husband's behest. Two seconds, Lucas calculated, was just long enough for good manners. As he inhaled, he realized he'd been mistaken—the lady *was* wearing perfume.

No. That was soap. Lemon verbena.

Every muscle in his body contracted.

Georgie.

Not in bed, after all. In front of him. Beneath him. Soft, fragrant, and no doubt repulsed.

He tightened his grip to push her away. Instead, some perverse imp seized the reins, and goaded him to kiss her more deeply—to kiss her properly, as he'd never managed to do in Munich.

He brushed his lips over hers. *Madness.* She would slap him, soon enough. She did not consort with lowbred dogs like him.

And yet . . . her lips quivered beneath his. They felt . . . increasingly pliant. *Interested.*

Sensation redoubled, growing painfully acute: the warm velvet of her mouth. The ragged puff of her breath. The swell of her breasts against his chest . . . And that scent, God above, too pedestrian to belong to a lady in silk. It had poisoned his brain in Munich.

It was doing so again.

At the last moment, he could not resist tasting her, his tongue brushing against the seam of her mouth, simply to see . . .

Well, there was the answer he'd long wanted: she tasted like wine. Wine and want and wasted nights and an ache that should be dead, but which resurrected now as a solid knot in his throat. She tasted like stupidity. Regret, and a toxic blow to his pride: that was what Georgiana Trent tasted like.

He let go of her. He did not shove her away; he would congratulate himself later on his restraint. He withdrew in one long step as he shoved up his blindfold, and from that distance—too short; a continent would have served better—he stared at her.

She opened her eyes. It shocked him how much she looked the same—her face as round and pale as the moon; her hair the color of oak leaves in autumn, and her eyes as dark and soft as a doe's. He'd told himself he'd inflated her charms. Misremembered them.

He hadn't. Her eyes, however, did not look warm and appreciative, as his memories suggested. Instead, they *glared*.

"Forgive me," he heard himself say. "It seems you stumbled into our little game. I hope you aren't offended."

"Offended? Goodness, how could I be? You kiss like a grandfather." As he digested this blow to his vanity, she smiled. "Very good of you to join us, though. Four hours after you were expected." She wiped her mouth with her knuckles.

"Four hours?" He offered her a smile of his own, sharp on his lips. If she imagined he was here by choice—that her father's orders suited him—then she flattered herself extremely. "Curious. The journey felt far longer. Endless, really."

"Did it?" She shrugged. "You'll understand, then, why we did not hold supper for you."

"Yes, of course. That *is* a pity." This entire week had been nothing but one unhappy surprise after the next, but seeing her again—in *this* manner, with the feel of her mouth still burning through him—well, a playwright could not have scripted a blacker farce. He very much regretted missing dinner. So much easier to disdain her over the fish course. To study her coldly while picking bones out of his filet.

She was not beautiful, he told himself. Of middling height and slight build, she was perfectly *average*.

And yet . . . those eyes retained all the force that had once struck him dumb. Her low-necked evening gown of scarlet bared an entrancing expanse of creamy bosom. Worse yet, as she stepped toward him, she betrayed that peculiar grace that had riveted him in Munich. In his derangement, he had written verses that likened her to a wood nymph, daughter of the willow, her movements magically fluid.

Her subtle charms were traps for the unsuspecting. He knew that now.

He took her hand and sketched a low bow. "It *is* a pleasure to see you again, Miss Trent. Two years, has it been?" And one week, exactly.

"Only two years? Goodness. It feels ages longer." Her bland smile widened as she glanced beyond him to the encircling diplomats. "Well," she said as she pulled her hand free, "now we are all assembled, I am very happy to commence our merry little Christmas!"

Her cheer seemed misplaced, overstated. After a puzzled hesitation, a few of the guests offered halting applause. After all, they had already been in residence for three days.

Clearly Miss Trent had not inherited her father's bonhomie. She favored books over parties; she disdained common entertainments, much as she disdained the common man. She needed help here.

Girding himself to his duty, Lucas stepped in. "Yes," he said, "welcome to one and all. I am honored to preside in Sir Philip's place while he—"

A sharp elbow in his ribs sent his teeth slamming together. Miss Trent had developed some muscle. "As your hostess," she said sweetly, "I have designed a program of events for the next three days. You will find them waiting in your sitting rooms. We begin our formal festivities tomorrow, when we will rendezvous for breakfast at half six before we set out on our first expedition. Does that agree with everyone?"

"Half . . . six?" said Countess Obolenskaya. She looked aghast. "Six in the *morning*?"

"The English are a race of early birds," balding Mr. Lipscomb informed her. "Sir Trent is a rare night owl, but his daughter, you see, is English to the bone."

"That's right," said Miss Trent. "And my father has left me very clear instructions: I am to introduce you to all the local customs, the purely English way of celebrating the holidays."

"Half six," the countess repeated, dazed.

"Would half eight suit you better?" Lucas said. When Miss Trent turned on him with a scowl, pure malice made him add: "Yes, half eight, then. Everyone agreed?"

Eager exclamations, nods. "Splendid!" said Mr. Lipscomb, and tugged down his jacket. "Gives us a bit of time for dancing, tonight. Lord von Bittner—help me with the carpets?"

Lucas took Miss Trent's arm, ignoring her resistance as he pulled her toward the privacy of the far corner of the room. Every fixture had been trimmed in holly and fir; the walls veritably bristled with holiday cheer. He took a deep breath, letting the fragrance of the evergreens clear his thoughts. "We should come up with a plan," he said.

Miss Trent yanked free. "For what? Your orders are clear."

Lucas took a survey of the possible culprits. Lipscomb, currently kneeling to roll up one side of the carpet, was from the Home Office—beyond suspicion. Von Bittner, who was kicking at the other end of the rug, was the one whom Trent suspected of the theft. But Lucas would not rule out Sobieski and Obolensky—nor their wives. Diplomats were trained to be canny; their wives, in Lucas's experience, were born to it. "Your father suggests I start with the German. What's your opinion?"

"I have none."

He glanced at her sidelong. The woman *he* remembered had nursed opinions on every subject under the sun. But this one seemed content to bite her lip as she stared toward the piano, where Mrs. Lipscomb was testing the first notes of a reel.

Rouge would have helped Miss Trent's pallor. But she didn't require powder; her skin was flawless. It had felt like silk beneath his touch.

And that was the only time he would touch it. He cleared his throat. "You've spent the last three days with this lot. Surely you have an inkling of their characters."

"None whatsoever." Her great dark eyes flashed toward him. "I pray you find that letter quickly, though. I did not plan for a party of ten."

Her asperity startled him. He had imagined, at worst, mockery or contempt—not cold hostility.

No doubt she thought him an upstart for daring to have admired her in Munich. But what had she imagined her effect would be? When a woman looked at a man as she had done—when she listened to his thoughts so intently, proving warm, amused, even delighted in reply—

Well. She'd shown him a thousand different encouragements, none of them reflective of what she actually felt for him. At least she was being honest now. "I'll start tomorrow in the Germans' rooms," he said curtly. "With any luck, I'll find the letter by noon and be gone before dinner."

"Oh, dear. Will luck be required?" She laid a hand on his arm, gazing at him with overstated sympathy. "And here I imagined you'd have a talent for sneaking into places. After all, Mr. Godwin, you *excel* at sneaking out of them."

He gritted his teeth. She referred, of course, to his impromptu flight from Munich. Whose fault had *that* been? It took great restraint not to ask. "Luck can't hurt." There, a fine piece of neutrality: he truly was a diplomat, after all.

She continued to stare at him. "You're shorter than I remembered."

Delightful! "It must be from the grave burden of steering our nation's course overseas. The responsibility does weigh heavily."

"On the shoulders of a second secretary?" Paired with her words, her smile stung. He had moved up the ranks faster than any man in history without aristocratic patronage, but a second secretaryship hardly carried real power. "Of course, you take your duties very seriously," she went on. "Marvelous, how you manage to balance them with all the time you spend drinking absinthe at the Chat Noir!"

Lucas inwardly cursed. That single night's excursion to Montmartre would hound his reputation forever. He would never again go exploring in the company of poets! As a breed, they seemed to derive their inspiration from bar brawls. "You've been keeping track of me? How flattering."

"Oh, one could not ignore you if she tried. Newspapers these days have no notion of what is fit to print. All manner of rubbish collects in the social columns!"

"Indeed?" he said. "I suppose you must take particular interest in that section, since you so rarely find yourself included in it." As her eyes narrowed, Lucas added with feigned haste, "Not for want of invitations, I expect. Surely not! You simply prefer . . . books."

Her color rose. No longer pale, she. In a minute, she would match the cluster of holly berries tapping at her shoulder. "As Sir Philip's daughter, I am naturally forced to be selective with my time. Otherwise, between this soiree and that ball, I would never get anything done."

"Sir Philip's daughter, of course." He gave her a very kind smile. "I expect Sir Philip's daughter would be in demand even if she sported horns and a tail." Here he paused, casting a questioning look down her figure.

When he glanced up again, she had fixed him with a glare that might well have conjured hellfire. "You're right," she said, deadly sweet. "I rarely go into company. I find the diplomatic crowd very tedious. All talk, no substance. I suppose that is what such circles require. No wonder you flourish there!"

"Will you join us?" called Mr. Sobieski. At the piano, Mrs. Lipscomb had finally found her rhythm; the couples were lining up in the middle of the room.

"*No,*" said Lucas, as Miss Trent snapped, "Indeed not."

He swallowed a laugh, then could not resist leaning toward her to murmur in her ear, "Ah, how like-minded we are. Birds of a feather, after all."

She glanced up at him through her lashes. Too late, he realized his stupidity. From this close, the resplendence of her eyes, the fragrance of her skin, were unavoidable.

In that moment, he remembered everything he'd tried so long to forget. How fondly she had once gazed on him. How badly he'd ached to win her laughter, and to keep her good opinion.

But he'd never had it in the first place. That had been made very clear to him.

His gut tightened; his hand fisted to resist the sudden, astonishingly fierce urge to touch her face, to force her to speak to him honestly. *What happened, two years ago?* He swallowed down the words like rocks.

For her own part, a shadow darkened her expression. She looked away. "Birds of a feather?" she said softly. "Well, Mr. Godwin, you certainly do have a talent for taking flight. I will follow your example now, I think."

Without another word to the company, she turned on her heel and walked out.

Chapter Three

December 23

She'd let him drive her out of her own drawing room last night. This morning, Georgie was determined not to repeat her mistake. She pounded at his door, heedless of the noise it made. By her instruction, he'd been lodged in the oldest and shabbiest wing, far away from the comforts of the other guest suites. Nobody would overhear.

At long last, the lock scraped, and the door swung open. Mr. Godwin, bleary-eyed, his square jaw darkened by stubble, blinked at her. "What time is it?" he asked in a graveled voice as he yanked at the knot that held his robe closed.

His throat was bare. She could see the hollow where his clavicle joined. His tan did not fade below his neck. Perhaps he was perfectly golden . . . everywhere.

She yanked her gaze away. "A quarter to six." Was he wearing anything beneath that garment? "I'll wait while you dress."

"We said half eight for breakfast."

She had not said it. She turned back, scowling. With his

black hair disordered and that stubble shadowing his face, he looked like a pirate. The robe clung too closely to his body: despite his shenanigans at vulgar Parisian stews, he retained the physique of an athlete, broad-shouldered and irritatingly muscular.

To think she had once esteemed his wit and learning! A man like him traded only on his looks. "Go back to sleep," she said, "by all means. You were ordered here to find a letter, but yes, why not laze about? The von Bittners were up before dawn and have gone into the woods to find a Christmas tree. *I* shall search their rooms. I already had a brief look yesterday."

He dragged a hand through his black hair. Then, without another word, he stepped backward and slammed shut the door.

She crossed her arms and stood tapping her foot for several long minutes before he emerged again, dressed in a dark walking suit, his jaw still unshaven.

She turned on her heel and started for the stairs. His footsteps announced his pursuit. "Goodness," she said without looking back, "you took so long, I imagined you had made time to shave. Do *all* gentlemen take such care with their attire, or are you particularly . . . peacockish?"

He made an ill-tempered grunt. "Look here, Georgie—"

Everything in her contracted. "*Miss Trent.*"

His pause seemed to last forever. She kept her eyes fastened on the path ahead, cutting through a hallway festooned with red ribbon and fragrant pine boughs.

"Pardon me," came his voice at last, very gruff. "I am not quite awake yet."

A strange nervousness churned through her. She pressed her hand over her belly, crushing the commotion as she walked more quickly yet. What was she to make of such a statement? In his sleep, he still called her Georgie?

Did that mean he *dreamed* of her?

A peculiar habit, for a man who had forgotten her so easily!

She came to a stop by the von Bittners' door, knocking for good measure. When no answer came, she pulled a key ring from her pocket. "A fine state of affairs," she muttered as she fumbled with the lock. He certainly did not dream of her. She felt irritated with herself, with him, with this dreadful situation. "Breaking into my own guests' rooms."

"You needn't help with this."

His voice came very near to her ear, making her flinch. "The sooner done, the better." She sounded breathless. Her nape prickled with awareness of how closely he stood. He did not smell like cologne this morning. That delicious scent was male skin, nothing more.

Curse him.

When she fumbled the key again, his hand closed over hers. She froze. How large his palm was. How hot his bare skin felt against hers.

I never thought to meet a woman like you, he'd told her once.

Did he really dream of her?

He turned her hand, and the key with it. The door opened, and she stepped free, mouth dry, and walked onward into the von Bittners' sitting room.

The mess gave her pause. The room had not been so disordered last night. Valises lay open, shawls and gloves strewn across the carpet. Through the door ajar to the bedchamber, she glimpsed a dress sagging from the wardrobe.

Outside, a bird warbled, startling her. Best get to it. On a deep breath, she knelt by an open valise. "You take the bedchamber," she said.

He walked past her. "How long ago did they leave the house?"

"Twenty minutes or so." She picked through the jumbled bric-a-brac: handkerchiefs, hairpins, letters—all addressed to Lady von Bittner. "A footman is watching the path for them; he'll fetch us as soon as he spots them."

"A *footman?*"

His sharp tone drew her attention upward. Naturally, the sun chose that very moment to break free of the clouds, spilling through the windows, illuminating Lucas Godwin in a blaze. Light gleamed off his black hair and his long, curled lashes; it washed like honey down the perfect bones of his face.

Her gut gave a pained twist. The first time she had seen him, across a crowded ballroom in Munich, she'd supposed him vain. The smooth fall of his black hair, the quick readiness of his smiles, even the way he moved—his easy, powerful grace—had made her conscious of the clumsiness of her own body. She had no rhythm for dancing.

But on their introduction, he had surprised her with a compliment to her essays in the diplomatic circular. *I've a fondness for Shakespeare myself,* he'd said. *You claimed this week that he has lessons to teach us about diplomacy. But I always thought his finest works concerned warfare.*

She had shrugged. *Diplomacy is warfare, sir. Its weapons are words, to be certain; but its aim is the same as that of any other battle: to force the other side to surrender ground.*

His smile had faded briefly, then redoubled. *Would you care to waltz?* he'd asked. And then, as she'd taken his hand, he'd added, *A waltz, and a debate: for I mean to change your mind on certain matters.*

What would those be?

Dance with me, and find out.

And if you fail to change my mind?

Then I'll have to apply to you again tomorrow. He'd offered her a beautiful smile. *Perhaps I should aim for failure, then.*

She'd never imagined herself vulnerable to flirtation. But suddenly, she'd felt made of wax . . . melting, loosening, beneath the warmth of his regard.

You dance divinely, Miss Trent. So he'd said a minute later.

And you lie very smoothly, Mr. Godwin. For she had just tripped over his foot.

He'd laughed, flashing perfectly white teeth. *But I was to blame for that stumble. I confess, I was thinking again on your essays. The one published last month—do you really think Romeo and Juliet base fools?*

Such ordinary conversation. But polite banter had quickly yielded to quips, and quips to spirited debate. Romeo and Juliet, she said, had been driven not by love but infatuation. For Shakespeare's finest lovers, one must look to the pairs united by an intellectual as well as physical chemistry, chief among which were—

Beatrice and Benedict, he'd replied.

Yes. She'd felt as surprised as though he'd given her a gift. *Exactly.*

By the end of the waltz, she'd been dazzled and delighted, laughing with him like an old friend—she, Sir Philip's bookish daughter; he, the rising star of the diplomatic corps, whom everyone wished to know.

When, the next day, he had paid a call on her, her father had seemed quite astonished, asking the butler to repeat the message. *Here to see my daughter? Are you certain?* But to Georgie's amazement, she had not felt surprised at all. Many gentlemen found her dull and bookish, but Mr. Godwin was different. His interest felt *right* to her. Inevitable. A curious joy had seized her then, at once exhilarating and profoundly comforting. *At last,* she'd thought. *At last, here he is: the man who sees me as I am.*

And now, two years later, after abandoning her without a fare-thee-well, he stood before her again, scowling at her as though she were some idiotic child.

"You informed the *staff* of our plan to search these rooms?" Mr. Godwin sounded incredulous. "How could you possibly be so indis—"

"The staff," she said through her teeth as she rose, "are not your concern." With her father so often posted abroad, Georgie had all but grown up at Brisbon Hall. The butler and Cook, three footmen and six maids—they were as close to her as family. Closer, in fact. "I trust them implicitly."

He stared at her a moment longer. "Of course," he muttered, then turned back into the bedroom, digging through a bag slung haphazardly across a Chippendale chair. "I recall how fondly you spoke of them."

The muffled remark caught her off guard. Until now, they had behaved by tacit agreement as though they had never exchanged confidences. She frowned at his back. "You remember that conversation, do you?"

He shot her a brief, unreadable look. "Do I strike you as senile?"

She shoved away the valise. "No, certainly not." Shallow, deceitful, and fickle, on the other hand . . . "But I suppose you make a habit," she went on, "of befriending any number of people, and collecting any number of"—*heartfelt, private, painfully shared*—"intimacies from them. So it does surprise me, somewhat, that you should remember my trifling discussion of Brisbon Hall."

He laid down the bag and faced her, jaw squaring.

They were going to have it out, then. A great pressure swelled in her chest, shortening her breath. He would admit now that he'd misled her. Good! She was sick of feeling as though she were the fool for having mistaken his interest as romantic. He *had* encouraged her hopes. He would admit it and apologize for it now.

"We should hurry," he said flatly. "The sooner we find the letter, the sooner I can leave."

The words slapped her. She looked blindly down at the

valise. How she loathed him! "Naturally. You have better places to be, I suppose."

"I suppose," he said, and turned back to his work.

But perhaps he didn't. His parents had passed away within months of each other, during his first year of service abroad. He had told her of it during a stroll through Munich's Botanical Garden. His father had been a great inspiration to him, it was clear. *For so long, I aimed only to make him proud. Once he passed, I felt . . . lost, I suppose.*

Her heart had swelled so painfully for him then. She had wanted above anything to give him comfort.

I know what it means to feel alone, she'd told him. *Orphaned, in a way.* Her father was so rarely with her—and he *expected* her to live up to the Trent legacy; he did not congratulate her for doing what he considered to be her duty. *Treasure your memories of your parents' pride in you . . .*

Bitterness goaded her to her feet. She went to the sideboard, pulling out drawers with violent force. How expertly Godwin had cultivated her sympathy—and for what? He'd manipulated her for his own entertainment. Destroyed her vanity and pride for fun. She had never met a man better designed for diplomacy.

She cast a sharp look at him. He was rummaging through the wardrobe, pausing now and then to bat away the exuberant ruffles and flounces of Lady von Bittner's ball gown. "Surely," she said, "you have *some* friend who will miss you on Christmas. Just *one.*"

He looked up with a snort. "You certainly are Sir Philip's daughter."

She crossed her arms. "I can't imagine what you mean."

As he straightened, his smile looked unkind. "Your father has a talent for stiletto jabs." He mimed the action. "In-out, so quickly that his victims don't realize they're bleeding until after they've bowed their thanks."

She bit her cheek to prevent a protest. *She* was not the

villain here. "How remarkable! You would imagine my father your enemy, rather than your *superior.*"

"Oh, no," he said flatly. "I could never forget that, Miss Trent." The sunlight fell slantwise across his blue eyes, illuminating them like stained glass; two unjust pieces of beauty in his liar's face, which she'd briefly adored beyond anything.

Would she ever feel so about another man? She hadn't managed it yet. Thoughts of him—of what he'd *pretended* to be—had ruined her.

Suddenly she felt weighted by stones. "You should have refused to come." All she wanted was to forget him. Why was it so difficult? "You should have told him to send someone else." *If you had any shame, you would have done.*

His jaw flexed. "As you said. He is my superior. Far be it from me to challenge his orders."

"Of course." The words scoured her throat like copper. "For the sake of your career, you would do anything, I expect." He would court a naïve wallflower for her connections—and then drop her flat the moment opportunity called him elsewhere, promising to advance his career more expediently.

He gave a grim, humorless tug of his mouth. "It's the lot of us lowly commoners. We must look after our living, rather than count on an inheritance."

His veiled jabs grew tiring. Did he truly think to make *her* feel guilty? "Why, imagine it—you almost sound as if *you* were the injured party."

His brows drew together. But before he could speak, footsteps sounded in the hallway outside, and Lady von Bittner's laughter rang out.

Georgie threw a panicked look around the room. There was no way to escape—nowhere to hide.

On a soft curse, Mr. Godwin lunged for her wrist. "Come." He hauled her into the bedchamber, then lifted her by the waist and thrust her into the wardrobe.

Chapter Four

Hiding in the wardrobe had not been Lucas's finest idea. For one thing, it was crammed full of highly perfumed, deucedly scratchy gowns. For another, it was far too small to house those gowns and the two of them besides. Necessity compelled him to wrap his arms around Miss Trent; there was no other place to put them. Her waist was small, her breasts an intolerably conspicuous presence against his forearms. As for the rest of her . . .

She was not wearing a bustle. A fine time to prove bohemian! He prayed that her petticoats were thick enough to disguise his reaction. Certainly she made no sound or movement to suggest otherwise. A slight tremble ran through her occasionally—but that was surely due to fear of discovery. The von Bittners were in their sitting room, having a laughing conversation in German.

"What are they discussing?" she whispered. Her hair brushed against his chin, soft and ticklish.

"The most robust specimen imaginable," Lady von

Bittner was saying. "A broad build, but very perky. Handsome, I think everyone must agree."

He frowned. "They're . . . praising some man's features. Why? Have you forgotten your German?"

Miss Trent stiffened, which was not at all what he required, since it solidified her position against him. "It's a bit rusty," she said with dignity.

He was glad one of them felt dignified at the moment.

"Which man?" she asked.

He tuned his attention to the conversation. "Oh, indeed," Lord von Bittner was agreeing. "A bold, cheeky aspect all around. And such a muscular trunk!"

"I thought you would take three strokes to finish," Lady von Bittner replied. "But you did it in one! I don't think you broke a sweat."

"Well?" Miss Trent whispered.

Lucas felt very uncertain now of the wisdom of translating. "I'm not sure."

"I was surprised," Lord von Bittner said. "Such a sound bottom, too. A sound bottom is crucial, I find."

"Crucial," his wife agreed.

Lucas bit down hard on his cheek. Either the von Bittners shared a very peculiar interest, or . . .

"Particularly since they don't have the proper pot for it," Lady von Bittner went on. "Imagine if it should topple!"

Lucas grinned. "They're discussing the *Tannenbaum* they found."

"The Christmas tree?" Miss Trent sighed. "I do wish—"

Floorboards creaked. The von Bittners were on the move. Miss Trent squirmed, and Lucas swallowed a curse. His next deep breath was full of her—of her fragrance, the softness of her hair, her warmth. How well she fit against him! She had always fitted so; taking her into his arms for the first time had felt like a puzzle coming together at last.

He still vividly remembered that embrace. She had offered it in sympathy, during their stroll through the Botanical Garden in Munich.

I am so sorry, she'd whispered against his shoulder. *Your parents sound wonderful. I wish I could have met them.*

He'd realized then that she'd never heard the gossip; that he needed to tell her the whole of it. But the feel of her in his arms, like a revelation unfolding, had stopped him. *How could I risk losing this?* he'd thought. *Not now. Later . . .*

"Look at this mess!" Lady von Bittner's voice came very close, causing them both to flinch. "You would think the maids might have straightened up. The staff is poorly managed, I think."

Judging by the jerk of Miss Trent's shoulders, she understood *that* bit of German well enough.

"I'll ring for someone," said Lord von Bittner. Footsteps came closer yet. They were about to be found out—

A banging came at the door. An unfamiliar voice, a man with a country accent, announced that the von Bittners were wanted downstairs immediately.

"I'd thought to change before breakfast," Lady von Bittner said querulously. "But this place is such a tip!" Her voice faded as she headed toward the exit. "Fetch somebody to straighten it, boy. How the Trents put up with this—"

The sharp slam of the door cut off the rest of her words.

Miss Trent did not wait a moment after the couple's departure to exclaim, "Blaming my staff for this disorder! What gall!"

Lucas pushed open the wardrobe, taking a deep breath. In large doses, Lady von Bittner's perfume smelled more like poison.

Miss Trent leapt out of the wardrobe, then turned back, hands on her hips, to glare at him. "You're looking very relieved," she said. "I suppose you were dying of horror, imagining what should happen if we were caught." She tipped her head, her dudgeon fading to puzzlement. "Don't you mean to come out of there?"

"In a moment." He remained in his awkward crouch, forty pounds of ball gown crushing into his back, praying for his rampant condition to subside.

She rolled her eyes. "Paralyzed by panic, no doubt. Well, rest assured—I wouldn't have married you. I would rather be ruined."

It took a moment to follow her meaning. "You thought . . ." He laughed despite himself. "*That* was your worry? That the von Bittners would find us hiding in their wardrobe and think us overcome by passion?"

The color drained from her face. "No," she choked. "As you say—what a laughable idea!" She turned away, stalking out of the bedchamber.

Her reaction baffled him sufficiently to tame his bodily humors. He stepped out of the wardrobe and followed her into the sitting room, catching her by the elbow as she took hold of the outer doorknob. "What is it?" he said. "What did I say?"

"Absolutely nothing." She would not look at him. "Naturally, the thought is absurd. Carried away with passion? You, with me? The thought is absurd."

He dropped her arm. A very fine thing that she had no grasp of the male anatomy. "Indeed," he bit out. "God forbid! A more preposterous mésalliance, I'm sure nobody could imagine."

She twisted, spearing him with a blazing look. "Quite right. Why, I would rather consort with—with—"

"Keep thinking," he goaded. "I'm sure you'll eventually find someone worthy of you. The Prince of Wales?" When she wrinkled her nose, he said sarcastically, "Oh, pardon me. The bloodlines *are* rather suspect. Too *German* for a Trent."

She huffed out a breath. "If you imagine I am forced to look to a *married* man for attention, even a prince, I'll have you know that I—I am quite—"

"What?" He was burningly, bitterly curious to know. What pristine, incontrovertibly pedigreed gentleman qualified as worthy of Miss Georgiana Trent's approval?

"I am quite happily affianced!" The words exploded from her with such force that she herself looked shocked. "To a—a very upstanding gentleman of considerable charm *and* fortune!"

The news staggered him. For a moment, he could only goggle at her. But . . . of course she was betrothed. Had he imagined she would remain unwed forever? A woman as winsome as Georgiana Trent, whose family recommended itself not only by its age but also its wealth and influence, would have no shortage of suitors—even if her taste was selective indeed.

"Well," he managed to croak, "my felicitations. Who is the fortunate gentleman?"

Her gaze broke from his, wandering to the far corner of the room. Obviously, discussing her private affairs with one such as *him* mortified her extremely. "Mr. Augustus Brumkin," she said.

"Augustus Brumkin." The very name felt like death in his mouth. He did not want to picture the man, but an image sprang forth, so vivid that it might have been conjured by magic: resplendently blond; bluff and hale and irritatingly overfed. In Lucas's mind, Mr. Brumkin posed, one hand in his waistcoat, with his pack of hounds brawling at his heels, a fine horse of seventeen hands at his shoulder, and a bloody manor looming on the hilltop behind him, pennants flying.

"Yes," she said. "That is—no. *Sir* Augustus. He is a—baronet."

"Oh, very good," he said. "So you'll be Lady Brumkin." The Trents would settle for no less. "My congratulations to you." He took a step backward to sketch a mocking bow and nearly slipped on one of Lady von Bittner's shawls.

At the same time, they both recalled where they were. Miss Trent yanked open the door. "Hurry," she snapped.

But he felt curiously indifferent to his own escape. He waited until she had slipped down the hall, until her footsteps had faded from the stair, before stepping out.

And when he shut the door behind him, he had only the strength to lean against it, and remember again how to breathe.

Sir Augustus bloody Brumkin. Had there ever been a name better suited to buffoonish, inbred *idiocy*?

Chapter Five

What the devil had possessed her? Georgie asked herself this at regular intervals throughout the morning, as she led her conspicuously unenthused guests on a tour of two local farms. Judging by their reddened eyes and sallow complexions, the Sobieskis and Lipscombs were suffering from last night's excess of champagne. The Obolenskys, on the other hand, proved noxious in a different vein as they helped each other around piles of dung—pointing them out with increasingly loud giggles, as though dung were an affliction unique to English sheep. Nevertheless, of the whole group, Georgie felt certain that she proved the most pitiable specimen. Inventing a fiancé wholesale!

Her pride had demanded it. Seeing Lucas Godwin laugh derisively at the very prospect of seducing her—it had grated beyond her ability to bear. Still . . . *Augustus Brumkin*? Could she not have invented a more dignified name? Brumkin! Why not call him Bumpkin and be done with it?

After the agricultural tour came tea at the vicar's house.

As Georgie privately willed time to run backward so she could invent a better name for her betrothed (*Matthew Hill. Charles White.* Even *John Brown* would have sounded more distinguished), Mr. Sobieski asked the vicar where the gold was stored, as if this were a cathedral rather than a humble vicarage. Meanwhile, Count Obolensky *happened* across a bottle of sacramental wine, *happened* to take it into his possession, and then *happened* to pour it into his teacup—twice! As though nobody would notice!

The vicar noticed. He gave Georgie a shocked look, which she took as a sign that it was time to hurry the group along to the bakeshop. Perhaps she would not take them to church on Christmas, after all.

The village itself seemed to delight the diplomats. Swanhaven was no larger than a single long street, thatched houses and shingled shops winding sinuously along the riverbank toward the green. The sky was overcast, but every window glowed with the light of Christmas candles. The bare-branched trees lining the lane had been strung with ivy, their trunks wrapped in red ribbon. At the end of the road, a group of young girls stood on the green, singing "God Bless Ye Merry Gentlemen" in high, pure falsettos to a small crowd.

The rest of the village was crammed inside Mr. Tilney's bakeshop, where the atmosphere felt close and warm, rich with the scents of cinnamon and nutmeg. Perhaps the sacramental wine had been parceled out rather more widely than Georgie had noticed. As her flock crowded inside, they jostled each other and joked with unseemly familiarity to those already queued at the counter. Fearing a spectacle, Georgie stepped up to remind Mr. Tilney of his offer: he had agreed to provide her guests a sampling of culinary delicacies particular to an English Christmas.

Tilney was a squat, broad redhead who took his trade very seriously. "Right," he said, frowning at the lot. "But they'll buy, afterward, won't they? For they're driving out my customers."

"I assure you, Brisbon Hall will make a sizable purchase," she said.

"That was Mr. Jones what just left. He was on the hook for three trays of mince pies."

She glanced over her shoulder and saw the countess blowing kisses at Mr. Jones's retreating back. "Send them to the Hall instead," she said hastily as she turned back. "Indeed, mince pies are a fine idea. Let's start with them." She clapped to call her guests' attention.

Like errant children, they straggled into a semicircle around her. She introduced Mr. Tilney, then retreated to the back of the room to watch.

Mr. Tilney held up a mince pie, rotating it right and left to show its dimpled crust. Tilney, now there was a fine name. Far more respectable than Brumkin! Any woman could hold her head high, betrothed to a man by that surname.

The baker handed his pie to Mrs. Sobieska. "See the shape," he said. "What does it remind you of?

"A bean," said Mrs. Sobieska brightly, before taking a large bite.

"The human kidney," said Mr. Lipscomb.

Mrs. Sobieska gagged.

Mr. Tilney, scowling, said, "It's an oval, aye?"

"Bit lopsided for an oval," Mr. Lipscomb said.

"'Tis an *oval* in the shape of a *manger*," Mr. Tilney bit out. "Like the manger where the Christ child was born! And as for the savory bits inside"—here his livid gaze swung to Mrs. Sobieska, who froze mid-chew—"those be gifts of the Magi. So if you're Christian, swallow them down!"

Mr. Tilney's provenance seemed doubtful to Georgie, but among diplomats, facts meant little, so long as the story seemed persuasive. Mrs. Sobieska swallowed obediently. "Oh," she said. "Oh, it's quite delicious!"

Hands shot out. With a satisfied smirk, Mr. Tilney continued to distribute pies.

Relieved, Georgie settled her weight against the plate-glass window. The bell rang overhead, and Mr. Godwin stepped inside.

"No letter," he said curtly as he joined her along the wall. "Not in the von Bittners' rooms, nor the Sobieskis', either."

She sighed. "The Obolenskys next, then."

He jammed his hands into his pockets and nodded, his mouth a tight line. "Will you take them home after this?"

"Thank goodness, yes."

He glanced at her. "Given you trouble?"

She smiled faintly. "They're diplomats, Mr. Godwin. Their livelihood depends on trouble. When they find none, they must invent it, lest they be thrown out of a job."

He blinked. "A cynical view, from Sir Philip's daughter." But the hard set of his mouth loosened; after a moment, he leaned back against the wall.

Perhaps, she thought, she should try to strike a truce. Quarreling certainly hadn't served her. Why, if they argued again, she would probably invent a secret wedding for herself, and two well-behaved children besides.

She leaned back, too. "Pardon me," she said politely. "I recall that you were an idealist about the cause of diplomacy." He'd spoken most impassionedly in Munich about his hope to do good in the world; to temper the sharp edges of British power abroad. "I don't mean that all diplomats are so self-serving."

He snorted. "Perhaps I'm not an idealist so much as a pragmatist. As a second secretary, after all, I have little scope to enrich myself."

She recalled her unkind jab about his position last night. "I doubt you would abuse your power, regardless."

He cast her a sidelong, measuring glance. "That is kind of you," he said after a pause. "I suppose we may soon find out. I have it on rather good authority that if I remain in the— Well. There is a rumor that I might be made secretary of legation next year."

He spoke stiffly, as though prepared for her mockery. But such news did not deserve it. "Goodness," she murmured, making a rapid calculation. "By thirty? You would be the youngest in the history of the service, I believe."

His color rose. "A rumor only. It may be empty."

Truce, she reminded herself. "I doubt it." Now *she* sounded stiff. "Everyone always spoke of you so highly. And you have—" She cleared her throat. "You have charm, sir, in addition to your erudition. And charm, I fear, is the main thing for a diplomat."

He looked at her directly, his blue eyes somber. "You fear it, do you?"

The solemn weight of his attention made her pulse trip. *Yes,* she feared his charm. Any wise woman would fear charm when paired with looks like his.

She felt herself flush at the thought. "It's terribly warm in here, isn't it?" She made a show of fanning herself. "Mr. Tilney must be using all the ovens."

He glanced toward the counter, and she felt released, able to breathe again. "Gingerbread," Mr. Tilney barked, holding up a cookie in the rudimentary shape of a man. The diplomats murmured and nodded.

Lord von Bittner raised his hand. "That is not an English food," he volunteered. "That is a German tradition."

"German!" Mr. Tilney bared his teeth, then turned the gingerbread man upside down and snapped its head off.

Audible gasps followed.

"It's *English,*" he said.

Lord von Bittner cleared his throat. "Perhaps . . . it is both."

Tilney held out the gingerbread head to Lord von Bittner, who accepted it with great dignity.

"Ah, the spirit of Christmastide," muttered Mr. Godwin.

Her giggle startled her. She felt him glance over at her again, but kept her eyes trained on Mr. Tilney. "Watch them go back to Germany talking of our curious rituals," she said. "England, where they must behead their gingerbread man before they eat him."

"No stranger than the Swedes burning their straw Yule goats," he said.

"Perhaps we should make it a tradition, then!"

He made a sound of amusement. "If you told me it already was one, I might believe you. I haven't spent a Christmas in England for eight—no, nine years."

"And what a fine holiday for you, doing my father's dirty work." When his expression darkened, she wanted to kick herself. Why bring *that* up? Quickly she rushed on. "Of course, I imagine Paris has *much* to recommend itself during the holidays. Do you hope to stay there, once you're promoted?"

"Paris is lovely," he said. "Very comfortable. But I may request a farther-flung posting. The Ottoman Empire. China, perhaps."

"China!" She felt a strange clutching in her chest. That was very far away indeed.

He shrugged. "There's real work to be done there." His lips twitched. "And no absinthe, you'll be glad to know."

Hesitantly, she smiled. Perhaps this truce might work, after all. "Well, I suppose in your shoes, I would long for adventure, too." Imagine it, having the entire world ranged before you, any spot on the map open to your choice! Where on earth would she start? "I think I should choose Persia myself."

He turned to her, his weight braced by one shoulder against the wall. He had found time to shave, but his hair remained unruly, unfashionably long; he wiped a dark cowlick off his brow as he said, "Persia. Yes. Did you keep up with your studies of the language, then?"

She refused to let the question startle her. A truce meant speaking companionably, without bristling at each reference to the past. "I fear it proved too much for me. Anyway, I simply wanted to read the poetry, and it turns out that several gentlemen have undertaken studies recently. Mr. Whinfield has a lovely manuscript in press of Jalal al-din Rumi's verses—have you read it?"

"I'm afraid I haven't."

"Oh, it's remarkable. 'Did my beloved only touch me with his lips—'" She came to an abrupt stop, realizing that the verse was hardly suitable for public discussion. Her enthusiasm had always outstripped her mindfulness of decorum.

But he was watching, his expression intent. "Finish it," he said.

"I'll send you a copy," she muttered.

"Shy, Miss Trent?"

The challenging note in his voice made her spine stiffen. She locked eyes with him. "'Did my beloved only touch me with his lips, / I too, like the flute, would burst out in melody.'"

He stared at her a moment longer—oddly, searchingly. "That is very fine," he said quietly.

His gaze was too intense to hold. She slid her palms down her skirts, knocking away a stray speck of flour.

"Why don't you have the choice, Georgie?"

She caught her breath. But he was frowning slightly; she did not think he realized his own slip of the tongue. "What choice?" she asked.

"The choice to go," he said.

"To . . . Persia?" She tried to laugh. "All on my own? I should think my father would have something to say about that. I do depend on him for an allowance, you know."

"So find someone willing to go with you," he said. "A companion in adventure. That's what you always wanted."

She turned away from him blindly, fixing her face in the general direction of the others. *I tried, Lucas.*

I thought I had found you.

He broke the silence by clearing his throat. "God save us. It's come to goose pies, has it?"

For Mr. Tilney had hoisted aloft a fine specimen—the pastry crust gleaming with a coating of egg white. "But you love goose pie," Georgie said without thinking. "Eating the enemy!"

Their gazes caught again. He must be remembering the same moment—that enchanted discussion they'd had at a Christmas party in Munich, keeping to themselves the entire night, lost in their laughter. Would he deny recalling it?

After a moment, he offered her the faintest smile. "Yes," he said. "I'm a diplomat, after all. We never forgive or forget."

A strange relief swam through her, making her feel almost giddy. "Poor geese! They crossed the wrong man."

He cocked a dark brow. "Had you been attacked by them at the age of eight—for the mere sin of attempting to feed them!—you would nurse a grudge, too."

"They *are* dreadful creatures, aren't they? I—" She paused as Countess Obolenskaya approached to hand them each a slice of the pie.

Mr. Tilney was the finest baker in the realm; his crusts could not be rivaled. As Georgie swallowed, she exchanged an amazed look with Mr. Godwin. "I suppose revenge is a dish best served hot, after all."

He laughed. "Still fond of Shakespeare, I see."

"Oh, no, that isn't Shakespeare. Everybody thinks so, though. Do you know—" She hesitated, wondering at herself. Would she confide this in him, when she had not yet shared it with anyone? "I've been writing a series of essays, a study of the common phrases misattributed to him. Trying to track down their origins."

"A fine project," he said. "I had wondered if you'd stopped writing. That is . . ." He brushed his hands free of crumbs, cleared his throat. "I no longer see your essays in the diplomat circular."

Had he been looking for them? "I think the editors grew tired of the subject of Shakespeare."

"You had other subjects in mind," he said. "Your piece on Machiavelli in his humanist guise—that would have drawn a great deal of notice. Perhaps you never submitted it, though."

She stared at him. She had given that draft to him two days before he'd left Germany—the very last day she'd seen him. He had taken leave of her that day by kissing her fingers, with no word of his impending departure.

Her fingers, her skin, her entire body, had felt more alive that day than in any before it, or any to follow.

"Your final taste," Mr. Tilney announced. "Plum pudding. Gather round now; you'll each need a spoon."

Mr. Godwin made no motion to approach the counter. As for herself, Georgie felt curiously rooted in place. "You read that piece?" she asked.

Mr. Godwin's jaw flexed. He was staring very fixedly now at the pudding eaters. "Of course."

"You approved of it?"

He slid her a quick, unreadable glance. "I always had the highest esteem for your scholarship, Miss Trent."

Yes. Alone among the men of her acquaintance, he'd seemed to take a personal, deeply felt delight in her bookish pursuits.

"Yet you never wrote me to give your opinion," she said very softly.

"No," he said.

She waited, but he did not go on. After a moment, he

shrugged. "I expect everyone will retire after this excursion, yes? But later, when you call them downstairs to trim the tree, that should give me time to search the Obolenskys' suite for the letter."

She felt jarred by the transition. "I suppose they must be the ones who took it."

"I expect so." He paused. "I'll book a ticket on the morning train, then."

Her throat tightened. She would be deeply relieved when he left. Wouldn't she?

Misery tangled her fingers together at her waist. Suddenly she foresaw that she would not be relieved at all. Not if he left without giving an explanation for what had happened two years ago. Her pride could go rot: she needed to confront him. To clarify, once and for all, that she *had* mistaken the significance of their friendship in Munich— that the face he had shown her was false, and should no longer remain the singular standard by which she judged other gentlemen, and found them wanting.

"Why did you not write to me of the Machiavelli essay?" she blurted.

He sighed. "Would my opinion have been welcome?"

After his rude departure? "Perhaps not. So tell me this: why did you not write to inform me that you were leaving Munich?"

He turned toward her, his handsome face cold. "You think that odd?" he said. "That I should have left without a word? How else was I to go? Tell me, Miss Trent, was my offense so great, the injury to your sensibilities so severe, that you would have preferred an *apology* before I departed?"

Her breath caught. Here it was: the crux of the matter. *Say no,* she told herself. *Don't let him see how deeply he hurt you. Have pride. Say no!*

The breath exploded from her. *"Yes,"* she said. "Yes! An apology at the *least*!"

"An apology," he bit out furiously, and then stopped, his face flushing.

She recoiled, astonished by the look on his face. Anger, at *her*! If anybody deserved to feel anger, it was she! "Yes, an apology!" How dare he try to put *her* to shame?

"Ah!" Countess Obolenskaya swanned up, looping her arm through Georgie's. "Where do we go next, Mistress of Revelries?"

Chapter Six

Georgie stood on her tiptoes, straining to reach the uppermost boughs of the *Tannenbaum* as Lady von Bittner barked at her. "Higher. Yes, even higher! All the way to the top!"

"Perhaps somebody taller ought to step in." Georgie cast a speaking look across the room. Count Obolensky and Lord von Bittner were kneeling by the fire, roasting chestnuts under Mr. Lipscomb's supervision. "*Much* taller," she called pointedly. It had required all three footmen to cart the von Bittners' fir into the drawing room; the tree stood over seven feet high.

"No, only women decorate the *Tannenbaum*. Drape it so—" Lady von Bittner stepped forward, tugging at a loop of beaten silver. It slipped off the bough and fell straight into Georgie's face, making her sputter as she clawed it away. "The tinsel must hang in swags, else there will be no room for the candles."

"Candles, on a tree?" Mrs. Lipscomb, who stood to one

side clutching a tray of crystal baubles, looked dubious. "Is that not a fine way to start a fire?"

"Only rarely," said Lady von Bittner.

"What Miss Trent needs is a hook," Countess Obolenskaya said. She was sipping her third glass of local wassail—a spiced mixture of rum and cider—and sounded lazily amused. "I have one in my rooms, for tightening my laces. Shall I go fetch it?"

"No!" Georgie blurted. Mr. Godwin would be searching the Obolenskys' rooms. "That is—I'm determined to do this in the traditional fashion. But perhaps you could fetch over that chair?"

This small innovation was deemed acceptable by Lady von Bittner, who remained squinting until Georgie finally managed to lasso the top boughs. "Yes, that's precisely right," she announced, then promptly lost interest and wandered over to the fire to request a chestnut. The countess followed suit, leaving Georgie alone with Mrs. Lipscomb, who watched mutely as Georgie hauled the chair around the tree, clambering up and down like a monkey to arrange the tinsel in an elegant, looping pattern.

"It seems a bit pagan," said Mrs. Lipscomb at last. "To kill a tree to celebrate the Savior's birth."

"Her Majesty always has a Christmas tree," Georgie said. "I would not call her pagan."

"Hmph, well. She *was* married to a German." With a sour tug of her mouth, Mrs. Lipscomb laid her tray of ornaments onto the carpet. "I think I will roast chestnuts, too."

Thus did Georgie find herself alone by the tree as her guests disported themselves with wassail, chestnuts, and a game of dice—the last of which rather marred the holiday flavor. Sighing, she finished wrapping the tinsel, then took up the tray of baubles to hang.

"It's done."

She jumped out of her skin. Mr. Godwin had sneaked

up behind her. He looked grim-faced. Still sulking over her remonstrance at the bakery, no doubt. Scalawags had little practice with being called to task for their rudeness.

"Good," she bit out. "Bring the letter to me after supper."

"Oh, no, I didn't find it."

"What?" But who had stolen it, then? In her surprise, she fumbled the ornament.

Mr. Godwin made a swift, graceful lunge, and caught the bauble in midair. From their position by the fire, the other women took note. Hearing their appreciative coos, Georgie felt her general irritation sharpen into a particular and pointed resentment. "It's not *done,* then," she said in an undertone. "It's not *done* until you find the letter." And until he managed that, he would have no choice but to remain here, antagonizing her with his very presence—his athletic grace, his innate and effortless and infuriating ability to charm anybody who happened to glance at him.

Why, the countess and Mrs. Lipscomb were *still* mooning. Georgie scowled at them until they turned back toward the fire.

Mr. Godwin lifted the bauble to the light of a nearby stand of candles. The ornament was etched with miniature engravings, vines of ivy entwining around snowflakes and stars. "Lovely," he said.

"Factory-made," said Georgie.

His mouth twisted as he handed it back to her. She carefully hung the globe on a lower bough, then knelt to take up another. When he followed suit, she snapped, "Only women may decorate the tree."

Kneeling, he looked up at her. The candlelight flattered him; it had no standards or taste; it painted shifting shadows in the hollows beneath his cheekbones, and played in the curve beneath his full lower lip. "Is the tree a very modest specimen, then?" he asked cuttingly. "Heaven knows I would hate to offend its tender sensibilities."

She turned away. He was making a jab at her, alluding in some obscure way to her remonstrance in the bakeshop. But she would not be ashamed for what she had said there. As she hooked the bauble around a sprig of needles, she hissed, "If you wish to pretend that your departure from Munich was gentlemanly, very well. It fools nobody but you."

Out of the corner of her eye, she saw him rise and square his shoulders. "I suppose if you want *gentlemanliness*, you'll need to look to a better-bred man."

What nonsense was that? She was sick of his excuses. "Even children know how to bid a farewell. But perhaps it was my fault to expect one. Certainly it seems bizarre to imagine that I once considered you a friend—but I did. And friends owe each other *that* much, I think!"

"Friends, were we?" His laughter was jagged. "Tell me, Miss Trent. Did you truly expect me to look on you as a friend—to treat you as a friend—after instructing me to be ashamed for having pestered you with my attentions?"

She frowned up through the boughs at him. "What on earth are you talking about?"

His expression was grim. "You know very well what I mean."

"No, I do not!" She stepped around the tree to face him. "I have no idea what you mean! I never once—"

"Would you like some chestnuts?" called Countess Obolenskaya.

What a gift she had for interfering! "Not right now," Georgie said tightly.

"How marvelous the tree looks!" Lady von Bittner caroled. "Keep at it, Miss Trent!"

Georgie held out her hand for another ornament. Mr. Godwin shoved it into her palm with a dangerous degree of force. "I have no more interest than you in speaking of this," he said tightly. "It is not a memory I cherish. We can let it be."

And leave her with another festering mystery? "No," she said. "I want to know. When did I . . ." Her courage nearly faltered; she swallowed hard, taking great care to pin the ornament to the tree. "When did I instruct you on any matter to do with your . . . *attentions* to me? We never . . . You and I never spoke of . . . such things."

"Come now," he said sharply—halted, and then laughed again, a dark and awful laugh. Dragging a hand through his hair, he shook his head. "There is no need to spare *my* sensibilities. Your father will have told you I spoke to him." His voice roughened. "Certainly you told *him* how mortifying you found my interest."

"What?" For a moment, she could only gape at him. "My *father*? You spoke to my father of me? When?"

He gave a sharp tug of his mouth. "When I asked his permission to court you," he said, "and thereby discovered that my attentions had become an embarrassment to you. *That*, Miss Trent, is no inducement to pay 'friendly farewells,' I think you'll agree."

Glass shattered. Somebody by the fireplace called out in concern. Georgie could not answer. Speech was beyond her.

A line appeared between Mr. Godwin's brows. His glance dropped to the floor, where lay the shattered remnants of the Christmas bauble. As his gaze lifted again, his face seemed to loosen and sag, so that suddenly, briefly, he looked ancient.

"Do not tell me," he said slowly, "that you didn't know this."

She tried once, twice, to say it: "I didn't." *Never.* "I . . ." Her lips felt numb. "We never even spoke of you."

Suddenly he was gripping her arm. His hold was so tight, his hand so hot, that the sensation seemed to ripple out over her skin, the shock of it causing her to draw a strangled breath.

"And what of the rest?" he demanded. "That you found my suit distasteful?"

She opened her mouth. Her voice failed her again. She shook her head violently.

"I say," Mr. Lipscomb called. "Is everything all right, there?"

"That my parentage made me unfit for you," Mr. Godwin said rapidly. "What of that?"

"We never spoke of you," she said again in a whisper. "*Never*, Lucas. Not until you . . . left." She groped behind her for the chair; sank into it abruptly, dizzy.

He did not let go of her arm. He followed her down, kneeling in front of her, and opened his mouth as though to speak again—then closed it and studied her face as though he had never seen her before.

"He lied." The ragged words came from her—such a simple truth, to have rearranged her life entirely.

"He lied," he agreed, in a voice like gravel.

"Are you quite well?" Mr. Lipscomb had come to stand over them. "Miss Trent? Perhaps you require sustenance. A chestnut?"

Chapter Seven

Two years!

Why, he *had* asked permission to court her. Their friendship *had* meant something more to him. She hadn't been wrong! Georgie's spirits soared—then plummeted as she realized the implication.

She would have accepted his suit.

They would have been married by now.

She could not play hostess with this shock coursing through her. She could not lead the guests into the dining room and sit down across the table from Lucas Godwin and chatter idly about stocks and politics and fashions without leaning over and seizing his hand and spilling her heart to him. But with everyone's interest already piqued by her "swoon," she could not risk a private audience with him, either.

She took the coward's way out, pleading a headache. That Mr. Godwin did not do the same astonished her. His impassivity, as he watched her leave the drawing room, seemed more than heroic: it seemed superhuman.

Alone in her bedchamber, she stewed and paced, and time dragged. Once, a knock came at the door, Countess Obolenskaya's voice speaking kindly. "Miss Trent? I came to see how you're faring."

Panicked, irrationally convinced that she might be caught out, she changed into a nightdress and retreated to her bed. But of course the countess did not barge in to test whether she'd lied about her health. The lady took herself back downstairs. Dinner was laid at half seven. But not until eleven o'clock did Georgie at last hear the guests returning to their suites.

Once the house had settled into silence again, she stole out of her room, to the far wing where Mr. Godwin was lodged. But he did not answer her knock, and when she bent to peer through the keyhole, his room was dark.

Where had he gone? How could he not long to speak with her? She made a furtive survey of the likely spots—the billiards room, the smoking room, the drawing room and library. But he had vanished.

He could not have left!

In her turmoil, she found herself flying through the service passage, down into the kitchen. Here, in this warm, slate-floored chamber strung with drying herbs, bright copper pans glinting from hooks, and barrels of flour and sugar stacked against the walls—this was the place she felt most at home in the world, safest and most herself. The staff had just finished cleaning after the night's industry; the long table in the center of the room had been cleared and swept clean, and Gladys, the scullery maid, was polishing the last piece of glassware.

Cook came out of the pantry and spotted her with an exasperated sigh. "Never say they're up again? Fourteen bottles at dinner! They drink more than sailors on holiday."

"No," Georgie said numbly. "They're all in bed, I think. But—has anyone seen Mr. Godwin?"

Cook glanced toward Gladys, who laid down her broom, bobbed a curtsy, and left.

"That one went for a walk," Cook said, with a snort that bespoke her opinion of such affairs. "Barton had to scrounge up a lantern for him, for the moon's clouded over. Barely a star to see by tonight."

"Oh." Deflated, Georgie took a seat on the bench before the great hearth. The fireplace could hold two boars spitted side by side; two or three hundred years ago, it had done, no doubt. But more recently, it had been partitioned into three separate chambers, only the center of which was used. She held out her hands to the dying flames. The labor of the ranges, earlier, had left the kitchen toasty. Why did she feel so cold?

Perhaps she was falling sick in truth. She felt profoundly off-balance, hovering at the edge of a precipice—and the fall would pull her into a world of regret, wasted days and months and years . . .

A gentle touch landed on her shoulder. Cook took a seat beside her, her wrinkled face pinched with concern. "What's this?" she asked gently. "Barton says you took your supper in your rooms. What's got you so upset?"

Georgie pulled her hands back into her lap, fisting them. "Do you remember when my father sacked the Lyalls?"

"Aye," Cook said slowly. "That's old history. What of it?"

Sir Philip had come home early from a treaty talk in Antwerp. Nobody had expected him. Georgie's twelfth birthday had been approaching, but he never paid attention to holidays. After Georgie's mother had died, he'd gone off them entirely. "I was so surprised to see him," Georgie murmured. He'd found her playing chase in the garden with Jenny and Tom Lyall, the second coachman's children. He'd embraced her. Announced that he had a present for her, a grand birthday excursion to London, where they would visit the zoo. How delighted she'd been!

But on the way back from town, he'd deposited her at a girls' school, a very refined place with four tutors for every pupil. "I had no idea you were running so wild," he'd told her. "You are a Trent. You cannot mix with riffraff. I've neglected you, I fear."

The boarding school had not suited her. Moreover, she'd inherited her father's stubbornness. She'd run away twice before figuring out the train schedules. When she'd finally made it back to Brisbon Hall, the Lyalls had been gone. Her father had dismissed them for the temerity of not knowing their place.

"He thought he was protecting me," Georgie said. "But his protection . . . it always feels like a punishment."

Cook's hand slid to hers, tightened over her knuckles. "He does his best, Miss Georgie. He only ever wanted what's right for you."

Georgie's laugh felt rough. "That's what he tells himself, no doubt."

Cook sighed. "It's hard, in his shoes. To be a father, and a grand man like him, besides. What's got you thinking on all this?"

Georgie looked up, letting Cook see her fight not to weep. "Because I've just discovered that he 'protected' me once again. And this time, I don't think I can forgive him for it."

Cook blew out a breath. "That gent that went walking?"

Georgie nodded.

"Well." Cook studied her with rheumy eyes. "You're a grown girl," she said gruffly. "Seems to me that your father doesn't realize how grown you are. Perhaps you should tell him so."

"I mean to," Georgie said.

Cook opened her arms, and Georgie threw herself into them. Gone were the days when Cook's great belly had made such embraces smothering; the decades had shrunk and wizened her. But she still smelled of bread and cinnamon and soap, and Georgie breathed deeply, taking comfort, as she always did, from the care of one who knew her truly.

Cook cleared her throat and eased away. "Visitor," she said briefly, and rose.

Georgie twisted on the bench. Mr. Godwin stood in the arched doorway that led to the kitchen garden, a curious expression on his face. He lowered his lamp to the floor. "I thought to return this," he said quietly.

"Leave it there for the night," Cook said. As she untied her apron, she fixed Georgie with a solemn look. "Don't be up too late now," she said, and then turned and took herself out.

Georgie felt curiously frozen. As Mr. Godwin approached, he glanced over her figure, and a slight, rueful smile curved his mouth.

As simply as that, her heart bolted into a gallop. She was wearing a nightdress, shapeless and heavy, tied beneath her chin. Nothing flattering. But she could not mistake the appreciation on his face.

He had wanted to court her. To *marry* her.

"I like seeing you so," he said as he came to stand by the bench. "Curled up like a cat. Thoroughly at your ease. I had . . . imagined you sitting thus. Many times. But I've never seen it till now."

She felt a flush rise, but she did not look away from him. "One can't sit so, in a corset."

He lifted a dark brow. Bold of her, naturally, to acknowledge her dishabille—that she sat before him stripped of her layers and lacings, the complicated armor by which a woman's body was trussed up and locked away from touch.

But she held his gaze as he settled onto the bench beside her, until it was he who looked away, toward the fire. "I wonder," he said, "that you will trust me with such intimacies. What would Sir Augustus say?"

She flushed to her roots. "There is no Augustus Brumkin," she said haltingly. "As I think—I think you guessed."

He exhaled. "Ah. I *had* taken a look today through the *Debrett's* in your father's library. The Brumkins were not in evidence, but I feared . . ."

"I can't believe I made up such a ridiculous name," she whispered.

He offered her a sideways smile. "And I am rather grateful for it."

She felt herself relax. He made it so easy to have this conversation. "Anyway," she said, "I could never mistrust you in *that* way."

"Don't be so certain of that. You make quite a temptation, in the firelight. And . . ." He loosed a slow breath. "A man does not spend five hundred nights dreaming of a woman and find himself unmoved by the reality." He shook his head once. "*Unmoved*: a very pale word for it."

As simply as that, she felt acutely aware of her own body: how, within the voluminous folds of her wool nightdress, her breasts hung loose and heavy; her legs sprawled freely; her toes curled.

They had kissed only chastely, in Munich. Kisses on the cheek, in the continental style. But in her dreams, she had tasted his tongue. She had felt the hard planes of his belly, the brawn of his thighs. He had lain with her in dreams countless times by now—but never vividly enough to satisfy her. She had always woken aching and unsatisfied, jolted abruptly into recrimination. *How could you still hunger for a man who never wanted you at all?*

But he *had* wanted her. He still did. His steady, heated gaze told her so now.

"Two years," she whispered. So much time wasted.

"Your father," he growled—and then fell silent, his

mouth twisting. He clawed a hand through his night-dark hair, shaking his head. His fingers trembled.

Lucas Godwin, trembling for her. Two years. Two years, and these lies, and if not for them, then . . .

He took a deep breath, lowered his hand, and said, "What did he tell you? That I had abandoned you?"

"My father said very little about you." She pushed these words from her dry mouth, though the syllables barely captured what she felt. She felt native to no tongue that could translate *that*. "He said . . . you'd been offered a promotion. A better post. That I mustn't be surprised you hadn't made time to write me. He said that was your way—to charm ladies, without intending anything by it."

But . . . God above, Lucas *had* intended something by it. And her father had told a lie to destroy them.

Pain lanced through her—sudden and breathtaking. "And what he told *you*. That I found you distasteful. How could you believe him?"

For he had let her go so easily. A few words, and he had abandoned her to rush toward new possibilities—Paris, his career. Meanwhile, what had remained to her? Her father's disappointment. Munich's titillated whispers at her heartbreak.

"Georgie." He made her nickname sound like a melody, low and sweet. "Your father was very convincing. And . . . God save me, but I never thought to doubt him. My superior—my *mentor*. The man who had championed my rise through the service—saying you found me repellent! Forgive me, Georgie—*forgive* me; it never occurred to me that he might lie."

As she weighed those words, she felt her mouth twist. "Then you don't know him." Her father had made a career of meddling. He had manipulated kings, designed the downfall of nations. Beside that, his daughter's hopes were no challenge at all.

His hand closed on her arm. He stared into her eyes, his voice hushed and fierce: "Listen to me. Leaving was the greatest mistake of my life."

She closed her eyes to trap her tears. His forehead came to rest against hers. The smell of him—clean, male, the spice of bergamot rising from his clothing—snared her, held her immobile, so close to him that she could feel his breath against her mouth, his warmth all around her, this man she had adored . . .

"I would have fought for you," she said raggedly as she pulled back to wipe her nose. "Had it been me—I would have demanded to hear it from your lips."

The sight of her tears made him flinch. He leaned forward as though to touch her again—but she made a noise, and after a stubborn moment, he heeded the warning. Fisting his hands, he sat back, but his eyes remained fastened on hers.

To break the hushed tension, she reached over and plucked a leaf off the holly mounded by the hearth. She cast the leaf into the fire, where it popped loudly, then sputtered and hissed into ashes.

His laugh sounded raw. "My mother always loathed that sound," he said. "I drove her half mad at Yuletide, setting holly on fire."

The affection in his voice struck her. He had never shared any tales of his childhood with her. Why was that? In Munich, she had imagined she knew him better than anyone in the world—but all at once, her own ignorance was made plain to her.

They had been friends in Munich. He'd asked so many questions, listened with such rapt interest, as she'd told him about growing up at Brisbon Hall. But perhaps she'd not been so fine a friend in return. The heady thrill of his attention had made her selfish. She'd never thought to ask after *his* childhood.

All at once, their history looked different to her—full of gaps, mysteries yet to be bridged. There had been so much more left to learn when they'd been parted.

"What was your mother like?" she asked. "You never spoke much of her."

"Didn't I?" He hesitated, a shadow coming into his face. Then, with a curiously formal air, he faced her. "I didn't," he said evenly—an agreement, solemn. "My restraint was deliberate, if I'm to be honest."

She frowned. "But why? You sound so fond of her." She envied that fondness. Her own mother had died before her seventh birthday; what memories she retained were more impressions than facts: a soft touch; the fragrance of roses; the feeling of being safe, cherished.

"She was a wonderful woman," he said steadily. "I miss her still, every day. Tonight, while I was walking, I thought . . ." His lips moved, not quite a smile. "I thought that had she lived, this whole debacle would never have happened. She would have counseled me to put aside my pride and go to you; to ask for an accounting and apologize for any wrong I might have done you. Pride, she always warned me, was as much a weakness as a strength. Pride is nothing compared to happiness, she said."

"That sounds very wise." Georgie spoke softly, over the ache in her throat. What a might-have-been! Lucas coming to her in those early days, when the fresh wound had not yet festered. It would have gone differently indeed.

"Of course," he added flatly, "my father would have counseled the opposite. Pride was his mainstay. And that, Georgie, is the reason I never spoke of her. You'll know something of my parents, I think. How . . . ill-suited their marriage was considered."

Hesitantly she nodded. In Munich, people had spoken of Lucas's charm, his talents and great promise, in the same breath that they had bemoaned his breeding. *Such a bright star, to come from such a stew!* And her father—consoling her so deceitfully, in the wake of Lucas's departure—had laid it bare: the second son of an earl did not elope with the coachman's daughter from motives as pure as love. Some rottenness must characterize a line that would produce such a bizarre mésalliance—and, her father had added, this same rotten streak no doubt explained why Lucas made a habit of abandoning his friends, including those who were his better in every regard.

But he had been wrong there as well. She was no better than Lucas. For they had both made the mistake of believing her father—abandoning their faith in one another without a fight.

Why, she wasn't simply angry at her father. Her anger also encompassed herself.

She swallowed down the bitterness. It had no place in this discussion. Not when Lucas was watching her so gravely. *I still know him,* she thought—such a seductive notion. She saw the pain hidden in his face, the anxiety so expertly concealed beneath his easy, lounging posture. But he was running his thumb across his fingertips, a seemingly idle, absentminded gesture, which she recalled being a habit of his during deeply felt discussions.

He did not find it easy to discuss his parents' marriage. But he would do so, for her sake, if she wished it.

And she did. Suddenly, it seemed absurd, unimaginable, that they had not talked about this in Munich. How could she have imagined she loved him, without asking him about this wound at the heart of him? "It must have been very hard," she said, "enduring the gossip."

He gave a one-shouldered shrug. "I never minded it for my own sake. But for their sake—for my mother's—I resented it tremendously." He took a deep breath. "I knew I was fortunate in my birth, you see. No child has ever been better cherished. Yet . . . there was never a moment, in the world outside my parents' home, when the shadow of that scandal did not hang over me. At Eton—well, the scholarship did not cover everything. My parents had to scrimp and save so I might enjoy a perk—coal in the winter, a ticket home at the holidays. Everyone knew it. Moreover, they knew *why*. At Field Day, mine were the only parents not in attendance—and it did not go unnoticed. They could not afford the fare to come, the missed wages from a holiday. But even if they had managed it, they would not have been welcomed. Their very presence would have been counted a breach of etiquette; the very fact of their marriage an imposition on polite sensibilities. And so, too, with me—a gross offense, in others' eyes, by the mere fact of my existence."

She shook her head in mute denial. "You had friends at Eton. You spoke of them to me. You spoke very fondly of those days."

"Certainly," he said. "I have a skill for winning people over. But it's a *skill*, Georgie—not some inborn talent. My parents were frank with me: I would always have to work harder than the others. Prove myself, give others no reason by which to discount me. But topping the exams, taking a first in the tripos, winning entrance to the service—that was only the start. Far more important was to ingratiate myself to those in power—not simply in the service, but even, at ten or eleven, with the classmates who might one day advance my career. That was the only way I would ever succeed. And never for a moment did I forget it. I was never *allowed* to forget it—that my fortunes depended on other men's indulgence. Their gracious decision to *forgive* me my birth, even if I had the best parents a man ever knew."

A trace of bitterness colored his words—a very old bitterness, she sensed, dulled now like a disused blade. She swallowed the urge to apologize to him for the injustice of strangers, to speak words of comfort about their bigotry. For he would not want her pity. She knew that as intuitively as she knew that he was fighting a great battle to bare his soul to her like this.

"You've certainly succeeded," she said softly. "The chance at becoming secretary of legation by thirty!"

"Yes," he said, with a faint, fleeting smile. "I play the game better than anyone. But it hasn't been for my own sake, you know, so much as for my parents'. They put all their hopes on me. Worked themselves to the bone to give me a chance. For their sake, I learned to charm and pander. But never for a moment have I felt easy in doing so. Nor have I taken my gains for granted. It would only take one mistake for my colleagues to say, 'Blood tells, after all.' Some of them are still waiting for the chance." He paused. "Someone will always be waiting for it, Georgie. That is what success means, to a man like me—forever to be balanced at the edge of a great fall."

"Lucas." Her hand was atop his. When had that happened? She was leaning forward, hurting for him. "That sounds . . . exhausting."

He huffed out a breath, not quite a laugh. "Coal mining, that's exhausting. Learning to lick the right boots—it's merely a career."

Frowning, she shook her head. "That is not at all how people see you."

"No. But at times, it was certainly how I saw myself." He turned his hand in hers, their fingers twining; such a simple touch, but her breath caught and her pulse began to trip. He rubbed his thumb slowly over her palm. "You'll understand, I hope, that it also wasn't an image I wished to place in the head of the woman I hoped to marry." He glanced up from their linked hands, his deep blue eyes meeting hers. "So I made no mention of my mother, in Munich. And when your father told me that you had only just discovered my parentage . . . well, it seemed possible. Because certainly *I* hadn't told you."

Her mouth went dry. They were back on dangerous ground now. "I always knew."

"I had supposed so," he said levelly. "But when he said otherwise—when he said you were repelled by how grossly I had deceived you—by my presumption in thinking myself worthy of your hand . . ." He sighed. "Well, it felt as though my worst nightmare were coming true. For I could not disown my parents, even for you. But I also could not deny that you were right to be mortified. This shadow world I live in is no comfortable place for *me*. How much less pleasant it would feel for a woman whose birth entitles her to better."

She jerked her hand free, stung. "It never would have mattered to me."

"I see that now." He hesitated. "The woman who was comforting you, earlier . . ."

Color rushed into her face. "That was Mrs. Nichol," she said. "Our cook."

"I see." His voice was oddly gentle. Why, could it be that he mistook her blush for embarrassment? After all, the same polite world that slighted him for his birth would also disapprove strongly of such intimacies between a mistress and her servant.

But that was not the cause of her discomfort. She had never credited the niceties of rank. Lifting her chin, she said forcefully, "Cook is more a parent to me than my father ever was. If I blush to say that—if I am embarrassed to admit it—then I am embarrassed for *his* sake, not mine. Nor would I ever have asked you to disown your mother, Lucas—or felt mortified for a *moment* by her birth."

He slowly nodded. "I realize that, Georgie. And you're right—your father should never have managed to make me doubt you."

"He is a very clever liar."

"No." His head tipped; he studied her solemnly. "It wasn't all his doing. My own fears blinded me to the truth. They drove me to believe his lies. I think I must take the blame, after all—even the share you might wish to grant to him."

But that did not strike her as fair, either. She stared into the blurring fire. "Then two of us were blinded," she said with difficulty. "For I should have written to you, Lucas. Been braver, less careful of my pride. *Asked* why you left so hastily. But I confess . . . from the first moment you smiled at me in Munich, I never quite believed that it could be true. That a man like you—a man of every distinction, a man of beauty and charm and wit and learning, who captured every eye in the room—why would a man like you choose *me*? When my father told me you had a habit of meaningless flirtations, I felt . . . as though I were waking from a dream. Like I'd always known it would end so. That *I* had aimed too high. That I'd been a fool all along to believe you could have loved a plain, ordinary girl like me."

She heard the breath go from him. Suddenly he was in front of her, kneeling to look into her eyes.

"Are you mad?" He cupped her cheeks, swept her hair back from her eyes. "I could use ten thousand words to describe you—but never, even at my most disillusioned, would *plain* and *ordinary* have numbered among them. You are . . ." He shook his head as he gazed at her. "Georgie, you are a *miracle*. Clever without cruelty, kind without naïveté, beautiful without flaw. And I prayed nightly that you would be *my* miracle . . . and I felt, even at the height of my bitterness, that the outcome had only been just, after all—for your father was right. I had overreached greatly when I asked for your hand. *Any* man would have overreached, had you been his aim."

Amazement washed through her. "I don't . . . You never . . ."

He made some strained noise. "I never did many things," he said roughly. He caught her elbows, pulled her to her feet. "Many things I should have done the first moment I had a chance at them." His hands framed her face. "Like this."

He kissed her then, opening her mouth with his own, brooking no hesitation. His kiss was so bold—so commanding and instantaneously consuming—that it gave her brain no footing to protest.

Nor did she wish to. Gladly, hungrily, she kissed him back. Two years—two years of sleepless nights, of a pulsing aching want that had seemed destined to go unfulfilled—this ferocity she felt was only natural; it was inevitable. She cupped his face in *her* hands, greedy for the hot, fine-grained texture of his skin; the slight scratch of his oncoming beard; the elegant angles of his cheekbones. She slid her hands through the thick silk of his night-dark hair, tightened her grip until it must have hurt him—but he only kissed her more fiercely yet, encouraging her with lips and tongue and teeth, his hot, clever mouth.

He lifted her into his arms and carried her over to the table. Very gently he laid her down atop it, amidst the lingering fragrance of ginger. He came over her, worshiping her lips, her cheeks, and her throat with his mouth.

But it wasn't enough. She tugged at his hair, his shoulders, to pull him against her. His weight was heavy and sweet. She pushed her face into his throat and breathed deeply of him. That dark, masculine scent sank straight into her, plummeted deep into her bones and belly. It struck up a more primal hunger than she had ever known in her dreams.

His body was what she needed—against hers, skin to skin. She slid her palms to his upper arms, squeezing, feel-

ing the dense bunch of his contracting muscle. The full
contact of his broad chest against hers—the breadth of his
strong body, enfolding hers—felt more elemental even than
air. He found her mouth again, and the demanding, skilled
possession of his tongue was not gentlemanly in the least,
nothing like the kiss he had given that masked stranger beneath the mistletoe. Because he was kissing *her* now. The
only woman he should kiss, ever again.

The thought exploded through her brain, bringing a
brief cold moment of clarity: there was no future for them.
Her father had the power to ruin his career.

She would not be the cause of his downfall.

Abruptly she averted her face. "Lucas," she said raggedly.
"Wait."

He went still, breath rasping like a bellows in her ear.
His hands found her shoulders, flexed on them as though
to trammel some great straining battle within him. "Georgie," he said hoarsely against her temple. He eased off her,
straightening. "Forgive me. I . . . Are you all right?"

She sat up. His hair was mussed—her hands had done
that. The knot in his necktie had unraveled—dared she hope
she'd done that, too? She drank in greedily the sight of his
bare, tanned throat, the glimpse of dark hair above the first
button of his shirt.

"Lucas," she said, and the sound of her own voice startled her; the low sultry purring note in it seemed to belong
to some other woman—a woman, she decided in the next
breath, that she very much hoped to become.

Why think of the future? Tonight was upon them. Her
father never need know what had happened here.

But when she reached out to pull him toward her, he
stepped backward, introducing a new space between them,
air that felt shockingly cold in comparison to his touch.
"You're right," he said, very low. "This isn't proper."

Proper? She almost laughed. But the rigidity in his face

made her bite her tongue, take a deep breath, and gather her composure. "I'm not sure I care much for propriety."

His mouth softened. Very lightly, he tucked a lock of her hair behind her ear. Drew a lingering line down her jaw, smiling a little as he reached her chin.

"A thousand times I dreamed of touching you so," he whispered. "But the reality . . ." His glance passed briefly down her body, his mouth hardening again. When his gaze lifted, the smoldering quality of his look made her flush. "I won't sleep tonight."

She swallowed.

He took her hand, helping her slip off the table, then lifted her knuckles for a kiss. "Until tomorrow?"

"Of course." But the brief sweetness of that thought faded as she realized the date.

Tomorrow was Christmas Eve.

They had only two days remaining, to make up for two years of loss . . . unless she found some way to check her father.

Chapter Eight

December 24

The crack of gunfire made Georgie clamp her hands over her ears. A flock of grouse wheeled and darted through the sky; farther down the field, two plummeted, but Lucas's targets made a winging escape to the north.

Applause broke out. Georgie went on her tiptoes to look over the stone wall that blocked her view. A beater had gone running out to retrieve the felled birds. "Oh, well done!" shouted Countess Obolenskaya from her own hide, some fifty yards away.

A footman approached with a freshly loaded rifle. Lucas took it, then lifted it to sight over the wall.

"Are you a poor shot?" Georgie asked teasingly. "Or do grouse rank higher in your affections than geese?"

Lucas cast her a laughing, sidelong look. "Caught out," he said.

She swallowed a happy sigh. She could stand beside him all day. The morning had dawned bright and mild, and a playful, kicking wind flirted with the thick curls in his dark hair. The sun, not to be outdone, lit his eyes until they reflected the patches of cloudless blue sky overhead.

Gunshot cracked again. They remained staring at each other. His gaze dipped to her mouth, and her skin seemed to tighten pleasurably. The curved wall protected them from others' view. She could touch him, if she liked—could kiss him, even. Nobody would see.

But kissing him would not be enough.

She bit her cheek. She saw no way to satisfy this longing without endangering him. Not unless she found that letter.

She cleared her throat. "I asked the staff to search belowstairs," she said. "If the guests don't have the letter, perhaps they left it with one of their own servants."

His expression hardened. He turned away from her to make a study of the stray grouse still fluttering overhead. "Forget the letter today."

Were there more time remaining to them, she gladly would have done. But the guests would depart on Boxing Day. If they had not found the letter by then, she would have no way to keep her father in check. "Lucas, my father—"

"I find myself curiously indifferent to his concerns." He sighted his rifle. The gun cracked, and a grouse dropped to the ground.

Applause broke out again, encouragements and congratulations traveling dimly down the field. One of the beaters ran up to fetch the felled bird.

This time, when the footman appeared with a fresh rifle, Lucas shook his head. "Leave the ammunition," he said.

He knew his way with a weapon, reloading it and sighting with swift, efficient brutality. Another round of grouse exploded into flight, and his gun barked.

Down came a bird, its body thumping audibly against the grass.

"Crack shot!" came Obolensky's cry. Lucas, grim-faced,

reloaded his weapon. Georgie looked away from the tight line of his jaw to the dark huddled mass of the bird.

"Poor thing," she said softly.

She heard Lucas sigh. He laid down the gun and turned to face her, his expression stony.

She took a deep breath. "If we find that letter, we can use it to our advantage. We can name our own price in exchange for it. We can be . . . safe."

His eyes narrowed. As he studied her, she felt her color rise. It was a shameful thing to propose blackmail. But she was not above it now.

"Safe," he said evenly. "Safe from *what*, may I ask?"

"Lucas." She hesitated, her stomach knotting. She could not say what she feared more—that he would ignore the risk to himself, or that he would deem it too costly. "My father is not a man to tolerate being crossed. If he were to discover your . . . renewed interest in me, he might punish you for it. He could ruin your career."

The corner of his mouth twitched—a fleeting, humorless smile. "Yes," he said. "No doubt he could."

Frustration tightened her throat. "Then don't you understand why—"

He seized her elbows and dragged her against him. As she goggled up at him, he said, "*This* is what I understand." His mouth came down onto hers.

The kiss was hard, furious, a branding more than a caress; his lips ground against hers as his grip tightened to the point of pain around her upper arms. Confused, a little frightened, she gasped—and his mouth abruptly gentled. His lips soothed hers, stroking once, twice, until she relaxed against him. His grip eased, his fingers flexing around her elbows as he turned his face aside. His breath warmed her temple for a long, silent moment before he spoke.

"What I felt for you in Munich." His voice was low and harsh. "What I feel for you now. It is not *interest*."

Why, he was shaking—she could feel the fine tremors of his body where his chest pressed against hers, as though he were racked by some inward pressure too great for his flesh to contain.

Her own pulse was hammering. "I . . . I meant no insult."

He eased back from her. Their eyes met, his own intent and unblinking. "Interest fades," he said. "Interest dulls. Interest does not ruin a man. It does not blind him to other women. It does not catch in his chest like a hook. What I felt for you—what I feel for you—is far from *interest*."

The top of her head seemed to lift away. Wonder purled through her. "Yes," she breathed.

"So hear me now," he said. "I do not give a damn what your father has to say about this. Do you understand that?" When she hesitated a moment too long, he said, "*Answer* me."

Swallowing, she nodded.

"Good." His hands slid down her arms, his fingers stroking over her palms, raising goose bumps, causing her breath to catch and her knees to weaken. He lifted her hands to his mouth in turn, his gaze hot on hers as he pressed his lips to her knuckles. His nostrils flared as he breathed deeply, in and out. Then he returned her hands to her sides, squeezing them once before stepping backward. "Good," he said softly. "We understand each other."

Giddy delight washed through her. She crossed her arms to contain it, to prevent herself from reaching for him again. He could not know what he was saying. He had not thought it through. Would his conviction remain so steadfast once his career was stolen from him? She had no inheritance, apart from what her father might choose to leave her. She would not be able to help him regain his footing. She was no Countess Obolenskaya, to smooth his way by her own charm and beauty.

And yet, the look on his face . . . the resolution, the steadfast intensity of his regard . . . it made her drunk.

She forced herself to glance away, down the sloping grassland toward the stone towers of Brisbon Hall. "Why would he have sent you here?" Why would her father have risked the truth coming out? "It's so careless. So unlike him."

He made a low noise, almost a scoff. "About that." He reached into his pocket, withdrawing a crumpled slip of paper. "Cable came this morning."

Hesitantly she took it.

Lady L in labor STOP Advise you go directly to Harlboro Grange STOP

"Lady L?" She looked up, frowning.

"Lady Lilleston," he said flatly. "My aunt by marriage, for all that I've never met her. Her husband was my father's brother." He paused. "He died a week ago."

She gasped. "I'd no idea. Lucas, I'm so sorry for . . ." But she trailed off, realizing that her condolences were hardly wanted.

He offered her a faint smile. Another round of gunshot exploded; birds wheeled overhead, and cries of disappointment went up. "I'm sorry for those who loved him," he said. "Naturally, having known him only through his silence, and the insult it offered to my father—I don't number among his mourners."

"But who sent this, then?"

"Certainly none of the Godwins," he said. "But I have a suspicion who might have wished me informed of this matter." He raised his brows, inviting her to guess.

She shook her head; she had not the faintest inkling.

"Georgie." He sighed. "Lilleston has no son. If this babe is a girl, *I* will inherit his estates. His honors. His earldom. I think your father would take an interest in that."

Comprehension dawned. "You think my father arranged that telegram?"

"I think," he said dryly, "that he has great faith in your

appeal. Not a stupid man, Sir Philip. And he saw a chance to put a future earl in your path. It all depends on Lilleston's newborn." He tipped his head toward the telegram. "I expect he wants me at Harlboro Grange to make sure no trickery is played with the babe."

She crossed her arms, buffeted by a wave of violent distaste. "How . . . gothic."

His laughter was soft. "Indeed. But in your father's circles? No doubt there's been a babe switched here and there, to keep a crown in the family."

She sagged against the stone wall. "How can you sound so *amused* by it?" She was mortified, every inch of her skin prickling. "He's scheming again! You should—heavens!" She covered her face, feeling the great heat rushing into her cheeks. "How presumptuous! To think you would have any interest in me, after what he told you in Munich!"

"As I said, he's no fool," he said gently. "No doubt he guessed that with one look at you, I would be lost again."

The words were sweeter than she deserved. "If the babe is a boy, he'll still oppose you."

"Hence, I suppose, the secrecy. Gives him a fine cover to repudiate me, should I end up a commoner tomorrow."

"I think I would like to take a shot myself," she said through her teeth. "If only innocent birds weren't the target. Will you go to Harlboro Grange, then?"

"Of course not." His voice was perfectly neutral now. "I wouldn't be welcomed there."

She could not match his equanimity. A dark, poisonous feeling brewed in her chest at the notion of his family scorning him.

She shoved the telegram into her pocket. "We *must* find that letter."

"Must we?" He picked up the rifle, aimed once more.

"Yes!" How did he not understand this? She caught his elbow. "You've fought so hard," she said, "your whole *life*, to make this career for yourself. I won't let you throw it away!"

He laid down the gun. "And I wouldn't," he said. "Not if what you felt for me was *interest*. Is it?"

Anxiety welled in her throat. She turned, looking blindly over the hide toward the sun-dappled grass.

"I'll be braver than you," he said levelly. "It was love, in Munich."

She closed her eyes. The beauty of that admission—it dazzled her. "Yes," she whispered. "It was love."

"And last night, as I walked through these fields, I did not feel like a man mired in the past, Georgie. I was not mourning for what could have been. I felt like a man given a chance at a new future—a future with you."

She swallowed hard. "Then we *must* find that letter. There's no other way."

"No. That's not so." He cupped her cheek. Drew her around to face him. "With or without the letter," he said. "Answer me: what does your future look like?"

◆ ◆ ◆

Her expression shifted in some subtle, unquantifiable way. A moment ago, she had looked dazed and flush and achingly ripe for any proposal he might have put to her. But at his question, some spark went out of her face. He could feel her withdrawal as distinctly as the nip of the breeze.

"I would make my future with you," she whispered. "But not at such cost."

He bit back his frustration. He'd spoken truly to her. Now he knew that what they'd shared had been real, it changed everything—altered the very grounds on which he'd conceived his hopes. For it was one thing to strive to forget a humiliation, a humbling breach of judgment: that effort was only wise. But no wise man hoped to forget the only woman who had ever held his heart. No man had ever died peacefully in his bed, contented with his efforts, while knowing that he'd been robbed of the chance to share all his days with a woman like Georgiana Trent.

This desire—this *need*—did not seem a return to Munich so much as a rebirth, stronger, fiercer, for the years it had been wrongfully trammeled.

"That isn't your choice to make," he said. "I will weigh the consequences to myself. And I *have* done. I am asking what *you* want now."

Her cheek hollowed; she was biting it, he thought. If she was biting back even a fraction of what he felt, right now, then there was hope for him, surely.

She stood straighter. Smoothed her shawl over her shoulders. "Do you know," she said—pausing to clear her throat before she continued—"I'm not sure my father has ever passed a Christmas here at Brisbon Hall."

He frowned, thrown by this segue, but willing to try to follow it. "Ever? That seems unlikely."

"Well." She gave a one-shouldered shrug. "Perhaps when my mother was still living."

He studied her, trying to divine the source of the melancholy that shaded her expression now. "So you must not have spent many Christmases with him."

She glanced away, her face perfectly remote now. "His career came first. He does love me, of course; he reads my letters very carefully. He can quote them by heart, in fact. But he rarely replies—he's so busy, when abroad." She paused. "Still, it would mean a great deal if he managed to reply more regularly."

"I imagine so." He felt very uneasy now. Blind, disoriented, unable to guess where she would turn next.

"I wonder if he keeps all my letters," she said. "I keep his, but they're only fifty or so. Mine would be . . . why, there would be a thousand of them by now. I expect he couldn't travel with so great a number. He must have burned them, I think."

He wanted to take her in his arms so goddamned badly—and to keep her there, heedless of the gunfire all around them, and the beaters crying out. "He keeps them," he lied.

She blinked. Looked at him directly. "Did you keep my letters? The ones I wrote to you in Munich?"

His jaw clenched. He had burned them in a reckless, drunken despair, and regretted it the next morning, before he'd even opened his eyes, the smell of stale smoke clogging his bedroom. "Georgie. Yours wasn't the only heart that was shattered that winter."

She nodded, very pale. "I don't blame you for not keeping them. I thought about burning yours, too. But I couldn't manage to do it." Her smile trembled. "I worry about what that says of me. It seems I'm a person who can't let go, even when she ought. I'm glad if you're not like that, Lucas; it is better, healthier, to be able to let go."

"I never let go of you," he said fiercely. "Never, Georgiana. I will admit, I tried to do so. But I never succeeded."

"Then there is my point." She gazed at him steadily. "For I know you say you would give up your career for me. But you've wanted it far longer than you ever wanted me. You have never let go of *that* dream, even when the odds were against you. Perhaps, once you had lost it, you would realize your mistake. That you valued it above everything else, after all."

He silently cursed. "You are your father's daughter," he said gently, "to put hearts and careers on the same plane. But I was raised by a different father, who did give up his prospects for a woman, and never regretted it. *That* is *my* model."

The quick pull of her mouth suggested frustration. "But I would always know the price you had paid. And it would weigh on *me*."

He sighed. "I'm not sure how to convince you." God knew, if she could only see herself through his eyes . . . She was beautiful, in the pearlescent light. She stood but an arm's reach away, framed against the broad, sweeping vista of winter-bleached fields, the parkland rolling away behind her toward the gray towers of Brisbon Hall. Close enough for him to count the long, dark lashes that framed her soft brown eyes, and to trace, with his gaze, the sharp peaks of her upper lip, her mouth the shade of roses . . .

The wind struck up, calling fresh color to her full cheeks. He touched her face very lightly, and she flinched.

The recoil sliced him almost more deeply than he could bear. "Don't," he whispered. He would not allow it. He leaned down to kiss her—a gentler kiss than he had managed before.

Her mouth was sweet, startled, soft. He drew away before it tempted him to forget their surroundings again.

But there was nothing else here worth his attention but her. There never had been, when she was near.

The beaters were announcing the third drive. Down the field, the other guests were preparing for the trek to the next hides. Lucas took her by the hand and drew her after him.

She threw a startled glance over her shoulder. "You're leaving your rifle."

"Enough with that," he said. "Enough with your father, and the future, too. The day is ours, Georgie. Walk with me awhile."

❖ ❖ ❖

It took no more than an hour, alone with him in the country air, for Georgie to recall all the small details of affection that misery and heartbreak had scrubbed from her mind. How she felt more at ease with him than anyone she had ever known. How fluidly and freely their conversation ranged, from books to music to foreign cuisines; from politics to the new trend for "tea-tray" bustles—quite notorious, he said, in France. And the English fad for bicycles! Lucas did not know how to ride one. "But I do admire modern technology," he said as he helped her over a stile, "always inventing new ways for bones to be broken. Perhaps I'll give it a whirl sometime."

"Oh, it's grand fun," Georgie said, "and not nearly as dangerous as a horse. I'll be glad to teach you."

Only a fraction of a moment passed before he smiled at her, but it was enough to call her attention to the slip of her tongue—her unthinking mention of a future they would share together.

He put her at ease, then, sensing, no doubt, her inward turmoil. As they walked down the rutted country lane, he pointed out a rogue bluebird that showed an obsessive, nearly amorous interest in a nearby buckthorn bush. Lending the bluebird a gruff, husky voice, he mimed its ardent words of affection to the scruffy-looking plant.

And she, recalling how he had always made her laugh over even the smallest things, entered the game again as easily as though it had never been interrupted by two years of grieving. She pitched her voice high, imitating the plant's flustered protests, its shrill defense of its virtue. Amidst their laughter, they forgot entirely the shoot occurring a quarter mile behind them; when shots rang out, they both jumped, then fell back together, laughing harder yet.

Two hours later, it felt odd, an imposition, to rejoin the others at Brisbon Hall. In the morning room, Georgie felt unable to do more than smile by rote as the party recounted their triumphs. Sobieski and Obolensky's friendship seemed to have flourished; they teased each other by congratulating each other's wives on outshooting them. She felt acutely aware of Lucas, smiling so easily at the men's bluster, making a charming remark to pull the von Bittners into the repartee. But she kept her eyes elsewhere, knowing that if she looked at him now, everyone would read her face like a book.

Happily, it was the privilege of the hostess to excuse herself to check on the evening's preparations.

Downstairs, she found the kitchens in a state of organized chaos—Dorking fowl and Norfolk turkeys being plucked and dressed for roasting; goose pies and currant cakes cooling on the broad table, side by side with gingerbread and cheesecake. On the range, wassail bubbled. Pansy, one of the kitchen maids, came rushing up with the Yule log, delivered from the village not five minutes ago. "Waited long enough!" she said. "I thought we'd have to make do with Christmas candles!"

"Oh," Georgie said, startled and pleased by this idea. "Do bring those to the drawing room too, won't you?"

"You'll burn the place down," Cook warned. "They've already added candles to that . . . *shrub*."

Cook looked with great suspicion on the Christmas tree; she considered it the first wave of an all-out German invasion.

"Gladys and I had a look through the baggage," Cook added. "Found nothing, I'm sorry to say."

Georgie's spirits faltered. On a deep breath, she pushed through her disappointment, clinging instead to the magic of the morning. "Thank you," she managed. "And—yes, I want the entire room to glow tonight. As many candles as possible. You can hide buckets of sand in the corners, if it eases your mind."

"Don't think I won't," Cook grumbled, but she could not quite catch her smile as she waved Georgie off. "It's well in hand here, miss. And you look as though you've got better places to be." She lifted a suggestive brow. "With a certain gentleman, maybe?"

Georgie shook her head, smiling, and slipped back into the service passage.

But once on the stairs, she found herself touching her mouth, simply to feel the shape of this silly smile. She fooled nobody.

Some movement drew her attention toward the wall. Startled, she stepped closer to look at her reflection in the mirror. Why, if this was what everyone saw, she did not mind it. She looked . . . pretty. Remarkably so. Rosy and merry and full of life.

She would never be a famous beauty. But if this face forever looked back at her from every mirror she passed, she would never feel inadequate to any circumstance.

But she had looked so once before. And that happiness had melted away like a dream upon waking.

She watched her smile fade. Here, now, was how she would look if Lucas lost his own joy—as he surely would, if her father destroyed his career in punishment for his marrying her.

She forced that thought away as she continued up the stairs. She would not think on that today. Today was her Christmas gift to herself: a carefree celebration, in keeping with the season.

As she stepped out into the hallway, she caught sight of Lucas in conversation with Mr. Sobieski. As easily as that, her smile came back. Eagerly, she went forward to meet them.

Chapter Nine

"Ladies and gentlemen!" Countess Obolenskaya waved for attention. "Miss Trent has just told me of a very lovely tradition among the English. Who wishes to walk to the stables with me?"

Georgie shared a sideways smile with Lucas. They had been warming elder wine in a saucepan over the fire, Lucas's hand over hers holding the pan steady above the flames—a very respectable touch, to which nobody could object.

The rest of the group lounged in voluptuous abandon, glasses of wine and wassail dangling from their hands. It was half eleven: stockings had been hung amidst giggles, carols had been sung, and the remaining chestnuts roasted, but the Yule log still blazed, promising another hour or two of warmth. Nobody felt particularly inclined to venture into the cold.

But as the countess's face fell, Georgie bestirred herself to encourage the crowd. "No Christmas Eve is complete without going to see if the oxen kneel," she said. "Not in England, at any rate. And you are all honorary Englishmen, this Christmas."

"What is this?" asked Mr. Sobieski, sitting forward with a frown. "You talk of the livestock?"

"The oxen," the countess said. "They are said to kneel at midnight, as they did the night that Christ was born, to warm the babe with their breath."

Mr. Sobieski snorted. "Shall we take a wager on it? I'll stand against, for fifty pounds."

"I will take that wager," Georgie said.

"He'll hold you to that," Lucas murmured in her ear as Sobieski bounced to his feet.

"I hope so," she murmured back.

He gave her a mystified look, then helped her to rise. Meanwhile, the countess was reasoning with her husband, who proclaimed himself content to wait inside for their return.

"Oh, leave him be," said Mr. Sobieski. "Spoilsports are not welcomed."

"Oh, no," the count muttered. "I'll not be held to *that* account." He heaved himself up.

Thus did the entire party find themselves bundled against the chill, picking their way through a clear, starry night to the stables. By prearrangement, the stable master, Mr. Handy, was waiting; at their appearance, he smiled and hauled open the double doors.

As the group stepped inside, they loosed a chorus of delighted exclamations. The stable had been trimmed in evergreens and wreaths of rosemary, the scent of which mingled pleasantly with sweet dried hay. Moonlight streamed through the cracks in the wooden slats, illuminating motes of dust that shimmered like stars. A horse put his head out of his box stall, whickering curiously.

"This way," Mr. Handy said. He led them down the

aisle, floorboards creaking underfoot, to the pen at the end of the stable.

There waited a handsome Brown Swiss ox, with a wreath of silver tinsel twined about his neck, and two fat red bows tied to his horns.

Lucas laughed. "When did you plan this?"

"Me?" Georgie offered an innocent smile. "If it was not on the program of events, then I had nothing to do with it. It must be a Christmas miracle."

"We're drawing close to midnight now," Mr. Handy said. "Gather round, to see if this ox is a Christian!"

The diplomats crushed in, the countess leaning over the rail to pet the creature's nose before her husband grew nervous and pulled her back. Georgie and Lucas were pushed to the edge of the group; after a moment, she seized Lucas's elbow and pulled him away. "We'll have a better view from the hayloft," she said, and rucked up her skirts before mounting the ladder.

At the top, she turned back to find him still planted on the ground, gaping up at her. "Aren't you coming?"

"I was hoping you might come back down," he said, "and climb for me again."

The giggle that escaped her felt girlish and silly and drunken, though she'd refrained from more than a sip of the elder wine. "Come," she said, stretching out her hand to beckon him. "Hurry. Mr. Handy will only do this once— he's his own family waiting for him in Swanhaven."

He made quick work of the ladder. The moonlight through the small window showed his delighted smile as he looked around the loft, wide enough for four men, which usually held winter hay. "You planned this, too," he murmured, touching the blanket she'd spread across the scattered remnants of straw.

"I come here to read sometimes." As a girl, she had spent long hours dreaming in this hayloft. "Come, look!"

He followed her outstretched finger. Gasps rose from the diplomats. At a hidden signal from Mr. Handy, the ox had begun to kneel.

In the distance came the sound of the church bells in the village. The cascading silver-toned carol, a peal of jubilation, sent goose bumps chasing over her skin.

"Merry Christmas," Mr. Handy called, grinning.

The countess and Mrs. Sobieska burst into applause. Mr. Sobieski put his hands on his hips and turned around, casting a scowling look down the aisle.

Georgie yanked Lucas back, out of view.

"Fifty pounds the poorer," came Obolensky's taunt.

"This was a con," Sobieski complained. "That ox was trained!"

"Ha! Who's the spoilsport now?"

"Shall you go collect?" Lucas asked, amused. She shook her head and put a finger to her lips. Smiling, he sat back; they waited in silence as the diplomats and Mr. Handy walked out of the stable.

The doors groaned as Mr. Handy shut them. Below, the streamers of dust sank back into darkness, and a horse released a snorting sigh.

Lucas's hand cupped her cheek, the lightest touch. "Merry Christmas to you," he whispered.

She waited, breathless, for him to kiss her. But as her eyes adjusted, she saw from his expression that he had no intention of doing so. He was studying her with odd gravity—focused, it seemed, on his thumb stroking over her cheekbone. His thumb dipped lower; he watched himself trace the outline of her lips.

Her mouth went dry. "May I ask for a gift from you?"

His gaze lifted to hers. "Name it."

"Lie with me here."

His smile faded. She swallowed, knowing how brazen

she must seem. But here, now, was the only chance they might have. And she would not let her father take this from her, too.

Perhaps he divined her thoughts, for his hand slipped away. "I will leave with the others tomorrow," he said quietly, "only because I must. It would look odd for me to stay. But I am not leaving *you*, Georgie. I hope you haven't told yourself so."

He was going to argue. He was going to be honorable. She loved his honor. But had he possessed a shade less of it, he might have voiced his feelings to *her* in Munich, instead of asking her father's permission first.

Heaven knew she would have welcomed his words. That autumn in Munich—parties filled with candlelit nooks, lovers always embracing just out of sight—had made her grow so impatient. Fevered, desperate, longing for him to touch her. Had he declared himself to her, she would not have waited longer. She would have touched *him*.

They would have been inseparable then. Her father's trick would never have worked. They would not have doubted each other.

She was a quick learner. She never repeated a mistake twice.

"I imagined bringing you here on our honeymoon," she said. "I spent. . . a thousand afternoons hiding here, as a girl, reading romances and dreaming of the man I would marry. And I thought . . . how fitting it would be, to bring him here. To . . . have him here."

Her face was flaming now. She had never imagined she could be so bold.

"Georgie," he said, his voice strained. "That is . . ." He exhaled. "The most marvelous, extraordinary . . . *damnable* invitation. If we could but table it for a week—long enough to—"

"No." She leaned into the starlight to show him her face more clearly. "Lucas. Two years, I've waited. Will you keep me waiting longer? Or will you give me my gift?"

His inward battle played over his face—nostrils flaring, jaw tensing as he glanced toward the stable doors.

She reached for him. He caught her hand; pressed a hot kiss to her palm. "You *will* marry me," he said hoarsely.

"This is our honeymoon," she whispered. "You are mine."

Some sound came from him. Too sharp and low to be a sigh. And then his mouth was on hers; he was kissing her desperately as his arms came around her, as he laid her gently down on the blanket.

It might have been one of her dreams—his mouth, so hot and demanding; his hands bold, freed of irrelevant daylight ideals, no decency or hesitance in them as they wandered her body, shaped her waist through her clothes, felt roughly down the curve of her hip, pausing to knead the fullness there.

But her dreams never satisfied her. She knew how to avoid their mistakes.

She reached for his coat, shoving it off; then his jacket, and the waistcoat that kept him from her. He was broader than she had realized, and leaner, too; as she palmed his waist, the soft cloth of his shirt could not disguise the muscled flex of his abdomen. He groaned, his mouth breaking from hers to track down her throat; but that, too, was a daylight business.

"Undress me," she whispered.

Odd and so thrilling, to command him; to feel the roughness of his hands on bare skin that had never known a man's touch. But he was not so practiced as to manage her corset without assistance; she found herself laughing as she sat up and knocked his hands aside, and when he buried his face in her nape, she felt the smile on his own lips—and then felt it fade, as the corset loosened.

She lifted her arms, and he drew the corset over her head, took her beneath her arms, and pulled her bodily out of the sagging collapse of her gown.

They knelt pressed together in starlit darkness, only the thin film of her underlinens separating them. The sensation briefly shocked her, riveted her in place. His body radiated such warmth.

But then he kissed her again, and her hands closed on his back, and the delightful discovery of the smooth texture of his bare skin, the elegance of his spine as it curved, the tightly muscled hillocks of his bottom . . .

Desire knew no shame.

They lay down together, still kissing; kissing for long minutes in which time lost its hold on them. But at last he pulled away, going up on one elbow to look at her. The dim light revealed only a faint impression of his body, but the growl he made suggested that his eyes were better than hers. He touched her breast very lightly, with the back of his hand, and she shivered.

"You like that," he said, very low. He bent down and kissed her nipple, causing her to gasp; but before he could mistake that noise for one of protest, she threaded her hands through his hair to hold him where he was.

His lips curved against her breast. He opened his mouth and touched his tongue to her nipple, and she groaned.

"Oh, yes," he murmured, and closed his lips around her again, suckling now, with strong pulling movements that made her feel faint—and ferocious—and deliciously weak. His hand slid into her hair, cradled her skull as though he sensed that she required the support, as he laved her breast more intently yet.

Her dreams could not compare. Here was what she'd

craved, those many nights of frustration—or so she thought, until his hand smoothed down her belly, brushed lightly over the tops of her thighs, then delved between, finding a spot so sensitive that she gasped.

"Wait," she said. It was too much—perhaps there was something wrong with her—but the insistent stroke of his hand, paired with the tugging assault of his mouth, caused something to twist tightly, low in her belly; to coil and build, an unbearable aching weight. "I don't think—"

"You do," he said, and stroked her more quickly, until suddenly—the coil burst. Pleasure jerked through her, took control of her hips; she bucked against him as he murmured to her, low soothing words that she barely understood; but the heat of his breath against her skin as he spoke seemed to heighten the pleasure further yet, until she turned her face into his shoulder to muffle her own moan.

His hand found her face. Smoothed back her hair. "Is that what you'd imagined?" he asked roughly. "For God knows . . . if so, we shared the same dream."

She felt too shy to reply, at first. How odd, that one could feel shy when lying naked, pressed against a man, her face buried in the aphrodisiac scent of his damp throat.

But after a moment, the question nudged her, and she frowned a little. "There was more to it."

He levered himself off her, his face a blur in the darkness, but she had the sense that he was smiling at her, smiling in that dark, provocative way he sometimes had.

"Is that so? What else was there?"

His voice was a purr, stoking her most secret, brazen inclinations. On a deep breath for courage, she slid her hand down his body, until she found the firm length of his erection. "This," she whispered.

His forehead came against hers. "Georgie," he murmured. "You . . ." He took a breath. "You realize there is no going back."

She gripped him, amazed by this marvel of nature: that such soft, hot skin could sheath a protrusion so unyieldingly hard. Something animal, primitive, caused her to tighten her grip, to stroke him; and his hiss was her reward. "There is no going back," she agreed unsteadily. "And I am glad of it."

He pulled her into an openmouthed kiss, and she pushed her lower body against him, instinct taking over, seeking to fit herself against him. She felt the last measure of his restraint in the way his back tensed, muscles hardening beneath her grip, but she angled her hips again, and the head of his member pressed just where it ought, and he gasped as he pushed into her.

Pressure—increasing, burning now as she stretched to accommodate him; she had a brief fear that this wouldn't work—and then he was inside her, penetrating deeply, filling her completely.

She held still, adjusting to the foreign sensation—until he began to move. *Oh,* she thought, a stupid wondering amazement seizing her, causing her to laugh as she reached up to grip his face, to encourage him with kisses. *Oh,* as he moved deeper yet, slow and steady strokes that seemed to strike like flint against some spot deep inside her that was not done with him by far. *Oh, oh*—he twisted his hips in some way, and her entire body flamed, hunger like a hot wind. She wrapped herself around him, arms and legs, kissing him deeply, then whispering, to her dim amazement, only half understanding herself: "Please. Now."

"Forever," he growled into her mouth, and the pleasure overwhelmed her again.

They lay together afterward in a restful, sated silence.

Outside, from the distance, came the muffled sound of laughter. Perhaps the ox *had* been trained to kneel, but it seemed the magic of the season was spreading, regardless.

His thought had followed hers. "The season of miracles," he said huskily. "I will never doubt it again."

She felt her way along his face, tracing the outline of his brows, the slope of his cheekbones. "How will we rejoin the others? One look at my face, and they'll know everything."

"Let them look," he said huskily. "Let them come to the wedding, if they like."

Her hand paused—only for a fraction of a moment. But he felt it, and sat up.

"We are marrying," he said evenly.

She reached for the blanket, covering herself against the chill. "Lucas. Let's discuss this later."

"Once you know whether I'm to be an earl?"

The sharpness in his voice alarmed her. "Not for my sake, but for yours."

"No. We will not have this argument again. Especially not now."

Miserable, she made quick work of dressing. She should have said nothing. Should have let his mention of marriage pass unremarked—for tonight, at least.

But she would not go along with his plan. She would not allow her father to leave him in shreds again.

They walked in silence back toward the house. It made a lovely sight, the windows glowing with stands of Christmas candles. Their flames blurred and jumped before Georgie's eyes. She dashed a discreet hand over her eyes as Lucas rapped on the door.

Barton greeted them. "Sir," he said, "a message came by courier." He thrust out a sealed envelope.

Georgie held her breath as Lucas read the letter. He looked up at her, his face unreadable. "The baby is born."

"And . . . is it a boy?"

"This note doesn't say." His jaw flexed. "Can you lend me a horse? I'll find out tonight. I'll ride direct to Harlboro Grange."

Chapter Ten

What was keeping Lucas from writing to her? The telegraph office was closed on Christmas Day, but surely he could have hired a courier? Against her better judgment, Georgie took the guests to church, where they managed to sit soberly for an hour and change. Inspired by their restraint, she even managed a satisfactory degree of conversation over the Christmas feast that followed. But her thoughts were with Lucas, her future seeming to hang in the balance as the seconds dragged by.

The houseguests, too, seemed distracted. They made polite exclamations over the gifts she had stuffed into their Christmas stockings—Italian writing paper; tortoiseshell fountain pens—but her suggestion of an afternoon walk to the Roman ruins was met with sluggish nods. So much for Christmas cheer! It seemed everyone was waiting for the holiday to expire, so they might take their leave without unseemly haste on Boxing Day.

Why did Lucas not write?

Determined to take her mind off this agonizing wait, she decided to visit the ruins herself. The lonely beauty would suit her mood. But as she approached the entry hall, she heard the front door close, and her heart flew into her throat.

Her steps slowed as she gained a view of the foyer. A gentleman stood in the entry hall, making a leisurely survey of the surroundings. As he tipped his head to inspect the rafters, his top hat tipped; he snapped it off his head, baring hair as white as snow, his movements birdlike in their quickness—deeply familiar to her.

Not Lucas. Alas, it was her father.

Perhaps she made a noise, for he turned suddenly, a smile wreathing his handsome, rosy face. "Georgiana! My surprise to you—at last, I've come home for Christmas."

She stopped in the archway. She did not know what to feel. The sight of him made her curiously numb.

"And I'm here through the New Year," he went on. "Isn't that splendid?"

He had a rich, booming voice, and a dapper neatness to his diminutive, trim frame. His waist, he'd once told her, was the same size as on his wedding day.

He had always looked distinguished. But never before had she seen him look *jolly*.

She let him embrace her, accepted his kiss on her cheek. But she made no move to return his affections. When he drew back, he was frowning.

"I expected more joy than this," he said.

"Were you ever in Constantinople?" she asked. "Or was that a sham as well?"

"What on earth?" He cast her a severe look before he set to unbuttoning his gloves. "Of course I was *en route* to Constantinople. But I got word at Gibraltar that the negotiations had failed, and so I turned back. We'll need to hold a multilateral conference in January—another grand squandering of money, for the sake of squabbling dogs." He glanced past her. "Where is the staff? It's a disgrace that nobody met me at the door. I do hope you haven't let our guests be neglected."

"Naturally not," she said.

"And where are those guests?" His keen brown gaze settled on her face, shrewdly calculating. "Is Mr. Godwin among them?"

"Mr. Godwin has left," she said. "Why, did you hope to speak with him? He did not find your letter."

She almost did not recognize the look that came over his face then. She had never managed to puzzle him before.

He cleared his throat. "I hope his presence didn't fluster you overmuch," he said smoothly. "I confess, that was part of my call to hurry back here. I would hate to have been the cause of distress, having left you with this party to manage."

"Heaven forbid your party might go poorly," she said. "A pity you spared no thought for my distress two years ago, when you lied to me—and to Mr. Godwin as well."

"Ah." His expression eased. "So the truth came out, did it? Well, I am sorry for that, Georgiana. I feel a lightening of my conscience, now the matter is laid bare. But you understand, he was no fit match for you, in Munich. Every word I spoke of his parentage was true. It's a suspect line." He paused. "And not a fertile one. I don't suppose he confided in you about the mess with the earldom Lilleston?"

Her temper broke. "You lied to us! You broke your own daughter's heart, and toyed with me as though I were your enemy—"

"Georgiana!" Aghast, he took her by the arm and looked around. "If you mean to bellow, we'll do this privately."

"Yes. I do mean to bellow." She yanked free and stalked to the nearest door, which opened into the second-best drawing room, a shabby but comfortable place, not nearly grand enough for his *guests*.

He closed the door very quietly behind him. "I was wrong," he said. "I won't claim otherwise. I realized it once I saw how deeply it affected you. I do apologize for it, but I never imagined"—he grimaced—"that you would lose your head so over a man. A child of mine! I thought you had more steel at your core. But believe me, the sad spectacle you mounted afterward was very persuasive in proving otherwise."

"So cold," she said, marveling. "Is there blood in your veins, or only daggers and plots? You are the perfect diplomat, sir. But you make a very poor father."

He recoiled physically, staring at her with a shock that she could not believe was feigned. "Georgiana," he said. "I think you will regret those words later."

"You may comfort yourself by imagining so. But they're long overdue. My happiness was not yours to gamble."

"I know that," he said quietly. "I have just apologized for it."

Stiletto jabs. Lucas had warned her of it. Her father probably did believe he had offered a satisfactory apology, no matter that he'd insulted her in the same breath. It was his training and his habit, accrued over a lifetime of handling the affairs of state, never to cede the high ground entirely.

The thought deflated her. She was angry, yes; she was furiously disappointed in him. But that was nothing new. She'd been disappointed in him her entire life—and never more so than at this time of year, when a child should be with her father, not left to the care of a staff who, despite their every kindness, had family of their own to care for, and better things to do than entertain their employer's daughter.

But that wasn't fair to Cook or the others. Their love

was genuine and heartfelt. She would not let her father tar that, too.

"It's pointless," she said tiredly. "You are what you are. I cannot expect a leopard to change its spots. I only wish . . . that I had realized that two years ago. Had I remembered to suspect you, I could have saved myself so much pain."

He hesitated, studying her. Looking, no doubt, for the best inroad, the cleverest angle of manipulation. "I am sorry, Georgie."

She waited for the twist. But it did not come. He stepped closer to her but made no move to touch her—the diplomat's instinct guiding him, no doubt,

"I never thought to be your only parent," he said. "I imagined I would be able to depend on your mother's wisdom. She would have raised you better. She loved you to the ends of the earth. She was, in every way, my better half."

And now he would try to raise her sympathy, to soften her. "I have no doubt of that," she said.

He sighed. "And there, in your disapproval, I hear an echo of her. Well, I deserve it. I will accept your disapproval as my due. But . . . know that I do love you, my dear. And I thought I was protecting you, in Munich. You were lovely. So bright. You could have attracted any gentleman."

She snorted. "You're losing your talent," she said, "if you expect me to believe that."

His brows shot skyward. "Georgiana, I will accept a certain degree of foolishness from you, but you are, in the end, my daughter. Please use your brain. You are your mother come to life again. So you must believe me when I say that I thought you deserved no less than a prince. After all, your mother managed to win *me*."

That startled a black laugh from her. His arrogance was insufferable—but also, oddly, credible.

She eyed him warily. Perhaps he did believe what he was

saying. It made no difference. "You had no right to deceive me so."

"A father's right," he began, and then cut himself off with a sharp tug of his mouth when he saw her reaction. "Very well," he said with asperity. "I said I blundered, didn't I? But why you fancied the only mutt in a kennel of purebreds, I will never understand. Lucas Godwin could never have offered the kind of life you deserved. Not then, at least."

And now they came to the heart of it. "You arranged this," she said. "Our . . . reunion. On the hopes he would inherit his title."

"Yes," he said—smiling, to her disbelief.

Realization jolted through her. "Why—there never was a letter, was there? Nobody ever stole anything from you."

His smile widened. "So now you see: I was conspiring for *your* benefit, my dear."

She recoiled. "Have you no shame? We ransacked the guests' belongings! Of all the horrid, manipulative things—"

"Horrid? Come now! I was trying to make amends. Two years ago, Godwin wasn't fit for you. So I dispatched him. But now that he stands a good chance of coming up in the world, I thought I'd make amends. Effect your reacquaintance. A fine atonement, I thought." He quirked a hopeful brow. "Did it work?"

There was no point in trying to wrap her mind around his self-justifications. But his smugness was intolerable.

"It did," she said. "But . . ." Let *him* learn what it felt like to be deceived, for once. For a brief, sweet hour of justice, let *him* suffer. "He will not inherit. Lilleston's child was a boy."

"Ah." His shoulders sagged. "Too bad, then. Too bad."

"But it makes no difference." She brushed past him, seizing the doorknob. "I will marry him anyway."

He scowled as he turned after her. "Now, listen here, Georgiana. I—"

She wrested open the door. "We have already arranged for a license. I am going to meet him directly."

"By God, you will not!" Flushing a very satisfying red, he followed her into the hall. Forgotten, all his concerns for discretion! "The cheek of him—to come back here, to press his suit when I already forbade it once—without so much as a word to me! I am his superior! That he did not even ask my permission—"

She whirled, speaking as she walked backward, away from him. "He doesn't need your permission. I am a woman grown. And *you*, sir, are a tyrant. If you gave him your blessing, I would refuse his hand. I would rather live as his trollop than satisfy you!"

He lunged after her. "And I would ruin him for it! Why, I could have him sacked like—" He gave a smart snap of his fingers.

Georgie rolled her eyes and turned away. "See to your guests," she threw over her shoulder. "For I am done with your business—*all* of it."

Chapter Eleven

December 26

As Georgie stepped into the drawing room, the sight of the Christmas tree made her sigh. All the candles had burned down to stumps, and the servants' children had stripped away the tinsel to make garlands for themselves. The needles had begun to brown.

Here was the eternal problem with Christmas: it ended. Oh, in other places, the merriment continued till Twelfth Night, but by now the gaiety would have assumed a frenzied nature, everyone resisting the knowledge that come St. Distaff's Day, work would resume, with nothing to look forward to but the bleak depths of midwinter.

Georgie always felt melancholy as she braced for the New Year. This poor tree seemed to reflect her wilting spirits. Thirty-six hours, and she'd still had no word from Lucas.

She knelt to study the urn in which the tree rested. Should it be watered? The von Bittners had left no instruction for it before their departure this morning.

"Has everyone gone?"

She twisted around. Lucas stood in the doorway, still wearing his heavy leather coat and riding boots. She rose to fly to him—thought better of it—crossed her arms very tightly at her waist, as his smile faded to a puzzled frown.

"What is it?" he asked gently. He wore a satchel over his shoulder; he lifted off the strap now, placing the luggage on the chiffonier as he approached.

"My father is back." He had closeted himself with Mr. Sobieski and Count Obolensky after breakfast, to discuss his plan for the conference in Constantinople. But they would emerge soon enough. "He won't be happy to find you here."

"Georgie. How many times must I tell you? It no longer matters."

"But it *does*." She caught his wrist when he would have touched her. "I told him the whole of it—that we uncovered his deception; that I love you. And he made threats, Lucas. Unless—was the child a girl?"

Smiling, he turned her hand in his, lifted it to kiss. "I'll tell you everything in a moment," he said. "First, a late Christmas gift. Will you open it now? I had it couriered from Paris, at no small expense."

Mystified, she let him lead her over to the chairs drawn up by the darkened hearth. He unbuckled the satchel, withdrew a thick binder, and placed it in her hands. It weighed half a stone at least.

"What is this?" she asked.

"Open it."

Her fingers trembled as she unwound the twine. Inside lay a thick stack of papers. Her breath caught as she read the first line of the topmost page.

February 7, 1884

Dear Georgiana,
    I try to make sense of it all. A wasted effort. My

*new colleagues must imagine me a perfect fool, so
absentminded I must seem to them.*

The door opened. She glanced up, heart beating very
hard, and found Lucas on his feet, a military squareness to
his posture.

Her father stepped into the room. "A footman told me
of your arrival," he said to Lucas. "Generally speaking, it is
customary to pay your respects directly to the master of the
house." His dark gaze moved pointedly over Lucas's rumpled
wardrobe. "To say nothing," he added, "of knocking the
mud off your boots."

She laid down the letter and rose, bristling, but Lucas
took a restraining hold on her arm. "I am paying my respects," he said, "to the woman who has tended this house
better than you ever did. To you, sir, I have nothing to offer
but my sincere regret, for I had hoped to look on my father-
in-law with favor one day."

Georgie braced herself for an explosion. Instead, her father stepped farther into the room, pushing the door closed
behind him. "Ah. So Georgiana has managed to suborn you
into this madness."

She hissed. "If you ever had any love for me," she said,
"you will prove it now. You will put aside your pride, your
outmoded notions of a suitable gentleman, and recognize
this man as the most decent, honorable husband I could
ever hope to find."

"It has gone beyond your opposition," Lucas said quietly.
"You will consent to our marriage, or you will disapprove of
it; but either way, sir, I have acquired a license, and mean to
put it into use before the New Year."

Georgie turned to him, amazed. "You have a license?
How on earth?"

But her father gave him no chance to reply. "I have
no time for this nonsense," he said sharply. "Very well, go

ahead. A more stubborn girl, I've yet to encounter—unless it was her mother. In which case, I know how little my opinion signifies. You may have her, Godwin—if not with my blessing, then at least with my resigned tolerance. But I will not lift a finger to promote you. I hope you understand that. You will have her hand—but none of the advantages that you might have expected from it. Will that suffice?"

"I never wanted more," Lucas said.

"Georgiana?" Her father snapped her name. "Will that content you?"

For a moment, tears blurring her eyes, she was tempted to let the matter go. To take this peace offering, no matter how inadequate.

But something in her balked, hardened. "No," she said. "It will not suffice. I have never asked anything of you. I have never complained at your absences—your *neglect*. I respected your work; I knew it was important. But *I* was important, too. And if I can't have your blessing on my marriage, then I will have your apology—not only for what happened in Munich, but for everything before it. Every Christmas you spent without me. Every birthday you neglected to recognize. Then, perhaps, it will suffice. Perhaps."

"Ah." Her father sighed. He passed a hand over his face—and to her amazement, blinked away what looked, all too briefly, like a sheen in his eyes. "You may have that, too," he said. "I'm sorry, Georgie." As he glanced to Lucas, he took a deep breath. "Perhaps he is a blessing to you," he said grudgingly. "Surely he will never put his career before your welfare. He's already shown himself willing to throw it away with both hands, for your sake. But I shan't interfere with him, that way." He looked back to her, his face solemn. "You have my vow. I will take no hand in interfering with his professional accomplishments. And I think . . . Godwin will go far, if it matters."

"Lord Lilleston," said Lucas.

They both turned. "What?" asked Georgie.

He was staring at her father. "I am Lord Lilleston to you, sir. And my resignation has already been tendered to the service, so you may count yourself safe from any temptation to go back on your promise not to meddle."

"Well!" Her father's jaw sagged. Then, all at once, he beamed. "Well, that's a fine ending to this tale, after all! A very merry Christmas gift, I dare say!"

"Oh, just go," Georgie said in disgust. "Go and leave us in peace."

"Without argument," he said, and gave her a wink. "Congratulations—my lady."

The door shut again.

"He is incorrigible," she bit out. "And I do not mean that in the charming sense. He is a perfect dog."

"He's a schemer by nature," Lucas said. To her astonishment, he sounded almost amused. "We'll have him knocking at our door by next Christmas, I'll wager."

"I shan't open that door!"

"Not next year," he said. "But perhaps the Christmas after. We'll make him grovel before we invite him in. And he'll do it—I promise you that. I've seen him pander for less than an earl's favor."

"Forget about him." She grabbed his hands. "Is everything well at Harlboro Grange? Why didn't you write?"

"A very healthy baby girl," he said, "gifted with the unfortunate name of Pandora."

She wrinkled her nose. "A curious choice."

"A very sly one. I believe I'm meant to count as one of the troubles she's unleashed on the Godwins." He urged her to sit down again. "But our conversations were as cordial as one could have hoped," he went on. "With my uncle gone, there's nobody left who was instrumental in the quarrel between our families. And I've assured the dowager countess that she will be handsomely provided for. I thought—if you don't mind it—that we might let her remain at the Grange for a year or two, until the child is weaned."

We. The world suddenly dimmed as she stared at him—dimmed, and then came pulsing back into vivid clarity, colors brighter and clearer. Even the Christmas tree seemed to perk up. "You really have the license?" she asked softly.

He reached out to touch her face. "What else could have kept me away, my love?"

Blushing, she looked down into her lap. She noticed the folder, the letter she had laid aside at her father's entrance, and retrieved it.

He had written to her, after Munich. Had poured his heart onto a page that he'd never sent to her.

"You should have posted this," she whispered. "It . . ." Such ardent, agonized words. "It would have brought me flying to you."

"I should have posted all of them," he said, just as softly.

All . . . ? She frowned a question at him, and he nodded, his expression so tender. "Go ahead," he said. "Look."

The folder was full of letters—so many! All of them addressed to her. She glanced through the dates.

"You wrote to me every day." She could not quite grasp it. "Every day, you wrote me."

"I never let go of you," he said gently.

"No." She swallowed. "You did not."

"One more thing." He reached into his coat and laid the license atop the letters. "Shall we marry on New Year's Day?"

She glanced up, appalled. "That's five days from now!"

A line appeared between his brows. "Too soon? Of course, perhaps you wish a grand affair—"

"Far too long!" She grabbed his wrist, tugging him to his feet. "The vicar will be at home at this hour. What are you waiting for? Put on your coat!"

Laughing, he caught her in his arms. "It's noon. Perhaps

we should let the man take his dinner in peace, before we harass him with this spectacle."

"*Spectacle*? Is that what you call our marriage? I warn you, I mean for it to be far less dramatic than what preceded it—"

His kiss stopped her words. She ceased to struggle, threw her arms around his neck, and kissed him back. *Mine, mine, mine.*

At last, he eased back a little, his forehead against hers, their lashes tangling as he spoke with a smile:

"I expect we'll have a spectacle nightly, don't you think?"

She laughed. "Why not in the afternoon, too?" And with a heart full of perfect joy, she rose on her tiptoes to kiss him again.